SOUTHERN HOTSHOT

A North Carolina Highlands Novel

JESSICA PETERSON

ALSO BY JESSICA PETERSON

THE STUDY ABROAD SERIES

Studying Abroad Just Got a Whole Lot Sexier.

A Series of Sexy Interconnected Standalone Romances

FOLLOW ME, Y'ALL!

•Join my Facebook reader group, The City Girls, and hang out in one of the coolest spots on the internet. I'm biased, but I'm also pretty thrilled by how awesome the people in my group are.

•Follow my not-so-glamorous life as a romance author on Instagram @JessicaPAuthor

•Follow me on Goodreads

•Follow me on Bookbub

•Like my Facebook Author Page

Published by Peterson Paperbacks, LLC
Copyright 2020 by Peterson Paperbacks, LLC
Cover by Najla Qamber of Najla Qamber Designs
Photographer: Wong Sim
Cover Model: Mitchell Wick
Editor: Marion Archer
Copy Editor: Jenny Sims, Editing4Indies
Proofreading: Karen Lawson

All characters in this book are fiction and figments of the author's imagination.

www.jessicapeterson.com

❀ Created with Vellum

CHAT #1

Monday March 13 11:48 PM EST
   Lady V85 has accepted your chat request
   Lady V85 is now in the chat room

MyBoyBlue4: You come here often to have sex with strangers on the internet?

   LadyV76: Yes. This your first time?

   MyBoyBlue4: How'd you know?

   LadyV76: I can spot a cybersex virgin from a mile away. You're in good hands.

   MyBoyBlue4: I get the feeling I might be. Part of the reason I reached out to you. Also, your Tumblr is really fucking hot. You gonna show me the ropes, sweetheart?

   LadyV76: Only if you never call me sweetheart again.

   MyBoyBlue4: Yes ma'am.

   LadyV76: Tell me what you want.

   MyBoyBlue4: You cut to the chase. I like that. As far as what I want...something different. Something real.

   LadyV76: Sex that says something.

   MyBoyBlue4: Yeah. Yeah, I like that idea.

LadyV76: Let's set some ground rules real quick. First, I don't chat with married men.

MyBoyBlue4: I'm not married. Are you?

LadyV76: No. You okay with sending each other pics? No faces, no sharing outside this chat, and no cheating, e.g., sending me a pic of a dick that isn't yours.

MyBoyBlue4: My dick's already on the internet, so I got nothing to lose. Sure.

LadyV76: Good story?

MyBoyBlue4: Yeah. Maybe if you're nice I'll tell it to you one day. Wait, I actually don't want you to be nice.

LadyV76: Good, because I'm not. You okay with kink? Role play? Any hard limits?

MyBoyBlue4: Yes, yes, and no. Only request is that you push my limits. I'm bored. Give me something I haven't seen yet.

LadyV76: Open-minded. I like it. Safe word is RED if I go too far.

MyBoyBlue4: Got it.

LadyV76: Any other questions?

MyBoyBlue4: What does *your* sex say?

LadyV76: It says I know what I want. And I want you to take your dick out of your pants and send me a picture. Right. Fucking. Now.

MyBoyBlue4: Wow. Lol okay.

LadyV76: You're already hard, aren't you?

MyBoyBlue4: [Sends picture of his erect dick in his hand]

LadyV76: You've got a gorgeous dick, Blue. And look at that yummy drop of precum right there. Don't touch it. Take off your shirt.

MyBoyBlue4: Already off. Why can't I touch?

LadyV76: Because I fucking said so. I'm your college professor. You're my student. My innocent, impressionable student who's twenty years younger than I am. You've come to my office for help with an assignment. I tell you I'll help, but only if you eat my pussy.

MyBoyBlue4: That's so wrong and so hot.

LadyV76: I've been listening to a lot of Van Halen recently.

MyBoyBlue4: Whaaaattt? Jump was my jam for years.

LadyV76: So you whip out your cock because you're young and stupid, and I've been turning you on all semester. But that's not what I asked you to do. So I slap you across the face.

MyBoyBlue4: Hell yes! I mean, ouch.

LadyV76: And then, just to tease you, I lean down and lap up your precum with slow, firm strokes of my tongue. Mimic those strokes with your thumb. Get yourself nice and slick. Imagine your cock glistening with my spit. You groan, but I tell you to shut the fuck up because we can't get caught.

MyBoyBlue4: Can I just say this is already the best sex I've had in forever?

LadyV76: You cannot because I didn't ask. Tell me how my tongue feels.

MyBoyBlue4: It feels...ah...really good I'm typing with one hand god I wanna fuck you

LadyV76: Don't make me slap you again. Get your hand off your dick. I stand and lean back against my desk, sitting on the edge. I'm wearing a pencil skirt and heels.

MyBoyBlue4: What do I doooo?

LadyV76: I reach up. Play with your nipple. Are you playing with your nipple? Then I tilt my chin and lick it. I like to lick you. You taste...clean. You tell me you like my instruction.

MyBoyBlue4: I sure as hell do Professor. I'm REALLY hard.

LadyV76: You come, and I'll slap you again. Didn't I just tell you to take your hand off your dick?

MyBoyBlue4: You're killing me. Fine I'm playing with my nip. Feels nice.

LadyV76: You've never eaten pussy before, so I have to tell you how to do it. I hike up my skirt and spread my legs. I'm wearing...hmm, a red lace thong. You weren't expecting that. I pull it to the side and show you my pussy. I tell you to get on your knees and lick my clit. You obey, finally, and you actually do a pretty decent job.

MyBoyBlue4: Please tell me you're as close to coming as I am. Your pussy is BEAUTIFUL. I want it.

LadyV76: Too bad it's not yours to have. I'm touching myself now.

MyBoyBlue4: I bet I got you wet. Really, really wet. You like that I listen. You like that I'm hard for you.

LadyV76: I do. Bet you want to put that cock where you mouth is right now.

MyBoyBlue4: Like you even need to ask.

LadyV76: But I didn't. I grab your hair and pull it. You groan against my pussy, and I pull your hair again. We CANNOT get caught. Do you like the pain?

MyBoyBlue4: YES

LadyV76: We just might have a natural submissive on our hands.

MyBoyBlue4: Maybe. Or maybe I'm just trying something new.

LadyV76: That's sexy.

MyBoyBlue4: I know.

LadyV76: Cocky?

MyBoyBlue4: Yes.

LadyV76: Not with me. I show you how to finger me. How to hit my G-spot while eating me out. You get into it. Kissing me. Sucking my clit. I'm falling back on the desk now,

I'm spread out wide and you can't get enough of it. Tell me how I taste.

MyBoyBlue4: ?

LadyV76: C'mon. Use that imagination.

BoyBlue4: You taste...like that first fall morning. You know the one, that day when the summer heat has finally broken and you can sleep with the windows open. Air is crisp and the fire is going. Pun not intended but hopefully appreciated.

LadyV76: Wow.

MyBoyBlue4: What?

LadyV76: I like that image. Just wasn't expecting it from a guy with a screen name from Old School.

MyBoyBlue4: Hey. Just because I'm good-looking doesn't mean I don't have depth.

LadyV76: *eye roll*

[Pause]

MyBoyBlue4: Someone just came, didn't she?

LadyV76: I always come first. My way of evening out the karmic scales. You know, making up for all those female orgasms that never happened but should have.

MyBoyBlue4: Interesting.

LadyV76: What?

MyBoyBlue4: I think my cockiness turns you on, Professor.

LadyV76: Hmm.

MyBoyBlue4: I won't push it because I know that praising someone else's boldness may not be kosher for an alpha like yourself. But food for thought.

LadyV76: Put your hand back on your cock. I want you to come on my stomach. I tell you to stand, and you do. I grab your dick and give it a hard tug. You thrust into my hand, hanging your head. I thumb your slit.

MyBoyBlue4: I push up your shirt.

LadyV76: You taste me in your mouth, don't you?

MyBoyBlue4: Crisp and sweet. Yes.

LadyV76: I keep tugging. Faster. It has to be fast, or we'll get caught. I want to know your cum is on my skin when I go to my next meeting.

[Pause]

MyBoyBlue4: Fuck. So fucking good.

LadyV76: When was the last time?

MyBoyBlue4: I already told you I'm new to this.

LadyV76: No. I mean when was the last time you were honest about what you wanted?

MyBoyBlue4: You sure as hell don't hold any punches.

LadyV76: One of the things you like about me.

MyBoyBlue4: I like you?

LadyV76: You'll be back for more.

MyBoyBlue4: You free tomorrow? I can do late.

LadyV76: No, but the day after I am. Monday is my day off.

MyBoyBlue4: Mine too. You work in a restaurant?

LadyV76: I don't share details about my personal life.

MyBoyBlue4: You have a lot of rules.

LadyV76: You don't have enough. Ever consider that having rules not only keeps you in line but also makes the experience of breaking them that much more of a turn-on?

MyBoyBlue4: Christ.

LadyV76: What?

MyBoyBlue4: I'm hard again. I'm hot for you, teacher.

Chapter One

EMMA

He's a coworker, not a conquest.

But damn if Samuel Beauregard isn't exactly my type. Big. Broad.

Bold.

I try not to stare as I approach the man standing outside The Barn Door restaurant. An Internet search told me the former star quarterback is six-five and two-hundred-sixty pounds. Pictures of him dwarfing pretty much everyone he's ever been photographed with were all over Google: teammates, girlfriends, even his three brothers, all of whom played professional football too.

In real life, though, my new coworker and kinda-sorta boss looks massive. Standing beside the restaurant's entrance with his hands clasped in front of him, I notice how his shoulders and thighs strain against the fabric of his sharply cut suit.

His *lavender* suit. It sports a daring white-and-purple check pattern that would scream Barney the Friendly Dinosaur on anyone else. But on Samuel, it works. His enor-

1

mous physical presence lends the whole getup a gravitas it wouldn't otherwise have.

And while the suit is not at all subtle, the accessories he wears with it are: crisp white button-down, black Gucci loafers (the classic black ones), wildly expensive but understated platinum Patek Philippe watch that peeks out from his sleeve.

Interesting. He dresses to impress, that much is clear. He's flashing dollar signs left and right, but he's also flashing a willingness to experiment. To get the balance of bling and business just right.

To try new things, as Blue so succinctly put it last night.

I like that idea.

Something I don't like? The way Samuel glowers at me. I get closer, my heels crunching on the neatly kept gravel path, and he actually scowls. His blue eyes are cold.

Thankfully, the man standing next to him—his brother Beau—offers me a much warmer welcome.

"Emma! You're finally here." He takes my hand and gives it a firm shake. "Only took me, what, two years to convince you to come up to Blue Mountain?"

I grin, my chest lighting up with pride. "Had to get that Master Somm diploma first."

He grins too. "I'm glad you passed. It's an honor to have you."

"It's an honor to be here. Heading Blue Mountain's wine program is a dream job, and I can't wait to get started."

Beau nods at his brother. "This is Samuel. As the director of our food program, he'll be your partner in crime in all things culinary. You two will be the co-heads who take the resort's food and beverage programs to the next level."

Samuel grunts. "We'll see."

Beau cuts him a look that I'm guessing says *play nice or else*. It makes me wonder what the hell Samuel's deal is. Is he gunning for the wine job too? Or does he not think they need me here?

I stiffen my spine. Not exactly the welcome I was hoping for from my new co-head.

Holding out my hand, I say, "Nice to meet you, Samuel. I'm Emma Crawford." I don't force cheeriness into my voice because, well, I don't need to. If he wants to be a dick, fine. He's not the first asshole I've worked with, but hopefully he'll be the last. "I look forward to working together."

I don't, his expression says. Yep, can read that one loud and clear.

My training as a sommelier has made my nose extra sensitive, so it's not surprising that I catch a whiff of his cologne. I pick up notes of graphite. Wet granite. A heavy hit of saccharine spice. It's expensive and not at all subtle, just like his outfit.

Still, it doesn't stop the bolt of electricity from darting up my arm when his hand engulfs mine. The warmth of his palm is a startling counterpoint to the ice in his eyes.

Eyes that flash, just for a second. Just long enough for me to think he felt the electricity too.

The space between us thrums, but I try to ignore it. I'm not here to get laid. I'm here at Blue Mountain Farm to make my dreams come true.

Besides, I have Blue for sex. I usually chat with several partners at once, but lately, the proverbial well has run dry. So for now, I'm unintentionally monogamous with Blue.

"Right," he says, and drops my hand.

A beat of uncomfortable silence blooms between the three of us, along with the scent of rosemary. The herb borders the path in pretty blue-green swaths, along with a riot of azaleas and a gigantic magnolia tree. From the service to the grounds, everything about Blue Mountain Farm is impeccable.

Doesn't hurt that it's a beautiful spring day. It's another warm afternoon in what's been a remarkably mild winter. We never got the usual snowstorm or two we've come to expect, which makes me think we're due for a thumper at some point.

"Okay then." Beau claps his hands together. "Emma, you up for a quick behind-the-scenes tour of The Barn Door? Then we'll get you checked into your cottage."

"That would be great. I can't wait to see this wine cellar I keep hearing about."

"My cellar. Stocked with my bottles." Samuel sends a meaningful glance in his brother's direction. "The ones I began collecting long before I was Blue Mountain's food *and* wine director."

Ah. So he wants my job *and* he doesn't think the resort needs me.

Great.

Rolling his eyes, Beau opens the door for me. "Excuse my brother. He's still warming up to the idea of accepting much-needed help with our expanding programs. I promise he'll see the light."

I move through the doorway. "By the way, I appreciate that not-so-little perk of y'all putting me up in a cottage. I won't lie, I'm really excited about staying here for a couple of weeks. Beau, your resort is stunning."

"Of course. I wanted you to experience the farm as a guest so you can get a feel for the experience we're trying to create. I'll admit it's also part of my shameless ploy to get you to stay, well, forever."

As a part of my signing package, Beau offered me the chance to stay in one of Blue Mountain Farm's insanely luxurious cottages for a few weeks. Considering they go for north of two grand *a night*, I would've never been able to afford to stay here otherwise. As much as I love my loft back in Asheville, a twenty or so minute drive from here, I'm excited about the change of scenery. Especially when that scenery is some of the best in the Smokies.

I take in the quiet of The Barn Door restaurant. It's midafternoon on a Friday, and while a handful of diners linger over a late lunch, the place has the buzzy feel of a party about to begin. A small army of staff patrols the floor—front servers, busboys, a pair of hostesses.

The impeccable décor is beautifully designed without being stiff or overstuffed. A pair of enormous fireplaces anchor each end of the space, and antique beams that look to be as old—and weathered—as the structure itself cover the soaring ceiling. Leather booths curl around tables covered in pristine white tablecloths with artfully mismatched flatware and broken-in wooden chairs. The sign at the resort's entrance told me the farm has been here since the 1750s.

The restaurant is a study in contrasts. The fine crystal glassware against the bohemian arrangements of purple and yellow wildflowers set out on each table. The smell of a smoker, something you'd find at a barbecue joint, against the briny, wet slate smell of a dozen oysters passing by on a server's tray. The five-hundred-dollar bottle of California Cabernet on a table where a man and a woman are chowing down on fried chicken sandwiches.

This is not my first time inside these hallowed walls. As one of Asheville's many resident foodies, I couldn't resist the siren call of Chef Katie Gates's high-low combination of Southern classics with a decidedly down-home twist.

But it is the first time I'm appreciating it as a project. A living, breathing entity whose story I get to help shape.

A zippy little chill darts along my spine, lighting up my chest like an exclamation point.

Yeah, I want this job. And I'm not going to let an entitled jackass like Samuel Beauregard keep me from getting it. Who knows? Maybe if I stick around long enough and dig my heels in deep enough, Samuel will call it quits and go live that cushy, pro-athlete retirement life. I imagine he's got millions socked away.

I just have to outlast him.

Outsmart him.

"It's gorgeous," I say. "Seriously, one of the most romantic and beautiful restaurants I've seen. Ever."

"Samuel," Beau says, a note of warning in his tone. "Why don't you give Emma the inside scoop on how The Barn Door came to be?"

Samuel lets out an annoyed sigh. I glance to my right to see him standing on the other side of Beau. As far away from me as he can get.

"What is there to explain?" Samuel rolls back his shoulders. "I came up with the concept, I executed it, and now I run it. Pretty fucking well too. Isn't that right, Xavier?"

The passing server offers us a smile, despite the fact that his tray is weighed down by a sizable beverage order. "It's an honor to work at The Barn Door, sir."

I study Xavier's face. It's not that the server's smile is fake, necessarily. It's that it doesn't reach his eyes.

Interesting.

"What Samuel means to say"—Beau cuts his brother another look—"is that our family has lived on Blue Mountain for generations. We were known for many things—some of them great, some of them not so much—but one thing that always stood out was our Beauregard hospitality. Whoever visited the farm could count on a warm welcome and a square meal that stuck to your ribs. We're biased, but our mama is the best cook in these parts, hands down. Daddy wasn't so bad at breakfast, either. I inherited their good looks—"

Samuel lets out a scoff.

"While Samuel here inherited their love of sharing good

6

food with good friends and family. So when the farm passed to us, we knew we wanted to continue that tradition."

"And so The Barn Door was born," I say, glancing up at the beamed ceiling. "For y'all's first restaurant, I have to say you absolutely killed it."

"Chef Katie's killing it," Beau replies. "As is our staff. We're just along for the ride."

I like Beau. He's got fame, and he's got money, but he's still humble. He's not afraid to give praise where praise is due. He's clearly a smart guy who's surrounded himself with smart people.

But Samuel doesn't say a word. Just stands there in his lavender suit looking like a pissed-off, albeit finely sculpted, block of stone.

"How about the wine list?" I say. "Let's take a look at that."

Beau looks at his brother. "Samuel?"

With a heavy sigh, Samuel heads for the hostess stand. He comes back with a binder, its brown leather cover fashionably scuffed up like a well-loved pair of hunting boots.

"Quite the bible y'all have." I hold up the binder. The pages inside are a combined two, maybe two-and-a-half inches thick. I glance at Samuel before opening the cover. "So. What's your gospel?"

"My gospel?"

"What's your story? Why *this* wine"—I poke my finger into a page of pinot noir—"for *this* restaurant? The food you serve is second to none. It's interesting, it's innovative, and it's got a great story to tell. How does this wine enhance that story? How does it deepen the meaning of a shared meal at a place like The Barn Door?"

Samuel's expression goes blank. Pink smudges appear on his cheekbones.

I allow myself a small smile. I imagine not many people challenge him. He's used to having his way, and he's used to not having to explain why.

I look forward to disabusing him of that habit.

"The farm is and always has been a family place," Samuel says, slipping his hands inside the front pockets of his trousers. "Our hospitality is the best of the best. I wanted our cellar to reflect that."

I keep flipping. Page after page of big name, big-ticket wines. "Best of the best. Right. I can definitely see you went that direction."

"You don't sound impressed," Beau says.

"To be honest?" I glance up from the binder. "I'm not."

"That's the biggest and best collection in the state, if not the South. If you don't get that it's special, then you don't get wine." Samuel's reply is cold. But his eyes are suddenly hot.

"Bigger doesn't always equal better," I say.

I shouldn't take pleasure in pissing off the guy who has the power to make or break my future. Samuel is not only Blue Mountain's food director but he's also got a large ownership stake in the resort itself.

All six members of the Beauregard family own and operate Blue Mountain Farm, a five-star resort in the Great Smoky Mountains. The brainchild of Beau, the oldest Beauregard brother who retired several years ago from a successful pro football career, the resort has been developed over the past five or so years to encompass luxurious guest accommodations, a spa, stables, a smokehouse, gardens, outdoor entertaining spaces, and the South's most awarded new restaurant, The Barn Door.

Unsurprisingly, Beau's got plans to expand the resort even further. He hopes to build additional rooms, a sports complex, and another restaurant on the twenty acres of untouched land to the resort's east. Meaning I could one day be wine director of not one top-notch, James Beard Award-winning restaurant, but two.

Still, I can't help engaging in a little sharp banter with

Samuel. Could be the fact that I'm still a little keyed up from the exceptional cybersex I had with Blue last night. I thought he might just be another internet creeper with zero personality and even less imagination. But he was a pleasant surprise. Considering how lame my non-internet love and sex lives have been, the timing of our meeting couldn't be more perfect. Blue gave me a much-needed dash of hope—hope that not every guy I meet, virtually or otherwise, will make me feel ridiculous for being who I am and liking what I like.

I want more. I can't wait for tomorrow night.

A flicker of a smile moves over Samuel's lips. They're full and very pink against his dark reddish-brown scruff. "Course not. But when it's big, *and* you know what you're doing with it, it can be fucking magical."

If only he knew how far from the truth that misnomer is.

I want to take his dirty pun and run with it. Show him I can be just as dirty, if not more so. Quicker and wittier too.

But considering this is my first day on the job, I decide to rein in that impulse. I often think about what my hugely successful older sister, Lindsey, would do. Right now, she'd definitely continue being the consummate professional she is.

"You know what's magical? When you can blow a guest's mind with a wine they've never heard of at a price point that doesn't bankrupt them. When you tell them about the woman who grew the grapes and the four-year-old daughter who's following in her footsteps, and the footsteps of her grandmother, and her great-grandfather. When you serve just the right bottle to just the right table and make it a night they'll remember forever. Not because the wine cost so much, or because they get to brag about the label to their friends the next day at brunch, but because it made them think. It made them remember. Hope. Appreciate. It made them *feel something.*"

Beau smiles. "She's good."

Samuel just stares at me. I can't read his eyes now. The weight of his undivided attention is intense and uncomfortable, but I stand my ground. If I've mastered one thing besides wine over the past decade, it's resilience.

I hold up the binder. "I think this list needs to say something other than 'rich people eat here.' Let's tell a story. Let's honor small producers, the winemakers who are taking risks and doing the hard work of making interesting wines. Let's make wine approachable for everyone by taking the snobbery out of it. Let's make people think, talk, and linger the way Chef Katie's food does. Let's do the hard work, Samuel."

Samuel is still staring. A muscle in his jaw tics.

His intensity finally gets to be too much, and I look away. Glancing at Beau, I find the vote of confidence I need in his big, genuinely gleeful smile.

"I love it," he says.

"I don't," Samuel growls.

"I'm not saying you don't have something special here," I reply. "Or the beginnings of it, anyway. I'm just saying you've got a binder full of boring, unapproachable BSD wines."

He arches a brow. "BSD?"

"Big swinging dick. Trophy wines."

Beau lets out a bark of laughter. "If that doesn't describe you to a T, brother..."

Samuel, however, doesn't think it's very funny. In fact, he looks downright murderous.

"I'm outta here," Samuel says.

Beau slams the flat of his clipboard into his brother's chest. "No, you're not. You're going to show Emma to her cottage, remember? Maybe give her a tour of the grounds on your way there. Emma, follow Samuel to the main house in your car. A valet will park it there for the remainder of your stay. Every residence has a golf cart, as they're a more convenient way of getting around the resort."

11

Samuel glances at me. Glances at his brother.

"No tour. I don't have time," he says at last. "Let's go, Miss Crawford."

I thought The Barn Door was peak magical-and-romantic-setting-straight-out-of-a-movie, but I was wrong.

As I climb out of Samuel's golf cart, my breath catches. A beautifully carved wooden gate with lush green vines crowding the stone posts on either end marks the beginning of a meandering pebbled pathway. At the end of the pathway is a storybook "cottage"—really, a decent-sized house—with cedar shake siding painted a smart shade of gray-black. Smoke curls from one of the massive stone chimneys (yes, there are several), and I can just glimpse an A-frame screened-in porch at the back of the house.

The cozy smells of burning wood and pine trees hang heavy in the air.

Not to mention the 360-degree views of the Blue Ridge mountains. It's a clear day, so I can see for miles in every direction: swaths of bright green mountains beneath a flawless Carolina blue sky. The colors are so vibrant and the light so ardent, it makes my eyes water to take it all in.

My heart twists with longing. This is it. Or could be, anyway.

The good life.

The life I was told over and over again didn't exist for someone like me. An artist (of sorts), making a good living off her passion. Her art.

How wonderful it would be to prove the world wrong.

While my career path may be somewhat unconventional, my hopes and dreams aren't. I want to own a home. I want to work at a job I love that also provides the stability I crave: a good salary, benefits that include health insurance and a retirement plan, and hours that aren't insane. I began my career as a cellar rat at twenty-one, and I've been working restaurant hours (at an hourly wage) in the ten years since. The combination of seventy-hour weeks and night and weekend shifts has left me burned to a crisp.

Never thought I'd say this, but I'd love a regular old nine-to-five job. And being director of Blue Mountain's wine and beverage program affords me exactly that. Not at first, granted. I have to learn the ropes here at the restaurant, which means I'll be on the floor more often than not. But Beau promised I'd eventually get that sweet eight-or-nine-hour workday.

Climbing out of the golf cart, Samuel glances up the hill and lets out one of his aggrieved sighs.

"What is it now?" I ask, meeting his eyes over the roof of the cart. "I had some pointers for your wine list. But I'm legit blown away by your resort. Y'all are clearly the experts there."

He grabs my tote bag and jacket from the back seat. "It's nothing," he grumbles, and starts walking toward the cottage.

"I can carry that." I scurry to catch up to him, our footsteps crunching on the pea gravel.

"I got it," he says, keeping his eyes trained on his feet.

"Really, I—"

"I said I got it."

I roll my lips between my teeth. "Thanks."

I put the key into the lock on the front door—no key cards at Blue Mountain; they use old-fashioned brass ones with gorgeous silk tassels attached to them—and Samuel and I reach for the knob at the same time. The back of my hand collides with his palm, and we immediately pull back, like we've singed each other.

"Sorry," we blurt in tandem.

"You always in the habit of not letting people help you?" he asks.

"It's not that I don't let anyone help. It's that I don't expect it. Or need it."

He's looking at me like that again—like he doesn't know what to make of me.

This time, I let him open the door for me. Samuel may be a jackass, but apparently he's a jackass with manners. I'd say the combination intrigued me, but that seems like a bad precedent to set.

I devour things that intrigue me. Wine. Books. Men.

Samuel isn't available for me to devour. Not in the naked sense, anyway.

Still, my nipples prick to life as Samuel's gaze follows me inside. The heat of it pins a circle to my back as warmth seeps through my blazer and into my skin.

A target.

Angling my body away from him, I gape at the impeccably furnished room that opens up just off the cottage's entrance.

It's a large open-concept kitchen/breakfast nook/family room combination with high ceilings clad in reclaimed wood. A fire blazes in the fireplace on the farthest wall. Cozy sofas and armchairs surround a leather ottoman nearby while an antique metal lantern holds court just above a TV hidden in a painted bookshelf. A big wooden dining table, presumably for those family meals Beau was talking about, is set in front of the kitchen island.

The *kitchen*. I don't have time to cook, but if I did, I'd want to do it in there.

An industrial-style range, complete with six burners, a griddle, and two ovens, is set into a wall of gleaming white tile. Copper pots of every shape and size hang from strips of brass set into the tile. Cushy upholstered barstools line one side of the island.

Through a doorway to my right, I glimpse a massive four-poster king-sized bed. It's made up with crisp white linens, a fluffy duvet, and a small mountain of even fluffier pillows.

The whole place is chic and comfortable, and it clearly cost a fortune to construct and decorate.

It's a dream.

If only I didn't have a glowering beast of a man beside me, intent to take me out.

I look at him. He looks back.

No use beating around the bush. The guy is being a total jerk, but we need to work together. Time to smooth out the kinks.

Chapter Three

SAMUEL

"You don't want me here." Emma crosses her arms. "I have a good idea why, but I want to hear it from you."

On the outside, this little scrap of a girl is buttoned up.

She's wearing a prim black suit and low, sensible heels. Even with some help, she barely comes up to my chest. Her dark blond hair is coiled in a tight bun at the crown of her head, and she wears no jewelry save for the pearl studs in her ears.

But she's got this raspy, smoky, phone sex voice that's completely at odds with the bun and the pearls.

Fuck me. This is exactly what I don't need, a hate-boner for the sommelier I'm determined to kick to the curb. I know a threat when I see one. And Emma's got that gleam in her eye. That hunger for more. For bigger and better.

For knowledge.

I'll be damned if I let her know me.

"I don't want you here because I don't need you. I'm really fucking good at my job. One of the best in the business, if that James Beard Award is any indication."

"That award was for your chef."

"One, Chef Katie is amazingly talented, but I'm the one who came up with the restaurant and food concept at The Barn Door. She takes my ideas and runs with them—she likes the challenge, and she always delivers. And two, what about the other awards? *Bon Appetit?* And the World's Fifty Best List? Those were for the restaurant. You know, the one I conceptualized from soup to nuts and now run."

She crosses her arms, wearing a smug expression on her face.

"You're good at your job. So what? If you really loved the restaurant, and really believed that story y'all were telling me about family and food and hospitality, you'd welcome expertise like mine, not insult it. What are you afraid of?"

I stare at her. I keep doing that, I just—Christ, I haven't been around this kind of radical, balls-out honesty in a long time.

No one questions me.

No one *digs* the way she's digging. I make it a point to be the ballbuster so people don't have the chance to return the favor.

But Miss Crawford? She beat me to the punch.

I don't want to like the curiosity in her eyes. Because curiosity means she's going to keep digging.

It means she cares. Makes the hollow inside my chest hurt.

"I've worked my ass off to learn a whole new field after I retired," I grind out. "I started from scratch and took a lot of lumps along the way. But I did it for my family, and I'm damn proud of what we've built here. I'm proud of my cellar, and I know if I give you an inch of it, you'll take a mile."

"*Our* cellar. The resort's. And I'll take what I'm entitled to."

"It's mine. I spent a decade building it, and I'm not about to turn over the keys to a stranger. We don't need change. We need to keep doing what we've been doing—crushing it, in other words."

It's not the whole truth. But it's not a total lie, either.

"Stranger? I've known Beau for years."

"A stranger to the family."

"Right. But that doesn't explain why you keep working even though you seem to think the cellar is set. You obviously don't need the money." Her eyes flick to the watch on my wrist. "Why not ride off into the sunset and live on a yacht with Jennifer Lopez?"

My brother Hank strolls into the room, Emma's sensible black suitcases in hand.

"Because he enjoys being a pain in all our asses too much," he says with a smile. He sets down a suitcase and extends his hand. "I'm Hank, Beauregard brother number three. Welcome to Blue Mountain. I've heard so much about you— Beau's seriously impressed with your grape juice skills."

Emma takes his hand and laughs. The ache in my chest tightens. What in the world?

I'm just exhausted. Yeah. Yeah, that's gotta be it. When you work night and day like I do, weird stuff can happen to your body.

"Hank," Emma says. "I like you already."

"I'm the best of the bunch." Hank glances at me. "But it looks like I don't need to tell you that."

"Thanks for bringing my luggage over."

"Thank you for being the brave guest who stays in Pinehill Cottage."

Emma furrows her brow.

"It's the cottage closest to Samuel's house," Hank explains. "You're practically in Broody Batman's backyard."

Emma's eyes dart to my face. I run a hand over my scruff, averting my gaze.

Enough. I've had enough of her questions and her curiosity. I should go.

I need to go.

But I find myself rooted to the spot, two feet from where she's resting a stockinged knee on the arm of a chair. The image pops into my head and stays there: her slowly rolling her stockings down, revealing bare skin. I take that knee in my mouth. Bite down. She slaps me.

I blink.

Holy *shit* that's a bad case of wires crossing. Probably because I haven't stopped thinking about last night. I'm the first to admit I'm no angel. I like casual sex. Or used to, anyway. It's just gotten a little boring lately. I haven't liked the way it's made me feel. It's not guilt or shame that haunts me the morning after. It's more...loneliness, I guess. There's this voice in the back of my head that always wonders if a girl is coming home with me because she enjoys my company, or because she just wants to fuck an athlete.

Maybe that's why I haven't hit it off with anyone recently. Or maybe I'm just a dick.

Either way, I'm sick of never being alone but always feeling alone.

"Would you get gone?" I snap at Hank, crossing my arms. I turn back to Emma. She's taking too much pleasure in calling me out, and it's pissing me off to no end. "One, Jennifer Lopez is married, and I don't fuck married women. Although I did see her show in Vegas, and now I'm a big fan. Two, yachts are great. But their kitchens suck, and I like to cook."

Emma blinks. "You do?"

"You know, first impressions can be deceiving. Just because I've got a—what did you call it? A big swinging dick?"

I don't miss the way her brown eyes flick to the front of

my trousers. When they move back up to my face, they're different. Sharper.

"A big swinging dick *wine list*," she corrects. "I said you had a BSD wine list."

"Implying, of course, that I'm compensating for a lack in other, more private areas."

Her lips twitch. "Private areas. Brain areas."

"Right. Just because I've got a list of robust wines at robust prices doesn't mean I can't enjoy life's simpler pleasures, like making the world's tastiest bourbon braised short ribs or the best, moistest cornbread you've ever put in your mouth."

"You used moist on purpose, didn't you?" She spears me with a look. "Just to make me squirm."

"Yup," Hank says.

"What's wrong with moist?" I ask.

"You know what's wrong with—ugh, I won't say it again."

"I happen to think moist is a happy state of affairs. When it comes to cornbread and...well."

She tilts her head. "You like to put that in your mouth too?"

I let out a bark of laughter. "I eat it all, yes."

"But can you taste it? Really, thoroughly taste it? Tease out its nuances, appreciate its texture, name its flavors?"

What the fuck are we talking about now?

Cornbread? Pussy? Both?

I like both.

I like 'em a lot.

A tide of heat rises inside my skin. It gathers between my legs, morphing into this sweet, awful pressure, and my dick nudges against my zipper.

I promised Beau I wouldn't lay a finger on Emma, and I mean to honor that promise. But a little borderline-inappropriate banter never hurt anyone. Miss Crawford may look all uptight in her pencil skirt and pulled back hair, but clearly, there's a dirty mind at work behind those wicked brown eyes.

I want to know more. If only so I can maintain the upper hand in this game between us that's clearly begun.

"Would you like to find out?" I ask.

She turns her head to look at me over her shoulder. "I would, actually. Tonight?"

"Aren't you going to at least buy me dinner first?"

Her eyes rake down my body again. Then rake back up. This time, they flicker with appreciation.

Aw, yeah. She likes the purple suit. She may be a stuck-up sommelier, but the girl appreciates a well-dressed man.

"Yes, actually. I've got meetings with the finance team this afternoon, and then I'll be in the kitchen tonight with Chef and her staff. What about tomorrow? Eight PM-ish? I'll arrange a tasting of my current favorite wines. We could do it blind—see exactly what you can do to my...cornbread."

"Y'all," Hank says. "For the love of God, the explicit food metaphors have got to stop."

I don't know my way around blind tastings very well. But I do know I want to show this chick who she's dealing with. I may be a pro athlete, and yes, I may be wearing a purple suit (that I am clearly rocking). But that doesn't mean I'm not capable of crushing this little competition she wants to put together. I've been collecting wine for over a decade. I've tasted shit that was in Thomas Jefferson's cellar. Trophy vintages of Chateau Lafite Rothschild, the best Chilean Carménère ever produced, and Screaming Eagle's highest rated bottles.

And I'll admit the fact that Emma is willing to go toe to toe with me has piqued my interest. When was the last time someone challenged me?

Why, I want to ask her. Why the fuck do you care so much?

I'm gonna find out. And then I'm gonna get her ass fired. This is my restaurant. My resort.

My family.

"I'm in," I say, making a mental note to set my alarm for quarter till ten tomorrow. "We won't have much choice when it comes to the food at such short notice."

"I'll get in touch with Chef Katie and work with what she's got," Emma says, waving me away with a dismissive flick of her wrist.

Anger punches me square in the gut. "I'm the food guy."

"I'm the wine woman. And I need the courses to complement my selections. The food and the wine have to speak to each other. You can't serve duck with Riesling, or an arugula salad with a big, fruity Amarone."

I'm going to fucking hate this, I can already tell.

"Whatever." I turn to Hank. "We all set here?"

"Yup."

Emma takes her knee off the chair. "Can I make a quick suggestion?"

"What?"

"Skip the cologne tomorrow. It'll mess with your tongue."

A pulse of anger screams up my center. Or maybe it's embarrassment.

The girl practically radiates her desire to dominate, which makes me think my "co-head" will eventually push me out. What if the wine and beverage program isn't enough for her? What if she wants the food too? Where would that leave me?

Out of a job and up shit creek without a paddle, that's where. I've been pushed out by an ambitious upstart before. There may be fewer headlines this time around, but the sting would be the same.

The shame would be the fucking same.

I hate to be the guy who's threatened by an ambitious woman. Usually ambition turns me on. I like a girl who's got something cooking. But when those ambitions threaten *me* and my future and my place in my family—well, that's a different scenario, isn't it?

My brothers and sister and mama are Blue Mountain Farm, and they're my life. I think it shocked us all how much we enjoy working together. How *well* we work together. I love the idea of continuing my parents' legacy and of keeping Daddy's memory alive through a spirit of generosity.

I am not being generous right now.

But I was serious about the yacht. I had my fun. Blew off steam when things went south in my pro career. Now, though, I'm done with that shit. I like my life here. I want to keep it exactly as is. Change has never been kind to me.

And now Emma is here to shake things up.

Over my dead body. I've already reinvented myself once. I know how painful and long the process can be. And if there's one thing I've always known about myself, it's that I like to stay busy. As Daddy used to say, idle hands are the devil's workshop. Don't get me wrong, I am fucking great at enjoying my leisure time. But I also like to hustle. If I'm not hustling, trying to make my family's resort the best it can possibly be, if I'm not working my ass off to ensure the people and the heritage I love so much have a future, then I'd have no purpose.

And that seems like the worst outcome of all.

Chapter Four

SAMUEL

I spend a few hours in my office above the restaurant, twitchy as hell as I listen to Emma getting settled in the room next door.

A hard workout always clears my head. When I have a rare break later that afternoon, I head home and hit the gym in my basement for a quick sweat session.

On my way downstairs, I pass my trophy case. At twenty feet long and ten feet high, it takes up the length of an entire wall. Some of my own shit is in there. Two Super Bowl MVP awards, NFC Championship trophy, an ESPY for Best Dressed Athlete.

But Dad's trophies are the real stars. They're displayed front and center; his Super Bowl ring is probably my most prized possession.

That, and his cast-iron skillet.

I slow my steps, eyes raking over the massive ring in its black velvet box. That hollow ache returns, taking root in the center of my chest.

All I ever wanted was to make the man proud.

I don't think he'd be proud of me right now.

Taking a deep breath, I square my shoulders. I'm not proud of acting like a jackass, either. But it's a means to an end. I'm defending my place.

Family always came first in Daddy's book, and I know he'd like to see me follow his lead in that regard.

I just wish he were here to tell me what to do. He was a good man who gave good advice. Before he got sick, anyway. He was also an honest man, and one of the few I implicitly trusted. With him in my corner, I never felt lost.

I never felt alone, the way I do now.

Daddy passed from early-onset dementia almost fifteen years ago, but I still miss him every damn day. He and I were thick as thieves, probably because we're so much alike. We have the same build. Same love of feeding our people. We played the same position, and we even wore the same number, 4, on our jerseys.

But missing him ain't gonna make shit any better. I've made my call, and I'm sticking to it. I've tried being the good guy before, and look how that went—I lost my job, my team, and my career all in one fell swoop.

And really, I'm doing Emma a favor. She's a smart girl. She'll find a position that's better suited to her talents. One that allows her to soar, the way I want to soar on my own at Blue Mountain Farm.

The cellar is my happy place.

Ducking my head as I step through the door, I inhale a deep lungful of that familiar smell: oak, fruit, alcohol. All undercut by this smoky dampness I can only describe as history.

The history of the barn, which dates back to the late 1700s.

The history of the wine itself.

And my own history—from my first sip of the good stuff at a team dinner at Del Frisco's Philadelphia to buying my first bottle at auction to this. A world-class collection that's a draw in and of itself. I've had dozens of guests return to the resort just for the wine. A fact I'm pretty fucking proud of.

Immediately, the ache in my chest loosens. I have no clue why Emma put it there, or why it lingered well into the evening.

No surprise, though, that my cellar would be the thing to shake it.

We had the state-of-the-art space constructed in the barn's basement. It's a cavernous cellar, equal parts rustic and slickly modern, with a vaulted stone ceiling and walls paneled in reclaimed wood. Enormous tempered glass boxes, illuminated from the floor, hold the actual wine racks. Each box is carefully organized with particular varietals. Makes it easy for our waitstaff to navigate our enormous list quickly and efficiently.

Also makes the cellar look sexy as hell. When I met with the architect, I told him I wanted to build Tony Stark's wine cellar if Tony were the secret lovechild of Daenerys Stormborn and Drake.

And that's exactly the cellar I got.

The lighting is low and soft, giving the space a moody, sexy vibe, and the temperature is set at a perfect fifty-five degrees. There's a massive antique table in the center, which we use for private parties and tastings. I keep a few of my really special bottles—a Nebuchadnezzar of Ace of Spades champagne, a magnum of my favorite Napa Cab—on a shelf that runs the length of one wall, which we covered in antiqued mirror to reflect the light. We spared no expense. Same as I spared no expense on this collection.

I've got three thousand bottles down here. Everything

from Silver Oak to hundred-year-old Burgundy. Opening the glass door to my favorite box—big, meaty California Cabernets—I mentally catalogue each bottle's characteristics: alcohol, acidity, body. It's been a while since I did a blind tasting, and my vocabulary is a little rusty. I used to do them with my teammates back in the day. A friendly competition where the dollar price of the bottles we brought mattered more than our acumen in identifying them.

I wonder what Emma will pick. She mentioned she liked small producers. Not my specialty. Not my preference, either.

Grabbing a bottle by its neck, I pull it out. Opus One. I vaguely remember this vintage. I drank it with...that chick from HGTV? Maybe in Palm Springs? Or was it Palm Beach? God, I'm tired.

Blue fruits. No, stone fruits. Red? Red what? And the tannins. *What about the tannins?*

Fuck.

I shove the bottle back into its slot with more force than necessary. The entire rack trembles, making me want to puke for one agonizing heartbeat, then another.

"There a bee in your bonnet?"

I turn to see my sister, Milly, stride into the room, a wine menu and notebook tucked under one arm, phone in hand.

"Nah." I paste on a smile and turn away from the wine. "Just—"

"A certain sommelier's arrival got you out of sorts. Or so I hear."

Out of my four siblings, I meddle the most. So I have absolutely no right to be annoyed by Milly's line of questioning.

But I am.

I'm really, really annoyed. And I really, really wish Milly would go away. I want to be alone.

27

"You know how I feel about that." I nod at her notebook. "Need some help?"

"Actually, Emma already gave me a few great ideas for John and Celeste. I guess they went to Slovenia last week and fell in love with the wine there, so they requested a change in the menu for the wedding. Emma said we should try—wait, here, let me check"—Milly opens her notebook to a book-marked page—"something called Rebula? And she suggested we give Cabernet Franc a go for the red. Apparently that's cultivated in Slovenia too. She gave me a few bottles to inves-tigate down here."

The tightness in my chest returns with a vengeance. Emma's already fucking with my work. "But I already helped John and Celeste pick out the wine. Some really nice stuff too. You sure they want that other garbage served at their million-dollar wedding?"

"Million point two, thank you very much. And yes. They want the whole thing to feel 'personal' and 'different.' Emma says these wines should help accomplish that. She also says they can be really delicious."

Milly is Blue Mountain Farm's resident wedding planner. This year, we booked our biggest wedding yet, for Celeste Loo (supermodel, cookbook author, and expert of social media clap backs) and John Bevin, legendary R&B star famous for singing songs about Celeste. The wedding's about a month out, so Milly's been finalizing selections and placing orders like crazy. So have Chef Katie and I. We pull out all the stops for all our weddings, but this one is especially lavish and especially large. John and Celeste are hosting three hundred guests at the swanky outdoor pavilion we built down by the small lake on our property.

I was very much looking forward to serving a delicious champagne and a spicy Barolo. But now I'm going to be serving something that sounds like an infectious disease?

Hard pass.

"She's wrong," I say, grabbing the wine menu from my sister. "So fucking wrong."

Milly just smiles at me, a wicked gleam in her eyes. "You hate her. Emma. And you don't hate anyone. Well, with one notable exception. Which makes me think you *like* her."

I busy myself by flipping through the Chardonnay section. *Far Niente: butter, melon. Chateau Montelena: lemon, no, lime, medium body, slight acidity (maybe?).* "That makes absolutely no sense."

"You make absolutely no sense. You're all smiles and swagger for the rest of the world. But with her, apparently, you're a broody, growly jerk. Yes, I talked to Beau, and yes, he told me how you showed your ass earlier today. Hank said there were some dirty puns being thrown around?"

I draw a sharp breath through my nose. "Y'all are gonna put me in an early grave, you know that?"

Milly's grin deepens. "She's pretty."

"She's not what the farm needs."

"She's staying really close to your house."

"You know I can do this, right?" I pause my flipping to meet her gaze. "You know I can run this restaurant and fill this cellar, and do it for any other restaurants and cellars we may open in the future?"

Milly's brows curve upward, making her look so much like Mama that for a second I can't breathe. Even though she's well into her sixties, Mama could almost be Milly's twin.

"Don't compare this situation to that one," she replies. "That was just a string of bad timing and worse luck."

I scoff. "If that's true, fate must've had it out for me. I was the unluckiest asshole in pro sports."

"Were. You *were* the unluckiest asshole. That was in the past. Leave it there. This is about our future, Samuel. Think about how lucky you are these days to be working with your kind, loving, amazing family."

"Did you miss my comment about the early grave?"

Milly just grins. "Of course you can run this place. But that's not what bringing Emma onboard is about. It's not about pushing you out. It's just a way of stepping up our game. When Beau first got the idea for the resort, we all agreed we wanted it to be the best of the best. You don't get to the top by resting on your laurels. We have to keep pushing forward, always."

I grunt. "From the feedback I've gotten, I'd say we're at the top already. But if need be, I can always expand the cellar. Get more wine. Better wine."

Milly shakes her head, putting a hand on my shoulder. "You're gonna burn yourself out working the way you do. That's another reason Beau wanted to hire a sommelier. To help you."

"Beau's worked his balls off for this resort. He's the one who needs a break, and I think Annabel's gonna give him one." Beau's best friend, Annabel, arrived yesterday at Blue Mountain with her four-month-old baby in tow. Beau and Bel have been in love since they were back in college, but they have yet to admit it to themselves or to each other. "I ran into her earlier, by the way."

Milly's face lights up. "You did? I'm jealous. How's she doing?"

"Well, she cried when she saw Beau, so...yeah, he wasn't joking when he said motherhood's been giving her a tough time. And yes"—I hold up my hand—"we are absolutely pulling out all the stops for her. Hank's arranging a spa day, and I made sure her fridge was stocked with lots of goodies. I've got dinner being delivered to her in"—I bend my arm and check my watch—"twenty minutes. I asked Chef Katie to send over four of her favorite entrees from tonight's menu, plus enough pimiento cheese and crackers to feed a small army. A couple of pints of ice cream too."

My sister smiles. "I won't pretend to understand how you can be such a great brother while also being the world's worst coworker."

"Isn't your motto 'you do you'?"

"It is." She looks down at a chirp from her phone. A text? Whatever it is, it's making her smile.

Now that I think about it, she's been smiling a lot since Nate Kingsley, owner of a famous local whiskey distillery, visited recently.

"Something good?" I ask.

Still smiling, Milly types a quick reply, then blanks the screen with a *click*. "Yes. Anyway, 'you do you' doesn't apply when you're being a complete and utter jerk. Give Emma a chance, all right? It won't kill you, and it would make Beau happy. Hell, maybe it'll even make you happy too."

"I am happy," I growl.

Milly points a finger at me. "Growling isn't a good look on you. Quit it. And have fun at your tasting tomorrow."

Fun. Ha.

Like I even know what that is anymore.

Chapter Five

SAMUEL

"Ready to get your ass kicked?" Emma asks the next night.

No greeting. Just a pretty smile and eyes that burn with a challenge she's unabashedly excited about.

Why does she enjoy brutalizing me this way?

And how does she look prettier than she did yesterday, even though she's standing in the same restaurant wearing almost the same damn outfit?

Despite my best effort to avoid her, I've seen a lot of Emma over the past twenty-four hours. She's popped into my office more times than I can count, and was all over the floor last night shadowing me as I selected wines for guests and served them.

She's thorough, I'll give her that.

My hand curls into a fist at my side. The sooner we start, the sooner we get this over with.

Taking a quick glance around the restaurant, my annoyance fades. The place is packed. People are chowing down on the food, smiling as they chat with their loved ones and sip their drinks. The waitstaff crisscrosses the floor, arms loaded with trays of beautiful food and bottles of excellent wine. A couple laughs in a booth in the corner. Another hold hands across their table. A family of five digs into Chef's insanely delicious take on rabbit ragu with homemade pasta and aged pecorino. Hank is chatting with a pair of older women at the bar.

The food, the wine, the people—it all comes together to create this heady buzz that's heaven on earth.

And to think that I made it happen. Yes, I got lucky hiring some of the best staff on the planet, starting with Chef Katie. Beau was there for every meeting, every round of interviews, and Milly played a big part in planning our food and beverage programs too. But I went from quarterback to food and wine director in the space of a few years. During those years, I studied the hospitality industry like a madman. I traveled all over to spend my Saturday nights in the kitchens of the world's best restaurants. I took courses, shadowed waiters, washed dishes. I cooked. I networked. I filled close to a dozen notebooks with my notes on everything from the proper way to slice prosciutto to how I wanted our guests to feel while dining at Blue Mountain Farm.

When we finally opened The Barn Door, I wanted to take the position of food and wine director knowing I left nothing on the table. I tried my best.

I still try my best. And I'm damn proud of the result. In that respect, I've done my family proud.

"Josie," I clip.

A hostess immediately appears at my elbow. "Yes, Samuel?"

"Take us to our table, please."

"Right away. We have y'all at seventeen."

I cut Emma a glance. She shrugs, this smug little thing that enrages me. Olly, my former backup-turned-traitor teammate, was smug like that too. At first, I thought it was just playful indifference, but I learned the hard way it was something much more sinister.

"Heard you had a thing for the night sky," she says, "so I guessed seventeen was your favorite table. You can see the stars through the window if you blow out the candles. It's also private and quite cushy. Perfect for a big swinging dick celebrity like yourself."

I can tell Josie is trying very hard not to laugh as she seats us at the table. It is my favorite, for exactly the reasons Emma mentioned. The booth is a circular swath of butter soft leather tucked into the far corner of the barn. A high window follows the curve of the booth, allowing diners to glimpse nearly three hundred sixty degrees of sky. At night, when the light's just right, it can be downright magical.

It can also be hell on earth when you're experiencing it beside Miss Know-It-All. Seeing the flight of wineglasses set out at each place setting is an unwelcome reminder of how long I'll be stuck here.

I could leave. Walk away. That might even be the smart thing to do.

But just like I was glued to the spot at Emma's cottage yesterday, I find my legs unwilling to move. I glance across the table and watch Emma settle her napkin on her lap. Her movements are elegant. Restrained. But her eyes flash in the low light, alive and eager.

I sit, my clothes feeling a size too tight as I grab my own napkin.

"I heard you gave Milly some pointers today," I say, careful to keep my voice even.

Emma nods. "The Slovenian wines, yes. What a cool request."

"You overstepped your bounds, Emma." When she opens her mouth to correct me, I hold up my hand. "I spent weeks helping John and Celeste put together a wine list. I pored over my entire cellar and went through every bottle until we found exactly what they envisioned. They want to change that now, fine. But you come to me first. Always. Have you ever planned a beverage menu for a wedding? What about a wedding that's happening in four weeks? Hundreds of moving parts are involved. You were just telling me how you can't pair duck with a Riesling. How do you think this is going to affect the food menu? What about the stemware we'll need? Milly knows her way around the logistics. And you may know your way around wine, but I'm the only one out of all three of us who can make those pieces, plus the hundred others, work together."

She blinks at me. Chastised. "You're right. I'm sorry. I just heard Slovenia, and Celeste Loo, and my excitement got the better of me."

My turn to blink. I wasn't expecting her to back down so easily.

"But"—*ah, here it is*—"I do have some great ideas for the revised menu. I think we can put together something really special."

"Of course it will be special. This is Blue Mountain Farm. And I'm in charge." I nod at the glasses in front of me. "Let's do this. I have to be out of here by quarter till ten."

Emma stiffens. "Right. I have a…call with a friend I have to get to as well." She looks up and nods with a smile, and Xavier approaches the table with an opened bottle wrapped in a serviette (that's cloth napkin in wine speak).

He pours us each a glass of sparkling wine. It's all I can do not to rub my hands together. After California Cabs, bubbly is my specialty. Back in my pro days, there was always a bottle being popped somewhere: locker rooms, flights, hungover mornings in Vegas that called for more than a little hair of the dog.

"A toast?" Emma holds out her glass.

I glare at her across the table, reaching for my glass but not holding it up. "I save my toasts for family and friends, thanks."

Undeterred, she continues to hold up her glass. "Fine. I'll toast myself. To our future partnership. I'm excited to see how far we can take this thing."

"You won't be touching my thing."

It's too far and entirely inappropriate. I want to send her running for the place she worked last, not a lawyer's office. But my lizard brain must consider being crass a legitimate way of pushing her away. The bun, the suit, the sensible heels —everything about her screams *I'm offended by your awfulness*.

But those eyes of hers tell a different story. They darken with mischief, a small smile working its way across her lips.

She unbuttons her blazer, revealing a white silk blouse that appeared to be all business when her lapels were closed. But now that they're open, I can see the damn thing is gossamer thin and slightly transparent.

Dear God.

"You can keep that thing." Her gaze flicks briefly to my crotch. "But this thing? The resort, everything it represents, showing your guests the best damn hospitality this side of the Appalachians? I'd very much like to play around with that."

My cock twitches.

The goddamn traitor actually moves inside my pants, thanks to the awareness—the blood—that gathers in my balls at her equally crass reply.

My fingers tighten around the stem of the glass. No fucking way Emma's perverted wittiness is gonna distract me.

No. Fucking. Way.

"Hey, y'all!" Hank appears at the table with a smile. "So, this tasting. I can only imagine how epic it will be. Emma, this guy being any nicer to you?"

Emma shoots me a look. "Not really."

Now Hank's looking at me too. "Dude, c'mon."

"Don't you have a job to do?" I reply.

"Be nice." He turns to Emma. "You need someone to talk some sense into him, you know who to call."

"Let's get this over with," I grunt, and hold my glass up to my nose as my brother thankfully disappears.

I watch Emma do the same. She really sticks her nose in the glass, looking like an idiot but not seeming to give two shits about it. Her tits rise on a deep inhale.

Look away. But is that the outline of her nipple?

Christ, it is her nipple, and it's hard. I can make out the whisper-thin cup of her bra through her blouse and the color of the pebbled point through it.

Her nipple is pink, lusciously sized, with those little fucking dots surrounding it in a tight, perfect circle.

My mouth fills with saliva as my cock full-on surges against my fly.

I look up to see Emma watching me. That gleam in her eye is still there. So is the smile.

The realization hits me with the force of a skillet to the head.

Emma did this on purpose. She unbuttoned her blazer, and wore *this* shirt with *this* bra, to tease me.

Taunt me.

Provoke me.

Fuck her. Two can play this game.

"I'm sorry," I say, setting down my glass without sipping. I place my fingertips on its stem.

She sets down her glass too. "Sorry?"

"I've been neglectful." I glide those fingers up the stem. Back down, Austin Powers style. Just to mess with her.

Just to see if she'll catch on.

She does, right away. Her gaze follows my movements.

37

She smirks, amused. But then her nostrils flare, and her eyes get a little hazy. Heated.

Aw, I like that heat. That hint of a chink in the armor of her impeccable professionalism.

But then she blinks and the heat is gone, smoothed over by something like victory.

We'll see about that.

"Xavier?" The waiter appears at my elbow in half a second flat. "Would you mind bringing some cornbread to the table?"

"Ah," Emma says, glancing up at my face. "You've been neglectful of that. Making it moist."

"I'm going to take my brother's advice and stop the food puns there. But I figure we could use some extra carbs to soak up five courses of wine."

"Six. I included a dessert course."

"I hate dessert wine."

"Trust me with this one? You'll like it."

"You have no idea what I like."

I run my fingers up the stem again. But this time, her eyes stay glued to mine.

"I'm learning," she replies steadily. "I'm good at reading the room. Good at reading people."

"Oh? And what kind of book am I?"

The gleam in her eyes darkens. "I'm not sure yet."

Her eyes keep flicking to my fingers. The ones wrapped around the elegant stem of my wineglass.

I gently glide them up the stem. Then I pick up the glass and bring it to my lips.

Time to get down to business.

Closing my eyes, I do my best to ignore the heaviness in my groin and focus on the wine instead.

I inhale. My nostrils sting at the immediate hit of alcohol. Behind that, I smell burnt sugar, an almost sticky strawberry note that brings to mind the kind of old, gooey candy you'd get at Grandma's house.

Emma sips, taking the lead, and I follow. Bubbles wash over my tongue. I wrinkle my nose. Oh, yeah, that sticky sweetness is there, and it is gross. Gotta be something young and cheap.

"You're smiling," Emma says, swallowing. "You know this one?"

"I'm smiling because your pick is downright awful. Reminds me of the crap I'd duct tape to my hands in college."

Emma cocks a brow. "You duct taped bottles of sparkling wine to your hands in college?"

"You've clearly never played Edward Forty Hands. It was forty-ounce bottles of malt liquor, actually, but it tasted the same."

"Right." She digs her teeth into her bottom lip, still smiling. Like she knows something I don't. "How about you save all your answers for the end? Make a note on your phone about what you think each wine is. Varietal, vintage, and location."

No need. I make a mental note—gotta be Prosecco, two or three years old, Italy—and raise my hand for the next round.

Emma's arm shoots out. She grabs my forearm, the heat of her touch seeping through the sleeve of my jacket, and guides it back down to the table.

Her grip is firm. Confident. So is her voice when she says, "This is my tasting, Beauregard. I call the shots."

My cock stands at attention as my vision goes red.

Who the hell does Emma think she is?

And since when does she call me Beauregard?

"Keep it moving," I grunt, slugging what's left of the sparkling.

Emma's paired it with a winter kale, Manchego, and

chili dusted pecan salad. We eat while we wait for the next pour. I can't help but notice how she eats like a European, fork in her left hand, knife in her right, and every time she takes a bite her lips linger on the tines of her fork. Gliding over them slowly as she savors every morsel.

When she moans, my knife slips against my plate and almost gouges my eye out.

"Wow," she says, shaking her head appreciatively. "We gotta give our compliments to Chef Katie. The play on texture in this salad is just—I mean, it's on a whole other level. The crunchy heat of the pecans with the creamy cheese and the tang of that warm bacon vinaigrette? Kill me now and I'd die happy."

There are two types of foodies in this world: those who like good food because they can post pictures of it on Instagram, and those who treasure food because they appreciate the art and effort and *heart* involved in creating dishes like this.

Emma's clearly the latter. Her phone's nowhere to be seen. She's sensitive to the most minute of flavors, brow furrowed as she chews thoughtfully. Eyes bright, like a light's been turned on inside her. Fully absorbed in the moment. The flavors. The feel of a shared meal.

Can't remember the last time I sat down with someone who radiated intelligent passion like this. Who wasn't putting on a front, a fake face.

Makes me realize how fake my smiles can be sometimes. A lot of the time, actually.

"I hear you feed your staff," she says, making me blink. Only then do I realize I've been staring at her. I look up and catch Hank staring at her too, hovering just out of arm's reach.

Looking away, I shove a forkful of kale into my mouth. If

anyone can make this leafy shit delicious, it's Katie. The chef *I* hired.

"And?"

"And I think that's really cool. Xavier was telling me how everyone eats together in the kitchen before service. Not many of the places I've worked for do that."

I grab my wine and finish it. I notice her eyes stray to my fingers on the stem again.

"Figured the best way to get the staff excited about our food would be to feed it to them. That way they can sell it honestly. Put a personal touch on their recommendations."

"You ever eat with them?" she asks, cleaning the last of her plate.

I shake my head. "I don't have time."

I lean back as our plates are cleared, replaced by a second course: spring vegetable risotto, featuring the peas, asparagus, and shallots grown right here on the farm. It's topped with a generous helping of freshly shaved parmesan, the nutty, umami smell making my stomach growl.

I worked out like a motherfucker earlier, which explains why I'm starving. Exercise makes me feel centered. I do it six days a week, fifty-two weeks a year, no exceptions, no excuses. But I don't usually go as hard as I did today. Guess I have a lot on my mind I needed to clear out, thanks to the girl who's currently torturing me from across the table.

The next wine is a white, straw colored. Cold enough to make the bowl of my glass frost over.

I follow Emma's lead and shove my nose deep into the glass. She watches me do it, something like pleasure in her gaze. Tonight she's the boss, and she digs it.

Exactly why she can't stay.

At last she tips back her glass and sips. I do it too, determined to hate this wine like I hated the first one.

Only problem? It's freaking delicious.

I'm not the biggest white wine fan, but I've tasted enough to know this one is *good*. It's sweet but not perfume-y, crisp but not astringent, dry but not boring. A little baked bread on the nose. There's so much going on here I can't tease it all out on one sip alone. I take another, moving it around my tongue the way Emma does.

We look like total assholes, gurgling our wine, swishing it around our mouths. But I could give a shit.

This wine, it's a whole mood. Makes me think of warm summer nights, cool water running over creek bottoms, the smell of fluffy lemon pancakes. The kind Daddy used to make on Sunday mornings. I feel grass under my feet. Lightness in my legs and chest. A sense of freedom and rightness I can't quite get my arms around.

Sounds nuts, I know. I'm never one to gush random bullshit when I'm drinking. But two sips in, and I already know this wine is really, really special. It's telling me a story—telling a version of *my* story back to me—making me sort through my memory to nail the exact feeling I get when I drink it.

Above all else, it makes me think of my past, which makes me think of Daddy.

My heart twists. Lungs clench. I set down my wine and reach for my water.

This little buzz I'm starting to get it is putting me in a weirdly poetic mood, and I am not here for it.

"You okay?" Emma asks. There's a knowing warmth in her eyes. I don't like that either.

"I'm fine. This is, uh, something new. The wine. Something I haven't had before I don't think."

"You say that like it's a bad thing, Beauregard."

"I don't like it when you call me that."

"I don't like it when you don't give credit where credit is due."

She doesn't ask permission. Doesn't try to win me over

with flattery and respect and deference, the way the rest of my employees do.

She just does and says what she wants.

I get that. What I don't get? Why she puts up with my rudeness. My scowly, shitty attitude. I want her to give *up* already, but she won't, and it's driving me up the goddamn wall.

Whatever. She'll break eventually. I'll just keep at it. So I chug my wine and clean my plate, bringing my blood back down to a simmer.

We finish that course. Dive right into the next one, and the next. All reds, all shit I'm pretty confident I know. Some are better than others. I fully expect a hearty, spicy red to go with our oxtail course, but I'm surprised when I'm served an inky Grenache (I think?) that, much as I hate to admit it, is juicy in all the best ways.

Emma keeps asking questions. I keep replying with one word answers, praying she'll take the hint.

She doesn't.

Her eyes flick to my fingers several times. So Emma here's clearly got a thing for my hands. Interesting.

Not that it matters. The sooner this girl is gone, the better.

Although the dessert wine she picked—yeah, I don't hate it.

It's the moment I've been waiting for all night: the reveal of the wines I've selected.

I resist the urge to rub my hands together with glee. I'm never one to gloat. But putting this guy in his place is going to be so, so satisfying.

"Thank you," I say to Xavier as he lines up all six bottles on the table. Their labels are still covered by serviettes, some of them damp on account of the old-school ice buckets I like to use for my sparkling and white wines.

I glance at Samuel. He's checking his watch. It's a different one tonight: a yellow gold Rolex that's a flashy pick against his (relatively) subdued navy-blue suit. As much as I hate to give him a win, this look is his best yet.

"Make this quick," he says, shooting his cuffs like the arrogant prick he is before settling his elbows on the table. "I'm about to turn into a pumpkin."

I'm about to turn into something much more interesting than that. Not that a blockheaded bully like him would appreciate it, but still. Victory calls for a special kind of celebration.

"First wine: the sparkling." I settle my first two fingers over the throat of the bottle. "What did you think?"

"Prosecco. Two to three years old, Italy. Garbage," he says with a smug smile.

I uncoil the serviette from around the bottle. I resist the urge to giggle like a kid in front of her birthday cake as I watch Samuel's smile flatten. His blue eyes widen in genuine shock.

"No," he blurts, grabbing the bottle. It looks laughably tiny in his enormous hands.

Those hands. They're this combination of nimble and thick that makes my mind short circuit.

I look away. "Oh, yes."

It's one of his trophy bottles—a 2002 Dom Perignon listed on the menu for north of eight hundred bucks—that I thought was pretty delicious.

I *knew* he'd hate my picks, no matter what they were. Testing that theory was unnecessary, but I'm glad I did it. Seeing the frantic look on his face as he pours what's left of the bottle into an empty glass to taste it again was worth the trouble.

I watch him swallow it down, heart thumping. He's gotta give in, right?

I really, really want this guy to give in already. Because maybe then he'll finally view me not as a threat but as a partner. I'm not here for a hostile takeover.

I'm here to help.

"That's not the wine I tasted," he tries.

Crossing my arms, I spear him with a look. "Now you're just embarrassing yourself."

"The bottle must be skunked." Samuel sniffs the mouth of said bottle, wrinkling his forehead. "Whatever. Next one?"

My heart thumps again, this time for a different reason. Something weird happened when Samuel sampled the Spring

Mountain Riesling I served for our second course. He got this look in his eyes, the one people usually get when a wine *does* something to them. When it not only touches something essential inside them but rearranges it too. Cracks it open. Makes it new.

It's the look of love.

Interestingly, Samuel quashed that look as soon as it appeared. But at that moment, his eyes had softened, and I'd almost felt a kinship with him. *See?* I'd wanted to say. *See how giving something new a chance pays off?*

Not all men are as evolved as MyBoyBlue, I guess. One of the five hundred reasons I prefer internet sex to the real-life version.

I grab the second bottle and hold it out to Samuel.

A spark of curiosity lights up his eyes. The firm line of his mouth twitches. He doesn't want to show interest. Appreciation. He's fighting it. But it's there, and it's the kind of reaction I live for as a sommelier.

"Riesling," he says. "Napa Valley? It's too dry for an old-world Riesling. I'm thinking 2015ish. 2017 maybe."

I could continue my gloating. But that would just give Samuel an excuse to replace that interest with annoyance, which would defeat the whole purpose of this tasting. So I try a different tack.

Unwrapping the serviette, I reveal a 2016 Riesling from the Spring Mountain district of Napa Valley.

"Well done," I say, holding up my hand for a high five. "One of the best wines I've had in the past five years. Different but totally delicious, right? And it retails for under thirty-five bucks a bottle. Not exactly a steal, but for a wine with this kind of complexity, it's still a great bargain."

Samuel glances at my hand. Glances at the bottle.

He leaves my high five hanging. But he does glide his glass forward—*those fingers, Jesus*—and raise his eyebrows.

"I'll have a little more."

I watch him taste it, biting the inside of my cheek to keep from smiling. He knows his wine, that much is clear, but I could tell at the start of our meal he wasn't as well versed in tasting. He wasn't smelling the wine correctly, and he gulped his wine instead of savoring it. Now he's shoving his nose into the glass like a pro, taking his time as he drinks to contemplate the Riesling's gorgeous flavor profile.

Clearly he watched me, took notes, and modified his behavior accordingly.

He actually learned something. Took a suggestion. *Changed*.

Hope rises in my chest like the sun. I don't want to jump the gun here. But I think Samuel's got a softer, more intelligent side. He may act like an unyielding asshole, but deep down maybe that's not who he really is.

Which begs the question: why the dissonance?

"I like this one." He tips back what's left in the glass. His eyes find mine, and he cocks a brow. "You know the winemaker?"

I finally allow myself to grin. "Sure do. Smith-Madrone is a family operation, same as Blue Mountain Resort. Their story is actually really cool. I'm happy to reach out to them and inquire about putting in an order. They have an Estate Riesling, too, that's baller. Pricier. But blow-your-mind amazing. Almost as good as a '76 German Riesling I had a few years back. It's still my favorite wine I've ever tasted."

"I'll think about it."

It's a small victory, but a victory nonetheless. I'll take it.

We're running out of time, so I hurry through the rest of the wines. Samuel only nails one of the reds, a Willamette Valley Pinot Noir. He completely misses the other three.

By the time we're finished, he's back to being a block of stone.

Two out of six. He's not happy about that. Tossing his napkin onto the table, he stands, letting out an annoyed sigh as he buttons his blazer. His gaze rakes over the bustling restaurant before it lands on me.

"You did well," I say. "That was a tough tasting."

"Now you're just embarrassing yourself," he replies, throwing my line back at me. "I bombed it. You proved your point. You're the expert and I'm the idiot. Happy now?"

I feel a pinch of guilt. It was a dick move, putting together a tasting of esoteric wines I knew he wouldn't be able to identify.

Then again, if he hadn't been such a jerk to begin with, I wouldn't have had to put together this tasting in the first place. I wouldn't have had to prove that I'm able to contribute something of value. If he'd been amenable to working together, we could already be on our way to creating something special and spectacular here on the farm, instead of staring each other down over a table littered with half-empty bottles.

The thought makes me angry.

It makes me sad.

"My cornbread *is* indeed moi—well, you know, if that's what you're asking," I reply, deflecting.

For half a heartbeat he squints his eyes, mirthful.

"Told you I was a food guy."

He stands there, looking at me. I look back.

It hits me that he's waiting for me to get up. Like the gentleman he most certainly is not.

Even more bewildering? When he holds out his hand.

"Need some help?" he asks. "I gotta get going."

I glance at his hand. Nails are neatly groomed—filed, not cut—which makes me think he gets manicures.

But the walnut-sized knuckles, the blunt calluses on his fingertips, the roadmap of thick, ropey veins that marks the back of his hand—that speaks to a roughness I like very much.

I blink, stopping that thought in its tracks. I have to keep my eyes on the prize. Which means keeping my eyes *off* this man.

"I've got it, thanks," I say, scooting out of the booth on my own. I grab my bag, and we head for the door.

I notice the servers and hostesses practically kowtow to Samuel as we pass.

I also notice how he turns the heads of nearly every woman in the restaurant. A few of the men too.

As for me, I try very hard not to stare at the breadth of his back. The guy is huge. And hugely confident. He prowls the floor like he owns it (I mean, he kind of does), massive shoulders rolling as he waves to one guest, then smiles at another.

He is all smiles for the world. But for me? Totally different story.

He holds the door open. I step outside, welcoming the slight chill in the air. I'm feeling overheated. Also a little trepidatious. It's dark out here.

I walked to the restaurant earlier. My cottage is close by, and I knew I'd be drinking, so I didn't want to take the golf cart provided with my accommodations. No big deal when it was light outside.

But now that it's dark, I'm not so sure. I'm not necessarily worried about a serial killer leaping out of the trees and grabbing me. But I imagine these woods are home to all kinds of animals. Bears. Mountain lions. Snakes.

Samuel's shoes catch on the flinty ground beside me.

Now that we're away from the smells of the restaurant, I can smell *him*.

My heart skips a beat.

"You didn't wear it," I say, looking up at him. "Your cologne."

The lights from the barn catch on his thick, stylishly parted dark hair. The expression in his eyes—I can't read it.

"You walk here?" he grunts, shoving his hands in his pockets.

"Yeah. You?"

He tips his chin toward the darkness. "C'mon. I'll make sure Eddie and David leave you alone." He starts walking.

"Eddie and David?" I ask, hesitating. The snakes, the fact that Samuel might actually be looking out for me—I don't know which one scares me more.

"The black bears that live up the hill here."

I hustle to catch up to him. "You're kidding, right?"

"I'm not," he says, slowing his steps a little. "For the most part, they leave us alone. Except for that one time."

"What happened? Did someone get hurt?" My heart skips again, but for a different reason. Small lights illuminate the path we're walking, but otherwise the darkness is complete. Makes me hyper aware of the steady sound of Samuel's footsteps. The pulsing of crickets around us.

Wait, what did I just hear? Was that a rustle in those bushes over there?

"David ate a baby."

Without thinking I grab his arm. "A baby? Like, a *human* baby?"

"Yup. Grabbed him right out of his stroller."

"Oh my God! How did I not hear about this? Is the baby okay?"

The arm I'm holding starts to shake, and I realize Samuel is laughing.

Jerk.

"God, you're easy to mess with," he says. "David likes blackberries more than babies. Obviously."

I shove him away. "Not cool, Beauregard."

"About as cool as that bullshit tasting you just put me through, Emma. But really, we tell all our guests to keep an eye out for wildlife, and to avoid walking around the resort alone if they can. Especially at night."

Oh, God, Samuel really is looking out for me.

He really is being a gentleman. Which absolutely does not square with the guy I met yesterday.

I thought I had this guy pinned as a self-absorbed egomaniac. But now? Now I'm not so sure.

I don't know what to say when we get to my cottage. I fully expect Samuel to leave me at the gate, but instead he opens it, allowing me to pass through first, and walks me all the way to the front door.

I root around my bag for the key and notice my hands are clammy. Like I'm nervous or something.

Like Samuel and I are on a date, and this is the will-he-or-won't-he-kiss-me moment.

I find the key and slide it into the lock. The heat of his gaze makes me feel like a teenager again—hot and sweaty and painfully self-conscious.

"So. Eight AM tomorrow at the barn." I keep my eyes on the lock.

I hear his feet shuffle on the gravel pathway. "You move fast."

"Me asking around to find out when your day starts is moving fast?" I glance at him over my shoulder. I'm a few steps up on the porch, but he's so tall that we see eye to eye. "Just trying to be a team player."

There's that look again. The one I can't read.

"I don't believe that," he says. "Not for one fucking second."

And then he turns and stalks into the night.

I usually reserve my sky-high stilettos for special occasions.

But I'm feeling all kinds of mixed up after my very long, very weird first couple of days at Blue Mountain Farm Resort. I need to gather myself before I start my chat with Blue.

And nothing makes me feel more gathered than slipping on a killer pair of heels and playing with sexual power dynamics.

Plus, I want to celebrate tonight's victory.

I take off my blazer and unzip my skirt. Next comes bra and undies. Then I step out of my stupid kitten heels, and step into the stilettos.

They're the most expensive thing I've ever bought for myself other than my car. Meghan Markle wore something similar to some fabulous event, and when I saw them on her I immediately started hunting online. An entire paycheck later, my Aquazzura pumps arrived. I've been obsessed with them ever since.

The shoes are black satin, with a delicate needle heel four inches high. There's a cutout at the instep that allows you to see my foot right where it curves seductively in the middle. But what makes the pumps really special are the tiny crystals that dot the back of the shoe and the heel itself, capped with this sexy little knot of fabric that glimmers every time I move.

They're just the right combination of understated and sexy, and I feel like a million bucks whenever I put them on.

I grab my laptop and hop into bed. I cue up some porn to get in the mood. Then I reach between my legs.

When my fingers graze my clit, I nearly jump off the mattress. I'm sensitive.

And wet.

Holy shit, did Samuel do this?

I circle the pads of my fingers over my clit again. My head falls back against the pillow, eyes fluttering shut. All I see behind my closed lids are the veins on the back of Samuel's hands. The broad tips of his fingers.

Samuel *definitely* did this. During the tasting, I was aware of my physical attraction to him. But that attraction was peppered with so much distaste and discomfort I hadn't realized how out of hand it'd gotten until now.

A part of me wants to be disgusted with myself. Another part wants to be afraid. This is my future on the line here. I can't risk it by indulging this nonsensical, downright dangerous interest in Samuel Beauregard.

I nearly jump again when the alarm on my phone goes off. 10 PM.

Letting out a sigh of relief, I hit my phone screen to quiet the alarm and enter the chat room. I smile when I see MyBoyBlue is already here, and he's already sent me a dick pic.

Bless his heart.

CHAT #2

MyBoyBlue4: [Sends picture of his engorged cock. It's standing straight up.]

LadyV76: [Sends picture of herself with her knees drawn up to her chest, feet on the mattress. Her pussy is spread and her heels are fully visible.]

MyBoyBlue4: Aw FUCK those heels. I like.

LadyV76: No love for the pussy?

MyBoyBlue4: You already know how pretty I think your pussy is. This is exactly what I needed.

LadyV76: Tough day at the office?

MyBoyBlue4: You could say that. I know you said you don't share personal details, but I feel like a dick not asking how your day was.

LadyV76: I don't share personal stuff. But because I had a rough one too, I'll say that I've very much been looking forward to tonight.

MyBoyBlue4: You got no idea. I need to blow off some major steam.

LadyV76: SAME. Okay so speaking of steam, smoke, whatever...I'm the mother of dragons. You're Jon Snow.

MyBoyBlue4: I was just thinking about Khaleesi!

LadyV76: Great minds. My Khaleesi wears stilettos. Got lube?

MyBoyBlue4: Yes. Thankfully lube is plentiful in Westeros.

LadyV76: Valar morghulis. I'm going to lube you up. And then you're going to fuck my tits, bastard.

MyBoyBlue4: Jesus.

LadyV76: What?

MyBoyBlue4: I like it when you call me a bastard.

LadyV76: I knew you would. So I push you down on the edge of our bed on the ship.

MyBoyBlue4: We're on a ship? Fuck yes, that's badass.

LadyV76: Ship sex is the best sex. So I push you down on the edge of the bed. I spread your legs and get down on my knees between them.

MyBoyBlue4: I'm there

LadyV76: I grab your dick and give it a good tug. At the same time, I reach for your balls and play with those.

MyBoyBlue4: YESSSSSSSSSS

LadyV76: I look you in the eye as I lean down and put your cock in my mouth. You're impatient, you've been waiting all day for this, so you buck your hips and shove yourself all the way into the back of my throat. But you're forgetting who's queen.

MyBoyBlue4: And who's the bastard. Uh-oh.

LadyV76: I shoot to my feet and grab your hair. I pull it, hard. I'm going to remind you that while I may have been on my knees, you're the one who'll bend the knee to me.

MyBoyBlue4: Go on.

LadyV76: I'm going to torture you. I'm going to make you go slowly, go gently, and I won't let you put yourself inside me until I'm satisfied you've learned your place.

MyBoyBlue4: Tell me what I need to do to make this right, Breaker of Chains.

LadyV76: I lie on the bed, my head facing the foot of the mattress. You're still going to fuck my tits, but you're going to eat me out while you're doing it.

MyBoyBlue4: Actual twenty-first century question: is that physically possible?

LadyV76: It is if I say so.

MyBoyBlue4: Fair enough.

LadyV76: We're basically sixty-nining. Only with tits involved.

MyBoyBlue4: Fuck.

LadyV76: So I'm facing the foot of the bed and you're facing the headboard. You straddle my head and put your hands on either side of my hips. I grab your dick and guide it down to lie between my breasts.

MyBoyBlue4: You gotta send me a pic. Please, V.

LadyV76: Since you asked nicely...[Sends picture of her tits squeezed together]

MyBoyBlue4: Wow. You have a beautiful body.

LadyV76: Thanks. I appreciate that. So you're holding yourself up above me. I press my tits together and tell you to move. Slow and steady. Since you're lubed up, you move easily. You're hissing because it feels so good. Stroke yourself and tell me how it feels.

MyBoyBlue4: I think you know how it feels.

LadyV76: Are you getting sassy with me, bastard?

MyBoyBlue4: I would never. I'm stroking myself softly and slowly, just like you told me to do.

LadyV76: Good boy. Now lean down and lick my pussy.

MyBoyBlue4: You taste magnificent. Like the moon and stars.

LadyV76: Your arms shake with the effort of holding yourself up while leaning down like you are, but you're strong.

MyBoyBlue4: All that white walker slaying has kept me in amazing shape, I must say.

LadyV76: You're funny.

MyBoyBlue4: I know.

LadyV76: You lick my clit. Circle it with the tip of your tongue. Someone's taught you how to do this, and do it well.

MyBoyBlue4: It was a teacher I had. Back in Night Watch College.

LadyV76: Cheesy.

MyBoyBlue4: Yeah, that one wasn't so great. A for effort, F for execution.

LadyV76: You get an A in both for oral. My legs shake and so do your arms. You're kissing my pussy and fucking my tits. I tell you to go faster, and you listen. Faster. Harder. I tilt my head back and use my tongue to play with your balls, because you seem to like that.

MyBoyBlue4: Aw shit, I'm gonna come but I want you to go first.

LadyV76: Jon Snow is a gentleman?

MyBoyBlue4: Layers, baby. I got 'em.

LadyV76: You kiss my clit, nick it with your teeth. Suck.
[A pause]

MyBoyBlue4: Please please please tell me you just came so I can go too?

LadyV76: Yes.
[Another pause]

MyBoyBlue4: [Sends pic of cum all over his belly]

LadyV76: Hot. So hot. Also, how many abs do you have? 800?

MyBoyBlue4: Full disclosure: I may have been flexing for that picture. But yeah, I take good care of myself.

LadyV76: *You* have a beautiful body, bastard.

MyBoyBlue4: You like the flex.

LadyV76: I do. Thanks for the orgasm. I feel a million times better.

MyBoyBlue4: Can this bastard be honest/personal for a sec?

LadyV76: I may be the breaker of chains, but you're the breaker of rules. My rules. But because you were such a good boy, I'll let it slide. Just this once.

MyBoyBlue4: You're good at this. The power play shit. I've never done it with anyone before, and I'm clearly enjoying the hell out of it. It's different, but a good different. I appreciate that about you.

[A pause]

MyBoyBlue4: Uh-oh. Did I get too personal?

LadyV76: No. I'm...pleasantly shocked is all.

MyBoyBlue4: By what? Me complimenting you?

LadyV76: More like you complimenting me for being different. Not everyone appreciates that side of me. Especially my new coworker. I'm not sure what his deal is. But I am sure he loathes me.

MyBoyBlue4: Fuck that guy for life. I think you're better 'n grits. And that's saying something, because I fucking love grits.

LadyV76: You're cute. Are you from the South?

MyBoyBlue4: Carolina born and bred.

LadyV76: Really? Me too. And no, I won't tell you where.

MyBoyBlue4: Girl, I get it. I'd never rush you, but I'm down to share more when you are. In the meantime...yeah, I also get the struggle of showing your real self to the world though. Different sides of yourself. This here, the side where I like to be fucked by a dragon lady, it's a side I honestly didn't know existed until I (virtually) met you. It's hard to put myself out there. The real me, I mean. Sometimes I don't know who the fuck the real me is.

LadyV76: I know who I am. I just question it more than I should.

MyBoyBlue4: Meaning?

LadyV76: I'm ashamed to admit it. I feel like I should be past it by this point in my life. Still...some days, I'm certain I'm doing the right thing by being true to who I am and what I love. But others, I wonder if I'll ever get where I want to go. And sometimes I wish I could change everything about myself.

MyBoyBlue4: I like who you are.

LadyV76: I like who you are too. Not a lot of guys are willing to submit themselves this way.

MyBoyBlue4: It's fun. Glad I gave it a shot. So when can we chat next?

LadyV76: Work is going to be crazy for the next couple of days. Want to play it by ear?

MyBoyBlue4: Sounds great. In the meantime, why don't you kick your coworker's ass the way you're kicking mine? He might like it.

LadyV76: Somehow I doubt that. Good night, Jon Snow.

MyBoyBlue4: Sweet dreams, Khalessi. I hope tomorrow gets better.

Chapter Seven

EMMA

I don't want to smile at Blue's endearment. But I do.

As I close my laptop, a weird feeling settles in the pit of my stomach.

I'm not tired. I feel equal parts full and empty. Nourished and starving.

Nourished: great wine, better orgasm, even better win over Samuel. I have a lot to celebrate.

Starving: I wish I had someone to celebrate with. Maybe the glaring dissonance between how full some parts of my life are, and how utterly empty the others can be, is what's keeping me awake.

I have the acute, unshakeable sense that I'm missing something. Because for the first time in forever, I'm wishing the sex I just had with Blue was real.

I wish he was really here, body wrapped around mine as we had that conversation in person. I've never felt this way about someone I've chatted online with. I've never connected like that with any of the guys I've met virtually.

I've also never been told what makes me different is also

what makes me awesome. A girl could get used to that kind of praise.

I startle at the distant sound of a splash, glancing over my shoulder at the windows beside the bed.

My stomach dips. I remember what Hank said about my cabin practically being in Samuel's backyard. From what I understand, each of the five Beauregard siblings has their own private residence here on the mountain.

Does Samuel have a pool?

Is he in it?

And why does the starving side of me crave the answer to that question?

Darting into the bathroom, I grab one of the fluffy robes hanging on the chrome hooks beside the shower. I shove my feet into my fur-lined boots and duck outside. It's even darker than before. The air is cold but my skin is hot, and it takes several beats for my mind to catch up to my body.

Am I really doing this?

I guess my chat with Blue has emboldened me. So I follow the sounds of splashes a little way up the hill. I dart through a thicket of pine trees, praying the predatory animals in the area are still hibernating.

A hulking building comes into view. It may be close to midnight, but the windows are lit up. The closer I get, the clearer I can make out just how massive the house is. It must be eight, hell, ten thousand square feet spread out over three floors. The roofline swoops elegantly into a stone terrace that I imagine has amazing views of the mountains beyond.

Below the terrace, there's a pool set into the hillside. It's also lit up with the kind of pool lights that change colors from green to pink to red to blue. I creep closer, hiding behind a tree twenty or so feet from the pool's edge. Steam rises off the surface of the water.

It's heated.

So is my blood when my eyes catch on the figure that suddenly pops up in the middle of the pool. His naked shoulders gleam, muscles rippling against the skin as he raises his arms to wipe the hair out of his eyes.

Those *arms*. They would make Wolverine weep. I swear to God the guy's bicep is the size of my thigh.

Heart pumping inside my chest, I watch him sink back into the water up to his chin. He turns, allowing me a perfect view of his profile. Sharp nose, full lips, scruffy jawline.

Oh, it's Samuel all right. Only this Samuel looks different. Could be the slicked-back hair or the way it gives him a Davidoff-model vibe.

Or it could be the lost, almost vulnerable look in his eyes. He swims to the edge of the pool with long, sure strokes, and rests his forearms on the stone ledge. He looks out into the blackness—guess the staff was right to tell me he likes the night sky.

He sighs. Shoulders slumping.

With me, he's got his dukes up. But here, he's pensive and sad.

I don't want to be curious about what that sadness is about or where it comes from. He's my coworker.

I never ever cross that line. I've seen workplace romances end badly at every single restaurant and bar I've worked at.

Those romances end especially badly for women. I can't tell you how many times my male colleagues stopped taking a woman seriously after discovering an indiscretion. Many of those women wound up leaving or getting fired, their reputations irreparably damaged.

But dammit, I am curious. The world knows Samuel as this flashy ex-athlete with a big smile and bigger bank account. You look at his Instagram, and that's what you'll see. He surrounds himself with wealth and beauty and success.

That sigh tells a different story.

Those eyes tell a really different story.

I can't stop staring at his back. An image materializes inside my head: the bunching of those back muscles as he works over me. Gliding his lubed-up cock up and down between my breasts. Lips parted, eyes vulnerable, he loses himself to me. I dig my fingernails into his shoulder blades and drag them down the length of his spine. He hisses. I smile. He half grunts, half speaks.

I. Thrust. *Appreciate.* Thrust. *Who you.* Thrust. *Really are.*

This bone-deep yearning settles in the center of my being. Samuel never said those words. But God, if he did—if he was that ardent, that open, that *real* with me—I'm not sure I could handle it.

The sound of a twig snapping startles me out of my reverie. To my horror, I look down to see I'm the one who made that noise—my foot rests on a broken branch.

Shit.

I look up to see Samuel glaring in my direction.

"Is someone there?" he calls, standing. A sheet of water glides down his chest, plastering the dark hair there to his skin. His nipples are erect. "This is private property."

I whirl around, back against the tree, and glue my arms to my sides. Oh, God, not only am I peeping my fellow employee like a total perv, but I'm also trespassing.

My heart nearly explodes when I hear Samuel climb out of the pool. He approaches, footsteps slapping against the wet concrete.

"Hello?" he calls, much closer than before.

I squeeze my eyes shut and pray like hell he turns back around.

After several excruciating beats, he does. Thank God. Pulse hammering, I listen to him pad up the steps back to the house.

I need to get out of here. Stat. But apparently, I have no

self-control when it comes to finding large men hanging out in pools at night because I glance toward the house one last time.

My pulse—it stops working.

Samuel is naked and turned away from me so I get a good view of his bare ass as he climbs the steps, using a towel to wipe his face. Like the rest of him, his ass is big and muscular. Two pale white globes that flex as he climbs, creating these delicious little indents just below his hip bones.

The whole thing is downright biteable. I imagine that's how the muscles flex when he fucks. He'd be athletic in bed, the kind of sex that'd have you down a few pounds after a weekend marathon of it.

He shoots one last look over his shoulder. This time, I don't take any chances. I scurry off, quiet as a mouse, careful to keep to places where pine needles cover the ground so they muffle the sound of my steps.

I'm out of breath by the time I get to my cottage. Closing the door behind me, I lean against it, struggling to get a grip on my runaway pulse.

I'm shaking, and I don't know why.

Thankfully, I have my phone to distract me. It's chiming from its perch on my nightstand.

My stomach dips the way it always does when I see a notification from Instagram, telling me my sister just posted a photo.

For a split second, I close my eyes. Overall, it's been a decent night. I bested Samuel at a tasting and had probably the best cybersex of my life. Why ruin it by hate scrolling through my feed?

But like the social-media-addicted millennial I am, I scroll anyway. Lindsey's is the first photo that pops up. Her feed is a beautifully curated collection of perfect images of her perfect life with her perfect husband, Palmer. Fabulous trips, fun-filled weekends, bright, sweaty smiles after a #Crossfit workout.

This particular post is a bright, cheery photo of her and Palmer, the two of them smiling on the sun-drenched patio of their beautiful home in Raleigh. My sister is, as always, impeccably put together, from her fashionable balloon-sleeved maxi dress to the stack of Cartier bracelets crowding her arm. She and Palmer are holding up flutes of sparkling wine. They're clearly celebrating something, and I have a sudden, almost panicky need to know what that something is.

Cheers to my promotion to partner! Ever since I was a little girl, I'd watch my dad come home from a day of work at the law firm bearing his name. For years, I've dreamed of following in his footsteps, and as of today, I've officially done it! No better way to celebrate than with the dude who makes my heart sing. @PalmerK I wouldn't have made it without you #BottomsUp #GirlBoss

Hashtag gross. Shit, I knew there had to be a reason she called earlier today. I haven't had a chance to call her back.

I'm still shaking as I type a quick text to Lindsey, congratulating her. Honestly, I'm glad I missed her call, and that it's too late to try chatting tonight. I'm happy for my sister. I'm proud of all that she's accomplished; making partner at a law firm is a big deal. But seeing her hit overachiever milestone after overachiever milestone while I'm over here trading dirty puns with coworkers in an effort to keep my first salaried position is...

Yeah, it's humbling to say the least.

A sharp-edged ache replaces the yearning in my center.

Envy.

And you know, I used to believe it was an unworthy emotion. But lately, I've come to realize that this particular kind of envy can actually be instructive.

It can show me what I want, and what I'm missing.

I don't want to be on the partner track, and I definitely don't want Lindsey's Cartier jewelry.

It's the success, the stability, the *happiness* that comes from making a good living doing something I love.

I try hard not to think about what my life would be like if I'd followed a similar path to Lindsey's. Back in college, we were both pre-law. But a lot changed for me my senior year, and while my mom and dad really wanted me to toe the family line—they're both attorneys—my heart led me elsewhere.

I don't regret becoming a sommelier. But I do wish I had more to show for all the hard work I've put in over the past ten years.

I do wish I didn't allow the world to make me feel like a joke as often as I do. I'm a lot less insecure than I used to be, but every so often, I can't help but think no one would ever give Lindsey the side-eye for her career choice.

I crawl into bed, tired but unable to sleep.

I really, *really* want to make this job work. Not to compete with or impress my sister, although maybe she'll finally stop looking at me with that condescending sympathy in her eyes every time I talk about my job.

I want to make it work for me. Because my gut is telling me that this is the one—the dream job that will give me the stability I want and the creative freedom I crave.

For a long time, I thought that was too much to ask. I know how the world works, and I realize how privileged I am to even be considering these goals, much less going after them.

But I figured hey, if I can imagine it, maybe I can make it happen.

So here I am. And unfortunately, I don't have a boss who believes in me. In fact, I have to prove my worth to him every damn minute of every damn day.

I think about Lindsey again, living in her perfect world. I don't need perfect. I don't need to *be* perfect. But I do have to find success in reaching my goals.

I've come this far. And I'm not going to let Samuel Beauregard keep me from making my dreams come true.

Chapter Eight

SAMUEL

I wake up with a woody.

What am I, a goddamn teenager?

Running a hand down my overgrown stubble, I blink the sleep from my eyes. I had dreams last night.

Vivid, explicit dreams. Someone's dark arts at work, no doubt.

Might as well revisit them this morning. Maybe starting the day with an orgasm will make it a little less miserable. The internet sex—it's been liberating.

Too often, I find myself playing into the fantasy of who my hookups think I am—the guy with the smile and the swagger—rather than just being myself. Almost makes me think I don't want them to know who I am.

Keeping girls at arm's-length gives me control over the situation. And I like control.

Only yielding that control, in certain situations anyway, has turned out to be the biggest fucking turn-on ever. For the first time in forever, I'm letting someone else take the lead, and I'm legit surprised it hasn't blown up in my face yet.

I'm not gonna begin to unpack what that says about me.

There's a lesson here, I know, but it's early days yet. Still, I like the sense of freedom I feel when I'm connecting with this girl. She's uncovered a side of me I've never shown to anyone else, and it's fun just being who I am with her. No expectations. No fear.

Reaching down, I grab my dick, hissing when I thumb the slit on the underside of my crown, and squeeze my eyes shut.

I fucked her tits last night. So this morning, I imagine I'm rocking into that pretty little cunt of hers as I start to give myself slow, lazy tugs, the heels of those wicked shoes digging into my bare ass.

It hurts.

I like it.

Goddammit, I like her.

My strokes become harder, more urgent. She knows I like it when she takes charge—she knows *me*—and I surrender when she pushes me off her, rough and raw and hot as hell. I land on my back, and she climbs onto my dick, reverse cowgirl style.

I can see the tops of her bent knees spreading as she rides me. This angle is deep, and I can tell she's adjusting to it because she goes slowly.

She feels *so* good. Tight, soft. Vulnerable. She's equal parts alpha and beta this way. Dominator and doe.

"My hair," she breathes, her head falling back. "Pull it."

Only then do I realize her hair is coiled tightly in a bun.

A bun I know well.

When I hesitate, she glances at me over her shoulder, and our eyes lock. Hers are light brown. They're heavy lidded, but they still burn with honesty. Real need, *vulnerability*.

My eyes fly open, my hand going still.

What the fuck?

How did Emma end up there? And why does my dick throb urgently at the idea that it's *her* fucking me?

I need a cold shower. Immediately. This is a dangerous road, one that leads nowhere.

But my cock is hard in my hand and my balls are screaming bloody murder, and something about the thought of leaving this unfinished is infinitely depressing.

I close my eyes. Working myself harder, faster, I imagine pulling the bobby pins out of her bun. Her hair cascades down her bare back, loose and wild, and when I wrap it around my fist and give it a tug, her pussy tightens around my cock.

No greater satisfaction than making a girl come on your dick.

She digs her fingernails into my thigh. "Harder," she pants. I can just glimpse her nipples as she arches her back. Pink. Puffy. Perfect. "Deeper. I know you can go deeper, Samuel. Do it."

I'm sweating now. Squeezing my cock so hard it hurts. I don't know if I can keep going like this.

"Yes, you can," she says, reading my thoughts. Her voice is breathy. Nothing held back. Nothing smoothed over. She rolls her hips, milking me and taking me deeper. "Follow me. Yes. Just like that."

It takes me a beat to get it. But then we fall into a deep, punishing, soul-baring rhythm, speaking our own language without saying a word. I read her: bucking my hips, I spear her on the crest of her thrust, making her whole body jerk. She slaps my thigh in approval. She reads me: noticing how I like it when she plays with my balls, she reaches between her legs and cups them. I pull her hair, lost in pleasure.

"Come with me, Samuel. Right. *Now*."

She clamps down on me, going still, and I come.

Hell, I fucking roar, sending the birds outside my window scattering. I jerk the sheets away, narrowly avoiding covering them in ropes of cum.

I climb out of bed on unsteady legs. I'm hollowed out.

I'm one sick bastard.

Hanging my head in the shower, I try to rationalize. Calm down. That weird fantasy—it was just my imagination going into overdrive. Doesn't help that I'm stressed as hell at work.

I have to get rid of Emma. She's fucking with my head, and now is not the time to lose my shit. I know what I'm doing. I don't need her and her lofty ideas.

I can do this job well *without* help. Because once that help takes over, I'm a goner.

This morning's fantasy is just me crushing on my new fuck buddy. I just—

Why can't I find that brand of fearless authenticity before now? Why don't I ever connect with anyone the way I connect with her?

Really, what the fuck am I doing wrong?

Bang.

Daddy's cast-iron skillet makes a loud noise as I drop it onto the burner. I should be more careful, but I'm feeling off-kilter today. My hands are unsteady. My entire body is unsteady, as evidenced by the way I keep tripping over my own damn feet.

"Whoa, whoa, whoa," a voice behind me says. "Samuel, are you rage cooking?"

I glance over my shoulder to see Hank standing beside my kitchen island. Beau is with him—they must've come in through the side door. My siblings and I stopped knocking on each other's doors years ago. It was a trend I started.

I regret that now.

"No," I grunt, turning back to the onions and asparagus

tips I got going. They pop, and I give the skillet a shove. "Maybe."

"Definitely," says another voice. "Whatcha makin'?"

"A frittata, asshole." I cut Beau a glance. "Better question: what happened to you? You look like hell. Insomnia strike again? Or something happen with Annabel?"

"I saw y'all dancing at the bonfire the other night," Hank says. "Looked awful cozy together."

My older brother flips his hat off his head and tugs a hand through his hair. Beau was recently diagnosed with CTE, the same degenerative brain disease that Daddy suffered from. One of the unfortunate symptoms is trouble sleeping. He always looks tired. But now he looks strung out too.

It's a feeling I know well.

"Nothing," he says. "It's nothing. So, this rage cooking—"

"I'll save you the trouble." I pour a bowl of whisked eggs into the skillet, along with a handful of freshly grated white cheddar cheese. I put the skillet in the oven, then I throw the whisk and wooden spoon I've been using into the sink. Hank jumps at the clatter. "Yes, I'm pissed, and yes, it has to do with Emma. She's gotta go."

Beau's shoulders rise on an aggrieved inhale. Remorse arrows through my chest. The man's got a lot on his plate. It's one reason I'm so adamant about maintaining control over my little corner of the Blue Mountain universe. I want to help as much as I can.

"Why?" Hank asks. "I think she's great."

"Not helping," I say.

Beau crosses his arms. "Why not Emma? The staff at The Barn Door said she's been a total dream so far."

My hands tighten on the chair. "You really think someone as ambitious as that is going to be content as a co-head? She wants the whole damn thing."

"Did she say as much?"

"Well, no, but I know when—"

"This have anything to do with the blind tasting y'all did last night? Heard you panned one of your favorite trophy wines."

"What? No. No, that's not—Good Lord." I run a hand down my face, cradling my jaw in my hand. "Rumors sure do fly up here."

Beau tilts his head. "You getting smoked at a blind tasting is not a rumor. It's a fact. C'mon. You should know how to have your ass handed to you with a little more grace."

"Ouch."

Beau's expression softens. "You know I didn't mean it like that. But she stays, Samuel. As a matter of fact, I have a project for y'all to work on together."

"Whatever it is, I'm sure I can do it myself."

Hank wrinkles his brow. "She's really got your panties in a bunch, huh? You didn't, like, sleep with her or anything, did you?"

"Jesus Christ!" Beau stares at me. "Samuel, you promised—"

"I did promise. And I'm offended you'd assume I'd break that promise. I'm a man of my word, same as you are, brother, so you best believe me when I say I haven't laid a fucking finger on that girl. I'm not stupid."

"Good." Hank looks relieved. "I'm glad to hear it."

"What, you got a crush on her or something?" I spit out.

Hank just looks at me sideways. "You really are raging today, huh?"

"Y'all." Beau slaps his hand against the counter. "Emma is staying, no one is sleeping with her or crushing on her, and you two are gonna work together in goddamn peace and harmony or I'll be firing both your asses. Got it?"

"Got it," I grumble.

"Good. So, the project. We have Chef Elijah Jackson—

yes, that Eli Jackson—coming into town with some of his buddies for a guys' weekend. He requested a boozy lunch on Saturday, family style, preferably outside. Thought you and Emma could put together a wine tasting and food menu for them."

I scoff. "No pressure or anything."

Eli Jackson is Charleston's most famous chef at its most famous restaurant, The Pearl. He's one of the greats who put Southern cuisine on the map. Serving him is the equivalent of me picking up a guitar and playing for Eddie Van Halen (RIP to that dude, he is missed).

To be fair, I do have a bit more experience putting together a meal than I do playing eighties rock. But still. This luncheon's a tall order.

Beau cuts me a look. "Y'all can handle it. And yeah, maybe I'm hoping it'll show you how much easier your job will be with someone as excellent as Emma at your side."

"I beg to differ." I can just imagine how hoity-toity Emma will be about my ideas. No doubt she'll shoot down everything. Take over, the way she's already trying to take over Celeste and John's wedding.

But Beau is the boss. He's also my brother, and whatever he's going through that he's not telling me about is clearly taking a toll on him. I don't want to add to that burden.

So I'll do the boozy lunch with Emma. Grit my teeth and get through it. Hopefully, she'll hate working with me so much she'll quit before the weekend's through.

"Fine. I'll sit down with Emma this afternoon." I take the frittata out of the oven and slice it four ways—I always make way too much damn food, and for once that's a good thing—and plate it, dropping the plates on the island. "Now eat. No, Hank, I don't give a damn if you already had breakfast, you're gonna finish those eggs."

He grins, putting a forkful into his mouth. "Yes, sir."

Grabbing his plate, Beau stands beside me and puts a hand on my shoulder. "Trust me, okay?"

I drop the skillet into the sink, creating an even louder clatter than the one before. "Everyone's always asking me to trust them. Why the hell don't y'all return the favor and trust me for once?"

Beau sighs. Again.

"I'm sorry," I say, curling my hands around the lip of the sink. "I don't mean to create a headache for you. I'll get it done, all right? You don't have to worry."

"But I do." He puts a hand on my shoulder. "I always worry about you, Samuel."

Chapter Nine

EMMA

Hank is the first to greet me when I arrive outside The Barn Door at quarter till eight.

"Morning, Emma," he says. "I was hoping I'd get to witness your victory lap today."

I grin. "I saw you peeking over Samuel's shoulder last night."

It's a crisp spring morning, and the sun is already vibrant in the early gray-blue sky. Hank squints as he smiles at me, this big, unguarded thing that makes me think he and Samuel are in no way related. Hank's also a lot smaller than his older brother.

He's still ripped as all get-out. His biceps are on the verge of splitting the sleeves of his T-shirt, Hulk style.

From what I gather, all the Beauregard brothers are incredibly well-built. Must be their genes. It makes sense, considering their father was also a football great.

"Couldn't help myself. Your mastery is a thing of beauty, Emma. I've never seen anything quite like it. The wines you picked? And that thing you did with the champagne? I knew you were something special from the way Beau talked about you. But damn, girl, you know your shit, and you're not afraid to use that knowledge as a weapon."

Warmth blooms inside my chest. "Wow. Thanks for that. I'm worried I took it a little too far, but overall, I'd like to think I did well."

"You dominated, no question. And let's be real, it was fun to watch you put Samuel in his place. I'm sorry he's been such a moody SOB. I promise he's not usually like this."

I scoff. "I'm glad you said that. I wish he could be a little more like you. You know, *nice*."

"You think I'm nice?"

"I do, yeah. I hope you don't mind me asking," I say, "but what is Samuel's deal? He seems to get along with everyone else. What sore spot am I hitting?"

"Fuck if I know." Hank puts his hands in his pockets. "On the surface, Samuel can be a big bullshitter. But when it comes down to it, I think he has trouble trusting new people. Letting them in. Be patient."

I nod. "I can do that."

"Anything I can help with in the meantime? I'd be happy to show you around the resort. I'm sure I could finagle you an appointment at the spa if you're into that stuff. We've got plenty of outdoor activities too. Just say the word and I'll line it up, free of charge. I'll tell Beau—I mean, my boss—that you're doing 'resort research.'"

I laugh. "Is that a real thing?"

"Nope. But I can make it one if you want."

"Thanks." I grin. "I appreciate the offer, really. I see why Beau put you in charge of guest relations. You're good at making people feel at home here. Me included. Makes Blue Mountain Farm stand out."

He grins too, handsome and glowing and clearly proud. "I appreciate the kind words. A lot of what I do is kinda invisible work, you know? It's not as sexy as, say, one of Milly's weddings, or Samuel's Tony Stark wine cellar."

"Did he actually have the cellar built in *Iron Man* style?"

"Yup."

"Of course he did." I roll my eyes, and Hank laughs. "But yeah, I see what you mean. You're the glue that holds it all together. The food, the weddings, the activities, the accommodations—I've worked in hospitality long enough to know it all only runs smoothly if there's a shit ton of work that happens behind the scenes."

Hank's gaze meets mine. "I like you, Emma."

"I like you, too, Hank."

"So, hey." He rocks back on his heels, and at that moment, I see a teddy bear, not a mountain man. Really, why can't Samuel have Hank's personality? It would certainly make my life a lot easier. "I know you're super busy, but if you ever have time for another tasting, I'd love to do one with you."

"Anytime. But you have to promise not to freak out the way Samuel did if I outmaneuver you."

His smile broadens. "Wouldn't dream of it."

Samuel walks into the restaurant at eight o'clock on the dot. He smiles at the restaurant's manager, Raquel, and nods at one of the dishwashers heading into the kitchen.

His greeting isn't exactly warm or personal. But it gets the job done. The hum of activity surrounding us is a testament to the respect Samuel's employees have for him. So are The Barn Door's stats: turnover is very, very low—much of the kitchen and waitstaff has been with the Beauregards since the resort opened a few years ago—and employees consistently give him the highest rating on Blue Mountain's biannual performance reviews.

He's not wearing a suit this morning. Instead, he's wearing jeans and a long-sleeved white thermal. His white and neon orange sneakers would look ridiculous on anyone else. But on Samuel, they're sexy. Probably because he wears them with I-don't-give-a-fuck-what-you-think swagger.

Guy's got balls of steel, I'll give him that.

His eyes lock on mine and despite my best efforts to remain calm, cool, and steady—*this is not your first rodeo, Em*—my stomach somersaults.

The image of his bare ass immediately flashes across my thoughts. Did I really trespass on Samuel's property last night to peep him in his pool?

Thinking about your co-head's naked, perfectly pert ass is not the best way to start your third day on the job.

As if he can read my dirty mind, Samuel's smile disappears.

"Emma," he says.

I clear my throat. "Morning, Beauregard."

A muscle in his jaw ticks. "Have a moment?"

"Of course."

"My office."

Notebook and pen in hand, I follow him up to the suite of offices on the second floor. His is surprisingly cozy, tidy too, with the same reclaimed wood walls and beamed ceilings as downstairs. Samuel takes a seat behind the massive desk in the center of the room.

He does not invite me to sit.

"Elijah Jackson is coming to the resort this weekend." He opens a drawer, takes out a leather folio, and tosses it onto the desk. "Beau wants us to put together a lunch-tasting combo for him and his guests on Saturday."

I smile, excitement fluttering inside my chest. Okay, working with Samuel has not been awesome. But the clientele Blue Mountain Farm attracts most certainly is. So is the idea of introducing one of my favorite chefs of all time to my favorite wines.

"*The* Eli Jackson?"

"Yup." Rummaging through the folio, his gaze flicks up to meet mine. "You a fan?"

"Love him. His breakfast bowls? And the fact that he fell in love with his wife by making her food while she wrote her first romance novel? I mean, he's an icon in every sense of the word."

Samuel grunts. "So you read that *Garden and Gun* profile too."

"I read everything food and wine related that I can get my hands on. The profile was a good one, right?"

Samuel's eyes flick to mine. They're intensely, almost supernaturally blue in the strident morning light. "Don't sound so surprised that I read. I know you think I'm just a dumb jock—"

"I never said that."

"That gleam in your eye last night when you showed me the label on that bottle of Dom? Yeah, that definitely said 'you're dumb.'"

"No." I cross my arms. "It said 'I want to open your mind, but since you're so hell-bent on thwarting me at every turn, this is the only way I know how.'"

He rolls his eyes. "Whatever. I reserved the Stag Pavilion from eleven till three. Eli's bringing his guy friends, fifteen guests total. Goes without saying we need to pull out all the stops."

My pulse kicks up a notch. This is my chance to show him that I really am a team player.

My chance to prove I'm trustworthy.

I take a seat in one of the chairs facing Samuel's desk and cross my legs, settling my notebook on my lap.

"Absolutely." I click my pen and start writing. "It'll be

something fabulous. Something different. Because he's well versed in southern classics, I say we stay away from that kind of thing. No one does grits quite like him—"

"You have yet to taste my grits."

It's all I can do not to roll my eyes. "So why try to top his mastery? It'd almost be an insult."

Samuel's eyes flick over my stockinged legs. That muscle in his jaw tics.

"I thought the same thing." We meet eyes, and my pulse kicks up *another* notch. "I gave Chef Katie a call this morning and floated the idea of doing a Spanish-style meal. I've always been a big fan of paella—"

"Me too," I say, my pen flying as ideas begin to take shape. "And you've got some pretty sweet wines from Spain in the cellar, so the pairings will be a breeze."

Samuel smirks, cocky and knowing and...actually kinda cute? "Exactly. And it just so happens our rice supplier is Luke Rodgers of Rodgers' Farms in South Carolina. He'll be at the lunch on Saturday. So not only do we get to do a southern riff on the dish with locally sourced ingredients, but we'll also be giving a guest a nod of appreciation."

"Perfect. I know Chef just harvested her first crop of peas from the garden, and a big-ass paella is the perfect place to show off our produce." When Samuel raises a brow, I grin. "Yes, I called Chef this morning too. I wanted to go over any changes to today's menu so I'll know which wines to recommend with each course."

He narrows his eyes at me. "Are you always so thorough?"

"Yes. The paella—what are you thinking? Seafood? Chicken? Chorizo? All of the above?"

Samuel blinks, like he's surprised by my questions. I bet the jerk expected me to run roughshod over him.

I allow my grin to deepen, meeting his gaze head-on. *See? Team player.*

I only run roughshod over men in the bedroom. Looking at Samuel, I wonder if he'd like that. Sometimes the guys who are as alpha as he is are secret submissives behind closed doors.

"You're the food guy." I hold out my hands, pen laced between my fingers. "Tell me what you want, and we'll make it happen."

"Chicken," he says automatically. "Chicken and chorizo."

I scribble in my notepad. "Love it. Classic combo that will be a total crowd pleaser. What about adding a crema to it? One of the best paellas I've had was at this place out in Santa Barbara. They paired theirs with this cool, tangy white sauce that was out of this world."

"The chorizo and chicken paella at Bonita?" Samuel is blinking again, brow furrowed.

"Yeah." I pull back, surprised myself. "You've been?"

"Probably my favorite restaurant on the West Coast."

I'm smiling now. "It's that good."

"It is that good. The gin and tonics? Christ."

"Oh yeah—love that one they do with the rosemary and cucumber. And the tapas? Insane. On my last trip out there, I may have emptied my bank account eating at that place four nights in a row. By the last night, all the bartenders were looking at me funny, but I was too drunk on gin and high on albóndigas to care."

He's doing that thing where he cocks his brow. Makes him look a little less angry, a little more approachable. "You got high on meatballs?"

"I'm only going to answer that question if you promise not to turn it into another gross food pun."

"Unfortunately I'm unable to make any such promise." He leans back in his chair and rests his clasped hands on his flat stomach.

"Then the conversation about meat and balls ends there.

Such a shame, because those were some pretty delicious ones."

It's an entirely inappropriate conversation to have at work. We're flirting with a line we probably shouldn't cross.

We're flirting, period. And that's a line we definitely shouldn't cross. But we've got some good energy going right now. Plus, it's fun trading banter with Samuel. He's quick and bold, and when we're exchanging bad puns, it means we're not exchanging barbs.

Which gives him the chance to actually listen to what I'm saying.

It's obvious Samuel likes what he's hearing.

For the first time, we're on the same page. Not only that —he's engaging me in meaningful (albeit slightly pervy) conversation about my love of food and wine and travel. I can't tell you how many people have made me feel like a joke for being passionate about things like gin and paella. Like I'm ridiculous for loving the things I do.

But right now, Samuel Beauregard of all people is smiling as we chat about those very things.

The man actually smiles, a cocky flash of white teeth and gleaming blue eyes that seems to melt the ice between us so quickly it's as if it was never there to begin with.

"I'm struggling not to make a crack about your corn-bread," he replies. "So let's keep talking about the menu. How about we add balls—pardon, albóndigas—as an appetizer?"

"Throw in some manchego croquetas and I think we have a solid start to what's going to be an epic meal."

Samuel runs a hand across his scruff. "Manchego. That shit is so good. Should we add some tasso ham? Just because we can? Our butcher smokes a mean ham."

"Done. I love that we have our own butcher on-site. I'm thinking we pair the croquetas with...hmm..."

I look up. He looks at me.

"Albariño," we say at the same moment.

"The acidity will complement the cheese really nicely," I say.

"The lemon-lime note will make a fried dish like that feel less heavy. I was thinking the—"

"Juan Luis?"

Samuel nods. "Great little wine. I discovered it years ago and have had it on the menu ever since."

"I couldn't agree more," I say, smiling so hard my face hurts. "Although I have to say I was surprised to see it pop up in your bible. It's a sleeper—not many people know about it. And it's cheap. Relatively speaking, anyway."

His lips twitch as he surveys me across his desk. "And you thought you had me pegged."

Chapter Ten

SAMUEL

"All right," Emma says, uncrossing and crossing her legs. "Since we're doing something light and different for the tapas, let's go BSD for the paella pairing. You have some really nice Riojas that would work beautifully. Which one is your favorite?"

Sweet savior in heaven, *why* does she gotta have those *legs*?

I also wanna know why she can't be easier to hate today. Yesterday she made me look like a humongous idiot, so wanting her gone was easy. But today she's playing by every freaking rule. She's full of good ideas and better energy, and she's not only asking for my input, she's also excited about what I have to say.

For the first time, I feel like we're real partners doing really great work.

I never felt that sense of camaraderie with Olly and Coach Kravinsky. Granted, after my injury I spent the better part of a season either in bed or at physical therapy, so I wasn't with the team for months on end.

But still. This chemistry I have with Emma is something I

didn't experience with my coach or my backup, ever. Which means—

Well, it means what, exactly? I know better than to trust Emma.

But what choice do I have? Beau is forcing me to trust her by working together on this event.

Those legs. Must. Stop. Looking. Or I'm gonna get hard. Who gets a stiffy at a work meeting?

Guys who don't have jobs, that's who.

I have V for that shit. Just gonna have to chat with her more often.

Tearing my gaze from Emma's body, I pretend to write something on my notepad. "The, uh, Canción de Sangre."

"Oooh, song of blood. Sounds dangerous. I like it." She jots down a note. "I assume it's big and meaty?"

I slap my hand down on my desk. Emma startles, those pretty brown eyes going wide in genuine shock.

Shit, did I scare her?

"I swear to God I didn't say that to be gross." She holds up her hands. "It just came out. Cross my heart and hope to die."

"It's good," I manage. "The wine is very...good. Spice and, uh, stuff."

Fuck me, this girl's turned me into a blabbering idiot.

It's her third day on the job. How mushy will my brain be after a week? A month?

A goddamn year?

"Hey, y'all! Can I come in?"

I look up and see my sister poke her head through the door. Without waiting for an answer, she strides into my office, smiling broadly at Emma.

I should be relieved Milly's here. She could very well be saving me from embarrassing myself any further.

But instead, I'm annoyed. Just like I was when Hank kept popping up at the tasting last night.

It's all I can do not to groan. Why does my family annoy me so much all of a sudden? If I didn't know better, I'd say I want Emma all to myself. Which is a joke. I don't want Emma. At all.

"Emma!" Milly extends her hand. "Great to see you again. I heard you guys are working on your first event together—"

"Who told you that?" I grind out.

Milly turns her smile on me, wagging her brows. "Beau. He wanted me to come by and referee. I mean, offer my services."

Emma laughs. My heart skips at the sound. It's deep. Throaty. Real.

Something tells me Emma would never fake it.

I shift in my chair, settling my elbows on the desk. "How great of him. We're doing just fine—"

"So." Milly grabs the chair beside Emma's and sits, turning to her. "As you know, I focus primarily on weddings. But I love to help out with smaller stuff when I can. Y'all are in luck—I don't have a wedding this weekend, so I'm free to help with the Charleston Heat Luncheon."

"So lucky," I deadpan. "Also, why are you calling it that?"

"Because, *Samuel*, apparently the gentlemen of this party are, shall we say, easy on the eyes." Milly grins conspiratorially at Emma. "I heard Elijah Jackson prefers to go shirtless."

"Even at mealtimes?" Emma says.

Milly's wagging her eyebrows again. "Especially at mealtimes. I've seen pictures, and the heat in his kitchen is very real. And Luke Rodgers, it's rumored he's grows the biggest zucchini on his farm and in his—"

"Stop," I beg. "Please? Just—so many food puns, I can't—topic. Stay on top of me. Stay on *topic*."

Milly peers at me. "Did you not have your coffee yet?"

"Out." I tear both hands through my hair. "Get out before I hurl myself through that window."

Emma wrinkles her forehead. "Are you really not okay?"

"He's fine." Milly waves me away. "So, back to this weekend. I do it all—decor, lighting, china and glassware, flowers, linens. Let's make this thing magical."

"Let's," Emma says. She glances at me. "Since the group's coming up from Charleston, they'll probably dig a change of scenery. What if we played up the whole rustic, wine by the fire on a bearskin rug angle you guys have going up here?"

My brain, that bastard, conjures an image of Emma on the bearskin rug I just happen to have in front of my fireplace at home. She's naked. Her legs are wrapped around me as I kiss her mouth. She tastes like the Rioja. Juicy stone fruit and heat.

"I love it," Milly says, eyes lighting up. "We could keep it simple but exquisite—springtime in the mountains. I don't know if you've been out to the Stag Pavilion yet, but it's got a huge fireplace and these beamed ceilings that really don't need much embellishment. We'll have a fire going, and some greenery and white flowers on the tables. Gerbera daisies, peonies. Oh! And tulips."

Emma's writing feverishly in her notebook. "I love tulips."

"I love running my own damn meetings," I say.

"Mr. Beauregard, I'm speaking." My sister shoots me a glare. "We'll do white linens and these cool metal chairs that just came in. Throw some matching blankets on a few of them in case someone catches a chill."

"Genius," Emma says, not looking up from her notes.

"I know."

Emma finally stops writing and glances at me. "Anything you'd like to add, Samuel?"

She's the one who's the genius. Her ideas, her mature

brand of enthusiasm, the way she confidently offers suggestions *and* asks questions…

I don't know why she doesn't take an eye for an eye and be a jerk right back to me. But instead, she's including me in the conversation.

She's doing it again—she's giving a shit. Genuinely, unabashedly inviting my input.

In doing that, she's putting herself out there. Making herself vulnerable in a way I sure as fuck never will.

Never again, anyway.

But damn if I'm not tempted to put my guard down. Just a little. Just enough for Emma to glimpse my non-asshole side. Because she makes caring look good.

She makes *me* want to care too.

My head's telling me to run. Caring means letting her in, and I know better than to do that.

But my gut is telling me Emma is different. Maybe that's why I'm drawn to her. I'm Frodo and she's the ring. I gotta resist. Gotta keep my head on straight. But she's got this willingness to subject herself to the ass kicking she visited on me last night that's a fucking siren song.

"Let's do the tapas family style," I say. "Everything passed around the table. Chef Katie's gonna kill me, but I think it's the right call for this group."

Emma makes a note. Milly looks from me to Emma and back again.

What? I mouth.

Milly just shakes her head. *You're in trouble*, she mouths back.

The three of us flesh out the menu. Emma defers to me on the food. Takes charge on the wine. She gets bolder and firmer with each pick.

I like them all.

I especially like that she takes no shit. When I suggest a

red to accompany the dessert course—cinnamon sugar churros with chocolate ganache dipping sauce—Emma calls me out.

"You don't pair a decadent wine with a decadent dessert like that," she says. "We want a punchy counterpoint to the creaminess of the chocolate. The richness. Something that's easy to drink. I say sparkling—a cava."

Milly looks at me, eyes wide with glee. "I say she's right."

Oh yeah, I'm in trouble.

Lots of it.

"Well." Milly taps her hands against her knees. "I gotta run. Emma, you have my number. Reach out anytime, day or night. We're thrilled to have you on the farm. Right, Samuel?"

I shoot Milly the darkest look I can muster.

"Good luck," she murmurs to Emma, patting her shoulder before heading out the door.

Emma smiles. "She's great."

"She's the worst, but I love her." I stand, closing my folio. "I have an eleven with the kitchen staff. Anything else you need?"

"Not at the moment, no. I'll follow up with Milly about the decor and pull the wines we discussed. Let's give them a try when you have a sec."

She moves to stand, her skirt gliding up her thighs as she leans forward. A surge of dark hunger moves through me. I shift on my feet, unsteady.

I do not like how this woman makes me so goddamn unsteady all the time.

"My schedule's packed for the next two days," I grunt. "Don't have time."

She draws to her full height—can't be more than five one, five two at most—and the look in her eyes turns flinty. For such a little thing, she's got real presence.

"You just saw what happens when you don't stonewall me, right? We not only get shit done, we crush it."

I run a hand over my stubble. "I always crush it. Whether or not you're here."

"We'll see about that." She tucks her notebook underneath her arm. "In the meantime, stop playing games, Beauregard. The pouting's just childish. Put on your big boy undies and let's see how far we can take this thing."

Without waiting for a reply, she turns and leaves. Head high, shoulders pulled back. Pert ass straining against the fabric of her slim skirt.

Those fucking skirts she wears. They're modest but...not.

Curling my hands into fists, I lean them against my desk. That hunger is everywhere now, throbbing inside my skin alongside the very real anger and annoyance I've felt since I first laid eyes on Emma. Was that really only seventy-two hours ago?

In my day-to-day life, I maintain an impeccable sense of control. It hasn't been a struggle. The people who work for me do what I say, and they do it exactly how I want them to. The Barn Door's success is no accident.

Now, though, I am struggling to maintain that control, thanks to Emma.

But I won't let her take me down. It's not in my DNA. I'll crush this challenge just like I always do, with strength, planning, and a shitload of determination.

Chapter Eleven

EMMA

The rest of the week flies by.

Introductions, tours, meetings, and my first real turn on the floor at The Barn Door. I shadowed Samuel and the wait-staff for a while, so it's nice to be out on my own again, doing what I do best.

It's love at first sight. The staff is friendly and incredibly well trained. It's a real pleasure serving food of this caliber and creativity, and an absolute honor to plunder Samuel's cellar in search of the perfect wine pairing for each lovingly crafted dish.

Of course, I can't help mentally choosing different wines —wines I'd stock—as I sell $27 glasses of chardonnay and $400 bottles of Burgundy.

The clientele at Blue Mountain Farm may be the most rarefied I've served. But that doesn't mean guests won't appreciate something different. Something they don't see at every high-dollar steakhouse and hotel they visit. I think it'd make the whole experience of staying here that much more memorable.

I manage to squeeze in that blind tasting with Hank.

"Australian Shiraz?" His eyes had widened adorably as he poured himself another glass of my favorite red from last year. "Not sure if I've ever had it before, but goddamn is it delicious. It's just the right amount of sweet."

"Right? The spice and hint of velvet evens out the sweetness nicely."

He'd run his tongue along the inside of his mouth. "Velvet. Yes. That's exactly how it feels. Good for chilly, cloudy days like this one—makes me feel all warm and cozy inside." His eyes flashed with understanding. Appreciation too. "Which is exactly why you picked it."

I'd smiled so hard my face hurt. "Yup. Originally, I selected an Israeli Grenache blend, but when it started to rain earlier, the Shiraz just felt right."

"There's such a thing as Israeli wine?"

"Heck yes, there is! They've been making wine there literally forever, and it can be really, really good. What do you think Jesus drank?"

He'd laughed at that, and so did I.

I meet Beau's friend Annabel and her daughter, Maisie, when they stop by the restaurant for an early dinner one night, and they're lucky enough to witness Samuel and me sparring over which wine she might want.

She went with a mocktail, and I went away rolling my eyes and biting back a smile. Samuel is not immune to the professional chemistry we have. I see it in the way his eyes gleam with appreciation when our ideas come together *just* right. I see it in the way he no longer greets me with a grunt. Granted, he doesn't say hello, either, but it's better than it was.

I also see it in the way he watches me. Every so often, I'll catch him looking at me as I pour wine, or converse with a guest, or take the mic at a meeting. A few times, he downright stares like he's trying to work me out inside his head.

The professional in me would say it's weird. But the woman doesn't mind it. In fact, she likes it.

Reason one hundred eighty-five why I'm grateful I have Blue in my back pocket.

"Ho-ly *shit*," I breathe.

I set my tote bag on the edge of the nearest table and stare at the gorgeousness that surrounds me.

Today is the Charleston Heat luncheon. It's barely half past seven in the morning, but the pavilion is a beehive of activity. A small army of staff in matching Blue Mountain Farm aprons crisscrosses the open-air space. They spear the stems of white peonies and limelight hydrangea into mason jars set out on a massive farm table and place locally crafted clay plates on brass chargers. Crisp white linens and embroidered napkins are an elegant counterpoint to the rustic wooden chairs and artfully mismatched silverware.

Excitement floods my chest as my eyes catch on the spotless wine glasses accompanying each place setting. Only a place like Blue Mountain Farm would have hundreds of mouth-blown Czech crystal glasses on hand, in more shapes and sizes than I could count. Milly and I pored over the collection earlier this week, selecting glasses that were just the right shape and size to complement the varietals we'll be serving.

For a wine nerd like me, it was nirvana.

In a corner, staff set up the station where Chef Katie will be making paella in a Kia-sized paella pan. Others decorate the dozen circular chandeliers hanging from the massive ceiling beams with garlands of greenery and hydrangea. Their light casts everything in a warm, cozy glow.

The smoky-savory smell emanating from the fire burning in the massive stone fireplace fills the crisp morning air.

It's such a picture-perfect moment—something out of a movie, if *Last of the Mohicans* had a feast scene it'd look and smell like this—that I get goosebumps.

Milly sidles up beside me. "What do you think?"

"Chills." I hold out my arm and pull up the sleeve of my jacket. "Milly, I have literal chills. This is magical. Thank you so damn much for your help."

"My pleasure. This kind of laid-back event is fun. Y'all are gonna have a ball, I can already tell." She cuts me a glance. "Things going okay? At the restaurant, I mean. I know Samuel's been less than accommodating."

"I'll make it work. Always do."

"The staff at The Barn Door already love her." Hank appears at my elbow, almost making me jump. "Can't tell you how many good things I've overheard in the past few days. Morning, Emma."

I look down at the cardboard cup of coffee he holds out. "Good morning. What's this?"

"Jet fuel. We like our coffee strong here on the farm. Thought you could use a boost before the big event."

Hank smiles, his hazel eyes warm.

"Thanks." I carefully peel the plastic top off the cup, grateful for the distraction. The silky, slightly bitter smell of the coffee fills my lungs. "That's really thoughtful of you."

"Took the liberty of adding cream and sugar." Hank lifts a shoulder. "Because it's Saturday and you're on the farm."

I grin, blowing on the coffee. "And Saturdays on the farm mean—"

"It's time to indulge. Enjoy."

"I can get on board with that."

"Laying it on a little thick, don't you think?" Milly eyes her brother.

Hank shrugs again. "I'm not afraid of bein' shameless. Beau said Emma was the best of the best, but now that I've seen her in action, I get how incredible it is to witness a master at work. If I gotta be the one to woo Emma to stay, well, I'll woo my ass off."

"Woo your ass on down to the cellar," a voice, deep and firm, says behind me. A shiver darts up my spine. "I've got five cases of wine down there that aren't gonna move themselves."

I look up and there he is. Samuel Beauregard in all his early morning glory, shoulders rolled back so they seem to take up the entirety of the pavilion's threshold. I don't know if it's the shoulders, the suit—double-breasted, Carolina blue with white check, pink tie that matches the face of his white gold Rolex—the smirk, or the way his hair is still wet from the shower. But damn does he look *good*.

The kind of good that makes the hum of activity around us come to a momentary standstill as everyone shamelessly checks him out.

He's looking at me. Eyes searing. My heart trips and falls inside my chest.

I can smell his shampoo. Sandalwood, smidge of musk. Expensive.

But no cologne.

Hank wrinkles his brow. "That makes absolutely no sense."

"This whole thing makes no sense." Milly loops her arm through Hank's, casting one last glance at Samuel and me. "C'mon. I'll help."

Blinking, I tear my gaze from Samuel's face and focus on my coffee. It takes more effort than I'm willing to admit.

I bring the cup to my lips, ready to sip when Samuel grabs the cup, calloused fingers rough against the back of my hand. That electricity—the one I felt when we shook hands the first time—zips through my blood again, a spark that starts at the place where skin meets skin.

Glancing up, I notice that his nostrils flare. Once. Twice.

"Careful," he says, dropping his hand. "Coffee from the main house is hot as fuck. And a burn will really mess with your tongue."

My lips twitch at the familiar line, even as my heart keeps doing that weird tripping thing. It's making my pulse blare inside my body, an insistent rhythm. *I want. I want.*

I want him to touch me again. I want to move closer and sniff his neck. Bite his shoulder.

I want to know if the chemistry that keeps crossing from professional to physical and back again is as hot as I think it is.

So what if it is, though? It's not like I could ever act on it. I have to keep my eyes on the prize. Not on Samuel's finely chiseled jawline or the freckles that dot his cheeks and forehead.

Not on how this is the second time he's looked out for me.

Still, I can't resist a little pervy banter to start the day.

"Thanks for the heads-up. My tongue might be my most treasured body part. Professionally speaking, anyway."

He's smirking again, shoving his hands in his pockets. "I hear it's the best in the business. Although I, for one, am not convinced that's true."

"It's not my job to convince you. My tongue is reserved for our guests and our guests only."

He lifts a brow. "You won't share? How ungenerous. Me, I'm the opposite. I always make sure to give before I receive."

Oh, God, he's talking about oral without talking about oral, and I can't help but fucking smile.

This is *not appropriate*. It shouldn't be fun. But it is.

It really is. And considering the only fun I have these days is in chat rooms on the internet, I am ripe for the picking.

"Somehow I doubt your tongue is as skilled as you think it is. Takes a lot of practice to get where I am. A lot of time, effort. Trial and error. Classes, tests, tastings..."

"You think I don't practice?" He shifts on his feet, leaning the tiniest bit closer to me. "I taste plenty, Emma. So much and so often I've been told I'm a connoisseur."

My turn to smirk. "I think you might need some new friends, Beauregard. Ones who tell it to you straight."

"I think you might need some new friends." He ducks, lowering his voice to a teasing growl. "Ones who give it to you right."

Oh, no, no, no, I want to say. *I'm the one who'd give it to* you, *hotshot. And you bet your bottom dollar it'd be right.*

Thankfully, Chef Katie appears. She's wearing a puffer vest over her chef whites and a big smile.

"I don't think y'all are ready for how delicious this paella is gonna be." She rubs her hands together. "I love mixing things up this way—been a spell since I brushed off my tapas skills. Great idea."

I tip my head toward Samuel. "I'm told he's a connoisseur."

His eyes flick to meet mine.

"What?" I ask. "I give credit where credit is due. Team player, remember?"

"Right," he replies. "I remember."

Only I don't feel right at all when he turns and stalks across the pavilion, the heels of his red-soled shoes marking a solid beat against the floorboards.

I want.

I want. But I won't allow myself to have.

Sipping my coffee, I'm glad I waited. It's still too hot.

"This," Elijah Jackson says, swirling the Albariño in his glass before tipping it back to drain what's left, "is fuckin' delicious. That green apple note? Damn if it don't play off the cheese and ham croqueta beautifully."

"Really nice combination of sweet and savory," Greyson Montgomery adds, holding out his glass for another pour. "What's the story behind this deliciousness?"

I smile as I refill their glasses, a bloom of lightness spreading through my center. I love this part of my job.

"I was lucky enough to meet the winemaker on a trip to Spain last year," I say, cradling the bottle label out so Chef Eli and his friends have a good view of it. "Carmen Garcia's vineyards date back to the fifteenth century—apparently, the nuns in a nearby convent liked to throw down while guzzling Garcia family wine by the barrel."

Luke Rodgers shakes his head. "Nuns. Gotta love 'em."

"If you had to wear hats like that every day, you'd drink your face off too. Anyway, when Carmen inherited the vines from her father, they were in pretty bad shape. She got a degree in microbiology and used her scientific background to bring the grapes back to life. I like to think you can taste that in her wines." I run my thumb along my fingertips, trying to capture just the right words. "That mashup of art and science. History and innovation. Her vines are ancient, but her methods are smart and new. You mentioned that crisp apple zippiness this Albariño has—that's sharp and sexy, yeah?"

"Very mod," Eli agrees.

"But then there's this backbone—yes, I know it's ridiculous to use words like 'backbone' when describing wine, but I'm doing it and I'm not sorry—that's got this earthiness, this minerality, that tastes ancient. It's timeless, really. A reminder of the bigger story we're all a part of."

Greyson nods, swallowing a sip of wine. "I'm not sorry either. I can totally taste what you're talking about. That sense of..." He pauses, thinking. Takes another sip. I can almost see the light bulb going off in his head. "Continuity."

"How essentially human and *right* it is to enjoy good wine with good food and good friends. We're taking part in an ancient tradition, getting fucked up with the people we love," Eli says.

Luke rolls his eyes. "You been hangin' out with a writer or something lately?"

"Married her." Eli turns to me and grins. "I'm a huge fan of my wife's torrid, kinky romance. Just like I'm a huge fan not only of this wine but of your storytellin' too, Miss Crawford."

I refill more glasses, wishing I could pour for events and people like this every day.

What if I made that happen? At a place like Blue Mountain Farm, anything is possible. I could bring in winemakers like Carmen. Organize whole weekends around regions, varietals, vineyards. Introduce guests to wines they would've never otherwise given a shot, expanding their horizons while giving them a good excuse to, as Eli so poetically put it, get fucked up with their people.

I can *bring people together*. At the end of the day, that's what I love most about wine.

"Please, call me Emma. And I love a good story, clearly. All the better if it's torrid. I actually just downloaded one of your wife's books—*My Enemy the Earl*. I'm always looking for titillating new adjectives to use to describe wine."

"You'll definitely find 'em in Olivia's romances," Ford Montgomery says. "They're very...descriptive."

"I'm game," I say. "In my line of work, being able to access the right vocabulary is just as important as being able to pour correctly."

People are buzzing and plates are licked clean. There's laughter. Conversation. Heat from the fire, relief from the breeze. Looking around the table to make sure no one needs another pour before we start the next course, I see smiles. The guests are enjoying themselves, especially the one dude at the far end who keeps laughing.

He also keeps looking at me, which makes my enjoyment dim ever so slightly, because I get the feeling I'm the one making him laugh. Not because I'm witty, but because I'm ridiculous. In his eyes, at least.

It's totally not okay for someone to laugh at me that way, but it's an unfortunate reality of my job. Over the years, I've learned that the sooner you stay away from people who just don't get it, the better.

Also helps to keep their water glass full and their wineglass mostly empty.

Making a mental note to keep his pours light from now on, I look away.

My gaze lands on Samuel, who's staring at me from the other side of the table. My stomach dips at the softness I see in his gaze. When he's looked before, it's been wolfish. Like he wants to eat me.

But this—this is open and honest and interested. Like he wants to know more.

About what? Wine? Me?

And why are butterflies taking flight inside my torso?

Chapter Twelve

SAMUEL

Fuck me, she's on fire.

Emma's burning with real, ardent passion, pride too, and I can't stop staring.

"She's incredible," one of the guys at the table murmurs to his neighbor.

She's better than that. She's extraordinary. She's knowledgeable and relatable and funny and warm.

She makes you *feel* something about the liquid in your glass that, on any other day, would just be wine. But today? Today the stuff is a story. A bridge between the past and present. A way to connect with people we love.

It's the meaning of life itself.

I have never, in all my years drinking the world's best wine, felt so much about a glass of grape juice, as Hank calls it. And I'm not even drinking it. I'm watching everyone else soak up the flavors while listening, rapt, to Emma's explanation of why it's important and what makes it special.

All the while thinking it isn't the wine that's the star here.

I should be threatened. Scared. I know this script all too

well. She's stealing the show. *My* show. The one I've poured years of my life into perfecting.

Only, I'm enthralled.

More. I want more of this, whatever it is. Her bravery, maybe? She's taking a deep dive into wine and nuns and history, wearing her heart on her sleeve as she gives the table full access to who she is and what she loves.

She's allowing them to know her in a way I never, ever let people know me. And I'm witnessing, firsthand, how the table connects with her vulnerability, and how it allows her to genuinely, joyfully connect with them.

This is what I've been missing.

Holy shit, how did I not see it sooner? I'm protective by nature. I'll protect my family at any cost.

I guess I've been protecting myself too. I thought I was doing the right thing, pasting on a smile so I could get through life without being pummeled again.

Beau once told me it's natural to want to protect yourself when you're a pro athlete, because the world—the media, the fans—believe nothing about our lives should be private. Like being an elite athlete means you aren't entitled to freedom anymore or something.

Is that why I'm so reticent?

Unlike Emma. Lord, does she make being open—transparent—look good.

She makes being known look like happiness. The kind of happy I saw in my parents' faces when I was young and times were good.

I want that. So damn bad. What if I trusted her and tried it on, her vulnerability? Dropping the bullshit smile and showing the world something else? Something real? I just—yeah, I'm scared shitless. Opening yourself up to joy also means opening up to pain. And I've had enough of that to last a lifetime.

Speaking of pain—I'm about to visit some on that prick at seat fourteen. He's been sneering at Emma all damn day.

Maybe the wine does taste like history. Or maybe it just tastes like tomorrow's hangover.

What's with the bun? She think she's got a real job or something?

Emma's not letting it ruffle her feathers, but I can tell by the way her shoulders stiffen every time he makes a snide comment that it bothers her. Eli and the other guys seem to be too absorbed in their own conversations to really notice.

But I notice. And that dickbag is one minute from getting hauled out of here by his hair.

Thankfully, the rich, starchy smell of the paella distracts him. Checking my watch, I glance at Chef Katie, who gives me the thumbs-up.

We're on time, which means the paella course is almost ready.

I glance at Emma who, like the veteran restaurant employee she is, glances back and forth between Chef and me.

I nod. Emma nods back and heads for the table on the other side of the pavilion serving as our makeshift service station.

I head for Chef. All the while stealing glances at Emma. She's got her wine tool in one hand and a bottle of Canción de Sangre in the other. She nudges the edge of the screw beneath the foil. Tries to pull it back but ends up jerking her hand away, catching her thumb on the screw instead.

"*Fuck*," she says.

The way she sinks her teeth into her bottom lip as she says it makes my pulse hiccup.

She brings the pad of her thumb to her mouth and sucks on it, her brow furrowed.

I grab a plastic glove at the kitchen station—Chef keeps a box of them around for mishaps like this—and next thing I know, I'm standing beside Emma. I take the wine and the tool in one hand. Pass her the glove and a few cocktail napkins with the other.

"You okay?"

She takes her thumb out of her mouth and wraps it in a napkin. "Thanks. I'll be all right. I don't—I've never done that before. Cut myself."

"Maybe you're too titillated to focus," I say, working my wrist as I guide the screw around the mouth of the bottle. I glide my thumb under the foil, pulling it back easily.

Emma watches me do it. Eyes glued to my fingers. For a second, her eyes lose focus.

She blinks, drawing a sharp, quick inhale through her nose. "Talking about wine does tend to get me hot and bothered."

"I noticed." I screw the tool into the cork and carefully give it a pull. The cork makes a muffled *pop* as it comes out.

"God, that's satisfying." Emma nods at the cork. "That sound. Probably not as satisfying as Chef's paella, though. It's your turn."

Pouring the bottle into one of the decanters lined up on the table, I say, "My turn?"

"To take the stage. You're the food guy, right? Go knock their socks off with your paella."

Now that was not what I expected.

In fact, apart from the wine tasting the other night, Emma hasn't undermined me in any way, shape, or form. She's literally handing me the reins, allowing me to showcase what I do best.

Extraordinary.

"One, Chef gets the credit for actually making the paella." I set down the empty bottle and reach for another. I have the sudden urge to touch Emma, and if I don't keep my hands busy, I'll wrap my fingers around her wrist and bring her thumb to my mouth and suck on it myself.

"And two—" Fuck, I forgot what two was.

Emma grins. "One, what's wrong with you *and* Chef taking the stage together? The cooking is hers, but the concept is all yours. And two, it's satisfying as all get-out to accept praise when praise is due. I speak from experience."

"Of course you do," I murmur, reaching for another bottle. "How many more of these do you want me to open?"

Her lips twitch.

"What?"

Her eyes flick to meet mine. "Are you being a team player, Beauregard?"

"I'm preparing wine for my guests to enjoy," I reply gruffly, nodding at the glove in her hand. "Put that on so you can help."

From the corner of my eye, I watch as Emma does what I tell her. She turns away, but she must forget that I'm so much taller than her I'm practically a satellite to her planet. I can see it all at any time.

And what I see is that her hands are shaking.

I frown. "You eat today?"

"What?" She throws me a look over her shoulder, snapping the glove into place. "Of course I ate. I'm not five. I can take care of myself."

"Better question: what did you eat?"

"Best question yet: why don't you mind your own damn business?" She grabs two decanters. "I had coffee. And a protein bar. And I guess half of another protein bar. Different flavor, though."

I stare at her, suddenly and deeply enraged. "What kind of garbage meal is that?"

"The kind I have time for working twelve-hour days. I'm

not starving, Beauregard. My hands...I'm, uh, nervous. New job, famous chef at our table—"

"Horseshit."

Her eyes flash with something I can't decipher. Surprise? Warmth? Both?

"When you're done serving this course, you go sit by Chef"—I nod in Katie's direction—"and eat some real food. Understood?"

"Whoa. Not only are you being a team player, but are you also *caring*? About me, of all people?"

"No," I grunt.

She grins. "Hey. If you can't be honest with me, at least make an attempt to be honest with yourself."

See, that's just the thing. Somewhere along the way, I forgot what honesty looks like. Feels like. I've been lied to so often and so well that I guess I started assuming it was a dead language. Like Latin or some shit.

But looking in Emma's eyes, I realize the truth feels like this. Like rage. Rightness. The combination is equal parts maddening and magnetic, and this time, it's my hands that shake as I grab two decanters and follow Emma to the table.

I know this is the first time I'm collaborating with her in a meaningful way. But I'd be lying if I said I wasn't already thinking about the really cool stuff we could do together going forward.

I think I'm actually seeing how working as co-heads might be a home run.

I think I'm actually trusting Emma. And not because Beau's making me but because she deserves it.

Try it on. Maybe I should try accepting that Emma isn't biding her time, waiting for the opportunity to manipulate me. To lie about her intentions.

My heart lifts the way it always does at the sight of a table of loud, happy people. The waitstaff has begun to set out the paella, and the smell is incredible. A little spice from the chorizo, starch from the rice, earthiness from the homemade chicken stock Chef and I spent the past two years getting just right.

I'm not the only one who appreciates just how fragrant and pretty the plates are.

"Y'all see that char on the rice?" Luke says, lifting his plate to get a better look. "Perfect."

Elijah nods, and my chest swells. "Damn fuckin' right it is."

"Chef Katie is all kinds of talented with a paella pan." I fill Greyson's glass, the scent of vanilla and stone fruit rising from the wine. Glancing across the table, I catch Emma looking at me. She tips her head.

Keep going, she's saying.

So I take a deep breath and gird my loins and put myself out there.

"Because I like to feed my ego, I'm gonna drop some knowledge on y'all." The table laughs. Emma smiles. "The crispy, toasted rice you got there on your plates is called socarrat."

"Socarrat," Eli repeats, tipping back his wineglass for a sniff. "The stuff of dreams."

I nod. "Exactly. Y'all give it a try. Notice how it's a little sweet? That's because the rice caramelizes in the pan. Add in that satisfying crunch, and you've got pure heaven. Well, for foodies like me, anyway."

Emma holds up her decanter. "This Rioja balances out that note of caramel nicely—taste the vanilla? A little more sweetness to go with all that savory happening on your plates."

Our eyes lock. Something urgent and sweet arrows through my center.

"Genius," Greyson says. "It's a beautiful pairing, truly."

Emma's at my side now, filling more glasses. Jen, a waitress, is right behind her. So I raise my arm and give Emma a nod. Lips twitching, she passes underneath it. Her elbow brushes against my belly, painting a brushstroke of heat across my torso.

I'm trying honesty on, and it feels *nice*.

"Nice casual mention of socarrat," Emma says when we're back at the service station. She's uncorking bottles for the next course, so I start lining up the appropriate decanters.

"Hey. Really good socarrat is a great way to enhance sobre mesa. Which, coincidentally, happens to be my favorite thing in life. Well"—I smirk—"my second favorite, but you get the idea."

She arches a brow. "Damn, Beauregard, bringing out the big guns today."

"Told you I'm good at this."

"You're the best." She meets my eyes. "Same as I'm the best at wine. Correct me if I'm wrong, but isn't sobre mesa the art of conversation over a meal? The way people connect and talk and, yeah, basically touch the divine while lingering over dinner?"

"It's a lost art here in the States, and one I'd love to bring back."

She pauses. The heat of her gaze coats my entire left side in this buzzy, prickly warmth. I've had women stare at me. A lot. Nothing new here. Except—

Except Emma's attention gives me sense of pride. I've worked hard to get where I am today, just like I worked hard on the field. But right now, I'm being acknowledged for my work in this world, at this event.

It's pretty fucking great.

"You do know that staring is rude, right?" I manage. When what I really want to ask is *Will you let me make you a meal so I can show you how nourishing real food can be?*

Speaking of getting crushed. A voice in my head screams *no* over and over again.

I listen. For now.

"You're full of surprises, Beauregard." I hear her smile in her voice. "And *you* know what the essential requirement for a solid sobre mesa is, right?"

"A pack of cheap French cigarettes. Obviously."

She's struggling with the wine tool again now that her thumb is tender. Wordlessly I take the tool and the bottle, the fingers of her gloved hand touching mine as she lets me take over. I curse the glove for being there because I want her skin. Her alive-ness, if that's even a word, because I'm suddenly feeling achingly alive myself.

"Well, obviously that, yes. But honesty too. A willingness to dig deep and bare your soul."

Pulling out a cork, I nod at the table. "Go see what seven wants to do about a refill. His glass is empty."

"On it."

She pours. I feed. Halfway through the next course she's beside me again. Before I can move to get out of the way, she's ducking underneath my arms again and shooting me a saucy, happy, satisfied grin. When the decanter I'm pouring from is empty, she's at my side with a full one ready to go.

I thank her, and she shimmies.

The girl fucking *shimmies*, a barely-there shake of her hips that's as playful as it is effortless.

No way putting myself out there is making *her* feel giddy too?

No fucking way.

Still, I can't help thinking that Emma could easily edge me out. Elbow me aside, roll her eyes, grab things out of my hand.

Instead, she's literally dancing while helping me out. Encouraging me. Injecting this heady sense of joy in what would otherwise be a routine luncheon at Blue Mountain Farm.

I suddenly feel like the world's biggest asshat for behaving the way I have this week.

Someone else who's a complete asshat? The guy at fourteen. From the gleam of thirst in his eyes, he witnessed Emma's shimmy, and he very much enjoyed the view.

Emma notices *him* noticing. Her mirth fades. My grip on the decanter tightens. Hers is empty. I run for a full one and hand it to her. She moves to take it, but I keep my hold on it firm.

"I'll ask him to leave," I murmur.

She shakes her head. "Don't. The meal is almost over. Hopefully, his friends will take him home and let him sleep it off. No need to cause a scene."

"Fuck that," I say. "He's the one who's making a scene."

"I don't disagree. But we're almost at the finish line, and I really want this event to be a home run for everybody. If he becomes a real problem, I'll let you know, all right? I'll pull on my ear or something. I don't need you playing Batman on my behalf."

"I'm more of an Iron Man."

"So I've been told. I got this."

Without waiting for a reply, she dives back in. I make up some bullshit about letting the wine in my decanter breathe for an extra minute, giving me the excuse to stand watch over the table.

But the only person I watch is Emma.

I may be protective, but I never get protective over girls I've just met, and I definitely don't get possessive.

But I feel a surge of both as I watch Emma approach the guy. She expertly trades her decanter for a pitcher of water from a passing server. Holding her body away from him, she tops off his water glass. He turns his head to look at her, and my pulse kicks up a notch when he lifts his empty wineglass, asking for more Rioja.

Emma politely but firmly refuses the request, suggesting a coffee instead.

That's when shit hits the fan. The guy digs a dollar bill out of his wallet, and he tucks it into Emma's lapel.

Somehow my spidey senses kick in, and I'm able to hear him say, "For your services. Because that's how much they're worth. A wine expert? What a joke. You may wear your little Lois Lane suit, but I think we all know what your real job is here. Which, yeah"—his gaze rakes over her curves—"I'll pay more than a dollar for that."

She stiffens, her cheeks burning pink.

But I see red. Is no one else catching this? The rest of the table is absorbed in other conversations. Every so often, Eli will shoot the guy a warning glance, but then someone tugs on his sleeve or calls his name, and he gets distracted.

I stare at Emma, silently begging her to look at me, to give me permission to suit up and kick some bad-guy ass. But she asked me not to intervene unless she gave me the signal. She's been so considerate today—all week—and returning that favor is the least I can do.

It goes against my every impulse, though. I set down the decanter I'm holding because I'm squeezing it so hard I'm worried it'll shatter. Emma steps back so that she's out of fourteen's reach. His hand falls and so does his face.

She removes the dollar bill from her lapel and slides it onto the table beside his plate.

"Trust me when I say you need that coffee now, sir," Emma replies steadily. I watch, pulse pounding, as Emma turns and heads to the back of the pavilion. She sets down the pitcher at the service station and slips out of the side entrance, which leads to the smoking patio.

My stomach drops. I may only have known the woman for

a week, but I can already tell tucking tail and running isn't like her.

Fourteen's clearly hit on a soft spot.

My feet move before my mind does. I don't know what I'm going to do or how I'm going to fix this or even if me following Emma outside is the right move. What if she just wants to be left alone?

But I do know I can't let some dickhead make her feel like an idiot for being real.

For being herself. Because now I understand the kind of bravery that takes.

Chapter Thirteen

EMMA

I know better than to let that douchebag get under my skin.

I'm thirty-one years old, for crying out loud. I've been in this business for almost a decade. Drunk assholes poking fun at who I am and what I do is nothing new. Usually, I can let their comments, their looks, roll right off my back. I'm good at my job. I'm passionate about it and proud of what I've accomplished.

But today's barbs are sticking. Maybe because something is going down between Samuel and me, something good and real and important, and it's got me feeling soft and mushy. He's opening up in a way he hasn't before, and it's incredibly satisfying to see how the Charleston Heat guests are connecting with that.

His vulnerability is making my own that much more poignant. That much softer. And since I'm so soft, this guy's jabs land hard.

What *if* this profession is a joke?

What if I never make it because finding success as a sommelier only happens for a chosen few?

What if I'm trying too hard?

Eyes burning, I make a beeline for the smoking patio.

A forest of nearby oak and pine trees cast the patio in shadow. The patio itself is set into a hill, bordered on one side with a tall retaining wall made of stone. Rocking chairs and upholstered benches face the unbelievable view. The cocktail tables between them are set with brass ashtrays and matching cigar cutters.

It's chilly, but the air feels good against my skin. Putting my hands on my face, I feel the literal burn of embarrassment. I close my eyes and take a long, deep breath, loosening the knot in my throat ever so slightly.

There's no crying in the wine expert world. In theory, at least. It's unprofessional, and it does nothing except embarrass whoever's doing it.

I haven't cried at work since I failed phase two of the Master Sommelier certification test five years ago. Once I passed on the second try and landed the enviable possession of head sommelier at one of Asheville's top restaurants, I thought I was finally past the hysterics-in-the-bathroom-during-break phase.

Guess I was wrong.

"He's wrong." The rumble of Samuel's voice makes my nipples harden. I look up and there he is, crowding out the late afternoon sky.

Is he reading my mind?

His voice is rough, but his eyes are soft.

"Clearly, I'm a fan of a well-tailored suit." He gives his lapels a tug. "While yours are not as awesome as mine, I happen to think they're less Lois Lane and more *Sex and the City* Samantha."

My lips twitch, and my throat loosens some more. "You watch *Sex and the City*?"

"Fuck yeah, I do. Samantha happens to be my favorite."

"Mine too."

"Go figure. Probably why you dress like the lovechild of her and a...librarian."

I laugh. Samuel's eyes smile as they search mine, and my heart does this lovely fluttering thing inside my chest.

"Point being, you're not ridiculous. That guy was. You put on one hell of a show today."

My thoughts scatter. Samuel is actually complimenting me. With actual words he's actually speaking out loud.

My hand rests against my thigh, and I pinch myself there, just to make sure this isn't some kind of stress-induced hallucination. Today's been wildly, unbelievably great. So great that my natural optimism is threaded with a strand of bright red doubt.

When, exactly, is the other shoe going to drop?

"What I do is not a show," I manage. "It's a job."

He holds up his hands. "You're right. I'm sorry."

I blink. Too startled to say anything else, I reply, "Thanks."

He shoots his cuffs. Picks at an invisible speck of lint on his sleeve, averting his gaze. "And while I'm being all confessional and shit, I happen to think it's a job you fucking annihilated. You know it, I know it, even that dickbag knows it. He acted a fool because he's not used to your kind of greatness."

I arch a brow, even as that fluttering inside my chest intensifies. "Sounds familiar."

"Hey. We're here to talk about you, not—"

Samuel twists at the sound of a voice behind us. Peeking around the bulk of his body, I see said dickbag spilling out of the pavilion. His eyes lock on me, and his gaze lights up with something sharp and lewd.

It lodges an ice pick of fear inside my breastbone.

Not thinking, I grab Samuel's arm. A charge rips through

me—longing? embarrassment?—and I quickly pull back my hand.

I square my shoulders, not daring to look at Samuel, and scramble to give myself a pep talk so I stand tall in front of this jerk. I won't allow myself to cower.

But before I even open my mouth, Samuel reaches back and puts *his* hand on my right hip. My body ignites at the contact, fire mingling with the fear in my veins. When he gently guides me to stand behind the shield of his body, my heart turns over.

That is definitely not embarrassment.

He keeps protecting me, and I don't know what the hell to make of it.

His fingers remain on my hip as I breathe in the breadth of him. I have never felt so small.

I've also never felt so safe. I resist the urge to put my hands on the small of his back and melt into his body. How good would it feel, to touch another human being and be touched in return? It's been so damn long.

His *skin*. I can smell it. Clean. A hint of spice, probably from the soap he uses.

The tiny space between my front and his back comes alive. My nose is an inch from his spine. My hips brush his backside with every breath I take. I could step back. I should step back.

Instead, I stand very still, caught in his gravity. The determined throb inside my skin coexists with the softness in my core. It's bewildering.

It's also somehow...affirming? The fear pounding through me fades. I don't need to be protected. But having someone on my side definitely helps me feel less afraid.

It makes me feel emboldened.

Samuel tilts his head to one side, then the other, making the sinews in his neck pop against the skin.

It's a *fuck off* signal if I ever saw one.

"Can I help you?" Samuel clips.

The guy draws up short. He eyes us, debating what his next move should be.

"Sir?" Samuel says. "I'm happy to escort you back to your room."

"No," he replies. "No, I'm good. I was coming out here to smoke." He pats the front of his pants. "Shit, I'm out of cigarettes. Never mind then."

I move to stand next to Samuel. His hand is still on my hip, arm extended across my torso.

I glance up at him. His eyes meet mine, and he dips his head in a barely perceptible nod. *Go for it.*

He wants me to take the lead. The idea that he's bending, that he's trusting me, sends a bolt of arousal through my center, as bright and fast as lightning.

"You know what's a joke?" I ask, turning back to fourteen. "Smoking. You may think what I do is ridiculous, but at least it doesn't kill me."

The guy has the balls to narrow his eyes at me.

"Whatever," he says, tucking his hands into his pockets.

I stare him down. "No, not 'whatever.' You insulted me this afternoon, and you made our other guests uncomfortable. Continue this behavior and I won't hesitate to ask you to leave the resort. Understood?"

A flush of embarrassment spreads across his cheeks. He looks away.

Looks downright sheepish. I bite back a grin.

"I'm done here," he says at last.

"You should've been done hours ago," I reply. "Good evening."

Samuel and I watch fourteen make his way around the pavilion toward the main house.

And then he's gone.

Without thinking I drop my head against Samuel's shoulder, the fabric of his suit jacket silky smooth against my skin. I take a long, deep breath, closing my eyes as I try to gather myself.

He smells so damn good.

My knee joints liquify. My heart hammers. My body is hollowed out and hungry.

Hungry for more of *this*. Touch. Electricity. Safety.

"I know David only likes babies," I manage. "But maybe Eddie has a thing for dickheads."

Samuel's massive shoulders shake as he laughs. I lift my head to find him looking at me.

Our eyes lock, and a beat of very real heat passes between us.

He holds up his free hand, the first two fingers crossed. "Let's hope so. You okay?"

"I am. You?"

"I'll be better when he's gone for good."

His fingers flex against my hip. I feel them around my heart. Squeezing. Probing.

I look down. Samuel is still touching me.

And somehow my hand is on his forearm, the heat of his body seeping into my own.

His eyes go hazy, and he turns around to face me.

He's standing close. Really close.

The fantasy blooms to life inside my head. I imagine him stepping into me, bold and unhurried, using the bulk of his body to plaster mine against the retaining wall. The feel of the stones bite into my back through my silk shirt. He puts one hand on the wall beside my head. The other he curls around my waist, just underneath my bra, and holds me against him, everything from my navel to my knees melting into his groin.

Heaviness gathers between my legs.

I imagine he ducks his head and puts his mouth on my neck. My head falls to the side, my breath coming in hot pants, as that heaviness throbs.

Yes.

My God, *yes*.

His teeth nick my skin, sharp and slow and arousing as fuck. He soothes the spot with his tongue, then his lips. His scruff is scratchy, but I like the sound it makes against my throat as he moves. He's not hard, not yet, but I still wonder what it would feel like. The crown of his erection thrust just where I want it, teasing my clit through our clothes.

I blink and the fantasy dissipates.

The arousal between my legs does not.

For the first time, I wonder if I bit off more than I can chew by coming up here.

Maybe this job—this man and this place—are more than I can handle.

"What are you thinking about when that happens?" Samuel asks. His voice is rougher than before.

"When what happens?"

"Your eyes." He searches them, his own alive with interest. "They're different. They...I don't know, darken or some shit. Makes me think—"

Think what?

I have to get out of here. Now.

"Thank you," I say, ignoring his question. "For the assist."

He pauses. For a horrible second, I think he's going to press me to answer. But then he smooths his expression and says, "You were the one with the killer lines and the determination. I just provided the muscle. Between your wine know-how and your smart mouth, I think it's fair to say you were the one who saved the day."

I bite the inside of my cheek to keep from grinning. "Does that make you the damsel?"

"I guess it does, yeah. Or maybe I was the damsel, but you were both the knight and the one in distress. The knight in distress." His eyes bore into mine. I get the feeling he hasn't finished that thought.

I am the damsel, yeah, and I hated every second of it.

I'm the damsel and I love it, give me more please and thank you.

My pulse spikes at the idea of this enormous, powerful man being even the tiniest bit submissive.

Even the tiniest bit into plays on power dynamics. I have yet to find a man *not* on the internet who is.

"There y'all are! I've been looking for you everywhere."

I turn my head and see Chef Katie standing on the pavilion's top step. She's squinting, like she can't quite see us against the glare of the sun.

My stomach drops a hundred stories. I quickly step away from Samuel and tuck nonexistent hairs behind my ears.

My hands are shaking again. I clasp them behind my back, pulse roaring in my ears as I paste on a smile.

"Just needed some air," I call back.

"I've got two plates of paella with your names on 'em," she replies. "Come on up."

She puts the flat of one hand against her brow and waves us in with the other.

Please, please tell me she didn't see me looking up at Samuel with stars in my eyes.

"Be right up," Samuel says. I feel him looking at me, but suddenly, I can't look back at him.

I feel like a coward, but I need time. I need to figure out —God, I need to figure out what's wrong with me.

How I feel about the fact that I feel safe and alive and *so* turned on when I'm with Samuel.

Is he a beta at heart?

Working with him today has stoked my attraction to new heights. What the hell am I going to do about that? What if this happens every time we're working together—me wanting him so badly I do something reckless that could jeopardize my career?

"We should go," I manage, and without looking back, I charge across the patio and up the steps into the pavilion.

All the while, I have a keen awareness of Samuel's presence two steps behind me. Close enough to let me know he's there, far enough to let me know he's allowing me the space I didn't say I needed, but that he's giving me anyway.

He knows I need it. And the fact he's paying such close attention makes me feel tender to the point of pain.

Chapter Fourteen

SAMUEL

I'm half naked when I open the door.

Hey, it's Saturday night. I don't usually have weekend nights off, but because Emma and I worked our fingers to the bone all day, we decided to give ourselves the rare treat of a free weekend evening. I'm celebrating by going commando in my coziest pair of sweats and nothing else.

Signals must cross inside my head, because my body lights up at the sight of Emma standing on my front stoop.

I still haven't recovered from how...intense that little interaction we had on the smoking patio was. I let my hand linger on her body way longer than I should have under the guise of keeping her close so I could protect her, and *she didn't pull away*.

In fact, she touched me right back. The way she put her head on my shoulder and her hand on my arm, like she was struggling just as hard as I was to keep her body in check—

Did she feel it too? That surge of desire and understanding between us? I think she did.

From the way her eyes darkened, she must have.

Then again, I don't exactly trust myself when it comes to Emma Crawford. I definitely don't trust my dick.

But I did trust her today. And she came through in a big way.

She's wearing leggings and neon pink sneakers, hands balled in the front pockets of her fitted black puffer jacket. Her hair, usually hidden in a coil, is gathered in a long ponytail at the crown of her head.

Her *hair*. It's thick and shiny and wavy. When it's kinda sorta free like this, she looks undone. A little wild.

She looks hot as fuck.

"I'd like to apologize," she blurts.

I pull back, startled. "Apologize? For what?"

Her eyes flick to my bare chest. She swallows audibly, and then she trains her gaze on my face. Her mouth flattens, like it takes effort not to keep looking down. "For today. I'm sorry I walked away like I did, but I needed time to think. So I took this really long hike, and I got lost, and I...I don't know why I touched you the way I did. You know, touching your arm and putting my head on your shoulder. I wasn't thinking, and I-I just wanted you to know how embarrassed I am. And I think we should clear the air before, you know..."

I blink. Out of all the things she could've told me, I wasn't expecting that.

I wasn't hoping for that.

The fact that I was hoping at all means I should thank her, tell her we'll figure it out in the morning, and close the damn door.

Instead, I open the door wider, and say, "Come in. Let's talk."

Yep, I must have a death wish. Or at the very least a masochistic streak. I know someone who would approve.

"You sure?" Emma asks, brow furrowing.

"Of course. By the way, I feel like I owe you an apology too. I touched you without asking—"

"You were just trying to do the right thing." Emma's eyes are steady on mine. "I appreciate that. No apology necessary."

"Okay. Good." I motion her inside.

Emma steps inside the foyer and glances around, eyes going wide.

"I thought your suits were ridiculous. But this—Beauregard, this is *sick*."

"It's baller, and I love it." I close the door without bothering to lock it because this is Blue Mountain, and you're more likely to run into Dave the Bear than a burglar. "By the way, how did you know this was my house?"

The color in her cheeks burns from pink to red. "Lucky guess. I picked the biggest one I could find and just...went with it."

"Yeah, you did. I was going to open a bottle of something good to celebrate us not killing each other today. Want a glass?"

She cuts me a look, her eyes slipping to my chest again. "May I request you put on a shirt first?"

"You may not. Kitchen's this way."

Emma follows me, steps slowing as we cross from the soaring sitting room into the kitchen.

She gapes. I smile. The kitchen is incredible, and it's the room I love the most in the house. The space is dominated by a pair of twelve-foot islands. One is for food prep, decked out with butcher block and two farm sinks, while the other is for dining, with several cushy barstools tucked underneath the marble countertop.

Emma is immediately drawn to the range, the centerpiece of the kitchen. Of the entire house, probably. At fifteen feet long, with two ovens, eight burners, a griddle, a warming plate, and a grill, it's the best range money can buy.

"This is the most beautiful stove I've ever seen." She gently runs her hand over the custom-made brass knobs. "Wow. Truly a work of art."

"It's the sexiest piece of machinery I've bought. The most expensive too."

"Tell me more."

"We had it custom-made in France. Took something like a month to build the whole thing by hand. I'd been dreaming about getting one of these beauties for years, so when I could finally swing it, I wanted it to be perfect."

"Why a stove? Why not, say, a Lamborghini? Or a Caribbean island?"

I lift a shoulder, very much enjoying the way her eyes move appreciatively over my bare skin. I may like to eat, but I also workout like a motherfucker. I've always been a work hard, play hard kinda guy.

I've also been thinking a fuck ton about how trying on Emma's honesty felt today.

I decide to try it again tonight.

"I love food. Grew up chubby 'cause my mama is the best damn cook this side of the Appalachians. Daddy wasn't so bad either. Wasn't long before I was bugging 'em to teach me how to make my own pancakes. Guess I just sorta took to it. I cooked for my siblings. Then my teammates and coaching staff. Now I cook for my family. Sunday supper's my favorite time of the week."

She furrows her brow. "That's sweet." She says it like she's confused.

I know the feeling. Here I am, welcoming into my home the sommelier I swore I'd kick to the curb.

Makes absolutely no fucking sense. But it feels right, so I go with it.

"Sit." I point at a stool. "I decanted some Screaming Eagle. Sound good?"

With her hand on the back of the stool, Emma cocks her head. "And here I thought I was winning you over with small producers and their stories of lushes who happen to be nuns."

I set the empty bottle and full decanter on the counter in front of her. Her eyes light up as she gives the decanter a sniff and inspects the label.

"I appreciate the nun lushes." I cross my arms over my chest, but even my biceps on full display don't distract her from the wine. "Just like I appreciate a solid bottle from my BSD collection."

"Solid? Samuel, you have a better chance of meeting the real Santa Claus than you do of finding a bottle of 2016 Screaming Eagle. Do you always open thousand-dollar bottles of wine on your nights off?"

"Yes." I fill the gigantic bowls of a pair of Cabernet glasses. "I woke up this morning thinking there was a very real possibility I'd end up in a shallow grave by dinner, so... yeah. The fact that I'm alive is kind of a miracle. If that isn't something to celebrate, I don't know what is."

"I'm not that scary."

"Yes, you are. You know it, and you like it."

Holding up her glass, she smiles at me, unguarded and warm, and damn if my heart doesn't turn over in my chest. "A toast to the truth. You're finally telling it, and I'm pretty sure you learned that from me."

I sip. "What makes you say that?"

"You're surrounded exclusively by yes men. Women. Yes *people*, I should say. Everyone but Beau."

Emma came here to apologize. And still she's unapologetically, brutally, *titillatingly* honest.

I tap my glass to hers. Keyed up and curious and *why* is my heart *doing* that aching thing? "What's wrong with being surrounded by yes people if they helped you build the best restaurant at the best resort in the South?"

"Chef Eli would beg to differ on the best restaurant bit. But I digress. What's wrong with surrounding yourself with people who never challenge you is that you never grow. You're not being pushed the way you need to be."

She's right. Deep down, I know she's right, and she's giving me something else to think about.

The girl's always making me think and making me question. I want to hate it, but I don't.

Looking away, I sniff my wine. I don't miss how Emma grins as she watches me dip my nose deep into the glass, just like she does. Whatever. It really does help you tease out the more subtle elements of the wine's flavor profile.

Case in point: I've had this same bottle several times over the past year (when you're able to get your hands on the Holy Grail of California Cabs, you buy it by the case). But tasting it Emma's way makes it a whole new experience. I pick up on notes of wet stone. Grass. Earth.

"Petrichor," she says, sniffing her own glass.

I snap my eyebrows together. "What the fuck is that?"

"What the world smells like after it rains."

The ache intensifies. "Yeah. Yes. I get that too. A little nutmeg on the nose?"

She smiles, the kind that touches her eyes, and my heart is doing full-on backflips now. "*Yes*. Nice way to liven up those earthy notes."

She sips. I sip. Our eyes lock as the flavors explode on my tongue. Watching her watching me, I feel joy rise inside me. Same as it did when I tasted her Riesling.

From the stunned look on her face, she's feeling it too.

It's autumn afternoons. The smell in the air on Sunday right before a game. Leaves and nerves and the feeling of carrying on a tradition that's gone unbroken for generations.

A tradition that broke me.

The joy that's flooded me all day dims. A prick of fear, familiar and hard, punctures the soft stuff inside my chest.

"Good God," Emma says, smacking her lips. "That's just... wow...no words..."

She sips again, this dreamy look coming over her expression. My skin tightens.

I like beautiful women. The curvier and flirtier, the sexier.

But a thinking woman? A girl who honestly and openly engages with the truth?

She might be the sexiest of all.

Also the most dangerous.

Clearing my throat, I give the wine in my glass a swirl. "I thought you didn't like my BSD wine."

She swallows and shakes her head. "I never said that. I did say most of it was uninteresting. But this—it's a cult wine for a reason. I get it, Beauregard."

"Look at us, proving each other wrong."

"Are you admitting that Riesling was the best fucking thing you've had this year?"

I swirl again. "Maybe."

She's smiling again, and Jesus Christ, so am I.

Danger.

Chapter Fifteen

SAMUEL

"So." I sip, the first stirrings of that red wine buzz I love so much tingling along my spine. "Didn't you come here to clear the air?"

Emma sets down her glass. "I did. I blurted out everything I came to say on your front step. But what went down on the smoking patio didn't sit right with me. I'm sorry."

"I'm going to use your line and say no apology necessary."

Looking down, she settles the stem of her glass between her first two fingers, palm flat against the base. "I saw it today —how you were opening up. I hope that means we can finally work through why things between us have been so...difficult." When she looks up, her eyes are serious. "I want this to work, Beauregard. The smoking patio incident notwithstanding, today went so damn well. I love the farm, I love the staff, and I love what we do together. It's special. With your passion for food, my knowledge of wine, and a stellar staff to work side by side with us, we can do amazing, transformative, *important* work. See what great things can happen when you play nice? I can't show you any more clearly. So please, for the love of

God, stop being a dick, and start being the guy you were today. The one who's kind and real and open to change."

My heart trips to a stop. The prick of fear becomes a full-on glacier of ice that lodges itself in my center.

Be open to change, Beauregard.

Those were the first words that came out of Coach's mouth the day I was released from the team.

Things are gonna change around here.

Those were the words Daddy said to me when he came home from the hospital after getting lost on a neighbor's farm.

I blink, the world around me snapping into focus. Like I'm waking from a stupor or something. The look I'm giving Emma morphs into a glare, and the ice inside me burns to anger.

I was kind once. I was real. I opened myself up to hope, but all I got was hurt.

"What exactly are you trying to prove here, Emma?" I challenge. She startles at my sudden change in mood. "You're at the top of your game, but you still try too damn hard. Here you are, trying to make me do things I don't do and see things I don't want to see. It's annoying. I may be a dick, but you're a pain in the ass."

Her shoulders set, and the look in her eyes turns to stone, even as the space between us electrifies. "I try hard because I care."

"No, you don't. You try hard because you're ashamed." *Oh, Lord, pot meet kettle.* I have absolutely no right to say these things, but the words are coming too fast for me to stop them. "That's why that drunk guy got to you. You're hard on yourself because you don't *like* yourself. Why do you think that is?"

I'm being a huge dick, and I know that. I'm angry with myself for taking it so far, and ashamed I'm letting fear win.

I'm angry that I'm ashamed. I'm angry that I have to put up with this barrage of inconvenient emotions at all.

I don't like being the angry guy. I've made it a point not to let my bitterness get the better of me. I'm the happy-go-lucky hotshot. But Emma's making me see just how big the disconnect is between who I want to be and who I really am.

Who I show the world, and who I show her.

Somewhere in the swirl of emotions barreling through me, I *know* Emma doesn't deserve this treatment. The up and down. The back and forth.

But that doesn't stop me from putting my dukes up.

Hell, maybe it's why I put 'em up in the first place. A shitty defense mechanism that's getting really fucking old.

Knowing that I'm wrong but not doing anything about it —that's what makes me angriest of all.

The red in her cheeks returns. She leaps up from her stool to stand in front of me. Without her heels, she's even shorter than normal, but her ballooning rage gives her an enormous presence. Jabbing a finger into my chest, she says, "You don't know a damn thing about me, Beauregard, so stop pretending you do. And let's be real, you're the one who tries too hard. You try to be something you're not, and that, in my *un*humble opinion, is much, much worse."

The rage that darts through my center tells me she's right.

Fucking hell, Emma's right. And she is *mad*. And...hot? Is that flash in her eyes the kind of heat I think it is?

Is this argument turning her on?

It'd be twisted if that were true. Then again, everything about my relationship with Emma is twisted.

She's twisting me up and turning me inside out, and I don't know how much more I can take.

"I'm fine with who I am," I say.

"That why you're all rage-y when I'm around? Because you're fine?"

I could be honest. But fuck it, honesty leads to hope, and hope leads to hurt. How many times do I need to learn that lesson?

"Are you fine after how I made you feel today?" I duck my head and lower my voice. "I saw it, Emma. I heard it, I felt it, and I saw how much you wanted me. You've wanted to touch me like that from day one, haven't you? And please, since you're so into the truth, be honest."

She stares back, not moving an inch. Eyes glowing like burning embers.

I smirk. "You want to do it again, don't you? Touch me?"

She keeps staring. A voice in my head keeps screaming *What the fuck, what the fuck, what the* fuck are you doing?

"Do it," I say. "Touch me again. You wanna slap me? Fuck me? Do it." I hold out my arms. "I dare you."

She stands there, two inches from a kiss, tits rising and falling on sharp breaths. My dick perks right up.

Emma isn't leaving.

Which means she wants to stay.

Aw, yeah.

Slowly—carefully—Emma lifts her arm. My entire being pulses when she wraps her hand around my throat. Her gaze, heated and hazy, moves to my mouth, like she can't look me in the eye.

Good. I won't be able to look myself in the eye after this either.

"You're full of shit," she whispers. And then she tightens her hand around my neck and pushes me against the wall and presses a bruising, hot kiss to my mouth.

My dick goes full salute in one second flat. She's strong for such a little thing, and my shoulder blades sting from the impact of being shoved against the wall.

"Give me permission to put my hands on you," she rasps.

"Already did," I murmur against her lips.

"No." I nearly jump out of my skin when her other hand skates down my belly to the waistband of my sweats. "I mean put my *hands on you*."

"Granted. Yes. Done."

Her hand slips inside my sweats and finds my dick. She gives it a tight, almost painful tug.

Goddamn, do I like all this pain.

I *like* how she gets right to it. She knows what she wants, and she wants my dick.

I ain't mad at it. When was the last time a woman was so fearlessly up front with me about what she likes? I could always tell when my partners were holding back. Playing a part, almost, as if they were feeling me out to see what *I* liked and what *I* wanted. They were putting on a show.

Hell, I'm certainly guilty of that sin. I'm guilty of it every damn day.

But Emma, per usual, isn't afraid to tell it like it is. She isn't afraid to be selfish in seeking out her pleasure. It's filthy and sexy and so damn great I want to do it too.

What if what pleases me pleases her?

I shove the thought from my head. This is hate sex, pure and simple. Nothing more.

She tugs me again, and again, and behind my closed eyelids I see stars. Her kiss tastes like wine. It's deep, urgent, our tongues and breath tangled. She bites my bottom lip, and I growl. She tightens her grip on my neck, and I do it again.

I don't think it's a sound I've ever made before.

She takes her hand off my cock.

"Emma—"

"Shut up," she says into my mouth. She grabs my hand and guides it inside her leggings. My entire being leaps when my fingertips meet her pussy.

Emma goes commando too? Fuck. My dick is in agony.

I jump the gun and try to part her lips with my fingers.

Immediately, her teeth come down on my tongue, and she pulls back my hand.

"Mine," she snaps, her voice smokier and raspier than ever.

Fuck. *Yes*.

I owe her this at least, the ability to punish my cowardice.

Her lips curve into a smile against mine. She pushes my finger inside her slit, and my eyes fly open.

Hers are open too, and they're on mine. For a second, we break the kiss to look at each other.

She's wet. So fucking wet and swollen I buck my hips, the heaven of sinking inside her almost too sweet to contemplate.

She's gotta let me do something. Taste her. Fuck her. See her.

She must read my mind because together, we circle the pad of my finger against her clit. Her breath catches.

Without a word, and her other hand still on my throat, she pulls me away from the wall and walks us closer to the edge of the island.

Yes.

If she's doing what I think she's doing, *yes*.

Since she's reading me so well, I try to return the favor. Her hips are rolling against my hand as her ass meets the countertop. She's bending one knee, pulling it up, and I instinctively take her leg in my free hand.

"Uh-huh," she breathes, dipping her head in a quick nod. She releases the hand I've got between her legs, and I use it to grab her other leg and lift her onto the counter. Her hand isn't on my throat, her hands are moving up my chest, stopping to play with my nipples. A direct wire of sensation between there and the head of my cock lights up.

She pushes my hands to the waistband of her leggings again. *Off*, her eyes say.

So off they go. I pull them down to her ankles and she spreads her knees, leaning back on her elbows.

It's my turn to stare. Emma's little landing strip is maddeningly hot.

"Gorgeous," I spit out, stepping between her legs. "You're fucking gorgeous, Emma."

She bites her lip. Propping herself up on one elbow, she reaches down and lazily plays with herself. Teasing me with her pink, slick, and ready pussy.

I'm going to scream if I don't get to fuck her soon.

"Why do you look so pissed?" she asks.

"Because you're a pain in the ass, remember?"

"I do." Her eyes flick to the floor. She raises her voice. "Get on your knees, Beauregard."

Fuuuuuuuuuck.

I drop down and she grabs me by the hair and yanks me to her. My blood roars at the way the hardwood floors bite into my knees.

This time she doesn't need to tell me what to do.

I lean in and gently suck on her clit. She hisses, head falling back. I sink one finger inside her, and my balls tighten. She's small and right, so fucking right, I want to weep.

She pulls my hair harder. *Another.*

I slowly push another finger inside her and feel her stretch around me. She sucks in a breath, and I almost stroke the fuck out when she lies all the way back on the counter-top. Her free hand disappears inside her shirt, and I can see the outline of her hand as she plucks at her nipple.

"Let me see," I grunt, shoving her shirt up her belly.

She's wearing a sports bra. She hasn't bothered to hike it up, so I do, exposing her breast. I thumb her nipple, and the crown of her head meets with the counter, her eyes squeezing shut.

I lick her clit and thrust my fingers, and her walls flutter, clamping down on me once.

"*Beauregard*," she yells, eyes still closed. "Where the hell did you learn to eat pussy like this?"

I just shake my head and continue my mission to make her come.

My cock is full-on tenting my sweats. I can feel the wet spot where my pre-cum's leaked through the fabric.

She's biting her lip, moaning as she rides my mouth and my fingers. Her pussy clamps down, hard this time. Her eyes open and find mine.

She comes, and it excites me so much—the sounds she makes, how her body arches off the counter, the way she looks me in the eye—that I almost come with her.

But scumbags don't deserve release. So I don't give in to mine.

I can't be punished enough for what I've done, and what I'm doing now.

Chapter Sixteen

EMMA

I come apart in Samuel's hands.

His tongue on my pussy, his fingers curled into my thighs, I come so hard it knocks the breath out of me. The force of the orgasm is propulsive, sending wave after wave of sensation crashing through my center. My entire being pulses in time to the tide, a quick, eviscerating drumbeat I feel down to my toes.

It's the best orgasm I've had in ages. Maybe because I shaved? I'm always experimenting with my grooming habits. Or maybe it's because I'm coming on someone else's fingers, with someone else's tongue on my clit. I don't have to try—to focus, to think, to fantasize—because the fantasy is happening right here, right now.

Granted, it's a fucked-up fantasy. Can you even call a hate hookup with a coworker a fantasy, especially after that coworker treats you like shit?

But the man knows what he's doing.

Those broad, strong fingers I've been staring at for days touched me just the way I like to be touched. His lips are as soft and full and knowledgeable as I imagined they'd be.

And there's something true about the way he's looking at me right now, blue eyes wide and full of emotion. He's not hiding or smirking or glowering. He's shocked, just as shocked as I am that he likes what I like.

He likes that I like being bossy. From the way he looks, and keeps *looking*, I can tell he's curious too. He's not afraid. He's not judging me.

I've met so few men outside the internet who don't judge me for being on the alpha side of the power dynamic scale I've started to believe they didn't exist.

But none of that matters when the guy in question treats you like garbage. Even a great orgasm doesn't change that.

It also doesn't change the fact that I never should've touched Samuel in the first place. This is wrong in a million ways.

He was wrong to taunt me, and I was wrong to let him.

How awkward is it going to be at work now? Will I be distracted and fuck up? What if Samuel runs his mouth, and it gets out I was (mostly) naked with a Beauregard brother?

I have so much to lose. My dream job. My reputation. My entire future.

Because here's the reality of the situation: I have a hell of a lot more at risk than Samuel does. He has an ownership stake in the resort, for crying out loud. His brother's the CEO. He'd have to do something pretty egregious to lose his position. But me? I'm new. No one really knows me, not yet anyway, so I'm vulnerable in ways Samuel will never be.

My orgasm fades, and the reality of what just went down sinks into my skin like a chill. I'm naked in Samuel Beauregard's kitchen. Tit out and legs spread, his handsome head between them. Mouth slick with my arousal.

Looking down at him, I'm overcome by anger like I've never known.

"What is it?" he asks, his brow crinkling. "Emma, talk to me."

My pulse thunders in my ears. I'm shaking. I'm needy. My body wants more, but I know better. I *fucking know better*.

I sit up. Tugging my bra over my breast, I look Samuel in the eyes. He has the nerve to appear concerned. Brows curved up, mouth curved down.

Longing rips through me. I want to believe him, to believe he cares, so very much. Today, I thought I saw a guy who cared. But clearly that was another front, another mask. Was he planning this all along?

Fuck him.

He reaches for me, but I flinch, pulling away.

His eyes go wide with confusion.

"Don't," I say, and I leap off the counter. Tugging up my leggings, I make a beeline for the front door.

I'm mortified by the sudden burn in my eyes. *Keep it together*. I have to keep it together until I'm safely out of this gorgeous hellhole. I will not let him see me cry. I won't give him the satisfaction.

But Samuel is hot on my heels, footsteps heavy on the hardwood floors.

"Hey," he says, reaching for my elbow. "Hey, look, whatever just happened, I'm sorry."

I pull out of his grasp. "Stop pretending you give a shit."

"Are you kidding? I just made you come. Of course I give a shit."

We're in the foyer now. He does this dip fake-out move thing and effortlessly overtakes me, putting himself between me and the door.

Athletes. Ugh.

"I'm not letting you leave until you tell me what's wrong."

"You know exactly what's wrong." I glare at him. "Step away, Beauregard. Now."

"Please." The pleading note in his voice gives me pause. He gestures to his impressive erection. "Look at me, Emma. I'm at your mercy here."

No, I think. *I'm at your mercy, and that's the problem.*

I reach for the doorknob, and he lets me. He steps aside, eyes following my every move, and I open the door.

"I really wish you wouldn't leave like this," he says.

"Why? Because you want to get off?"

His expression softens with hurt. "Because I know you don't feel good about what just went down, and neither do I."

Shaking my head, I scoff. "You take such pride in faking it. You're good at pretending, Beauregard, I'll give you that. Really, really good."

"You really think I'm proud of that?"

"I think you don't know who you are." I meet his eyes one last time. "Who the fuck are you, Samuel?"

He looks stricken. He looks away, a muscle in his jaw clenching against his carefully trimmed scruff. "I don't wanna be the kind of man who hurts you, I know that much."

"Horseshit," I say, throwing his earlier line back at him.

Before he can reply, I slip through the door and walk back to my cottage on unsteady legs. What the hell did I just do? I thought touching Samuel earlier today, and being touched by him, was inappropriate.

But I enjoyed it. I loved that Samuel didn't fight me when I had my hand around his throat. That he let me tell him where and how I wanted him.

Stop. I can't go down that path. This is my job, my future, my fucking career.

I cannot, under any circumstances, touch Samuel Beauregard again.

The only relationship I can have is one with Blue, especially while I'm proving myself here at the farm. But coming so hard with someone else's hands on me makes me wish I could actually meet my cybersex partner.

I want his cock inside me, rather than just imagining how good it would feel.

What if we did meet in person?

I recognize I'm not exactly in the best state of mind to be making big decisions about my romantic life, but I need something to look forward to.

Something to give me a sense of hope. Because my situation at work just started to feel pretty fucking hopeless.

Blue did say he's in the area. We could meet at a local restaurant or something. Have drinks and get to know each other. Chances are, the chemistry we have online won't translate to the world outside our computers. Still, it's worth a shot, right? He does have the body of a god. And a beautiful cock. Samuel's girthy, heavy dick felt exactly the way I imagined Blue's would feel in my hand.

I close the door behind me, then close my eyes. *Enough.* Enough of this Samuel bullshit. He's a coworker. End of story. Any other relationship we might've had—sexual, romantic, whatever—was never supposed to happen.

That's what Blue is for.

In the meantime, I'll keep my relationship with Samuel strictly professional. No more attempts to get him to open up. No more opening up to him. We don't need to be close to do our work, although it would've certainly helped.

That ship has sailed.

CHAT #3

MyBoyBlue4: Confession: I just defeated the worst case of blue balls I've had in my life, so I'm not sure how much energy I have left.

LadyV76: You've been a very bad boy.

MyBoyBlue4: But really. I'm a piece of shit.

LadyV76: Hey. Don't beat yourself up, it's just internet sex. TBH, I'm not really in the mood to get down either. Bad day. Well, great day, but it ended on a pretty terrible note, so. Yeah. If you want to take a rain check, I understand.

MyBoyBlue4: Thanks for understanding. I had an awful night too.

LadyV76: Why don't you just jerk off?

MyBoyBlue4: Long story. I know you don't like to get personal, so I won't go there. Any chance you're free tomorrow for that rain check?

LadyV76: Wait, wait, wait. I know I'm breaking my own rules here, but I really don't want to be alone right now. I'm happy to hang around for a bit and chat if you are.

MyBoyBlue4: God yes. Talk to me, V. What's on your mind?

LadyV76: I try to follow my heart and take the right risks. But a couple of things happened today that made me question whether that's the right way to live.

MyBoyBlue4: Lol. Wow okay, you went deep right off the bat.

LadyV76: I do like it deep.

MyBoyBlue4: I do too. At least since I've met you. You talked about this before, second-guessing yourself, and it made me think. Like, until I started chatting with you, I never really questioned much at all. I was certain about who I was and what I liked. I never really bothered trying new things because I thought I'd done it all.

LadyV76: Why'd you start chatting with me then?

MyBoyBlue4: See, that's just it. On the outside, everything was perfect. But inside, I was lonely. Still am. For so long, I could ignore that loneliness because I was busy AF. But after a while, it got louder and wouldn't leave me alone. I guess the stuff I did to keep it quiet wasn't working anymore. So I thought hey, maybe I'll find what I'm looking for on the internet.

LadyV76: Typical millennial.

MyBoyBlue4: I know right? PS I'm 35, *am* I a millennial? Let me confer with Google.

LadyV76: I'm 31, and I'm definitely a millennial. You are too, I think.

MyBoyBlue4: Yep, Google tells me I'm right in the millennial range #facts. Anyway, I see that going to the internet was a bonehead move. But there's an element of anonymity here that I need. The universe must've been looking out for me because I found you, and you showed me I like to be dominated. Never would've thought it, but now that I know that about myself, it makes me wonder all the other things I'm wrong about. I'm wrong about a lot.

LadyV76: I love everything about this. I've made you

hungry for more! More sci-fi-based fantasy scenarios and more self-exploration.

MyBoyBlue4: Exactly. But it's scary. I find myself doing stupid stuff, like lashing out and shit, when I'm pushed out of my comfort zone. I've got this one coworker in particular... she's constantly pushing me, and while part of me hates her for it, another part of me knows she's right.

LadyV76: I like this coworker.

MyBoyBlue4: I like you.

[A pause]

MyBoyBlue4: Shit, I went too far, didn't I?

LadyV76: It's nice to hear. I like you too, Blue. I like how uncomplicated this feels, you know? It's a welcome antidote to how messy my life feels right now.

MyBoyBlue4: Look at us, two sad sacks.

LadyV76: Misery loves company.

MyBoyBlue4: I'm not miserable when I'm with you. I didn't think I was miserable in my real life until I met you. But now, the difference between how free I feel in this chat room and how trapped I feel outside of it...

LadyV76: It's making you think. That's not a bad thing. It just sucks at first. I'm trying to wrap my head around the idea that actually living the dream I've been after for years is so much harder than I anticipated.

MyBoyBlue4: Maybe that's the point?

LadyV76: I just need to catch a fucking break already. A little bit of sun.

MyBoyBlue4: I can relate. The rain keeps coming, doesn't it? I have this feeling that the storm's only just begun for me.

LadyV76: For me too. Only way out is through. Such a depressing thought, though.

MyBoyBlue4: How about I lighten the mood then? Tell me about your first.

LadyV76: My turn to LOL. My first sexual experience, you mean?

MyBoyBlue4: First anything. I want to know something true about you.

LadyV76: I'll take first orgasm for six hundred, please. This will surprise you, but I was actually a late bloomer. A friend in college was appalled when I told her (at the ripe age of nineteen, mind you) that I had never orgasmed OR masturbated. She gave me some pointers and sent me on my merry way.

MyBoyBlue4: Details, please.

LadyV76: I thought you said you didn't have any juice left?

MyBoyBlue4: The half chub I'm getting thinking about you touching yourself says otherwise. Give me some visuals, woman.

LadyV76: I got naked, climbed onto my bathroom counter, and looked at myself in the mirror.

MyBoyBlue4: Yep, I'm hard.

LadyV76: How about we flip the script? You tell me what you want me to do.

MyBoyBlue4: Hey, wasn't I just telling you how I liked to be bossed around?

LadyV76: Yeah. But maybe you'll like to do the bossing around too. And sometimes even alphas need to be taken care of.

MyBoyBlue4: Baby, I'd love to look after you. Start with your nipples. You'll find that playing with them makes you wet. You've got pretty tits, firm and full, with these puffy pink nipples that are silky when they're soft. But I want 'em hard. Use your thumbs. Then pinch them. You feel it yet? Your pussy wanting more?

LadyV76: Oh yeah. I do like that.

MyBoyBlue4: Reach between your legs. You're watching

yourself in the mirror, right? Good. See that little thing at the top there, where your lips come together? That's your clit. And that's what you want to go for. But first, you gotta reach a little lower and find where you're wet.

LadyV76: In the center? That's where I'm getting wet. I have to go inside to find it.

MyBoyBlue4: Yep. Spread the moisture around. Get yourself nice and slick everywhere. Use your first three fingers and go slowly.

LadyV76: Oh. OH.

MyBoyBlue4: I know, baby. I know. Now take your forefinger and glide it over your clit.

LadyV76: How do I know if I've found it?

MyBoyBlue4: You'll know.

LadyV76: Found it. Nearly jumped off the counter.

MyBoyBlue4: Fuck, baby, I'm hard AF now. By the way, is it ok if I call you baby? I know you didn't like sweetheart.

LadyV76: Yeah. Yeah, I actually like baby.

MyBoyBlue4: The longer you hold off, the better the orgasm will be. So we're gonna play around a little. First, tell me how wet you are.

LadyV76: Dripping.

MyBoyBlue4: God, I want to eat you up right now.

LadyV76: Ohhhh...

MyBoyBlue4: Take your hand and play with your nipples again. This time, you've got some natural lube to work with. You like?

LadyV76: Oh, wow. Yes, I do

MyBoyBlue4: Don't put your fingers back on your clit. I know you wanna keep touching yourself there, but you'll come too soon. So glide those fingers through your folds, baby. Take the middle one and put it inside you. Press it against the front wall of your pussy. You feel that spongy bit? Keep pressing on that.

LadyV76: Ohhhhhhhhhhhh

MyBoyBlue4: It's hot, right, watching yourself in the mirror?

LadyV76: Yeah but dirty too

MyBoyBlue4: Dirty doesn't equal bad. If it turns you on, it's all good, baby. Tell me how you're feeling. I need you to talk to me, always.

LadyV76: I'm feeling like...like I'm getting closer to something. Like I'm rising, or it's rising to meet me. I'm afraid but not, and now I'm wondering, wow, *this* is what I've been missing out on.

MyBoyBlue4: I get it. I was a late bloomer too. My parents were awesome, but they were strict too. No parties, no booze, and definitely no girls or porn. Needless to say, I've gone the opposite way in my adult life.

LadyV76: When it's good, porn is the best. Oh wait, I don't know that because I'm nineteen and virginal in every way imaginable. Baby, I'm getting close. Please, please let me come.

MyBoyBlue4: I like it when you call me that. Okay, I'll stop torturing you. Take your finger out of your pussy and use your first two fingers on that hand to circle your clit. Play with your nipples with the other hand.

LadyV76: Magic!

MyBoyBlue4: See? Life isn't all bad. Keep circling. And when you feel the pressure, surrender.

[A pause]

LadyV76: So. Freaking. Good.

MyBoyBlue4: I know.

LadyV76: Blue?

MyBoyBlue4: Yeah?

LadyV76: That was my first time willingly playing the submissive. I liked it.

MyBoyBlue4: Willingly? Explain.

LadyV76: For a long time, I thought that was what men wanted from women. Submission. So I played along and pretended to enjoy it and faked every orgasm I had after that one on the bathroom counter.

MyBoyBlue4: God, that's bleak.

LadyV76: I know! Anyway, I happened upon some deliciously feminist romance novels, and they convinced me to put my needs and my pleasure at the forefront of my own story. So I tried on my alpha suit, and the rest, as they say, is history. Speaking of...I'd like to make you come if you'd let me.

MyBoyBlue4: YES

LadyV76: Imagine you're the one who helps me learn I'm a natural alpha. You're the first guy who's willing to let me fuck him sideways in pursuit of my true pervy self.

[Pause]

MyBoyBlue4: Yeah, you can stop there. I came halfway through that second sentence. Right around "sideways."

LadyV76: Success! Your mind off the coworker yet?

MyBoyBlue4: No, actually. But because you just gave my imagination a good workout, I have an idea how to fix the situation. Well, make it less of a train wreck, anyway. Thank you for that.

LadyV76: Good luck. So, I'm going to go out on a limb here and ask where you are. You don't have to give me specifics, but since we both are from Carolina, and we just might be close by, any chance you'd be down to meet in person?

MyBoyBlue4: Hell YES. I'm happy to keep having the best cybersex ever with you. But I've felt so confused lately, and the only time I seem to find clarity is when I'm chatting with you. I'm in North Carolina.

LadyV76: NO SHIT. Me too! Asheville area.

MyBoyBlue4: Fuck off. I'm ten miles from downtown. You're kidding, right?

LadyV76: I'm not. Are you?

MyBoyBlue4: Nope. Wow. It's almost like we're meant to be. Let's do it. Name the time and place, and I'll make it happen.

LadyV76: Next weekend? Right now, they're calling for snow (!) on Friday, but let's be real, it's almost April so the chances of that actually happening are slim to none. I should be able to get that day off…

MyBoyBlue4: Yeah, I saw that…I was born and raised here in the mountains and lemme say April snowstorms are few and far between. I usually work Friday and Saturday nights, but I'll try to get Friday off too. What's your favorite bar? Restaurant?

LadyV76: Let's do downtown. You know, so people will be around to save me if you really are a serial killer. Cucina is a favorite. Great drinks.

MyBoyBlue4: Love that spot. I know the owner, so I'll get us a table. 8 PM? I'll confirm Fri or Sat tomorrow at work.

LadyV76: I'll do the same.

MyBoyBlue4: Holy shit, do we actually have a date?

LadyV76: We actually have a date. I can't tell you how much I'm looking forward to it.

MyBoyBlue4: Same, girl, same

LadyV76: PS: I'm glad I could help you make some sense of yourself. Lately, the few times I feel certain in the choices I've made are when I'm with you too. Thanks for that.

MyBoyBlue4: Good night, baby.

LadyV76: I'll end with this: Clearly, I don't know you, but from what I've gathered, I don't think you're a piece of shit deep down. You've got a creative, thoughtful, kind side to you that I'm guessing you don't show the world (why else would millennials like us seek solace with strangers on the internet?). Whoever you think you're going to lose or disappoint by being the real you wasn't meant to be in your life anyway. You do you, boo, and fuck what everyone else thinks.

MyBoyBlue4: How do you feel about me calling you boo?

LadyV76: Nah, I'm claiming that as mine. Night, boo.

Chapter Seventeen

SAMUEL

My brother Rhett eyes me over the small mountain of foil-covered casserole dishes I've set in his arms. "Why do you need me to help you deliver this stuff again?"

"Because I need a second if she challenges me to a duel."

I grab my keys and silently inventory the dishes. Short ribs, collards, cornbread. Strawberry and brown sugar buckle for dessert. Should be enough, right?

Lord above, I hope it's enough to at least get Emma to talk to me again. Really talk. At this morning's brunch service, she was maddeningly professional. Polite as all get-out, per usual, but beneath her calm exterior, I could tell a cauldron of rage and hurt was bubbling.

She refused to look me in the eye, and that was the worst of all. I have never in all my thirty-five years felt like more of a douchebag.

I have never felt more *wrong*. I don't ever want to feel this way again.

Which means I've gotta make some changes. Starting with figuring out who I am behind the bullshit smile I've worn for the past fifteen years.

Last night, I realized the freedom I felt has less to do with the sex than it does with the ability to be myself with someone. Not the smiling bullshitter, but the guy who's on the sub side of the scale, who likes Van Halen and *Game of Thrones* and admitting when things are less than perfect. I like who I am when I'm being open-minded. Brave. Playful.

What else could I be if kept opening up that way in real life? Who else could I connect with the way I connected with Emma yesterday? Yes, it's scary. Yes, I'm risking loss. Real, painful loss. But sharing truths last night, and then with Emma too, has shown me that I can't keep living my life so closed off from everyone and everything. The loneliness I felt when Emma walked out of my house after giving me the cold shoulder I absolutely deserved—yeah, it was the worst I've felt in a long time.

Made me think that whether I open up or not, life's gonna hurt. So why not pick the path that allows me to experience joy along with the pain? It'll take practice, but I'm willing to try.

The first thing that came up when I started to think about who I really am: I'm a guy who plays fair. And I haven't played fair with Emma. Not by a long shot. After the Charleston Heat luncheon, I realized what an asset she truly is. When I think about her quitting now, I get a legit stomachache. I just hope it's not too late to repair the damage I've done.

Second thing: I'm a guy who loves to feed people. So I'm going to feed Emma. At the very least, her hands might stop shaking at work. I know better than to hope for more than that, but...yeah, I'm praying my peace offering will at least get her to look at me.

"Who's 'she'?" Rhett asks. He's at the farm for a weekend visit. His primary residence is in Vegas, but during the off-season, he comes up here often.

"Our new somm." I meet my brother's eyes in all seriousness. "I think she may want to kill me."

"Ah, right. Hank wouldn't shut up about her. Said she's great." He tilts his head. "You deserve it?"

"Yup."

He crosses himself. "Baby Jesus, please bless our endeavor with Your divine favor, Amen."

We load up my favorite pickup truck. It's a 1967 Chevy, impeccably restored in cobalt blue to match my alma mater.

It's also my least obnoxious ride. A Tesla, a Rolls, and a G-Wagon painted a custom shade of matte black with bright gold rims are lined up beside it. If I pulled up at Emma's door in the G-Wagon, I can guarantee you she'd tell me to go fuck myself. I need her to see that I can be flashy *and* down to earth. I can be a dick, but there's also a hidden damsel inside me. I contain multitudes. If only I could figure out how to manage those multitudes so they don't piss me off or drive me to push everyone away.

"You got flour in your hair," Rhett says as we head down the road to Emma's cottage. "Want to talk about it?"

"Meh," I reply, keeping my eyes glued to the windshield.

"Cool," he replies. "I'll be right here when you're ready." I shove the truck in park in front of Emma's place.

"Whatever happens, we do not leave here until she takes this food. Understood?"

Rhett dips his head. "Yessir. Is it cool if I ask if y'all are sleeping together? You and the somm?"

Heat floods my face. "No, Rhett, it is absolutely not cool to ask about my sex life."

"You haven't boned yet, but you want to." Rhett grins. "Y'all both got it bad, huh?"

Hand on the door latch, I shoot daggers at my baby brother with my glare. The lie's on the tip of my tongue. It'd be easy. So damn easy to deny and ignore and go on my merry way.

But instead, I fall back on the seat and close my eyes, plucking at my swollen eyelids with my thumb and forefinger. I'm tired, so damn tired of pretending. Living that way hasn't made me feel merry in a long-ass time, which is why I'm determined to change.

"Please don't tell Beau," I say, keeping my voice low. "I promised him I'd keep it in my pants. But things with Emma —they just keep getting out of hand. I don't know what to do, Rhett."

Rhett puts a hand on my shoulder. "I won't say a thing. I'm sorry, brother, that you've gotten yourself into a pickle. It's not like you."

"I know," I say. "I feel like I met her and hated her, and now all of a sudden, I adore her and I'm in deep. She's doing everything right while I'm over here getting it all wrong. I'm gonna fix it. Well, I hope I can fix it, anyway, but I'm not entirely sure how."

"You're scared." He squeezes my shoulder. "That's a totally natural response. But you being a prick? That isn't. You're better than that."

Pushing the heel of my hand into the steering wheel, I curl my fingers around it and hold it in a death grip. "Mama and Daddy raised us better than that. Yes, I know."

"You really do know." Rhett holds up the casseroles. "Exhibit A. See? You're headed in the right direction. I think maybe you're getting overwhelmed by the bigger picture here. Coach is always using this metaphor of, you know, how do you eat an elephant? You do it one bite at a time. How do you engage in sexual relations with your coworker without it blowing up in your faces? You move in the right direction one step at a time."

"Listen, Bill Clinton, I'm not sure we'll be continuing said relations."

"Why not?"

"Because I was an asshole, and I don't deserve her. Also, there's this other girl I've been talking to. Not sure what'll come of it, but it'd be a hell of a lot less complicated than what's gone down with Emma."

Rhett nods. "That's fair. But you still need to make things right with Em. I've only heard great things about her somm skills, so we don't want to lose her."

"Exactly."

"So be thoughtful. Be intentional. And be you—the man Mama and Daddy raised."

I look at my brother. "That was a pretty solid speech."

"Thank you kindly," Rhett says. "Just because I'm the youngest Beauregard brother doesn't mean I can't be the wisest."

"You think it's wise to keep playing the game that gave your father and your brother a degenerative brain disease?"

Rhett just rolls his eyes. "Stop trying to change the subject. This is about you. C'mon, let's go win your girl back with some signature Samuel Beauregard hospitality."

"She's not my girl, and I'm not winning her back. But the short ribs did turn out pretty damn good."

"Samuel, anything you make is good. Let's go."

My heart hammers as we wait for Emma to answer the door. I knock once. Twice. I start to sweat. I can't just leave all this food on her doorstep. One, Dave and Eddie might catch a whiff and come visit. And two, I really want to see Emma outside of work. I want to look her in the eye and tell her how fucking sorry I am.

We get lucky. Just when I'm about to call it quits, Emma answers the door. Sheer terror flashes across her eyes at the same moment it darts through my chest.

She's scared. I'm scared. The intense vulnerability of the moment makes me want to run and hide.

Instead, I stand still with a bowl of collards in one hand and a Pyrex dish of cornbread in the other.

The first few seconds are excruciating. But I know I'm on to something good when the terror in her gaze dissolves into confusion.

"What's this?" she asks, brow furrowing as she takes in the dishes.

"Dinner. And, hopefully, lunch tomorrow and the next day. I made enough to last most of the week, actually."

Emma blinks. She looks cute as hell in her leggings and hoodie. Her hair is loose, falling in waves past her shoulders. For half a heartbeat, I can taste her pussy in my mouth. Sweet, salty, and hot.

"Why?"

"Because I won't have you living off garbage protein bars when you're on our farm." I intentionally use the word *our*. Judging by the way Emma's eyes flick up to meet mine, she notices. "I'd like to feed you proper food. I made short ribs in pecan-bourbon sauce, my mama's collards with bacon and butter, and, because I know you're curious, my famous cornbread."

Her lips twitch. I love it when they do that. "You make it extra you-know-what?"

"For you? Always."

Rhett barks with laughter. "Who are you, and why don't I know you yet?"

"I'm Emma." She extends her hand. "You must be Rhett."

"Yes, ma'am. So, about this cornbread—"

"We should be going," I say, cutting my brother a warning glance. "I don't want to interrupt your plans for the evening, Emma. Everything here is warm and ready to eat."

We load up Emma's arms. Rhett, actually being wise

again, heads for the truck, leaving me alone with Emma on her porch.

I don't waste a second. Sliding my hands into the front pockets of my jeans, I say, "My turn to apologize. I am so fucking sorry about last night. I acted a fool, and I have no excuse. Baiting you like that, using your apology against you that way—it was wrong, stupid, and mean, and I feel horrible about hurting you. I'm sorry, Emma. Really, truly sorry."

Moving in the right direction feels like giving Emma time to absorb what I'm saying. Time to respond. So I let uncomfortable silence bloom between us, melting into a Wicked Witch of the West puddle inside while trying my damnedest to keep it together on the outside.

She's studying me with a thoughtful expression on her face, like she wants to ask me more probing questions. Deeper ones. Like why I acted the way I did.

A part of me yearns for questions like that.

Another part wants to run from them. What if I don't like the answers? What if they push me up against something I'm only just now learning to let myself have?

"You were awful," she finally says. "That stunt you pulled was shitty in the extreme. And the things you said…"

I reach out and take the collards back. All this shit is heavy, and she shouldn't have to carry it alone while I beg for her forgiveness.

"I'm sorry. I can't take them back, but I would if I could. You're not annoying, and you're not a pain in the ass. You're just doing your job. Doing it really fucking well, might I add. After seeing you in action at the restaurant and at the Charleston Heat event…Emma, you're remarkable."

She's staring at me, eyes full. "Thanks. I appreciate you saying that."

"I understand if you can't forgive me. I crossed so many lines."

"We. *We* crossed those lines. Yesterday—" She shakes her head, blinking against the way the light glints of the tin foil covering the collards in her hand. "None of that was supposed to happen, Samuel. The stuff on the smoking patio. And then at your house. I make it a point never to engage in personal relationships with coworkers. From my experience, it never ends well." She looks up at me. "Can we agree to keep things professional going forward?"

The fierceness of the disappointment that grips my heart and squeezes takes me off guard. She's right.

She's calling me Samuel. Goddammit, I love her smile, and I love the sound of my name on her lips.

See, this is where I get tripped up. Rationally, it makes perfect sense for us to maintain a strictly professional relationship. But if I'm being honest—I'm really trying hard to be honest here—I want more.

Is it possible to have it bad for two people at once?

Because now that I'm on Emma's front step, her brown eyes on my face and her hair fluttering in the breeze, I realize just how right Rhett is. I do have it bad for Emma. But now more than ever, I need to keep my crush in check and my dick in my pants. Emma is right—relationships between fellow employees rarely work out.

Emma can be my friend. Just a friend.

I tell myself I'm okay with that.

"Absolutely," I hear myself saying. "I'll do whatever it takes to keep you happy and keep you around."

Her eyes flicker with surprise. "Are you saying what I think you're saying?"

"Yes. Emma, I want to *try* to work together as co-heads of Blue Mountain's wine and food programs. Yesterday, you convinced me you really are a team player. Let's see if you can keep it up."

"Wow." She crosses an arm awkwardly over her chest.

"You must feel really bad if you're not only willing to give me a chance, but you've come to offer that chance in person. With a side of some pretty sweet food."

"I'm giving you a chance because you deserve it."

She eyes me. "I'll believe it when I see it."

The idea pops into my head, and it feels right. I'm sick of feeling like the bad guy, so I go with it. "Let me prove it to you. Come to Sunday supper. My family gets together at the same time every week to catch up. We talk a little shop, but more than that, we talk shit about each other. Since you'll hopefully be staying at the farm for a while, join the gossip fest. That way you can really get to know everyone. I'm running the risk they'll scare you off, but"—I shrug—"sometimes my family can be cool. *Sometimes*."

Emma smiles.

A real smile that lights up her eyes and rearranges the soft parts inside my chest.

God, she's gorgeous when she's relaxed.

"Your family is something else. I'd love to," she replies. She holds up the cornbread. "Should I bring the food back to your place then?"

I wave her away. "Nah, I always make enough to feed an army. Keep that stuff for the rest of the week. So help me God, if I hear about you eating another protein bar, we'll be having words, you hear?"

She bites her lip, and I have to shove my hand back in my pocket to keep from reaching for her. "I'll consider it, yes."

"I'll take it."

"All right," I say.

"Okay," she replies.

"Five o'clock at Beau's place. It's the brown house a little ways up the hill—can't miss it. I've gotta go grab everything from my house, but I can give you a ride if you want?"

"I'll walk, thanks. And yes, I'll watch out for your favorite bears, David and Eddie."

I turn and find Rhett practically hanging out the truck's open window with wide eyes and a shit-eating grin on his face.

"Shut up," I say, climbing into the driver's seat.

He holds up his hands. "I didn't say a damn thing."

"Yeah, well, I know what you're thinking."

"How'd you know what I'm thinking?"

"Because I'm thinking it too." I turn the key in the ignition and the car roars to life. "But she requested that we keep things professional—"

"Bummer."

"So my official line is that I invited her to supper so she can get to know the family she'll be working with a little better."

Rhett raises his brows. "And you're okay with that?"

"Doesn't matter if I'm okay with it or not. It is what it is."

"God, I hate that expression."

"Me too." I put the truck in park. "Remind me to bring the bourbon. I'm gonna need it."

Chapter Eighteen

EMMA

I'd equate the decibel level inside Beau's house to a live Van Halen show.

Granted, I'm too young to have ever actually *been* to a Van Halen show. But this is exactly what I'd imagine it would sound like in a stadium circa 1986.

There's a high-pitched scream coming from the back of the house. Someone in the dining room to my right is calling someone else a stupid shithead.

The homey smell of a meal in the oven is everywhere. My stomach rumbles. I'm *hungry*.

Per Samuel's request, I've let myself into Beau's house. Bottle of wine in hand—I brought the Riesling that knocked Samuel on his ass—I make my way inside.

The scream gets louder. There's a bang. A shout.

I smooth back my hair and wonder for the eightieth time if this was a bad idea. I need to see Samuel outside work like I need a hole in my head. But how could I say no when he showed up at my door with a feast in his hands and this contrition in his eyes that was so sheepish and shy it had to be genuine?

Don't get me wrong, I'm still mad as hell at him for what he did. I'm still hurt by the things he said. But I snuck a taste of the short ribs and cornbread, and let me just say his apology is definitely on the right track.

I also really do want to get to know the Beauregards. I hope they'll be my employers for a long time to come, so getting in a little face time can't hurt.

"Emma!" Milly rounds a corner and wraps me in a hug. "I'm so glad you're here. When Samuel told us he invited you—"

"We all nearly shit a brick because we were so surprised," Hank adds, appearing at his sister's side. "Hey, Emma. We're really, really glad you came. I'll take your jacket."

An older woman with Samuel's blue eyes hands me a rocks glass. "And I'll give you a cocktail, just because. It's Samuel's whiskey sour. Welcome, Emma. I'm June Beauregard. You wouldn't know it from their dirty mouths and less-than-stellar manners, but these are my children. I tried, I really did."

I smile, a rush of warmth flaring to life in my cheeks even as the chill of the glass seeps through my palm. "It's so nice to meet you, Mrs. Beauregard. Thanks for the cocktail, and for having me. Judging by the work your kids have done on Blue Mountain Farm, I'd say you did a pretty solid job raising them."

"We'll see if you feel that way after supper." She tilts her head. "Come on back to the porch. Everyone's here. And please, call me June."

It's all I can do not to gawk at Beau's house as we pass through it. It's just as impressive as Samuel's, only on a smaller scale. It's tastefully rustic and beautifully furnished with shiplap walls, beamed ceilings, and a curated collection of art that had to have cost more than what I've made in the past decade.

I've been around wealth before. But the Beauregards are a whole new level of loaded.

It's the view that's the real star of Beau's house. When I step out onto the massive back porch, the breath leaves my lungs. The house is set on top of a ridge, affording it a sweeping view of the mountains beyond. Purple peaks and green valleys undulate against a backdrop of fiery sunset. The sky is spotless and the air is crisp, and I take it all in, reminding myself that while life may be a bit of a clusterfuck right now, at least I have this.

This is where I get to come to work every day.

The porch spans the length of the house. A fire crackles merrily in the gigantic fireplace at one end, the scent of burning logs about as cozy as it gets. I scan the faces of the people who sit by the fire in rocking chairs and on a sleek sectional sofa. My heart falls when I don't see Samuel.

I say hello to Rhett. He's got the Beauregard blue eyes and biceps, and he's got Samuel's swagger.

I shouldn't like that about him. But I do.

"Emma!" Beau smiles when he sees me and gets up from his seat. A tiny baby is nestled in the cradle of his arm. "Not gonna lie, I half expected you to be on your way back to Asheville by now. I'm glad—and relieved, so damn relieved—you've stayed."

"I'm glad too." I grin at the baby. "And how is Miss Maisie doing today?"

Annabel sidles up to Beau, resting her head on his shoulder. He turns his head and presses a kiss to her temple. "She slept nine hours last night, so we're all happy campers today. It's great to see you, Emma. Work going okay?"

I met Annabel and Maisie when they recently dined at the restaurant. I know she and Beau call each other friends, but judging by the way Beau's looking at her, hearts practically popping out of his eyes, I'm guessing they're more than that.

My grin tightens. "Work is going well, thanks. Samuel and I had our first event together yesterday, and I'm really proud of how it turned out."

Beau taps his glass to mine. "As you should be. I ran into Eli Jackson this morning, and he said it was hands down the best meal he's had all year. Y'all absolutely killed it. Now if the two of us can just refrain from actually killing my brother, we just might have a win on our hands."

"Y'all talking shit about me again?"

Samuel appears in the doorway, wiping his hands on a kitchen towel. He's wearing the same jeans and ivory sweater as before.

And just like before, he looks really fucking good.

As I take him in, my stomach bottoms out. He fills out the sweater to perfection, looking like an especially beefy Ralph Lauren model. Because I'm clearly a pervert with no self-control, my eyes flick to the fly of his jeans. I remember the shape and size of his dick in my hand. How he growled when I tugged the velvety skin back and forth, his eyes going hazy.

At that moment, I had him. He was mine. I felt powerful and beautiful and in control.

"Hey, Emma," he says.

Honestly, why do my nipples get hard every time he says my name?

I cross my arms. Samuel watches me do it, his eyes flashing darkly.

"If you didn't want us to talk shit about you," I say, "then you should behave yourself."

"Good luck," June says, taking the baby from Beau. "I've been trying to get him to behave for thirty-five years."

The number catches inside my head. Samuel and Blue are the same age. Go figure. Maybe the fact that they were born under the same star or something explains why I'm insanely attracted to both of them.

"If I behaved, I'd be boring, and y'all would like that even less."

"I'd take boring over boorish."

"I'd take bossy over boring," he replies steadily, "but you already know that."

A tingly, almost glittery rush fills my skin. He's being honest, and it's so damn hot. As hot as the fact that he really does like to be bossed around. The kind of bossing I like to do.

But so does Blue. I have to keep reminding myself of that. Just because he's out of sight doesn't mean he has to be out of mind.

It's just hard to think about someone I've never met when Samuel Beauregard's eyes are on my face.

I try to remember what a jerk he was last night. The things he said and how awful they made me feel.

Annabel looks between Samuel and me, a knowing grin tugging at the corners of her mouth. "You two seem to be equally matched. Conversationally speaking, anyway. Which makes you very fun to watch."

"We're here for your enjoyment." Samuel keeps his eyes on me. "I'd love your help with the wine, Emma. I brought a few options and I can't decide what would work best with the short ribs. I was thinking a Merlot, but then I just got this Amarone—"

"I *love* Amarone!"

He grins. "Thought you might, you grape weirdo. C'mon, let's give it a try."

I follow him inside, the tingles growing stronger as my eyes rove over the expanse of his back. Heaven above, the way the muscles there press against his sweater, how they *move*—

I close my eyes.

Remember he was a jerk.

Remember you made him promise to keep it professional.

If only my body would get the memo. But that's difficult when this man has given me, hands down, the best orgasm of my life not by my own hand. I had no idea I could come so hard with someone else.

Ugh, can't go there. I'm at Sunday supper. There will be absolutely no thoughts of orgasms or penises in hand or fucking gorgeous bodies.

None. Zero. Zilch.

We head into the kitchen as I try to get a grip on my raging libido. I pause on the threshold, heart beginning to pound as I take it all in.

The island is covered in cutting boards and casseroles. The skins of onions, carrot peels, and a freshly grated mound of cheddar cheese crowd a large cutting board. Something bubbles in a pot on the stove; the oven lights are on, and I can just glimpse an enormous cast-iron pot through the door.

The smell is insane. Butter and braised meat and the starchy-sweet smell of roasted vegetables.

Samuel navigates the fray effortlessly. Pointing me toward the case of wine set on the far countertop, he lifts the lid on the pot and gives whatever's bubbling a whisk. Then he grabs the knife on the cutting board and gives a bunch of parsley a quick, expert chop, the muscles in his massive forearm flexing as he moves.

"You always cook for Sunday supper?" I ask.

"Yup. Everyone pitches in, but I don't mind doing the heavy lifting. It's fun cooking for a crowd. It's also relaxing. After brunch service on Sundays, I go home, throw on some jeans and a playlist, pour a glass of something good, and then get to work."

I decant the Amarone in a daze, stuck on the way his

hands look as they gather the cheese mountain and dump it in the pot.

"What's that?" I ask, nearly losing an eye in my effort to uncork a second bottle. I pour myself a taste. Amarone is an Italian grape known for its raisin, candied fruit deliciousness. It's been around for a while but has only appeared on menus here in the States in the past couple of years.

This one delivers in a big way.

"The cheesiest, butteriest, most decadent grits you're ever gonna have in your life. That guy Luke at yesterday's luncheon, he brought a whole truck's worth of his grits up with him. Eli gave me some pointers on how to cook 'em." He whisks in the cheese. "Also, Annabel's nursing the baby, which apparently makes her really hungry. I thought some old-fashioned, stick-to-your-ribs grits would be good for her. For you too. When you're on your feet all day like we are, you gotta eat. It's a good way to start the week. Plus, grits'll go real nice with the gravy from the short ribs. I put a little brown sugar in the gravy to make it the tiniest bit sweet. That sweet and savory combo—or, should I say, that Albariño and ham croqueta combo—well, it's fuckin' ridiculous."

He taps the whisk on the side of the pot. Grabbing two spoons, he dips one in the pot and blows on it before offering it to me. With eyes bright, his grin is somehow rakish and cute all at once.

"What?" he asks, furrowing his brow. "You not like grits?"

I need to stop staring, and I really need to stop my heart from swelling so much and so quickly it explodes. But I can't.

This is a Samuel I've only caught glimpses of—a guy who's relaxed, effusive, *joyful*. He looked this way talking about soccarat and sobre mesa. His grin is so different from the big, flashing smiles he gives the rest of the world. It's soft. Sweet.

It's real.

"I love grits," I manage as I take the spoon. Our fingers brush, and I'm suddenly short of breath. "Thank you."

He grabs a spoon for himself, and we eat our grits at the same time.

I would never in a million years think of grits as an aphrodisiac. But Samuel's grits?

Lord Almighty, they're making me feel all kinds of sensual. They're just the right balance of toothsome and creamy. Perfectly seasoned. I savor them and I taste the bite of the sharp cheddar, the slight sweetness of the heavy cream he must've used, and the salt and starch and the satisfying richness of the corn.

I can't help it.

I moan.

I actually moan, and then turn bright red because I'm in a nice family house at a nice family dinner, but here I am having a downright explicit moment all thanks to *grits*.

Samuel's chest barrels out on a laugh. The sound is deep, satisfied, contagious, and I laugh too, holding a hand over my mouth so I don't spew food everywhere.

"So you're saying they give Eli Jackson's grits a run for their money?" he asks.

"The last thing I want to do is add hot air to your ego. But yeah. Yeah, those are really, really good. And with this?" I pour him a taste of the Amarone and pass it to him. "It'll take the entire meal over the top."

He sips, then moves the wine around his mouth.

Then *he* moans, rolling his eyes in exaggerated pleasure.

"Am I interrupting something?" Annabel walks into the kitchen, baby on her hip, and heads for the refrigerator. "Or is the wine really that orgasmic?"

Samuel sets down his glass and nods at me for more. "I'll definitely be drinking it at my orgy later."

"Wow," I say. "Your Sunday nights sound a lot more interesting than mine."

"Right?" Annabel takes a teething ring out of the freezer and holds it up. "This about sums up my plans for today and really every day from now until forever."

"I hope some good food will help."

"It definitely helps." She puts a hand on Samuel's arm. "Thank you. For everything. I really appreciate all that you're doing for Beau and me."

He lowers his voice. Looking out the window at Beau, who's chatting with Rhett by the fire outside, he says, "I'm trying my best to get my brother to see some sense."

Annabel's smile fades. "I'm trying, but so far I'm failing."

"He'll get there. I'll keep reminding him what a bonehead he's being. You keep being you. And Miss Maisie, you just keep being the cutest damn baby ever, all right?" He tickles Maisie's foot, making her smile.

I'm not the biggest kid person. But not gonna lie, it makes my heart melt to see Samuel being so affectionate and playful with Maisie. I'm seeing a whole other side of him tonight, and it's working some kind of murder on my resolve to keep things fucking *professional*.

Chapter Nineteen

EMMA

"In the meantime," Samuel continues, glancing at Annabel, "you let me know if Beau needs some new breakfast recipes to make for you. He told me how much you liked the bread pudding. I've got some good ones up my sleeve. As a matter of fact, why don't I drop off some lemon and thyme scones in the morning? I've got homemade dough ready to go in my freezer—my own riff on Daddy's lemon pancakes. You'll just have to pop 'em in the oven and have a cup of coffee while you wait. Beau's making you coffee, right?"

"The scones sound amazing. And yes, Beau makes a pot of coffee every morning," Annabel replies, laughing. "He's totally spoiling us."

"The fact that your man makes you real food and good coffee doesn't mean you're spoiled. Means he's taking care of you right. The way you should be cared for."

Be still my beating heart.

Watching Bel and Samuel, I can see they have a genuine friendship. That surprises me, considering what a curmudgeon Samuel can be.

Then again, when he's like this—happy and at home and

generous—I get how he could be a great friend. I get how he and Bel could be close. If there's one thing I'm getting from Sunday supper so far, it's that Samuel loves his family. I can see him being the type of guy who'd do anything for them and the people *they* love, Annabel and Maisie included.

I'm more curious than I should be about what's going down between Bel and Beau, and how Samuel is helping them out. Not because I'm jealous. But because a guy who cares that much about his people is quite possibly the sexiest thing ever.

And those scones? I wouldn't mind having one for breakfast. After I had Samuel, of course.

He feeds his people, and he works hard for them, but most of all, he seems to *get* them. He doesn't judge them or try to change them. He wants them to be happy.

Why doesn't he want that for himself?

And how could such a good guy be such an asshole too?

"Speaking of good food, dinner's about ready." Samuel grunts as he lifts the cast-iron pot out of the oven and sets it on a trivet beside the stove. "Why don't y'all go grab a seat?"

I push up the sleeves of my sweater. "I'll help."

"You don't have—"

"I want to. I may even let you boss *me* around a little bit."

"Don't you dare," Milly says, coming in from the porch. "I hope you'll give him the swift kick in the ass he deserves."

Samuel rolls his eyes, but he's grinning. "You do that on the daily, sweet sister, so I'm set, thank you very much."

I help, but so does everyone else. Samuel garnishes the food. I pour the wine. Hank changes the music, and June helps Annabel change Maisie's diaper. Beau lights candles, and Milly fills water glasses.

And while it's pure chaos getting everyone seated, served, and settled, it's a fun kind of chaos. At one point, Samuel is coming out of the kitchen carrying that giant cast-iron pot while I'm heading back in for Maisie's bottle, which Bel left on the table out on the porch. I'm about to step aside to let Samuel pass, but instead, he raises his arms, just like he did yesterday.

And just like I did yesterday, I grin and duck underneath them. I decide a beat too late that it's a bad idea to let my arm graze his stomach like it did at the luncheon.

So it grazes. My body electrifying at the contact. I could be imagining it, but Samuel leans into the touch, close enough that I can smell the detergent on his clothes.

Again. He's not wearing his cologne again.

A bubble of light is rapidly expanding inside my torso by the time I actually sit down to eat.

"Brother, you did it again," Hank says, wiping his mouth with a monogrammed napkin that could only belong to Milly. "Best thing I've eaten all week."

Rhett snickers. June elbows him. "Don't be crude."

"I try, Mama, but it ain't easy."

"You're the one who's easy," Milly says, wagging her brows at him as she eats a forkful of collards.

Rhett smiles. "I am as God made me."

"Y'all," June says.

Maisie starts to fuss in Annabel's lap. Swallowing his first bite, Samuel sets down his utensils and holds out his arms. "Hand her over. I'll play uncle while y'all eat."

"You sure? She's pretty unfun this time of day," Bel says.

"Of course I'm sure. Eat." Samuel's eyes find mind across the table. "That goes for you too, Emma. Did y'all know our new sommelier here has exquisite taste in wine but thinks protein bars count as real food?"

"No!" Beau gasps.

June takes my hand and gives it a squeeze. "I'll pray for you."

Milly just solemnly shakes her head.

"Thank God you're here," Hank says. "I hope we've saved you before it's too late. Eat up, girl."

So I eat. And I answer questions and ask some of my own between bites.

"Why wine?" Milly asks. "I mean, I totally get being obsessed with it. But what made you decide to, you know, devote your life to the stuff?"

I feel the heat of Samuel's gaze as I ponder my response. He's had to get up from his chair in the hopes of helping Maisie chill out, and now he's doing laps around the dining room while bouncing Maisie in his arms. Every so often, I'll glance up, and he's looking at me with this funny gleam in his eyes.

"I was pre-law throughout all of undergrad," I say. "I took the LSAT, got into law school, and was set to enroll the fall after graduation. Everyone in my family is a lawyer, so it just seemed like the thing to do."

Hank's eyebrows pop up. "Literally every member of your family?"

"Literally. My grandparents, my mom, my dad, my sister... everyone. Needless to say, I felt a lot of pressure to follow in their footsteps. I wasn't crazy about going into law. As a matter of fact, when I committed to law school, I had this terrible feeling in the pit of my stomach, like I knew it wasn't the right move. It just didn't feel very *me*."

Milly winces. "I don't like where this is going."

I shrug. "I just didn't have a particular calling or passion for anything else. My sister had gone to law school a few years before, and my parents were ecstatic about how well she was doing. So I figured I'd go to law school, keep everyone happy, and go from there. And then Spain happened."

I glance up to see Samuel looking at me again. "What happened in Spain?" he asks. His eyes are intent on my face, his jaw tight, like he really wants—needs—to know where this story goes.

"It was spring break my senior year. United was running this insane sale on tickets to Europe, so my friends and I hopped on a plane to Madrid. We took a train to Grenada, which is this cool town in the south famous for its Moorish architecture. On our first night out, we met some of these cute Spaniards at a bar—"

"Okay, I changed my mind. I really like where this is going," Milly says, leaning an elbow on the table and resting her chin in her hand.

I smile. "I wish I had a better ending for you. Nothing crazy happened, but the eight of us sat at this table outside a tiny restaurant overlooking the Alhambra, a gorgeous medieval Moorish palace right out of a *Game of Thrones* episode. We ate tapas and talked for hours and drank bottle after bottle of this red wine that was maybe ten euros a pop. I still remember how it tasted, how warm the air was while I tasted it, and the happy buzz it gave me. It made us philosophical. Funny. It allowed us to bare ourselves, our true selves, in a way we never had before. As I drank and ate, I realized I'd never talked so frankly with my friends like that. I finally shared how I was feeling about law school, how I had that awful feeling in the pit of my stomach. Saying it out loud made me realize just how wrong the whole thing was. And a lot of that had to do with the fact I was falling in love at that table. Not with a person, but with the truth."

"That's beautiful," Samuel says. The look in his eyes turns my heart inside out.

"And naïve." I swallow. I notice Hank is looking at me too. "I followed that feeling I got at the table—the warm, deep, happy peace that filled me. Again and again, it led me back to wine. Food. A table full of friends. Sharing stories and truths and fears. Look, I get it. At the end of the day, wine is grape juice that gets you drunk. But when I drink it—even just a taste, a sip—I feel seen. Or maybe I allow myself to be seen. It liberated me. When I came back from Spain, I kept following that feeling. It led me to drop out of law school to work in a restaurant cellar instead."

Hank's eyes go wide. "Bet your parents loved that."

"They did not." I smile tightly. "But I get it. They want me to have a nice life, you know? I want that for myself too. So I've worked hard to put myself in a position where I can get it. I know that will make them a little proud at least. Still, it's taken me a long, long time to come to grips with the fact that following my heart meant letting down the people I love. It's something I still struggle with, especially when I see how my sister's crushing it in her law career."

"Ballsy," Samuel says. He's full-on staring at me now, and I have to remember what a dick he was when I first met him or I'll be falling hook, line, and sinker for the naked admiration in his eyes. "Such a ballsy move, Emma. I mean that as a compliment. I got lucky—my dad and I loved the same things, and were good at the same things, right down to the position we played. If that hadn't been the case, I don't think I would've been brave enough to do what you did."

I meet his eyes. "Give yourself more credit. You're braver than you think."

He holds my gaze for one long, heated beat. I can feel the entire table watching us. I want to look away, but I like this sensation—the feeling of Samuel and me being the only people in the room.

The sense of belonging and safety that gives me.

Grabbing my wine, I break eye contact and take a long, thirsty sip. Milly's looking between Samuel and me with a knowing expression on her face.

My own face burns.

"Moral of the story, you fell in love with what wine represented," Hank says, breaking the silence. "Not necessarily the wine itself."

"Exactly." I clear my throat. "So, Hank. Tell me how you got into guest relations."

I get seconds, then thirds of cornbread, using it to sop up the ridiculous gravy Samuel was talking about. Everything is insanely delicious. We go through four bottles of the Amarone, everyone getting just tipsy enough to let loose and laugh. June tells a story about the time she found several pairs of Samuel's Ninja Turtle underwear underneath the kitchen sink. Upon closer inspection, she discovered they were covered in brown skid marks.

"Apparently, Samuel was afraid to tell me he pooped his pants," she says. "So, at the age of six, he hid his undies, thinking I wouldn't find out."

Samuel shrugs. Maisie is asleep on his shoulder. "What? I still hide my dirty undies there. Sometimes, I just get scared shitless."

"Seriously, dude, you need to stop getting poopy pants drunk," Rhett says, howling.

Beau slaps the table. "What a shitty thing to do."

Milly's rolling her eyes and biting back laughter. "Y'all and the poop jokes. They're not that funny."

"They're not," June says, wiping the tears from her eyes.

I'm laughing so hard the sides of my torso ache.

By the time we finish dessert, this particularly delicious strawberry strudel type thing, I'm painfully, happily full. Despite working in some of the best restaurants in the Carolinas, I don't normally eat this well. I don't have the time or the energy to cook for myself, and Blue Mountain is one of the few places that serves its staff a meal before service.

"Need a ride home?" Hank asks, handing me the pot he just washed.

I'm in the kitchen helping clean up. Again, everyone plays

a part. Milly wipes down the counters while Rhett loads the dishwasher. Samuel's filling dishes with leftovers for everyone to take home with them, and Bel and Beau are using dining room clean up duty as an excuse to make out with each other. Hank washes dishes and I'm drying them. There are people and plates everywhere, but it's weirdly soothing to be in on the action.

"I'll take her," Samuel says.

"That's okay," I reply a little too quickly. "I want to pick Hank's brain anyway about room service stuff."

It's not a lie. But the whole truth is I don't trust myself to be alone with Samuel right now.

I've seen so many sides of the man today. Fierce, loving, funny, generous, cocky. Sensual. I'm attracted to the whole package.

But I need to accept that we can only be friends. I need to commit to the fact that another man I can have is interested in meeting me.

With that in mind, I'll try chalking up my attraction to Samuel to a simple case of shared passions—food, wine, sobre mesa.

There.

Done.

I hope.

Chapter Twenty

SAMUEL

I give Milly a ride home after supper.

"Why are you following Hank so closely?" She turns her head to look at me. "You're gonna rear-end him."

My headlights don't do shit to illuminate what's happening in Hank's vintage Bronco ahead of us. I still try to creep closer, thinking if I hit just the right angle, I'll be able to see what he and Emma are doing. Laughing? Touching?

So what if they are? But they wouldn't be, would they, because Emma doesn't get involved with coworkers.

Then again, she got involved with me.

I tighten my grip on the steering wheel. I hate this jealousy, especially when it's aimed at my little brother. It's unworthy of the man I'm trying to become.

"Hello? Earth to Samuel."

"Sorry." I blink, easing up on the gas. "There. That better?"

Milly's looking at me. I look back.

"What?" I ask.

"You and Emma seem to be getting along."

"What about you and Nate Kingsley? I hear y'all are getting friendly."

"Stop trying to change the subject. You've been happier than usual lately. Since Emma arrived, as a matter of fact. With the exception of right now. Right now, you look kinda...scary."

"What? No, I don't."

"Why are you playing coy?"

"Because." I let out a sigh. Once again, the truth wins because I'm just too damn tired to keep up with the lies. "I know what you're getting at, Milly, and it ain't gonna happen. Me and Emma, I mean."

"Why not?"

"Because that's what she wants. It's what I want." I watch Hank pull off the main road and head up the lane that leads to Emma's cottage. "And I'm kinda sorta into someone else, anyway."

"Really?"

The tightness in my chest loosens at the change in subject. I may not know her real name, and I may be having sex with her in a way I've never had before, but that somehow feels more straightforward than my relationship with Emma. "Promise not to judge?"

"Absolutely not."

"Whatever. I met a girl on the internet. We've been chatting for a while, and I really like her. I think we're gonna meet up. Meet in person, I mean."

I pull up to Milly's house and put the car in park. She unbuckles her seat belt and leans back against the passenger side door, cutting me a look. "That's...interesting."

"Goddammit, Milly, you can judge me, just—I need a sympathetic ear here for a minute."

"I'm not judging the internet girlfriend thing. I *am* curious about why you think you're into someone you've never met when you're so clearly into someone else. Like, why invite Emma to Sunday supper if you're crushing on your internet girlfriend? You had to have known seeing Emma interact with us would only make you want her more."

I sigh. Again.

And feel like a douche canoe. Again.

"You're not wrong. It's a long story, one that I'm not exactly at liberty to share, but I thought inviting her was the right thing to do. I figured, hey, I can be the good guy for once, and she can hang with the family and get to know everyone a little better. Kill two birds with one stone kinda thing."

"So you *don't* think Emma is out to steal your job anymore?"

"Honestly?" I run a hand over my face. "After working with her this week, I don't think I do. She's wonderful, Milly, like, really fucking amazing at what she does—and she's been nothing but a team player. But it's still hard to let go of that grudge, you know? That knee-jerk reaction I have not to trust a damn soul after Olly."

Milly claps her palms against her thighs. "Well, Olly was a dude. A straight dude. Which meant he didn't look at you the way Emma does."

I'm holding the wheel in a death grip. "What does that mean?"

"I mean Emma's into you, Samuel. She watched you the whole time back at Beau's. And you watched her. You try to hide it, but both y'all have that look in your eyes—the look of love."

"Shut up." I wave her away. "Now you're just teasing me."

"I'm not. She's into you, but she's also into who you are and what you have to say. She respects your opinion. She's hungry for it—that sense of certainty you have. And you're hungry for her ballsiness, as you so eloquently put it."

"The ballsy thing is hot."

"Hell yeah, it is. You know how much I admire a woman who knows what she wants and goes after it the way Emma does. This is just me talking, but I don't think she's gonna stab you in the back. I think, if anything, she *has* your back. How many times are you gonna make her prove it?"

I slump onto the bench, feeling suddenly deflated. "How fucked up does this sound? But what if I'm making her prove it as many times as it takes for her to show me I'm right? Because I want her, and I can't have her, and the only thing that will get that memo through my thick skull is if she betrays me the way Olly did?"

Milly's gaze softens. "Betrays you the way Daddy did by dying too young, you mean?"

I haven't felt the burn of tears in...Christ, it's gotta be a decade. More than that.

Now that I think about it, I haven't cried since the day we buried him.

The sensation startles me. I blink hard and turn my head to look out my window. My throat tightens at the same time my grip on my self-control loosens.

How the hell did we go from talking about internet sex to our dad dying? My life—conversations, emotions, desires—is giving me insane whiplash lately.

"Hey." Milly rubs my back. "It's okay if you're not over it. I'm not sure any of us will ever get over losing him the way we did. But you and Daddy—y'all were really close. I knew from the second we found out Daddy was sick that losing him would be hardest on you."

It has been hard. Really fucking hard.

Even harder to pretend I'm okay when deep down, I know I'm not.

I remember what Emma said back at Beau's—that I'm

braver than I think. What did she mean by that? That I'm brave enough to do what? Face the facts?

Brave enough to be honest with myself about how much losing the man I loved hurts? And how he was the last person who knew the real me because I've been too scared to let anyone in since?

"But how?" I manage. "How do I let it hurt without drowning in the pain?"

"I wish I could answer that for you. I think you start with the idea that acknowledging the truth welcomes awful, awful pain. But it can also welcome an incredible kind of love too. The kind maybe you're looking for with your internet lover. Or Emma. Or both."

"And if Emma *isn't* looking for that? Not with me, anyway. She says she wants to keep things professional."

Milly grins. "I think y'all blew right on past that when you hooked up."

"What?" My eyes bulge, a welcome relief from the burn there. "We—uh—"

She pats my leg. "You and Beau must think we're all blind or something. You don't look at a girl the way you looked at Emma if you don't have, shall we say, carnal knowledge of her."

"Cool. Well, not cool, but I have no idea what the fuck else to say." I tap my hand against the steering wheel. "So I'm gonna kick you out of my truck now because that is not my story to tell. If there was a story, I mean."

"I'm offended y'all think I'm such an idiot. Night, Samuel." Milly opens the door. "Love you."

"Love you too, Milly."

I drive home alone in the dark. Windows rolled down, nighttime breeze in my face. I put the truck in park in my driveway and turn off the ignition and sit in silence. Just me and the truth.

I think back to the darkest time of my life. The day they told us Dad had committed suicide after a years-long battle with a degenerative brain disease. That moment when I looked into my mother's eyes and saw stark, agonizing pain. When I watched my incredibly strong sister crumple in shock. When I realized I'd never again be able to look into someone else's eyes and allow myself to be completely, compassionately understood.

The day I felt betrayal that eclipsed sadness because Dad had left us.

Left me.

"Why?" I shake my head. "Why'd you go? I hate that you fucking left me."

The burn in my chest makes my eyes smart.

I don't want to feel this way. I don't want to be alone anymore.

It's time to make some changes.

"This was you, wasn't it?"

I look up from my laptop. Emma is carrying the lemon scone and coffee I set on her desk when I got in this morning.

Biting back a grin, I turn back to my computer. "Why, yes, Emma, I did bring you breakfast. Being thoughtful and kind is a crime, I know, but I couldn't help myself."

"But you already made me dinner. And lunch. And dinner tonight too."

"Eat it."

"What if I already ate?"

I glance back up. "We've been over this. Consider it a token of my appreciation for helping out with Beau and Annabel." Over the weekend, the two of them had a date night at The Barn Door. Emma helped create a special tasting menu for their dinner. "Now eat some real food and get back to work, dammit."

A pause. My skin prickles with awareness the way it always does when I'm around Emma. I'm not looking at her, but I mentally revisit the outfit she's wearing. My favorite skirt—it's black, tightly fitted, the kind of sophisticated sexy Samantha would definitely approve of—and a black blouse that's just the right amount of see-through. She looks like a French businesswoman intent to bend you over the table in the boardroom and have her way with you.

And Lord, does it work for her.

It works for me too.

"Fine," she sniffs. "Don't you dare do this again."

"Fine. Actually, not fine. I'm going to do it again tomorrow just to piss you off. Or feed you because real food matters."

"You're the worst. Also, the best." She lowers her voice. "Thank you."

"Welcome."

"Your family is great, by the way. I'd kill to have that kind of relationship with mine. You know that's rare, right?"

"I do, yeah."

"Oh! I meant to ask. Are you taking any time off this weekend?"

I settle my elbows on the table. "I was going to ask if you'd cover for me on Friday."

"I was actually going to take Friday off too." She frowns. "Shoot."

"You have a hot date or something?"

She grins. "I do, actually."

I have a date too, so I have absolutely no right to be jealous. But I am. The kind of jealous that makes you inappropriately curious. It's all I can do not to play a game of twenty questions with her about this asshole she's going to see.

But because I'm trying to change, dammit, I give Emma the night off instead. "Both managers will be on the floor that night. As much as we'd like to believe our little planet up here will stop spinning if we're not around, I think the two of us can take the night off. I'll just keep my phone at the ready."

"I was going to say the same thing."

"Great."

She nods, then hesitates. Nods again. "Do you? Have a date?"

My stomach dips. I shouldn't read too much into the fact she asked the question. But I do. Is she jealous? If she is, does it mean what I think it does?

"Yes."

"Good for you."

"Thanks."

Charged silence stretches between us.

Emma lets out a breath. "Well, I should get back upstairs." She lifts the plate. "Thanks again for breakfast."

She turns and goes. Her heels mark a steady, deep-throated beat against the cellar's flagstone floor. *Do not look up*. Do not look at her ass—

Fuck, too late. I'm looking. And her backside is just as glorious as it's been the other eighty-five hundred times I've checked it out.

I'm overwhelmed by the urge to ask her to turn around and sit down and share another meal with me right now. But that goes against her wish to keep things friendly.

But what's more friendly than eating together? And what if I can show her how sharing a meal with me is a far superior experience to sharing one with the douche she's seeing Friday night? Yes, I can't say for certain if he's actually an asshole or a douche. But envisioning her date being a total dud makes my jealousy burn a little less brightly.

I only had my fingers and tongue inside her a week ago. Now she has a date? Had she met the guy before she allowed me to see and taste her? Because Emma's not someone who plays with men. She's not the type to string someone along. Is she?

Before I can think better of it, I leap to my feet. Emma turns around at the same time.

"Samuel—"

"Emma—"

Our eyes lock across the cellar. Her lips twitch.

I nod. "You first."

"I was going to say you should make breakfast for the staff one day. Keep it simple—a tray of these lemon and thyme scones would be perfect—and I can do a little Irish coffee or something to accompany it. If we're feeling especially sassy, I could do lemon drop martinis."

Grinning, I reply, "Because what's sassier than martinis in the morning?"

"Exactly. We can all eat and drink together. You know, as a chance for everyone to get to know you better."

My pulse thumps. One hard, decisive beat. "How about now?"

Not what I was going to ask, but I'll go with it.

"You have time to make that many scones?" she asks, brows raised.

"No. But I have you to help."

Emma smiles, and I feel something crack open inside my chest.

"I'll get the vodka," she says.

I close my laptop and head for the elevator.

Chapter Twenty-One

SAMUEL

The lemon scones are delicious. So are Emma's martinis. They're strong, the sweetness softened by just the right amount of tartness.

The conversation, however, is awkward as hell.

"So, Xavier," I say, chowing down on my third scone. Because I can't do awkward, I keep eating. It's not a good look. But at least it keeps my hands and my mouth busy. "Tell me about...you."

Fourteen pairs of eyes seem to blink in unison as they watch me make horrific attempts at real conversation.

Breezy, how-are-you-I-don't-really-care-to-know conversation I can do. Bullshit is an art I've perfected over the years. So is sticking to business.

But genuine conversation? The personal kind that leads to a real connection?

I'm re-learning how to do it from Emma. But saying I'm rusty in that department is a kindness I do not deserve.

I'm downright awful at it. Daddy is rolling over in his grave right now.

But I gotta keep trying.

Xavier wipes his mouth and smiles. It's different, some-how, from the polite smiles he's always given me. It's amused, kind, and a little embarrassed, not because he's awkward but because I am.

He's sympathizing, and I appreciate that more than he knows.

"How about this," he says. "We did this ice breaker back in college called two truths and a lie. You give three facts about yourself, and everyone has to guess which one is the lie."

I clap my hands together, making one of our hostesses Bianca jump. "Yes. Thank you. Let's do it. Who wants to start?"

"I will." Emma grins from her seat beside mine. "Okay, three facts: one, I dropped out of law school to become a cellar rat. Two, the most expensive things I've ever bought myself are a car and a pair of killer stilettos. Three, the best wine I've had all year is a Riesling from a Spring Mountain producer."

"Two," I blurt. "Definitely two."

Emma's grin becomes a smile. "Anyone else?"

"One," Jen says.

"I'd guess three, actually," Xavier replies.

Bianca narrows her eyes at Emma, pondering. She picks up her martini and sips. "You're sharp as a tack and a great storyteller, so I don't doubt you went to law school. You wear boring heels to work—"

"Hey! They're *sensible* heels. And sensible doesn't always equal boring."

"I beg to differ," Bianca says, and the entire table laughs, Emma laughing right along with them. "You know they're boring and so do I."

"Fine, fine, they're boring. But when you're on your feet eight hours a day, killer heels really will kill you. Unless you're

Bianca Jimenez, and then you're just a freak of nature who makes walking in boots with four-inch heels look easy."

Bianca uncrosses her legs and crosses them again, flashing said boots in the process. "You know I love my kick-ass boots."

"I wouldn't want you to kick my ass wearing those heels, that's for damn sure," I say, and the table laughs again.

I look around in wonder, a funny little feeling nudging underneath my breastbone.

Holy shit, I made my coworkers laugh.

I'm laughing with them.

It actually is kinda easy. Nice too.

"So?" Bianca asks. "Which one is the lie?"

Emma points at Xavier. "Three."

"Stop it!" I put my hands on the table and gape at Emma. "That's gotta be the lie. You said that Riesling was your favorite when we did your tasting."

She curls her lips between her teeth, then lifts a shoulder in this adorable little shrug. "It was. Until I tried that Screaming Eagle."

I nearly jump out of my chair. "*What?*"

Also: she has a killer pair of heels she's hiding?

"I know."

"But that's one of my BSD wines. You know, the ones you said 'didn't tell a story' and 'weren't that interesting.'"

She covers her face with her hand. "I know!"

"Does that mean I win?"

Emma glides her fingers apart so I can see her eyes. "Never. I'd settle for a tie, though."

"A tie? Are you serious?"

She does that shrugging thing again. She's smiling, and I'm smiling, and the entire room is watching us with laughter and curiosity in their eyes.

"Yes, sir. You introduced me to my favorite wine of the

year, and I introduced you to yours. I'd say we're even. Right, y'all?"

Xavier looks at me. Looks at Emma.

"Ugh." I tug my hand across my stubble. "Be honest."

He grins. "That's a tie, yeah."

"Totally agreed," Fi, a sous chef, agrees.

I lift my hands to wave them off. "Y'all are biased."

"Yup," Jen says. "Sorry, Samuel."

"I'm not," Emma says.

"Of course you're not." I let out a sigh. "Fine. It's a tie."

Emma offers me a hand for a high five. "See? Now we're all satisfied."

"Satisfied," I reply, "but not finished."

"You want to make it last, huh?"

I smirk. "Good things come to those who wait."

Jen peers at us. "Do y'all always talk in sexual innuendo, or..."

Oh, yeah, we should definitely stop this. Right the fuck now. Emma "I don't do workplace romance" would definitely not approve of public flirtation.

But this Emma—the one sitting beside me with her legs crossed, giving me a maddening glimpse of her stockinged calf—she just smiles and shrugs.

"That's exactly why I'd make a terrible lawyer," she says, eyes on mine. "And why I'm a fucking great sommelier. Because really, is there anything sexier than a great glass of wine?"

I feel the table's eyes turn to me as they wait on my response. I know they've picked up on the less-than-friendly vibes between Emma and me.

I know *they* know that I wanted her gone. I only said as much, out loud and in front of employees, about five dozen times.

I don't want that anymore. But am I ready to admit that

not only to my staff but to myself too? That's some terrifying territory right there.

But I have to try.

"I'll go next," I say. "Two truths and a lie. One, I think Emma is the best damn sommelier I've had the pleasure of working with, and I think she's insanely talented with both wine and sexual innuendos, and I hope she'll be with us at the farm for a long time. Two, the word moist grosses me out. And three, I have a favorite sibling."

Emma's smiling so hard it lights up her whole face. The kind of excitement she was talking about when we traded ideas about truth and honesty and authenticity.

And I did that.

I lit her up because I'm touching things inside her that matter. Or maybe I'm helping *her* touch those things.

Speaking of sexual innuendo—I'd love to touch her things. All of them. Inside and out.

Only, I can't. I understand now why she's so adamant about not engaging in workplace relationships. She's staked her entire life on this job.

It's important she not only keeps her position but thrives in it too. Which means she shouldn't be taking stupid risks like hooking up with me.

Because, really, what if it blows up in our faces? What if one of us falls in lust and the other in love? How horrific would that be, coming to work every day knowing you'll be side by side with the person who doesn't want you back? It'd make me hate the job, no matter how much I love food or Emma loves wine.

It's a disaster waiting to happen.

Besides, I have my date with V to look forward to. Who's to say we won't hit it off? I'm really, really hoping it goes well. If only so I have someone else to think about besides Emma Crawford.

"Three," Emma says softly. "You hate all your siblings. Only because you love them so much that you smother them with your curiosity and your cooking, which makes them lash out at you often and with great vehemence."

Bianca furrows her brow. "Samuel, you like the m word? Ew!"

The table's laughing. Emma's lit up.

And me? I keep finding more reasons to dig the woman I can't have.

I throw the casserole dish onto the range and coat it with butter.

Tossing a cutting board onto the counter, I mince a couple scallions while I wait for the spinach to cool, cursing when my knife comes down on my thumbnail.

It makes me think of the time Emma cut her thumb with her wine tool. Her lips had ducked out ever so slightly as she sucked on it.

She'd be great at sucking dick. I know she would be. The idea of being at her mercy with my dick in her mouth—she'd be on her knees, but I'd be the one begging—makes my balls tighten.

Why does everything have to make me think of her? I need to be moving away from this shit, not toward it. This isn't high school, and we aren't hormonal teenagers with questionable self-control. I can defeat these feelings if I try hard enough.

But that's the problem. I am trying. I try every fucking minute of every hour not to think about Emma, not to feel what I feel for her. But it seems the harder I try, the more I realize I'm a hopeless case.

I throw the knife across the island. It skitters across the countertop and lands with a *bang* on the floor.

Hank, who's apparently let himself into my house, bends down to pick it up.

Holding it in his hand, he says, "Rage cooking again?"

Wrapping my thumb in a paper towel, I cut him a glare. "What do you want?"

He nods at a stool. "Why don't you sit and let me handle the scallions?"

"Fine." I sit. "You know what you're doing?"

Hank sidles up to the cutting board and shrugs. "Not really. But better I mess up the garlic than you lose a finger. What are you making, anyway?"

"Quiche. Chef Katie just harvested our first crop of spinach, and we've got that ridiculous house-made feta. Thought it'd make a nice combo."

His eyes rove over the pantry's worth of eggs, sour cream, butter, and half-and-half I have set out. "Are you cooking for the staff again?"

I deflect. Because I'm cooking for Emma even though I shouldn't be. "How do you know about that? The breakfast I made for everyone, I mean."

"Dude, the whole restaurant won't shut up about your scones and how you like the word moist." He glances at me over his shoulder. "Who *are* you, and how, as manager of guest relations here at Blue Mountain Farm, can I get you to stay?"

"Throw in the scallions." I nod at the dish on the stove. "I'll add the eggs next."

Hank scoops up the scallions and tosses them in the pot. Half of it ends up on the floor. What-the fuck-ever.

"A lot of the staff also mentioned you and Emma have, uh, a special rapport."

I can't tell if it's the heat from the range or if it's emotion that's making Hank's cheeks turn red. Is he embarrassed? Does he have something he wants to say?

"Say it."

He doesn't look up from the pot, gathering a few stray chopped scallions from the cutting board. "Say what?"

"Whatever you came here to talk about."

Dropping the scallions into the dish, he turns around and crosses his arms. "Is there something going on between you and Emma?"

"No," I say a little too quickly. "Absolutely not. Why?"

He scratches the underside of his clean-shaven jaw. "No reason. Just wanted to make sure we, uh, didn't have a...situation on our hands is all." He looks at me. "You sure you don't have feelings for her?"

"That's not what you asked."

"Well, I'm asking it now," he says. Hank's an easygoing guy, so it surprises me that he's getting angry. "Do you have feelings for Emma?"

Be honest.

But what if I'm honest about how I want to feel? Does that count?

"I don't, no." Self-loathing crawls up my throat as the words leave my mouth.

Still. Maybe if I say them, I'll actually start to believe them. I'm that desperate. And Hank doesn't need to know about how I really feel.

What if confessing it somehow blows back on Emma? I'd trust Hank with my life. But I've been around long enough to know shit like this grows legs and gets around more often than not.

Admitting my feelings would just reopen a closed case.

But because I'm an asshole, and because this whole conversation is rubbing me the wrong way, I still can't help asking Hank the same question.

"Do you? Have feelings for her?"

A beat passes between us. His eyes are locked on mine, but they're a little vacant. Like he's somewhere else.

"No," he says.

Abandoning the scallions, he leaves my house.

CHAT #4

MyBoyBlue4: Friday night it is! That still work for you?

LadyV76: Sure does. I'm trying to keep my expectations in check here, but...yeah, I am really looking forward to meeting up. Although I admit I'm terrified of disappointing you.

MyBoyBlue4: I'm scared of the same. Taking this offline is definitely a leap of faith. But I'm trying to be more honest and brave and shit. And I honestly really, really want to meet you.

LadyV76: The fact that you're saying that makes me even more excited to meet *you.* Things with work are actually smoothing out. Well, they are, and they aren't.

MyBoyBlue4: Care to explain?

LadyV76: Maybe when I see you. It's quite the story. And it has nothing to do with us, except that I think I'm finally able to, you know, do something nice for myself. Like go on a date with a dude I like.

MyBoyBlue4: Whoa, whoa, whoa, you like me?

LadyV76: I like your dick. I hope I'll like you.

MyBoyBlue4: Fair.

LadyV76: Let's agree to some ground rules. We've already agreed to meet in a public place. No phone numbers are exchanged until after we meet. I may have a friend tag along, at least for the beginning.

MyBoyBlue4: Right. Just to make sure I'm not that serial killer. How will I know it's you?

LadyV76: I'll be wearing my heels. The ones you've seen. What about you?

MyBoyBlue4: I'll be wearing...hm. Let me think about this.

LadyV76: Really?

MyBoyBlue4: Hey now Miss I Love to Subvert Gender Norms. I like clothes. So what? I make 'em look good.

LadyV76: Funny, but my coworker, the one I'm always complaining about, likes clothes too.

MyBoyBlue4: Ha. If I were your coworker, you wouldn't be complaining.

LadyV76: I'd probably be fired, considering how much sex we'd be having.

MyBoyBlue4: Oh, yeah. All over the place. Shit, I just got hard. But let's figure out the details of our date before we get down. I need this. Both the date and the orgasm.

LadyV76: Something on your mind, Blue?

MyBoyBlue4: Yeah. I can't figure out what to wear. What's your favorite color?

LadyV76: I have two: black and blue.

MyBoyBlue4: You were born to dominate, weren't you?

LadyV76: Indeed.

MyBoyBlue4: Okay. I'll wear blue then. But it won't be like a bullshit French blue collared shirt or anything. I hope you weren't expecting a banker.

LadyV76: Nope. So basically, you'll be hard to miss in your unique shade of blue.

MyBoyBlue4: And you'll definitely stand out in those fucking heels. Can we throw in something cheesy and expected?

LadyV76: Like?

MyBoyBlue4: Hm. What if you bring...an apple?

LadyV76: Oh ha, the naughty teacher thing from our first chat. Good memory. Okay, I'll be holding an apple. What about you?

MyBoyBlue4: I'll have a Van Halen CD on the table.

LadyV76: You still have a CD?

MyBoyBlue4: It was my dad's. VH was his favorite band, so I kept all their cassette tapes and CDs he collected over the years.

LadyV76: Van Halen was one of my dad's favorite bands too! He's very square, very uptight, the kind of guy who wears khakis and cuff links on the weekend. But he had this secret love for eighties hair bands. Well, it wasn't secret per se, but he definitely didn't advertise it. You go for a ride in his Lexus, though? You bet he had Panama blasting.

MyBoyBlue4: I like your dad.

LadyV76: He and I are pretty much opposites. But sometimes I think I got my weird, artsy feely wild streak from him. I guess he could just hide his better.

MyBoyBlue4: Maybe his didn't sing as loud as yours.

LadyV76: Cool thought. Yeah, maybe.

[A pause]

MyBoyBlue4: I'm more nervous than I want to admit.

LadyV76: But you're admitting it, which is hot. I'm nervous too. While we're being honest...this is the first date I've gone on in over a year. In real life, I mean. Not on the internet. I'm worried I forget how.

MyBoyBlue4: How to what?

LadyV76: Date. Have fun. Do something other than work.

MyBoyBlue4: I get it. My hobby is my work. Which is awesome most of the time, but it really blurs the line between my professional and personal lives. As in, I don't really have a personal life anymore. Insert wincing emoji here.

LadyV76: The more we talk, the more I feel like we're the same person. Well, except for the whole alpha/beta thing. Although you made a pretty good alpha the other night. But I digress. My point is, my hobby is my work too, and the lines have definitely been blurring lately. Which is one of the (many) reasons I'm so excited to meet you. I think you might be just what I need to get over this weird hump.

MyBoyBlue4: Jeez no pressure or anything. Just kidding. Speaking of hump...what happens if we meet each other and we totally hit it off and we want to bone?

LadyV76: Then we get a fancy hotel room and we bone until our bodies give out. Yes, I'll keep my heels on. Everything else comes off.

MyBoyBlue4: I got a shiver just thinking about it.

LadyV76: Me too. I also got scared.

MyBoyBlue4: You know what I like most about you?

LadyV76: What's that?

MyBoyBlue4: You keep it real. I'm trying to do the same, but it's not easy.

LadyV76: It's never easy. But I'd like to think it requires a lot less effort than pretending to be perfect all the time.

MyBoyBlue4: Good point. So...next time we talk, it will be in person.

LadyV76: Pretty crazy. Please don't kill me.

MyBoyBlue4: Hey. What if you end up being the serial killer?

LadyV76: These heels can definitely be used as weapons...

MyBoyBlue4: Wait, you're wearing them now?

LadyV76: [sends picture of her feet crossed on the bed, legs bare, stilettos on]

MyBoyBlue4: Boing.

Chapter Twenty-Two

EMMA

On Monday, forecasters give the freak winter storm sweeping through the Rockies a twenty percent chance of making it to Asheville by the weekend.

On Friday, winter storm warnings are issued across Buncombe County.

That's right. On the night I'm supposed to head into town for my first date with Blue, blizzard conditions are expected. They're calling for up to eight inches of snow and forty mile-per-hour wind gusts.

It's *April*.

If I were superstitious, I'd say the universe was conspiring against Blue and me meeting. Good thing I'm not.

So on Friday morning, I put my head down and hope for the best, and thank the powers that be that my Toyota has four-wheel drive. Luckily, the snow isn't supposed to start in earnest until after seven. I figure worst-case scenario, I'll make it downtown for dinner but get snowed in there, in which case I'll just grab a hotel room. And if Blue and I hit it off, that definitely wouldn't be a bad thing.

I'm really hoping we hit it off. I wasn't lying when I told

Blue I need this—need to get out and lust after someone other than Samuel Beauregard. Maybe that's all it will take. A night out with someone new to help me forget about my crush on the guy who has life or death authority over my dream job.

Maybe I'm being overly idealistic, believing one date with someone new will do the trick. But I have to do something, or I'm going to lose my fucking mind.

Schools close early, but we're fully booked for the weekend at the farm. Thanks to the approaching storm, guest arrivals begin earlier than usual, and we get a steady stream of diners and drinkers at the barn from breakfast onward.

I tell myself that busy is good as I run to the cellar to grab a pricey bottle of Muscadet. Busy means I won't have time to think about...well, how much I try to think about Blue but end up thinking about Samuel instead.

How much he's changed since I arrived.

How his tongue felt between my legs.

How fucking handsome he is today in his cobalt suit and black tie. He was the first person I saw when I came in this morning, looking fresh and sharp, if a little subdued. He didn't smile at me, but his eyes did, and my heart dropped, and my lips throbbed, and I wondered if I'd taste the coffee on his mouth if I kissed him.

Stop. I try to stop thoughts like that in their tracks. Samuel's respected my wish to keep things friendly, and it's only fair my imagination does the same.

Trusting my feet to guide me down the stairs—I could run up and down this staircase in my sleep I do it so often—I close my eyes and try to imagine what Blue will look like. Granted, I've only seen his thighs, dick, and stomach, but it's obvious he's in great shape. He had a light brown, almost red happy trail, so maybe his hair will be a lighter shade of that? Or darker? And his eyes, I bet they're—

"Whoa!"

I bump into something hard at the same moment I hear Samuel's voice. My eyes fly open and the spicy smell of masculine shampoo fills my head. Suddenly, I find myself pressed against his broad chest with my nose buried in his shirt. He's close enough that I can make out the different shades of blue that speck his irises—slate, sky, ocean.

"Wow, I am so sorry," I manage, leaning back.

"Are you trying to break a leg? Or do you always walk down staircases with your eyes closed?"

"I'm, um, practicing. For the time you inevitably challenge me to find a specific bottle down here blindfolded. I refuse to accept another tie, so..."

He smiles. With his eyes *and* his mouth this time.

An ache unfurls along the sides of my torso, so strong and persistent it makes me short of breath. My heart is popping around again.

I want to put my mouth on this man so very badly.

"Game on. But seriously, I don't want you breaking those legs, okay?"

"Ha," I say. But the universe must really be conspiring against me because my left leg buckles.

My knee literally gives out, and I feel myself going down like a heroine in a Regency novel. I didn't think swooning was a real thing until this moment.

And just like in a Regency novel, Samuel curls an arm around my waist and holds me up—holds me against him—the motion quick and effortless.

"Whoa," he repeats, brow furrowed. "Emma, I was joking, but if you're really not okay, let's sit you down and get you some water. If you tell me this involves a protein bar—"

"No protein bars." I put my hands on his chest and gently push him away. "Just busy. I'll see you around."

I hobble into the cellar and leave Samuel staring after me.

It's rude, and it's weird, but I'm worried if I stood there one second longer, I would've done something stupid.

I almost run into Samuel again upstairs. And again, in the hallway outside our offices when I'm shrugging into my coat after a meeting with our managers to make sure everything goes smoothly tonight. My nose somehow ends up in his shirt again.

"If I didn't know any better, I would say you're trying to sniff me. I smell that good, huh?"

He's smiling again, real and warm.

It shouldn't be this hard, not wanting to strip your coworker naked and fuck him six ways to Sunday.

It shouldn't be this hard not wanting someone, period.

"Get over yourself," I mutter and dash out of there like the barn's on fire. My pulse is hammering, and I feel lightheaded.

I see flurries on my short walk home. It's also windy. The sky is getting dark, and the smell of cold stone and dampness fills the air. I've lived in the mountains long enough to recognize it as the smell before a good snow.

My stomach twists, and I walk faster. I know the worst of the storm isn't supposed to hit until later tonight. But the weather changes quickly at higher altitudes, and the farm tops out at almost four thousand feet above sea level.

Shit.

I hurry inside my cottage. I throw my jacket, boots, and bag on the bench beside the front door and make a mad dash for the bedroom. I have my outfit picked out, but I didn't have time to pack an overnight bag in case I get stuck. Truth be told, I also didn't want to jinx myself. Is packing for a night away bravely optimistic or embarrassingly naïve?

Either way, I didn't do it yet, so I scramble to throw something together. Protein bars: check. Samuel would not approve, but this isn't about him. In fact, this is about *forget-*

ting him. Plus, if I really do get stuck, it can't hurt to have some food on hand.

Aquazzura heels: check. I'll wear boots on the way there, then slip into the stilettos when I get to the restaurant.

Condoms: most likely checking the embarrassingly naïve box, but whatever. If Blue and I are gonna bone, we're gonna do it safely.

I throw on some eyeliner and lip gloss. Then I wiggle into my jeans. It's the first time I've worn them since I came to the farm, and they've definitely gotten tighter.

Gotta be all that food Samuel keeps feeding me. Despite the fact that these jeans are cutting off my circulation, I smile.

Worth it. That quiche he left on my desk the other day? The stuff of dreams.

So I leave the button undone and plug in my curling wand. I feel sexiest when I'm rocking long, loose waves, so I'd planned to curl my hair after work. Glancing out my window, I see it's getting dark, and the snow is really picking up.

I try to be quick, but I also want my hair to be perfect. I don't know what it says about me that a great hair day gives me a bigger boost of confidence than pretty much anything else, but I don't care.

Only when I'm halfway done with my head, I lose power. Literally. As in the lights go out and the heat cuts off and the world goes dark around me.

"What the hell?" I say out loud. "You've got to be kidding me!"

I come up with plan B. I'll pack my wand, cross my fingers and toes there's an outlet in the restaurant bathroom, and finish my hair there. But I have to leave *now* if I'm going to have time to do it.

I don't realize just how hard it's snowing until I'm making a run for my car but find a golf cart instead.

Because my car is parked in the lot up by the main house. *Of course.* Hank took it up there when I arrived, and I haven't needed it since. How did I forget that large detail? Maybe because being on Blue Mountain makes you forget the real world and all its conveniences—cars, men who aren't distractingly beautiful—even exists.

For a second, I consider calling Hank. Should I have him bring the car here? But with the amount of arrivals we're having, everyone at the main house will be busy. My guess is it'll be much quicker for me to run up there and get the car myself.

No use taking the golf cart. Those tiny tires definitely won't cut it on the slick road.

Cursing the day I was born, I pull up my hood, hike a bag over each shoulder, and start walking. It's barely five o'clock, but it's already pretty dark, and I have to squint to see through the snow. The path is mostly uphill, and as I huff and puff, my lungs and heart burn from the cold air. The snow is coming down sideways, blowing inside my hood. My curls are already wet, and I can tell my jeans are gonna be soaked by the time I get to my car. This bums me out more than it should.

Still, I keep going.

Think about what a great story this will make, I think to myself, legs aching. *You and Blue can tell your grandchildren how you literally had to walk uphill in a snowstorm to meet him.*

That's dangerously naïve, but hey, my hair and my outfit are already ruined, and I don't want my eye makeup to go too. So I do what I must to keep from dissolving into tears.

The snow is coming down so hard now I can barely see two feet in front of me. The realization, sudden and awful, settles like a brick in my stomach.

This date isn't going to happen.

It's just too risky trying to make it down the mountain in

weather like this. The narrow road connecting Blue Mountain to the rest of civilization is precarious in even the best weather. In snow like this? It'll be downright treacherous.

Somewhere in the back of my mind, my rational self is telling me it's no big deal. Blue and I will just reschedule. The disappointment is temporary. If the date is meant to happen, it'll happen.

Still. The disappointment may be temporary, but damn is it crushing. I blink against the sting in my eyes, embarrassed that I'm crying over a scrapped date with a virtual (heh) stranger but too exhausted to give myself another pep talk.

That's when I see an unfamiliar pair of headlights moving my way. They're halogen, so bright it hurts to look at them. An enormous black SUV materializes out of the darkness. I take one look at the shiny gold rims and know—*oh, shit*—it's Samuel.

My stomach plummets. I tug my hood over my eyes and keep my head down. A beat later, I hear the whirr of a window rolling down, followed by—wait, is that Van Halen's "Why Can't This Be Love" I'm hearing?

"Emma? Is that you?"

I hold up a hand but don't stop walking. "Hi. And bye. I don't mean to be rude, but I gotta go."

A beat. The idling engine of his truck throbs.

I hear him change gears, and the next thing, I know he's reversing the vehicle, following me.

Yeah, that's definitely Van Halen. For a second, my stride falters. What are the chances Samuel's listening to the band that always comes up in my chats with Blue?

Speaking of blue—Samuel's still wearing that cobalt suit. And he said he had a date tonight.

Now it's my heart that's faltering.

No way.

No way Samuel is Blue. Right? Samuel may have come

around to kindness recently, but Blue has been excellent from the beginning. Samuel was rude and narrow-minded and didn't listen. Blue always listened. Blue always had an open mind. More than that, Blue has a grip on who he is and what he wants. Samuel didn't, at least when we met. I'm not sure he does now.

My heart starts beating again. They can't be the same person. It just doesn't make sense. The music and the suit and the date—they're coincidences, that's all. For all I know, Samuel lied about having a date to make me jealous. Let's not forget his history of being a dick.

Right.

"Where are you going?" Samuel asks.

"The main house," I say.

"Why?"

I go with the truth. A version of it, anyway. "My power went out."

"It did? Dammit. I'll give maintenance a call. In the meantime, let me give you a ride."

I'm freezing and tired and wet, but getting even more freezing and tired and wet is preferable to Samuel seeing me on the verge of tears in the close quarters of his truck. Who knows what will happen if I get in?

If I keep walking, I'll make it to the main house. If I make it there, I can dry off and maybe warm up by one of the fireplaces while I shoot Blue a message to reschedule our date.

"I'm good, thanks. You'd better get where you're headed anyway. It's bad out here."

"Emma, get in the truck."

I'm wracked by a full-body shiver. My hands and nose are numb.

"Look at you, you're gonna get yourself sick. Don't make me come out there."

I keep going.

"God*damm*it." I hear the clank of Samuel putting the SUV in park. My heart skips. Eyes burn.

He rounds the truck, as big and broad as a bear in his sharply cut coat. His breath billows around his head in a cloud.

"If you don't stop walking, I'm gonna throw you over my shoulder. You have three seconds. One. Two—"

I round on him, tears blurring my eyes. "*Please.*"

He studies me for a stunned second. Then he slowly holds up his hands, eyebrows snapped together. "I was just kidding. I won't touch you without your consent. But I get the feeling that's not what you're upset about."

We're trapped in our own little snow globe, the snow falling silently around us. Snowflakes catch on his eyelashes and eyebrows. He's standing a couple of feet away, but I can still feel the warmth radiating off his body.

I want to curl into his chest and live there forever.

How do I tell him I can't stop falling for this nice guy he's turned into? That he's putting me between a rock and a hard place, and I feel like I'm going to break? That my one chance to get some breathing room was dashed by this fucking storm?

"I'm not okay," I blurt, eyes stinging, throat burning.

"I know," he says quietly. "Walk if you want to. But if you'd let me, I'd love to give you a ride. Warm you up a little bit. And if you wanna talk about whatever's on your mind... well, I've got a generator at my place, and a whole tray of lasagna with your name on it. I used Mama's recipe with sides of Caesar salad, homemade dressing, of course, and garlic knots. I'll throw in a couple of bottles of that 2016 Screaming Eagle to sweeten the deal."

Fuck him.

Seriously, fuck this guy for life. How does he know what I want—need—before I do?

Think about your career.

But then I shiver, drawing a sharp breath through my teeth. I am so cold. And hungry.

Really, really hungry.

"That's it," he says, his expression hardening as he takes a step forward. "You're coming home with me. Give me permission to put my hands on you."

I grin, despite the fact I can't stop shivering. It's a fun little inside joke Samuel and I have, throwing each other's lines back and forth.

Samuel and I *have inside jokes*. I don't know how it happened or when, but I love it, and I want more of it.

That's when I give up.

Or maybe it's just giving in to the truth. And the truth is that I want to go home with Samuel.

Chapter Twenty-Three

SAMUEL

I move quickly.

Shrugging out of my coat, I wrap it around Emma. Poor thing is shaking like a fucking leaf. Her teeth chatter. Anger grips my heart. What was she thinking, coming out in this weather? She should've called the main house.

She should've called me.

I'll have time to be mad at her later. Right now, I need to get her warm.

I open the passenger side door and hustle her inside. Thankfully, I already had the heat blasting, and I adjust the vents so they're pointing directly at her. She closes her eyes and exhales, wrapping her arms around the bag she's set in her lap.

I furrow my brow. Was she planning on staying the night at the main house? Leaning in to make sure she buckles her seat belt, I get a good look at her face. She's wearing more makeup than usual. And her hair—it's down, wild, wavy.

"What's up with the Van Halen?" she asks when I climb into the driver's seat.

I glance at the center console. "Am I not allowed to like

eighties rock? Where do you think Eddie and David's names came from?"

"Ha! I get it now." She looks at me from the corner of her eye. "Indulge my totally inappropriate curiosity for a sec."

"Shoot."

"You said you had a date tonight. Where were y'all going?"

Settling my left hand on the top of the wheel, I use the other to put the truck in gear.

"I cancelled it," I say. Which is and isn't true. When I saw how bad the weather was leaving The Barn Door, I knew my date with V wasn't happening. I don't doubt the restaurant where we were supposed to meet will be closing early anyway. I just haven't officially cancelled our date yet. Chances are she already did anyway, but I haven't had a minute to check our chat since this morning.

"Oh. Oh, okay." Emma almost sounds...relieved?

I try not to think too much about what that means on the drive back to my house. I also try not to drive like a lunatic. The roads are already starting to get slick. But my girl clearly needs to get out of her wet clothes and into a hot shower stat, so I hit the gas.

Having Emma over is not a good idea. But for starters, I wasn't gonna leave her struggling on the side of the road in a snowstorm. And it's a distraction from the disappointment of having to cancel my date with V.

By the time Emma and I pull into my driveway, the snow is coming down so hard and so fast I can barely see three feet in front of the truck. I park in the garage. The wind howls above the sound of the door closing behind us.

Blizzard conditions are minutes away.

"Phew," I say, grabbing Emma's bag from her lap. "That was lucky timing. I haven't seen a storm this bad up here in years."

Emma nods, unbuckling her seat belt with fingers that

tremble. "As much as I didn't want you to rescue me, I'm glad you did." Her eyes meet mine. "Thanks."

The space between us thrums.

Must. Get. Her. Inside.

"Right," I say, climbing out of the truck. "How about a shower?"

Her eyes go wide, and I don't miss the flicker of heat in them.

I open her door for her and hold out my hand, laughing. "Not together. Unless—"

"Don't go there."

I was joking, but clearly she's not.

We kick off our boots when we're inside, and I lead her to the nearest shower. Which just so happens to be the one in my bathroom.

Emma stares at the expanse of glass and tile. Then she looks at the sink nearby, my toiletries neatly arranged on the marble countertop. A beat of charged silence fills the room.

Yeah, my bathroom is legit. But that's not what this silence is about.

She's standing in the inner sanctum. Probably the most private room in the house. Now she knows I use Crest toothpaste and an electric razor. She knows I like Molton Brown soap. She knows I'm a secret neat freak.

These are intimate things. The stuff only a girlfriend or wife would know.

The stuff I'd only share with someone who means something to me.

Judging by the way her expression softens, that's not lost on Emma.

But then she's shivering again, and she's trying to peel her clothes off, but she can't because she's shaking so hard.

"Help?"

She doesn't need to ask twice. I gently unbutton her

jacket and fold it, draping it over the edge of the nearby tub. Together, we guide her sweater over her head, revealing a black bra with delicate, transparent cups.

Christ Almighty. Her nipples poke against the fabric, tight, pink buds that are just begging to be sucked. A rush of warmth moves through my groin, gathering in the head of my dick.

Draping her sweater over my arm, I turn away. "I'll let you finish."

"But my jeans." I glance over my shoulder to see her unzipping her fly. "I think I'm gonna need your help getting them off."

I just stare at her, mouth going dry.

Lord Jesus, what am I supposed to do here?

I catch a glimpse of her panties through her fly. They match her bra: black, tiny, see-through.

"Uh," I say.

Emma is trying to shimmy out of her jeans now, doing that little shake of her hips that's playful and sexy, but they're not moving. Her jeans, I mean. She really does need help.

And I'm gonna need to cut off my dick while I prep dinner because I'm hard as a goddamn tree.

Clearing my throat, I discreetly adjust my trousers and nod at the tub. "Sit."

Emma sits. I squat in front of her, knees cracking. I pull her jeans down one leg at a time, going slowly so I don't startle or hurt her.

The muscles in her legs convulse as she trembles.

I frown. Her legs are covered in goosebumps.

"But really," I say. "Is it okay if I put my hands on you?"

She dips her head in a nod. I run my palm over her bare thigh and give it a good, warm squeeze. Emma goes still. Her skin is cold to the touch, and the need to make this better fills me. Her belly rises on an inhale, and I imagine leaning in and kissing her there. Kissing my way down her hip, between her legs. Pushing those fucking panties aside and kissing her pussy.

Emma is (mostly) naked.

She's in my house.

And she's trusting me to do the right thing.

Groaning, I rise to my feet. I set her jeans beside her sweater on the tub. Then I strip off my socks and turn on the shower.

Immediately, it fills with steam. Holding the door open, I look at the ceiling.

"Take your time," I manage. "It's a good shower. Water pressure's excellent."

I glance down at Emma to see her peering inside. "Are those multiple showerheads?"

I bite the inside of my cheek. *Yes. And yes, I put them in there for exactly the reason you're thinking.*

Shower sex—actual dick into pussy action—is not worth the hassle. But getting or giving head in the shower? Nothing hotter.

My dick throbs. I shove a towel into Emma's arms. "Enjoy. Don't turn that water off until you're thawed out, all right?"

I head for my closet, where I grab the softest, warmest sweats and sweatshirt I own. Emma will be swimming in 'em, but at least she'll be warm and dry.

I put on my second softest sweatsuit, an ivory Balenciaga set I recently bought, and try my best to make a beeline through the bathroom again.

"Don't worry," I say, cupping my hand over the side of my face as I pass the shower. She's inside it now, the door closed behind her. "I won't look."

"I thought you were being honest these days," she shoots back, voice echoing off the tile.

"Fine. I'll look." And I do.

The glass is fogged up, but I can still see Emma's outline as she reaches behind her and unhooks her bra. She hangs it over the door, its lacy straps dangling, and then she steps out of her panties. She hangs those over the door too, only they fall to the floor. A tiny black heap that may just be the death of me.

Emma Crawford is in my shower. Naked as the day she was born.

Her see-through panties are on my floor.

Do I have time for a quick tug in the guest bath?

I definitely don't. But watching Emma shimmy through the glass—yeah, she knows I'm looking, and she doesn't care—makes me think I might have to.

"Blow-dryer's on the counter over there," I say huskily. "Help yourself to whatever else you need."

Thankfully, I prepped the lasagna last night, so I just have to pop it in the oven. Then I get started on the rest of the meal.

Being in the kitchen, I feel more steady. A little less like I'm gonna die from want. Food is something I'm good at. Food is what I know.

Without exception, food makes me feel centered.

So I decant a bottle of Emma's Screaming Eagle (I'll never not think of it as hers). I grill some romaine hearts. Shred a block of aged parmesan and toast day-old focaccia, then cut it into cubes that I'll use as croutons.

I put the garlic knots in the oven beside the lasagna. Put on a Top 50 playlist I pray is not romantic in any way, shape, or form.

I light a fire in the family room.

All the while silently chanting a litany of affirmations.

You can be friendly.

You can be honest.

You can keep it in your pants.

Emma said living this way may be worth it in the end. But right now, it's a kick in the balls.

Especially when Emma emerges from the shower. Her wet hair is brushed back from her face. Color in her cheeks. Eyes puffy.

Her vulnerable beauty knocks the wind out of me. She's not trying to hide.

She's not trying, period. She's Emma *as is*.

She looks fucking adorable in my clothes.

"Hi," she says. She's got her phone in her hand.

I nod at it. "Hear from your date?"

"Not yet. I just sent him a message to cancel."

"Bummer. You warm?"

"Getting there."

I nod at the fireplace. "Sit by the fire. I'll bring you some wine."

"Samuel." Taking a seat on the raised edge of the hearth, she meets my eyes. "Go easy on me, okay?"

"What do you mean?"

"Don't be so"—she gestures to the fire, the glass of wine I hand her, the food on the kitchen island—"awesome. I know I told you I hated him, but if you could bring back a little Samuel-from-before, you know, the jackass, I would appreciate it."

I smile tightly. "Too late. That guy's gone forever."

We're in trouble, her eyes say.

I know, mine say back.

I want her, I fucking *want her*, and from the way she's looking at me, burning need written all over her face, she wants me too.

It doesn't matter. What matters is making her feel better.

Honesty, bravery, authenticity—those are the things that

light her up. She's got something to share, something to get off her chest, but she's tired and scared. It's my turn to do the heavy lifting. Maybe after I bare my soul to her, she'll feel comfortable baring hers to me.

So I tap my wineglass to hers and dive into the deep end.

"A friend and a teammate stabbed me in the back and ended my career."

Emma's eyes bulge, and she chokes on her wine. Pounding the side of her fist against her chest, she says, "What? Samuel, my God, I'm so sorry. I had no idea. I—"

"Look, if you don't want to talk about this shit, I'll understand. But I want you to know I'm making an effort not to bullshit anymore. We can do small talk. But after meeting you, I gotta say it bores the hell out of me. It's like you taught me how to talk to people. Really *talk* to them."

She smiles down at her wine. "I didn't have to teach you that."

"Fine. You reminded me how to do it because somewhere along the way I'd forgotten."

"That's really cool of you to say," she replies, looking up. She pats the hearth beside her. "So talk to me."

I sit, careful to keep a good twelve inches or so between us, and talk.

The truth comes out in a torrent. How Olly Welch played the part of supportive teammate as second-string quarterback after Carolina drafted him five years into my career. He was wet behind the ears, but he was hungry, and he worked hard, and he took a real interest in learning what I had to teach him. He reminded me a lot of myself at his age.

We also shared an agent, so it wasn't long before Olly and I became friends. When a torn ACL sidelined me halfway through my fifth season in Carolina, Olly checked in on me daily. He was great. He sent me food and kept me smiling with texts and calls.

I tried to hurry back to the team, speed up whatever I could in my recovery. Fans—and coaches and owners—have a short memory. I was hell-bent on getting back in the game as soon as possible. My dad never missed a game in his twelve-year career, and I hated that I wouldn't be sharing that statistic.

I also hated the idea of being forgotten. Eclipsed. Olly was starting games while I was out, and he began playing really fucking well. He knew it, I knew it, the organization knew it.

Still, when I got back, everyone assured me I'd start again. Olly most of all.

"He looked me in the eye and said he had my back one hundred percent," I tell Emma. "Little did I know he'd end up stabbing me there instead."

Emma gasps, hand going to her mouth. "Oh my God, Samuel, what happened?"

"It turns out, Olly was playing games behind my back with my agent, Lina," I reply grimly. "Apparently he told Lina that I told him my heart wasn't in the game anymore. He said to her, 'hey, the docs say Samuel will be cleared, but he's still in a lot of pain and he told me point-blank he doesn't want to start anymore. He doesn't even want to come back at all.' Olly told her I didn't want to go through all that again if I got injured a second time—the surgery, the rehab. Said it 'took too much out of me.' He also told her not to tell me that I shared everything with him."

Emma furrows her brow. "Why?"

"Because I was"—air quotes—"'brokenhearted,' and I was ashamed over losing my love for the game. I'd rather be asked to leave than publicly admit I didn't want to play anymore. He claimed I felt like I'd be letting the team down, like I was a coward. So Olly pushed her to take the information to our coaching staff without saying a word to me."

"Oh my God, Samuel."

"No kidding."

"I don't know the world of pro sports that well, but isn't that illegal? At the very least, it has to be a serious breach of ethics."

"Absolutely." I nod. "Didn't stop it from happening, though. I walk into training camp my first day back, and Coach pulls me aside. Says the team will be okay without me, and that they were 'moving in a different direction' with their new starting quarterback, Olly Welch."

Emma gasps. "Wow. I googled you, obviously, before I met you. I read a much different version of this story—"

"The PR people fed the media that bullshit about the team and I 'amicably' parting ways. I rode the bench for another year to the end of my contract. And then...yeah. My career in the pros was over."

Emma is shaking her head. "But what about Lina? What about the rest of the people working for you?"

"I went right to my manager after my conversation with Coach. And he said he'd been told that Lina was working hard to help me retire from football, and that thanks to Olly, they both knew that's what I wanted."

"Holy shit." She's still shaking her head. "But you fought it, right?"

I shrug. "I did for a little while. I was *angry*. But the wheels were already in motion, and Olly was playing so fucking well. He took the team far that year." I swallow. "At the time, it was devastating. Football had been my life for so long. But by then Beau had retired, and he'd started putting his plans in motion to develop Blue Mountain. My siblings and I, we'd always planned to come back to the farm one day and make it the place it was always meant to be. Beau asked me if I was ready to lend a hand, and, well...seemed like the fresh start I needed. The way things ended in Carolina made me hate the sport for a while there."

Emma pushes the sleeves of my sweatshirt up to her elbows. Her skin there is covered in freckles. "Understandable."

"This is something I've never told anyone," I say. I'm already in over my head here, so no point in holding back now. "But there's another reason I didn't fight longer than I did. The rumors Olly spread about me—they weren't entirely untrue. I knew in my gut that my body wasn't the same after the injury. Neither was my head. I couldn't get into the game the way I had before. Maybe I was scared or tired or whatever, but the first thing I felt after the rage died down was relief."

Emma frowns. "Why keep that a secret?"

I search her eyes. Heart thumping inside my chest. "Why do you always ask such good, awful questions?"

"Because I care."

"I really did feel ashamed." I tip back my wine. Emma's already halfway through her glass, and I need to catch up. "I did feel like I was letting the team down. Although the reality is my gut very likely saved me from the kind of injury Beau's dealing with right now. But still, that shame, the feeling that I fell short—it's real."

"You don't need to tell me. Shame's been my constant companion for as long as I can remember."

"How did you finally kick its ass?"

Emma's throat dips as she swallows her wine. My body pulses. She smells like me—my shampoo and my soap.

"When I do, I'll let you know." She smiles. "Therapy helps. So does time. I give way fewer shits about what people think of me as I've gotten older. But I guess it comes down to being brave enough to acknowledge who you really are and what you really want, and honoring that instead of fighting it.

Thinking of it as sacred and good, rather than something that's shameful, something that should be ignored or swept under the rug or bottled up. It's living your truth."

I'm full-on gulping my wine now. "And what's my truth?"

She thinks for a minute before responding. "You talk a lot about your dad. I don't know much about him, except that he passed when y'all were young."

Aw, shit, I'm gonna cry again. "I was eighteen."

"That's awful. I don't know what else to say except that I'm really, really sorry."

"Thanks."

"But I have a sneaking suspicion it's got to do with him—who you are, and what you feel like you're missing. When he died, what died with him?"

My eyes won't quit burning. The sensation is familiar now, and I don't fight it.

Emma and I both startle at the ding of the timer in the kitchen.

"Saved by lasagna," I say, getting up. Just because I don't fight the tears doesn't mean I'm not glad I don't have to explain why they're there in the first place.

What I don't say is the loneliness I've felt for years goes away whenever I'm with Emma.

I don't say it's because I think she's the only person who's cared enough to get to know me—to dig past the bullshit to the real me—since Daddy.

Chapter Twenty-Four

EMMA

I know I'm going to sleep with Samuel one bite into my lasagna.

It's like the cheesy, carby goodness meets my tongue and the last of my defenses comes tumbling down.

Maybe I knew it the minute I climbed into his truck.

The minute he told me what he'd never told anyone else.

Or maybe I knew it the minute we met.

Whatever the case, it's happening. I want to fight it. And right up until the end of my shower, I *was* fighting, valiantly, reminding myself over and over that my whole life is at stake. Every dream. Every dollar.

I fought to remind myself of how he behaved that night in his kitchen.

But then his confession happened, and now this lasagna and this fucking wine, and I have never wanted in my life something more than to be with this man in every sense of the word.

I'm begging you, I silently tell him as I sink my teeth into a garlic knot, *don't break me.*

"Good?" Samuel asks, blue eyes flicking to mine.

He looks eager. A little nervous. Totally fucking adorable.

"Insane. You're a pretty amazing cook, Samuel."

He suggested we do dinner indoor picnic style, which I was totally on board with. So we're eating on a bear skin rug —"it's fake, I promise"—in front of the family room's massive fireplace. It's laughably over the top and incredibly, temptingly romantic. Snow falling outside the picture windows, the frozen swirl a delicious contrast to the cozy, buzzy warmth sinking into my bones.

Samuel wants to take good care of me. Tonight, I'll let him.

Just tonight.

Something deep down tells me that's a promise I won't be able to keep. But it's the assurance I need to make my professional and personal desires square up right now.

I go with it.

The disappointment I felt earlier is nowhere to be seen.

I eat my lasagna and I gather my courage, Samuel's elbow brushing mine every time he lifts his fork to his mouth.

Jesus, even the way he eats is sexy. He takes his time, thoughtfully savoring every bite. I try to do the same, although it's hard because this stuff is so delicious I want to devour it in giant bites. But slowing down does heighten the experience. This is not a meal to be rushed through. Lasagna is time-consuming to make, and I'd bet my life everything in it is homemade, from the sauce to the noodles to the ricotta cheese.

As trite as it sounds, everything Samuel cooks is made with fierce, real love.

"It's truth," I say, sipping my wine.

Samuel cuts me a confused look, his blue eyes glowing in the dim light of the fire. "The lasagna?"

"Yes. My God." I scoff. "How did I not see it sooner? Your truth—it's in your food."

He grins. "See? I'm not all bad."

"You were a jerk for a minute there, yes, but...what if food is your way of showing love? You put a lot of effort into feeding the people who mean something to you. Filling them up fills you up. That's why you adore sobre mesa so much. It's people eating what you love and connecting over it, connecting with each other. Your food brings them together. See? You're honest *here*"—I hold up my empty plate—"and you always have been. That love and that authenticity and the courage to put yourself out there, it's been *here*"—I press my finger into the center of his chest—"all along."

His eyes soften, and so does everything inside my body. "That's beautiful, Emma. It's beautiful that's what you see in a plate of noodles and way too much cheese."

"It's more than that, and you know it."

"You know it." His eyes hold mine. "You know how much I want to kiss you, Emma Crawford."

My heart leaps, and my stomach drops, and I sit, waiting for him to finish that thought.

He sets down his plate and tugs a hand through his hair. "Since we're on the subject of honesty. I know you said you wanted to keep things professional, and I have every intention of respecting your wishes. But I couldn't not—" He groans. "I'm trying to be a better man here, and right now that feels like being up front about what's going on inside my head."

Those fingers of his tighten on the stem of his wineglass, but he doesn't move. Doesn't break eye contact. He's feeling his feelings, and he's not running away from them like he did when we first met.

He's trying for *me*.

It's affirming and arousing in a way I can't quite describe.

"Samuel Beauregard," I say, setting down my wineglass on the hearth. "I'd very much like to kiss you too."

His eyebrows pop up. "Really?"

"Really."

"And you're okay with it?"

"I am." I flatten my palm on the floor beside Samuel's hip and lean into it. "Right now, I really am. In fact, I'm okay doing a lot more than that too."

"Promise me. Promise me that no matter what happens, you'll stay on the farm."

I meet his eyes. "That's quite the commitment."

He curls a hand around the nape of my neck. My body ignites at the feel of his fingers on my skin. His palm is huge and warm, and I already feel myself melting into a kiss that hasn't even happened yet.

"Promise," he repeats.

I look at his lips. They're full, dark from the wine. "I promise."

My initial impulse is always to take charge in sexual situations. If I'm in control, no one gets hurt. Not if they don't want to, anyway.

Ceding that control, surrendering rather conquering—it's scary. But I try it on anyway.

I let Samuel lean in and angle his head. I tilt my chin, lips parting, welcoming his kiss.

I let him in.

The moment his mouth finally comes down on mine is a rush. He's confident right off the bat, his tongue licking my bottom lip before moving into my mouth. His lips are soft, sure, and he tastes clean, like water and wine. His scruff catches on my chin and I bring my hand to his face, unfurling my fingers through his beard. He groans, this half helpless, half rowdy sound, and my nipples harden to tight points. They brush against the inside of his sweatshirt, making my clit pulse.

He goes slowly but my heart still thunders inside my

chest, blood running wild inside my skin. A beat tightens between my legs. He deepens the kiss, drawing me up to him, and I meet him stroke for stroke, his tongue licking into my mouth, my teeth coming down on his bottom lip before I give it a quick, hard suck.

Samuel groans again, his other hand finding my hip. He guides his fingers inside my—his—sweatshirt, not stopping until he finds skin. He glides his hand up my bare side, my body arching into his touch.

Keep going, I silently plead.

His thumb trails a ribbon of fire up my stomach and stops just beneath my breast.

"Where the fuck is your bra?" he rasps against my mouth.

I smirk. "Somewhere in your bathroom, I think."

"Aw, baby, you're *killin'* me," he murmurs, gliding his thumb up over the curve of my tit.

A shockwave of need rips through me when his thumb finds my nipple. The heat from the fire, the heat between my legs—it's overwhelming.

I like it when he calls me baby.

I also like it when he circles his thumb over my nipple. Gentle and slow and soft. My kiss becomes eager, and Samuel gives me what I want, deepening the kiss without making it messy.

It's sexy, and it's romantic, and it's exactly how I hoped kissing would feel when I was a confused fifteen-year-old making out with my pillow.

He doesn't try to dominate. Doesn't rush and doesn't show off. He just kisses and touches me the way I want to be kissed and touched. He's just a guy and I'm just a girl, and we're trying on *real* together for the first time. No pretense. No lies.

Just breaths and heartbeats. And what's truer than that?

My heart tells me I want more of his touch. So I moan

and he says, "This has gotta come off," and then I'm pulling back and holding up my arms as Samuel lifts the sweatshirt over my head.

The sudden rush of air makes my skin pebble. Samuel's eyes rake hungrily over my bare torso, my lips and my clit throbbing. His gaze becomes hooded. It moves to meet mine, and he curls both hands around my torso, just underneath my armpits, and guides his thumbs over my nipples.

I see stars. Electricity zips from my nipples to my clit, and I roll my hips, breath coming in pants. He's touching me *well* and *carefully*. Like he's treasuring rather than taking me.

I don't know if I've ever been touched that way before.

I shiver.

"Samuel," I manage. I don't recognize my own voice. It bares the need making me weak...everywhere. My knees. My resolve.

And you know what? I don't hate it.

I especially don't hate it when Samuel's brow curves upward and he reaches behind his head to grab the neck of his sweatshirt. He tugs it off, and no joke, I think I black out for a heartbeat.

He is fit. In the American and the British sense of the word. He's on the thick side of ripped with muscles everywhere. But it's the tiny details of his physique that light me on fire. The sharp lines of his collarbones. The vein that runs vertically up his bicep. The whorls of hair covering his chest.

I shiver.

He frowns and pats his lap. "Come here."

I push off my hand and lift my knee over his crossed legs. Straddling his hips, I hold myself up a little ways from his groin. He's not pitching a tent—not yet—but if he's as turned on as I am, he's got something going on down there, and I don't want to inadvertently hurt him.

Samuel, apparently, isn't worried about that.

"Come *here*." He puts his hands on my hips and guides them down until I'm settled snugly against him. My pussy comes alive at the slight pressure, making need coil tightly in my core.

My nipples brush against his chest. His skin is warm. Really warm.

My stomach aches at the way the muscles in his chest bunch against the skin as he wraps his arms around my waist and pulls me to him.

In an instant, I'm surrounded by his heat. With my face buried in the crook of his neck, he places his palm on my nape again, holding me there. My shoulders relax away from my ears, bit by bit until they're languid and soft.

"Warmer?" he murmurs into my hair.

I turn my head to press a kiss to his neck. I feel his stomach tense. "You're a human furnace."

"I run hot."

"I like hot."

"Good thing you have me around then," he says, and then he kisses my mouth.

Chapter Twenty-Five

SAMUEL

Emma wraps her arms around my neck and falls into the kiss.

I wait for warning bells to go off in my head. *Danger. Stop. Don't.*

But my thoughts are strangely calm. And while I'm nervous about...well, fucking everything, my gut's telling me I've gotta give Emma what she needs.

Luckily, her body is responsive to even the smallest touches, the tiniest changes in pace, so I take my time and learn her.

I learn she's got a spine of steel but the softest skin.

I learn she likes to linger. Her kiss is deep and searching, and her body rises into my touch when I tease her a little, when I go slowly, intentionally.

I learn that turning me on turns her on. She kisses my neck, and I growl, and she does it again, nicking me with her teeth as her fingertips glide into the hair at the nape of my neck. I tighten my arms around her—I want her close, I've gotta keep her warm—and she starts playing with my hair, moving up and down ever so slightly, just enough that her nipples rub against my chest.

I'm hard, and I want to fuck. But for the first time, I want to make it last longer. Who knows when Emma will let me touch her like this again? I don't want to think about what happens tomorrow, but I realize I'm at her mercy. I may be holding her, but she's holding all the cards.

The last time we hooked up was intense. This time is soft. Slow.

It's different, and I like it.

I've fucked plenty in my day. And while that was satisfying in its own right, now I understand that I never let it go deeper because I was too scared to let anyone in.

I'm still scared. But I'm letting Emma in anyway.

I let her learn me. She trails her mouth down my throat, stopping to linger on my collarbones. When she flicks her tongue over my nipples, I grab her hair and fist it. I feel her lips move into a smile against my skin.

Her hands wander over every inch of me. Caressing me, like what she finds is a wonder. Her fingers dance over my abs, and my stomach caves. The heaviness between my legs hurts.

"Stand up," she commands.

My cock leaps. I like it when she gets bossy.

I also like where this is going.

Getting to my feet, I look down at Emma. I guide her onto her knees and take her face in my hand. She's fucking gorgeous. Tits high, nipples puckered and perfect, brown eyes liquid and warm. Skin on her chest flushed.

She curls her fingers into the waistband of my sweats and pulls them down. Her eyes widen at the sight of my dick. It juts out from between my hips, rock hard and huge.

Emma's lips twitch. "Wow."

Smirking, I give myself a lazy tug with my free hand. "You're welcome."

"Hey." She grabs my wrist, stilling the motion. "Did I say you could touch yourself?"

Aw, yeah.

Yeah, I really like where this is going.

I kick off my sweats and hold up my hands. "Tell me what to do, baby."

She grabs my ass, fingers curling into my flesh as she jerks me forward.

"Come here." Emma is eye level with my cock. She glances up at me. "You touch me, and I stop. Understand?"

"Yes, ma'am."

"Keep your arms up," she says. Then she opens her mouth, tongue darting between her lips, and licks my shaft. Starting at the base, she drags the tip of her tongue along the vein that runs up the side. I grit my teeth, sparks igniting deep in my core.

She circles her tongue around my crown. I want her to take my head in her mouth so badly. I'm leaking already, and I need to fuck the back of her throat right now.

Only Emma seems intent to take her time. My fingers curl into fists as she teases me, brushing her nipples against the tops of my thighs. I want to fist her hair, shove my cock into her mouth. But I don't.

And the waiting, the unbearable tension—it's hot.

When she does finally taste my head, my hips jerk. The sight of her lips ducked out over my cock might be the sexiest thing I've ever seen. Her mouth is warm and slick, and Lord does she know what she's doing with that fucking tongue of hers.

But it's her willingness to look me in the eye while she sucks my cock that gets me. Bobbing her head, taking me a little deeper, then a little deeper still, her gaze finds mine and stays there.

Her words were firm, but the look she gives me is soft. Heavy lidded. I have to bite the inside of my cheek to keep from coming, but it's obvious she's turned on to the max too. She laps at me, drinking me in, her grip on my ass loosening as she loves me. She swallows me, taking me to the back of her throat, and I moan.

Her eyes glisten. Pulling back, she takes a deep breath and does it again. And again. Her head moves sensually now, slowly, and she wraps a hand around my shaft, giving me a tug as she goes up and down, up and down. She wants this to be good for me because she cares.

Still she looks at me. She lets me see her feeling, falling, and I know, I just fucking *know*, she wants me to do the same.

I want to too.

I let the dam inside me break. I want to close my eyes, to bear witness to the moment alone, but I resist the urge, and I look my girl in the eye. My stomach does a hundred backflips in the space of a single heartbeat.

My legs are Jell-O. I reach for her, grabbing her hand, saying, "I'm sorry, Em, I'm sorry, but I need—"

I need you.

I half expect her to pull away. Instead, she tangles her fingers with mine, palms flush, and gives my hand a squeeze.

There's a pull at my feet, like gravity is sucking me into the floor. My vision goes blurry at the edges. The room spins.

It stops. All that's left inside is Emma and me, and this feeling that moves between us.

We're lost.

We move together, giving and taking in equal measure. I roll my hips, and she bobs her head. We do this until I feel a familiar twist at the base of my spine.

"Baby." I cup her face again, thumbing up her chin. "I wanna come inside you."

Curling her tongue around me one last time, she slowly pulls back. Her saliva covers my cock and her swollen lips. It's lewd and it's beautiful, and I take a mental snapshot so I can remember her like this.

"I have condoms in my bag by the garage door," she says. "I'll go get a few."

It's wrong that I wonder why she's got condoms and who she was planning to use them with. I know that. But I'm past knowing, I'm just feeling now, and what I feel for this woman is deep and raw and primal. The idea of her fucking someone else makes me burn with jealousy.

I do my best to shove it aside. Em and I can have that discussion later.

Right now, I need to be between her thighs, or I'm gonna die.

Bending down, I bring our joined hands to my lips and kiss hers. "I've got condoms in my bathroom. I think. I may have to do some digging—"

"My bag is close, and it's a sure thing." She squeezes my hand again. "Hurry."

The fact that she's as needy as I am has me darting for the back hallway.

It's chillier over here away from the fire, and dark, but I don't bother turning on the light. I make a beeline for the outline of her bag on the bench beside the door, unzipping it. I dig around inside. Something pokes the back of my hand—a heel? Thing's a fucking weapon.

I dig blindly until I hear the crinkle of foil packets. Sleeve of Trojans in hand, I sprint back to the living room.

And nearly come right then and there when I see Em waiting for me on all fours. Light of the fire catching on the bare skin of her back, her ass toward me, knees together.

I stand, and I stare. I don't know where her pants went,

and I don't care. Glancing over her shoulder, she shoots me a little grin and gets down on her forearms, making her back arch and her ass shoot straight up.

"Fuck," I say, tearing a packet off the sleeve and opening it. "Not fair, Em."

"I never promised to play fair."

"Spread your knees."

"Make me."

"You want me to hurt you?"

Her grin fades. "I just want you to be with me."

I roll the condom on with shaky hands.

Getting on my knees behind her, I lean down and press a kiss to the base of her spine. "I'm here, baby."

I straighten, my cock brushing her hip. I cover her ass cheek with my hand. Then I use my thumb to pull her cheek aside, revealing just the tiniest sliver of her asshole and pussy. Pink. Wet.

I suck in a breath through my teeth.

"Em," I whisper, gliding my middle finger through her folds. Back to front. She's so wet and swollen I move easily, dipping two fingers inside her. "You're so fucking right for me. You're *right*."

Her hips cant, rising into my touch, and she glances over her shoulder to meet my eyes. Hair loose and wavy. Her brow's wrinkled, lips parted.

"Samuel," she pants. "Please. Don't stop. I need you."

She's hot and soft against my finger, and to be honest, I'm a little dizzy at the prospect of being allowed to have her this way.

She's giving this to me.

She's holding absolutely nothing back.

She's also shaking. Tiny tremors that make her skin tremble beneath my touch.

"Hey." Curling my arm around her waist, I use my knee to gently part her legs. "I've got you. I'm here."

The lines of her throat work as she swallows. "I'm sorry. I don't usually get like this. I just..."

"You need. I know." I glide my fingers forward and circle her clit, whispering, "Thank you."

"For what?" she whispers back, hips rolling. I move my hand up her belly and cup her breast, plucking at her nipple. She moans.

I replace the fingers of my other hand with the wide head of my cock. She moans. I say, "For letting your guard down with me. I'm honored. And inspired."

Emma pauses, mid-roll. Her eyes say what her words cannot. That she's happy and scared and so turned on it hurts.

I sink a little inside her, her pussy swallowing my crown. Seeing stars at how sweet she already feels.

Her breath catches, eyes squeezing shut.

I'm big. She's small. This position is probably not the best call for our first time, but it's what she wants. So I nudge her legs a little wider and grit my teeth and go slowly. I move my hand back to her clit, gently massaging her there while I sink inside her millimeter by millimeter.

It's heaven and hell, all at once. She's so tight I wanna scream. I wanna jackhammer my hips and have my way.

I put the other hand on the floor beside Emma's torso and lean forward so that I surround her. She's so little she fits inside the shelter of my body perfectly. I kiss her neck and suck on her shoulder. I gather her slickness on my fingertips and spread it on her nipple, making her pussy flutter around my cock.

"You that close?" I nip at her earlobe.

"The pain," she replies thickly. "The contrast with your gentleness—it's hot as hell, Samuel."

That's the story her body's telling too, so I go with it.

She pushes up onto her hands when I am sunk to the hilt.

"Okay?" I ask.

Running her fingers through her hair, she nods. "Start slow?"

I kiss her shoulder blade. "Keep talking to me."

But it's her body that does the talking. I do a mini-thrust, a slow in-and-out motion. My free hand still on her clit.

Her pussy flutters again. Stronger this time.

Her arms start to shake.

"Aw, baby," I murmur against her skin. "You are close. Tell me what you need me to do to get there."

She opens her eyes. *I already said it,* they reply. *I need you.*

I thrust again, a little harder this time. Her tits bounce and her head rears up. My thighs are flush against hers. She cries out when I take my hand off her pussy, but I need to find our rhythm so I can catch her when she falls.

Hand now on her hip, I guide her back and forth in time to my thrusts. We begin to move. I watch my cock glide in and out of her, my skin growing clammy with sweat. Holding back like this takes a fuck ton of effort, but I would rather light myself on fire than hurt Emma.

Plus, I have a feeling her orgasm is gonna be really, really good.

I want it to be her best ever.

Doesn't take long for Emma to meet me stroke for stroke. She's eager, athletic, and we set a good, sweaty pace, our bodies slapping with every thrust. When I'm confident she's okay, I curl my arm around her waist again and hold her tight against me.

I love the feel of her body against mine.

By the way the walls of her pussy clamp down on my dick, so does she.

"I want to see your face when you come," I say in her ear. "Roll over."

She obeys, my dick slipping out of her as she settles onto her back. I want to devour her with my eyes, the way her cheeks are flushed, the lines of her belly, but she's reaching for me, wrapping a hand around my cock and guiding it back to her center.

I smile at her impatience and hike her leg over my shoulder. Sinking inside her, I lean over her and play with her clit.

But it's when I kiss her mouth that she comes.

Her pussy tightens, milking my dick. She breaks the kiss and closes her eyes, body arching into mine. She cries out, head falling back. Neck bared.

In my arms, she lets go.

I watch, heart in my throat, with my eyes on her face. The sinews of her neck pop against her skin, and I lean down to kiss them. She curls her hands into the muscles on my chest, nails biting into the skin, and the place between my blood and bones sings at the ferociousness of her desire.

She wants to be held so I hold her. I pump into her, my balls tightening. I keep my gaze on her face as she rides out her orgasm.

At last, Emma opens her eyes. They're stormy, sated. Full.

She's falling.

I kiss her, and I come, growling into her mouth as my entire being implodes. Pulse after pulse of pounding sweetness I can barely breathe through. But I keep my eyes open and watch her watching me lose my shit.

Emma strokes my face, tucking my hair away from my forehead. The shockwaves flatten me, and for several seconds, my heart stops working even as the pulses keep coming.

The orgasm goes on for forty-eight years.

When my heart finally starts beating again, it feels

different inside my chest. Like it's worked itself into a new shape. Or maybe just untied itself from its perpetual knot.

I let out a breath.

Emma keeps playing with my hair. It feels nice. She smiles.

I do too. A real smile. Because finally, fucking *finally*, I don't feel lonely anymore.

Chapter Twenty-Six

EMMA

I wake up naked, horny, and sore.

I am sore everywhere—between my legs and inside my chest. The first one isn't new, but the second one is. My pulse skips a beat.

Oh, God, this feeling. It's lovely and it's terrifying, and in the darkness, my heart begins to pound.

I forgot myself with Samuel. I don't always play the alpha, but my tendencies always show through.

Tonight, though? Tonight, I forgot about power dynamics. I forgot to play or that control even existed. Because the sex was so good, and I was so into it that I barely had time to catch my breath, much less plot out what my next move should be. And that sort of freedom—that sort of ease, of comfort—is something I've never felt before with another person.

I felt connected with Samuel during sex without being worried about keeping my guard up. I felt appreciated for who I was in the moment. Not who I could be or should be.

He adores me for who I am.

Against my better judgment, I'm falling in love with Samuel Beauregard.

Not only that, I told him as much on that bearskin rug in front of the fire. Granted, I didn't say the words out loud. But he knew, and I knew, and now it's not only my career in his hands, but my heart too.

I want him. I want to be with him.

I am so fucked it's not even funny. Although having sex on a bearskin rug in front of a roaring fire is a cliché for a reason. It is *awesome*.

The worst slash best part? I'm pretty damn sure Samuel's falling for me too. He didn't say so either, not explicitly. But there was a tenderness in his lovemaking, an earnestness in his eyes, that I know he wanted me to notice. My insides do a happy dance at the idea that *we are in love*. My pussy clenches, and I can tell I'm already wet.

I start to panic.

Putting my hand on my forehead, I turn my head a little on the pillow. I can just make out the slumbering shadow of Samuel's massive body. He breathes deeply, evenly, making my rapid, shallow breaths sound all the more distressed. Turning away, I reach for my phone on the nightstand. It's 1:08 AM.

I pull up my chat app because I don't know what else to do. Blue hasn't sent me a message since I cancelled. I can't tell if I'm relieved or bummed he hasn't reached out since. I feel messy inside. Stirred up and swirling.

"Hey," Samuel says in a sleep-roughed voice, making me jump.

I turn back to him. My eyes have adjusted to the darkness so I can see his face now. The swollen fullness of his lips makes my heart twist.

"Hi."

"You okay?"

"No."

He furrows his brow. "Are you hurting?"

"I'm a little sore, but nothing too bad."

"Can I get you anything? Tylenol?"

Christ, why does he have to care so much? "That would be great, yeah."

He sits up and turns on the light beside the bed. The muscles in his back and butt flex as he stands. He's gloriously naked, and when he turns toward the bathroom, I can see he's fully, unashamedly erect.

I want.

Samuel returns with the Tylenol, a glass of water, and some lube.

"The lube's not for that," he says, handing me the water and Tylenol. "It's a little cooling, you know? Thought it might soothe your soreness."

He's not wrong. I gulp the medicine, grateful to have some water too. "All right."

I figure he'll pass the lube and let me apply it. But instead, he makes his way around the bed and sits beside me, erect penis and all, and squeezes a good bit of lube onto his fingers.

Sensation spikes through my clit at the image of him touching me.

"I can do it," I say.

He cocks his head. "Let me? I'll be gentle, I promise."

I love how he looks out for me.

"I know," I say, knowing exactly where this is headed. "All right."

I shouldn't go for round two. Actually, I should get my ass out of Samuel's bed and go home to process what's going down between us.

But I want him too badly. I need him to hold me and love me, if only for tonight.

Because let's be real, maybe tonight is all we have. I can love Samuel and be loved by him here in the privacy of his exquisite home, but when we're back at the barn surrounded by employees and expectations—I mean, that's a totally different scenario.

But for tonight, I can play pretend. The rest of the world doesn't exist. It's just him and me until forever. There will be no fallout, only orgasms and great food.

Samuel pulls back the covers. He's naked, and I'm naked, and I'm parting my legs for him, I'm watching with bated breath as he leans down and kisses my stomach before reaching between my thighs.

He touches me, and I jump, the desire in my core tightening. His first two fingers glide down my slit, making my breath catch, and his nostrils flare again.

"Did you wake up this wet?"

The lube does feel nice, but that doesn't stop my heart from swelling.

"You say that like it's a bad thing."

"It is when you need me, but you don't say anything," he replies, meeting my eyes. Shit, he's angry. "Why didn't you tell me? We don't have to fuck. I can get you off a million other ways, Em."

Em. I love all these nicknames he suddenly has for me.

"I know you can," I shoot back, seeing stars when his fingers find my clit. "Doesn't mean it's the right thing to do."

His fingers go still. "You think what we're doing is wrong?"

"I don't know," I say softly. "But it feels nice. Samuel, it feels—" I hiss when he touches my clit again.

"You feel what?" he says.

"I feel like fucking you."

I expect him to maul me right then and there. Instead, he pins me with a glare. Fingers still moving between my legs, he shakes his head. "I'm not fucking you."

"Why not?"

"You know why. I want to make love to you. But it doesn't matter what I want, because you're sore and you think this is wrong and I won't—"

"I want that," I say quickly, a different kind of panic rising in my chest. "I want you to make love to me, Samuel. The lube is helping. You won't hurt me, I promise. And this isn't wrong. It's just...complicated."

"Complicated doesn't equal right. I need you to be okay with this, or I'm not going any further."

I roll my eyes. "Sometimes complicated equals delicious. And that's what this is. Right now, Samuel, this is fucking delicious." I firm my voice. "Give me what I want."

He looks at me for a long beat. "Can I tell you what I want?"

"Sho-*oot*," I manage when he slips a single finger inside me.

"That hurt?"

"No. It felt good. Really good." I'm panting now, eyes glued to the place where he's touching me. His fingers—*those fingers*—move slowly over my slick folds, making sticky sounds that only turn me on more.

"I love condoms. Well, I don't love them, but I always use them. Like, *always*. But with you, I kinda...don't. Want to use them, I mean."

I go still, and my heart flips. For a second, I feel like I'm going to cry. Not because he's being careless, but because he wants it to be different with me.

The idea is arousing in the extreme to the point that it overwhelms me. Fuck, how am I supposed to pretend these feelings will just...go away tomorrow?

"Samuel—"

"Forget it." He leans in and presses a hot, quick kiss to my lips. "I'm sorry I brought it up."

"Why did you bring it up?"

"Because I want you to trust me the way I trust you. Because I want to feel you. Because I'm the best lay you've ever had, and I want to show you how the sex can get even better. Because—"

A beat of silence stretches between us, filling with the words he didn't say.

The words I'm too scared to hear.

"I'm sorry," he says again. "It was wrong of me to ask. To put pressure on you."

"It's okay. I just...I don't think I'm ready for that yet."

He nods, climbing onto the bed so that he's on his haunches between my legs. "I'm glad you told me. Just keep talking to me, okay?"

"Of course."

He slips his hands underneath my knees and spreads my legs wider. He looks down at my pussy, then looks up at me. The earnestness in his gaze, the hunger, is so real and so sharp it takes my breath away. "May I?"

I sink my teeth into my bottom lip, throat suddenly tight. "You may."

Then he ducks down and gives my slit a long, slow lick that has my hips curling off the bed and my fingers fisting in his hair. "My clit," I say. "Go there. Now."

His eyes flash as he does what I tell him, pressing the flat of his tongue to my clit. He stays there, waiting for further instruction.

The need inside my blood roars. Maybe if I reach for my inner alpha, if I grab at whatever control I can get my hands on at this point, I won't cry. "Now circle it. Yes, just like that, just the tip of your—" My breath catches. "I forgot how good you are at this. Now kiss me. Slow and deep. Like you mean it, Samuel. Yes. *Yes.*" I reach for the Trojans on the bedside table. I grab one and tear it open with my teeth. "I want to come on your dick."

Samuel groans against my pussy in reply, the vibration making me see stars.

I grab his hair and pull him away from my pussy. "On your knees."

He straightens to an impressive height even on his knees, towering over me. His body radiates heat. I drink him in, starting at his thighs. He's muscle and girth and strength, sinews tight against his skin. His mouth and the tip of his cock glisten. A cock that's enormous, its velvet length protruding obscenely from between his sculpted hips.

All this power. He's surrendering all this beauty *to me*.

My eyes film over. Hands shake as I pull the condom out of the wrapper and wrap my fingers around the underside of his shaft, giving him a firm, slow tug.

Oh my *God*, how am I supposed to maintain control when he's so fucking beautiful?

When I can be exactly who I want to be with him because he makes me feel so damn at home in his arms?

I roll the condom onto his dick.

"Hey." He curls his first finger underneath my chin, tilting my head to look up at him. "What's wrong?"

Samuel's brows are drawn together. Curving upward ever so slightly above his nose. His eyes are soft. His whole expression is sweetly concerned.

I shake my head. Sniff. "You're pretty, that's all."

His belly bows out on a quiet laugh. "You're the pretty one, Em. But thank you."

He's fully sheathed now. Ready to go. But I can't help running my palm up his belly, fingers moving over the smooth skin just above his hips.

Rising up onto my own knees, I move up to his ribs, his breath quickening when I brush my fingers across his nipple. His pectoral muscles tighten, making him look even bigger and firmer.

I can feel the need thrumming inside his skin. He's hot to the touch, breath coming in pants now. But still I go slowly, doing my best to savor the moment. Savor the fact that he's flesh and blood and he's *here*, and how that makes this encounter so much more intense than any I've had online.

It's more intense than any encounter I've had, ever.

Our eyes meet. He reaches up and thumbs a tear off my cheek.

"I know," he says. And then he cups my face in my hands and kisses me deeply, tenderly, the thickness of his erection pressing into my stomach. I can taste myself on his lips.

He breaks the kiss and sits on the mattress, straightening his legs. Without a word I climb onto his lap, knees straddling his hips, and taking his dick in my hand, I notch it at my center. His hands skim up my sides, thumbs flicking over my nipples as I lean my forehead against his. Our eyes lock. His breath is warm on my skin, our noses brushing when I wrap my arms around his neck.

Lowering the cradle of my hips, I sink onto his length. But then I stop, hissing when his head fully breaches my entrance.

He goes still. "Too much?"

"The angle," I pant. "It's different. I'll be okay."

In reply, he curls his arms around my waist, offering me support as I lower myself bit by bit. There's some resistance, and I feel myself stretching to accommodate him. There's a burning twinge that reminds me we've already done this once tonight, and beneath that, a calm certainty that we'll do it again.

I sink as far as I can go. Samuel's eyes on mine the whole time. For several beats, I stay there, our breaths finding a matching rhythm as I adjust to the feel of him.

It doesn't take long until I'm soaked and soft and close to coming. I start rocking my hips, little circles at first. Samuel gives me a minute or two and then he starts moving too, thrusting his hips to meet mine. We go slowly at first, and then we keep going slow. The effort not to ride him hard and fast makes sweat break out on my skin, but I can see in his eyes that he wants to savor this too.

This isn't playful sex. This is serious I'm-so-into-you sex, and even though it scares the shit out of me, it's too wonderful not to enjoy.

Silent, I watch him rise to meet his orgasm, and he watches me. Brows curving upward again, he's reaching down to thumb my clit, and that's all it takes to send me over the edge. He cries out at the same moment my pussy fists around him, and I realize we're coming together.

We cling to each other as it happens, my body pulsing with exquisite, almost brutal release.

The wave subsides and Samuel and I are left wrapped up together. Breathing hard, and falling harder.

Chapter Twenty-Seven

SAMUEL

"Let's talk," I say the next morning, handing Emma her coffee.

She looks unkempt. Mouth swollen, cheeks bright, hair everywhere.

She looks like she's just been fucked all night by someone who knows how.

I grin, my dick twitching at the memory of her sucking me off in the shower ten minutes ago. We'd ended up on the floor, tiles cold against my ass as she rode my dick with abandon. She came in two seconds and then asked me to come on her tits.

Yep. Never waking up without Emma Crawford in my bed again.

I want to shower with her. Cook for her. Eat with her. Fuck her again before lunch.

Spend time with her outside work where she's my equal. My counterpoint.

I want that, even though the idea of living with someone should terrify me, given how much I value my privacy. But with Em—

With Em, I feel calm about changing my life, and the way I think.

She's wearing the sweatshirt I gave her and nothing else. Her bare legs are muscled, strong, and sexy as hell.

And I know she's going commando. I resist the urge to reach between her legs and find out if she woke up wet again.

"Can I have my coffee first?" she asks, tipping back the mug. "This is *good*, by the way."

"Of course it is. I made it. And no, I want to talk to you now, before you have a chance to escape."

She cocks a brow. "Are you holding me prisoner?"

"Only if you want me to." I look out over the snow. We got a good six inches, and it blankets everything around us in white. The overcast sky is white too, turning the world into a quiet winter paradise. "I want you to stay."

She smiles down at her mug. "We've been over this, remember? I am staying."

"Not on the farm." I take a breath. "I want you to stay with me. Here, in my house. For good."

She swallows another sip, smoothing her tongue along her bottom lip. My gut twists. She's hesitating.

Not the response I was hoping for.

"You know why I can't," she begins.

I dip my head. "I do. You've got a lot on the line, and I recognize how much you're risking to be with me. I'm not even sure it's right to make such a huge ask of you." I search her eyes. My heart is pounding so hard I feel sick. I take a deep breath and plunge forward. "But I have to ask anyway. What we have—it's once-in-a-lifetime stuff, Em. Last night, you asked me about my dad, and what went with him when he died. And I think it was my ability to trust people. That whole situation with Olly sure as hell didn't help."

"No kidding." Emma winces. "I can only imagine."

"Guess I learned that letting people in gives them the

253

power to hurt you. And they will hurt you. So I threw up some walls, figuring I could protect myself or whatever. Which they did—the walls did work for a while. But over time, I realized that keeping people out also meant not letting anyone in. I didn't let anyone know me, and I was lonely as hell." I swallow when I see Em's eyes fill with tears. "And then I met you. You live fearlessly, and even though it took a hot minute for the message to get through my thick skull, you eventually inspired me to do the same. You're different in all the right ways. I fucking adore that about you."

Emma blinks, hard, eyelashes fluttering. "You're killing me, Samuel."

"I know," I say, managing a smirk despite the lump in my throat. "So tell me to fuck off and I'll leave you alone. You'll break my goddamn heart, but if you can't see a way for us to be together, then say the word and I'll never bring this up again. But I really do believe this is a risk worth taking. Take it with me. Please. I want to wake up with you every morning. I want to fuck you without a condom. I want to be yours, Em."

She sniffles. Shit, she's crying. I reach over and catch a tear with my thumb. My body ignites at the contact. Judging by the way Emma's breath catches, she feels it too. The spark that remains alive between us despite the very real obstacles keeping us apart.

"But how? How would we make that work? And what would it look like?"

I gently thumb her chin, urging her to look up at me. "We take it one day at a time. We communicate. We gotta be intentional about everything, even the smallest decisions. Basically, we do what we can to explore this thing between us while minimizing the impact if—"

"If shit blows up in our faces." She digs her teeth into her bottom lip. "What then?"

I tug at that lip with my thumb. "We figure it out. Look, I wish I had a better answer for you. I know I've hurt you before, but I promise to try my best to never do it again. I'm done bullshitting people, you most of all. I'm done being angry and stupid. Will it suck if things don't work out? Yeah, absolutely. But could it be amazing if they do? Fuck. *Yes.*"

She grins at that. "I don't disagree with what you're saying. And I appreciate your honesty, Samuel. Really, I do. I can't tell you how refreshing it is, you being so up front about where you're at and what you want. It's kind of the biggest turn-on ever."

I reach for her free hand and put it on my chubby. She wags her brows. I growl.

"You're killing me," I say.

"I know," she replies. Her eyes flash with heat. For half a second, I really do think she'll set her coffee down and climb me like a tree and end this conversation with a quickie fuck on the counter.

Instead, she pulls her hand away and sips her coffee, taking a beat to gather herself. When she looks back, her eyes tell a different story. One that has me feeling hopeful and scared all at once.

"But here's the thing, Samuel. I have a hell of a lot more to lose than you do. The risk we'd each be taking isn't equal. Emotionally, yes, we both risk getting burned. But think about the professional and financial side of the equation." Her eyes flick to the kitchen around us. "You don't need your job. I do."

The words are on the tip of my tongue. *What if I promise to be the one to resign if we can't make it work?*

But something stops me from saying them. That would be a tidy solution to the problem. Whatever happened, I could take the blame and quietly go away, leaving Emma to crush it as both the wine and the food director here at the resort. She could go on working. And I could—

What? What the hell would I do?

I tug a hand over my face. It's important for Emma to keep her job, and I get that. She doesn't have the financial cushion I do to weather any storms.

But this job is important to me too. In different ways, granted, but it would still hurt like hell to lose it.

"There's a way we can both win," I say, as much to myself as to Emma. "There's gotta be. If anyone can figure that out, it's us. Who's to say we can't keep our professional relationship amicable if our personal one doesn't work out?"

She cuts me a look. "You'd really want to work side by side, day in and day out, after the horrific breakup we'll inevitably have *if* it happens?"

I sip my coffee, averting my gaze. "What makes you think it'll be horrific?"

"Because. Whatever this thing between us is, it's not casual. It's not forgettable or easy or clean. You say what we have is a once-in-a-life time connection, and with that comes this...this voraciousness for each other, I guess." She pauses, searching for the right words. "Something like that just doesn't go away. You can't stop feeling those feelings on command. We'll be jealous and hurt, and seeing each other every day will crush one or both of us. You know it. I know it."

Voracious is exactly how I'd describe this feeling I have for Emma. And the fact that she wants me as fiercely as I crave her is exactly what I need to push my case.

"I want you, Em. Badly. I don't know how else to say it. I'd love for you to give me a chance, but again, I understand if it's too risky for you. You're right to say I'm voracious for you. You're right to say the fallout wouldn't be pretty." I take her hand again, only this time I twine our fingers, same as she did last night. "But how beautiful could it be if we made it work?"

Emma's fingers curl around mine. Ever the courageous one, she doesn't break eye contact. She's just thoughtfully quiet.

"Give me time to think about it," she says at last, and lets out a breath. "Part of me wonders if it's already too late to go back. Like, have we crossed the Rubicon without knowing it?"

"I don't rightly know what the Rubicon is, but I think I get what you're saying. It's possible. If you decide you don't want to pursue this...yeah, I'll be really fucking bummed. Especially after last night. And this morning. You gotta believe me when I say I didn't mean for any of this"—I flick my eyes over her bare legs—"to happen. When I stopped to help you last night, I still had every intention of keeping things professional. I just wanted to feed you, Em."

"Then I tasted your lasagna—"

"And the rest is history." I lift our joined hands and kiss her wrist. "Take all the time you need, all right? I'm not going anywhere."

She nods. "Okay. Thanks. I have a lot to process. Some loose ends I need to figure out."

I want to ask about those loose ends, but instead I think about my own.

I have to end things with Lady V. She's great, and we had our fun, but Emma's the clear winner here. I'm not gonna go after one woman while keeping another in my back pocket, just in case. I feel like that's just begging karma to deliver swift justice to my faithless ass.

If I'm gonna do this thing with Emma, I'm going all in. No second-guesses. Definitely no second choices.

I'll get in touch with V later, when I have some time to myself.

I look at Emma. "Can I ask you to stay for the rest of the day? At least until the roads are clear?"

"But the restaurant—"

"Is closed. Beau called while you were in the bathroom— no doubt your phone's lighting up now too. We'll be offering in-room service only at the main house, at least until tomorrow. Then we'll see how the weather looks. I'll make you breakfast. And I'll make you come. And then lunch maybe?"

Her laughter is a low, husky sound. Not a belly laugh, but the kind of laughter you have over drinks with friends or over an inside joke with family told for the five millionth time.

I want to make her laugh this way every morning.

"Lunch may be tough because I have to go over some inventory today—yes, I'll be using my laptop, so I won't need to go into the office." She hesitates.

I reach for her hand. "Stay. Please."

She bites her lips, and meets my eyes for a beat, then another. "Okay."

I set down my coffee and reach between her legs.

"I thought breakfast came first," she breathes.

Aw, yeah, she's wet. "You always come first, Em."

And I make good on that promise right there in the kitchen. Only this time when she's finished, Emma rewards me with a smile.

Chapter Twenty-Eight

EMMA

My overnight bag draped over my shoulder, I draw up short when I see the navy-blue BMW SUV parked in front of my cottage.

I catch a familiar pair of brown eyes in the rearview mirror. The driver's side door opens and my sister emerges, dressed in impeccable athleisure: black sneakers, black leggings, black cashmere poncho.

Really, everything about her is impeccable. Her neatly styled short blond hair. The large diamonds winking in her earlobes. The enormous Louis Vuitton tote she hauls out of the passenger seat.

I glance down at my rumpled jeans and snow boots. My unzipped bag overflows with dirty, wet clothes. This morning I brushed my teeth with my finger (I forgot to pack my toothbrush) and washed cum out of my hair.

Deep down, I don't regret any of that. But seeing how beautifully put together my sister is—how expensively neat and organized—yeah, makes me feel less than great about the hot mess express I am at the moment.

"Lindsey!" I say, trying valiantly to keep the burn creeping up my face at bay while tucking my hair behind my ears. Her timing, like her clothes, has always been impeccable. "What are you doing here?"

She flashes me a smile before pulling me into a quick, tight hug. "I wanted to surprise you with a little weekend visit! You said you were off work because of the snow, so I figured I'd take a ride up to Blue Mountain. See how things were going at this dream job you keep talking about. How gorgeous is it up here? And this cottage? So cute. How long are they letting you use it?"

My antenna goes up. Lindsey's always on, but there's something almost...frantic about her energy today.

"Hey. Hi. Were the roads okay?"

Lindsey nods at her car. "That thing's amazing in the snow. It's the tires. They're ridiculously expensive, but damn, do they work."

I feel a flicker of envy. Followed in short order by shame, because it's not the good, constructive envy I've felt about Lindsey before. "Is it new? The car?"

"Yeah. I got it as a little promotion gift to myself. Sweet, right?"

"It's beautiful. You weren't waiting long, were you? You should've called."

"Got here twenty minutes ago. Took less time getting up here than I thought."

A beat of uncomfortable silence blooms between us. My face is on fire now. I tilt my head toward the cabin. "Come on in. I, um, wasn't expecting visitors, so it may be a little messy—"

"No worries." Lindsey's eyes flick to my bag. "I hope I'm not coming at a bad time?"

I'm tired as shit, and I was really looking forward to some time alone to think about what I should do about Samuel. Because thinking about him fills me with this warm, homey, achy feeling.

But I somehow manage a smile. Lindsey and I are always so crazy busy we rarely get to hang out, especially just the two of us, and I have a feeling something's up with her. As great as my sister can be, she wouldn't just "surprise me" with an unplanned visit. Is she pregnant? Did she and Palmer buy a beach house or something?

"Lindsey, please." I move toward my front door, and she follows. "There's never a bad time for you to visit. I'm glad you're here. How about I order some food from the main house? We can eat and catch up."

"Cool if I stay the night?"

I unlock the door and hold it open. "Sure. What's Palmer up to this weekend, other than missing you?"

"He's working." She sets her bag on the kitchen island, then looks around with her hands on her hips. "Wow, Em. This is beautiful. No wonder you love it up here so much."

"Thanks. It's...yeah, insanely gorgeous. Going back to an apartment after living here is gonna suck."

Unless I go live with Samuel instead.

Twenty-four hours ago, the idea would've been ridiculous. A month ago, it would've been laughable.

But now, I'm really considering Samuel's proposition. Things have moved quickly with Samuel in a way they never have with anyone else. Is that a sign our connection really is special? Or is it just lust leading us headlong into disaster?

"What have you been drinking these days?" My sister is combing through the bottles on my counter. "Anything special I should try?"

I blink. "Now?"

Bottle of sauvignon blanc in her hands, Lindsey shrugs. "Why not? It's Saturday. Plus, it's a snow day. What else are we going to do?"

"Linds, it's not even ten o'clock. *In the morning.*"

Smiling, she starts opening cabinets, clearly in search of wineglasses. "Exactly. When was the last time you just said fuck it and did what you wanted? C'mon, have a glass with me. I can't believe I'm having to beg a sommelier to drink."

I open the cabinet above the coffee maker and pull out two white wineglasses. Someone—I have a good guess who—stocked the kitchen with several kinds of wineglasses. Big balloons for meaty reds. Slim flutes for sparkling. Dainty glasses for white wine like this one.

"Here, you open it. Corkscrew's right there beside the stove. I'm gonna go change real quick."

My mind races while I slip into leggings and a sweatshirt. Mine, not Samuel's, although he gave me his to take home because I "look really fucking good" in it.

My heart flutters. Full-on *flutters*, like I'm a middle schooler with a crush.

But beside that flutter lies a sharp edge. One my excitement keeps catching on.

What about my job? My reputation?

My future?

A part of me thinks Samuel and I could make it all work. We're dedicated enough. Passionate enough too.

We're also well seasoned. We know what it's like to live alone, and we know what we'd be giving up to live together. To think about everything we'd gain, though...

I mean, it could be pretty incredible.

But then a part of me thinks I'm just being stupid. There's no way a relationship with Samuel doesn't end badly. He's got all the power. Not only is he rich as sin, but his family literally owns the company I'm working for. *He* owns it. So while he is my coworker, he's also kinda sorta my boss. And dating your boss is dicey territory in the best of circumstances.

Hell, I'm already blushing about seeing him tomorrow at the barn. What if it gets out that Samuel and I are sleeping together, and our employees, who've known Samuel a lot longer than they've known me, start to form less than great opinions about me? It's sexist and terrible, yeah, but sometimes it's how the world works.

What if having such a giant distraction around *all the damn time* makes me fuck up my work? What if it makes me self-conscious to the point I can't perform? What if we get sick of each other? We'll be around each other day and night. Will that make the magic wear off?

And was it wrong of Samuel to make such a proposition in the first place? And if it was, why does it make me feel so damn good?

He makes me feel good. And therein lies the problem. I don't need him to feel good about myself. But being around him definitely makes me feel great. Which means not only does he have power over the future of my career, but he's got power over my feelings too. If he can make me feel good, he can also make me feel like shit. He's certainly done it before.

He could destroy me.

I don't have time to be destroyed. I have goals. Big, scary, super ambitious things I am determined to get done.

It's terrifying, knowing that committing to Samuel could mean losing all that. I could always find another job. But if I leave Blue Mountain under...well, not great circumstances, who knows if they'll give me the reference I need to land a comparable position somewhere else? Beau is a great guy, and I know he's in my corner, but Samuel is blood. That's a kind of loyalty I can't compete with. If Beau ever had to choose between the two of us, I know without a doubt whose side he'd be on.

But God, I really do like it here. A lot. I like the people, the scenery, and the food. It's a special spot, the kind of place I dreamed of landing when I first started my career in wine.

I want to have my cake and eat it too. And I get that it may not be possible with Samuel.

But with Blue? I glance at my laptop, which I left on the nightstand beside the bed last night.

With Blue, I could have both. I could fall in love and keep my job, no problem.

That's assuming a lot. Mostly that Blue and I will not only hit it off but also connect as instantly and as deeply as Samuel and I have.

I'm in deep with Samuel. That much is obvious. And the fact that I'm thinking about someone else makes me feel slimy, sure. Can I really fall for two people at the same time? Am I delusional to think anyone will come remotely close to making me feel as accepted and sexy and valued as Samuel does?

But I gotta be smart. The smart thing is to explore my options, right? Especially the option that allows me to thrive in all areas of my life without being scared shitless I'll lose everything.

I guess I just need to know.

I need to know if my connection with Blue is real, or if it's just some internet-induced fantasy that exists only inside my head.

I need to know if Samuel really is the one, or if there's someone else out there. Because if I don't explore this option, I may be leaving my perfect future on the table. One that doesn't make me sweat the way I'm sweating now.

Also, Lindsey's here. Which means I'll have someone to come with me for my meetup with Blue. If anyone will be an honest judge of a guy and his potential, it's her.

I open my laptop and fire off a message to Blue. Feeling a million different things as I type.

Tonight. Let's meet.

Weirdly enough, my phone dings with a text message less than a minute later.

Even weirder? It's Samuel, asking me if I want to come over again tonight. He's thinking about firing up his wood-burning pizza oven—because of course he has one of those—and wants to know what toppings I like.

Emma: Sounds great, but my sister just arrived. She's staying the night. Wasn't expecting her...will explain later.

Samuel: Bring her too. All are welcome

Emma: You don't know Lindsey. Rain check for Wednesday?

Samuel: Wednesday?

Emma: It's the next night I have off.

Samuel: I am not waiting until Wednesday to see you.

Emma: You'll see me tomorrow bright and early at the barn.

Samuel: So you'll let me eat your pussy there?

Emma: No.

Samuel: My point exactly. I wanna see you again. Tonight. Sneak out. Don't make me beg.

Emma: Trust me, I'd love nothing more. But I gotta hang with Lindsey.

Samuel: Okay. Can I call you later?

Emma: Sure. I can't promise I'll be able to answer, but I'll try.

Samuel: I can't stop thinking about you. I hope you have a great day with your sister.

Reading that last text, my chest aches. What do I say? That I can't stop thinking about him either, but I'm not sure I can envision a future for us that doesn't threaten the financial and professional stability I want so badly for myself? That I'm actually meeting up with another man in the hopes I can envision that future with someone else?

Emma: I miss you.

I look up at the knock on my bedroom door. "Em? Hey, Em, you all right in there? You need any help?"

I'm about to slam my laptop shut when I see a message from Blue pop up. *Tonight works. Same place, maybe an earlier time so we get out before the roads ice over again?*

I quickly type *Yes. Think you can get a 6 PM at Cucina?*

He replies right away. *Absolutely. See you then.*

"Coming!" I say.

I hop off the bed and open the door. Lindsey's standing in the kitchen, wineglass tilted back.

"You okay?" she asks.

I grab the glass she's poured for me off the counter and take a fortifying swig. "I'm great. Hey, this is gonna sound nuts. But how would you feel about coming downtown with me tonight to meet this guy I've been sexting with on the internet?"

Chapter Twenty-Nine

SAMUEL

I had hoped to work out alone today.

Mostly because I want to think about Emma. How it felt waking up next to her. The sounds she made as she demolished the dinner I made for her. The weight of her tits in my hands and the taste of her skin and the way she looks me in the eye when she's giving me head.

I also need to figure out how I'm gonna tell V that not only does the cybersex have to end, but so does the possibility of dating outside our chat room. Do I go with the old, *it's not you, it's me* thing? Because that's not entirely a lie. It really is me.

I've fallen for someone else. It happened literally overnight.

Or, really, it happened slowly, over the course of several weeks. And then, just like that after a night of incredible sex and vulnerable truths, I'm head over heels for the woman I swore I'd always hate.

I feel a little guilty leading V on, which is part of the reason I agreed to meet her tonight. That, and the fact that Emma is busy. Regardless, this is a conversation I should probably have in person. I respect V, and I really have enjoyed the time we've spent chatting. She's special, and I want to tell her that face-to-face.

I also want to personally thank her for prying me open. She's the one who first encouraged me to be honest and real. Without her, I'm not sure I would've had the courage to open up to Emma. And if that hadn't happened...

Well, I wouldn't be where I am now. Falling for an incredible woman, feeling whole and happy for the first time in forever.

Passing Daddy's trophy case, I smile. I'm one hundred percent certain he'd be proud of me. I know I'm becoming the man he raised me to be.

And that feels pretty fucking great.

But it's not so great finding my brothers already hard at work in my gym. Beau is doing leg lifts in a corner; Hank is dripping sweat while kicking the shit out of my boxing dummy, who we've *un*-affectionately nicknamed Olly.

"What the fuck are y'all doing here?" I growl, grabbing a towel from the pile beside the door and flipping it over my shoulder. "Don't you have your own damn gyms to work out in?"

"Baby's sleeping," Beau grunts.

Hank keeps one gloved hand glued to his cheek while he begins pummeling Olly's eyeless face with the other. "I was overwhelmed with shit, so I needed to blow off some steam. This weekend's been *insane*."

"So y'all came here to harass me. Great."

"Hey." Beau spears me with a look. "It's only fair, considering you're the one who's always pestering everyone else. Where the hell have you been?"

Hank stops punching Olly. "Yeah. Where have you been? No one's heard a peep from you since you left the barn yesterday."

I look at Beau. "I picked up your call this morning, didn't I?"

"I mean none of *us* have heard from you. The family. Mom thought for sure you were dead somewhere on the side of the road."

Shit, how did I forget to text Mom back?

Because I was too busy making love to Em. Right.

I make a mental note to text Mom when I'm done with my workout, and then I grab a pair of dumbbells.

"I'm alive. But if y'all don't get gone, one or both of you might not be."

"You brought someone home, didn't you?" Beau asks, grinning.

But Hank's expression is wary. "Did you, Samuel?"

Beau wouldn't be grinning if he knew who I took home. In fact, he'd probably grab those gloves from Hank and punch *my* face.

I forgot I need to iron that little detail out too. Considering what a dope he's been about the whole Annabel situation, maybe he'll have a little sympathy for my less-than-stellar decision-making when it comes to Emma.

Wait. I refuse to think opening up to Emma was a bad decision. Telling her I wanted to fuck her without a condom? Meh, maybe that's a little reckless. But I stand by my decision to tell her how I feel, and to share what I want.

At the end of the day, I just want her.

Thankfully, I'm saved from answering my brothers' questions when Beau's phone chimes loudly. He immediately stops what he's doing and digs the phone out of his pocket.

"Baby's up, and Annabel's hungry." He blanks the screen and drops the phone back into his pocket. "Gotta run. Y'all be good. Samuel, I'll give you a call later to check in on how things are going in the kitchen."

"So far, so good," I reply, already breathless from the

seven bicep curls I've done. Granted, I'm using a fuck ton of weight. But damn, maybe sex with Em is exercise enough for the day. "They're slammed with room service requests, but I called in a few favors from friends downtown—most restaurants there are closed, so their employees are available for extra work. Got two dishwashers and four sous chefs, plus a pâtissier from that bakery you love so much on Biltmore. I offered to jump on the line myself, but Chef Katie just laughed at that. So I put calls in to our suppliers to assure them the roads on the way up here are plowed. Generators are operational, and we've got plenty of dry wood for the smokers. We're making it work."

Beau pats my shoulder on his way out of the room. "Good work, brother."

My heart twists. Part pride. Part guilt. If only he knew the kind of work I was doing with our sommelier this morning.

Whatever. I'll figure out how to make Beau see the light about Emma and me. In the meantime, I just gotta get through today.

Hank and I are quiet during our workouts. Normally, that silence doesn't bother me. Hell, most times I don't even notice it. But this afternoon, it feels off. Maybe because Hank is beating the shit out of Olly, throwing punch after punch after punch. Sweat flies everywhere, and his face is bright red.

"You okay?" I ask.

He cuts me a look. "Fine."

"You're not fine. Talk to me."

"I'd rather not."

I hold up my hands. "Your call. But I'm here if you want to tell me about this girl who's bothering you."

"Who says it's a girl?" Hank wipes his forehead with the back of his gloved hand.

"I do. I haven't seen you like this"—I nod at the sweat covering the floor at his feet—"in an age."

"It's nothing." He delivers a stinging blow to Olly's left kidney. "Just a shitty situation. Love sucks."

I arch a brow. "That all you're gonna give me?"

"Yup." He goes silent again, the only noise the slap of his gloves as they meet with Olly's increasingly battered body.

"Do you want some food? I've got leftover lasagna in my fridge. And a pint of that peanut butter cup ice cream I made for Milly's birthday."

"You don't have plans for dinner?"

"I didn't say that. I'm just offering you some good shit in your time of need, that's all."

"Do you?" He pauses. "Have plans tonight?"

I narrow my eyes at him. "I do. Why?"

He starts jabbing Olly again. "No reason."

I roll my eyes. Hank isn't usually a drama queen—in fact, he's the opposite—so I'll give him a little space to figure out whatever shit he's got going on. I grab my phone and turn on a playlist, Drake blasting through the speakers in the ceiling. Determined to mind my own damn business.

But as I watch Hank pummel Olly, I can't help but feel there's something desperate about the way he punishes the dummy.

He's punishing himself.

Clearly, he's hurting over this girl. Since he won't tell me what happened, all I can gather is that she broke his heart.

That does suck. As much of a pain in the ass as my brother can be, I love him, and I want him to be happy. Now that I know how fucking great love feels, I want him to find it too.

I arrive at the restaurant twenty minutes early. I order a Manhattan and a water, and try not to chug both as I wait.

Why am I so nervous? It's not like I fell for someone else on purpose. It just happened.

Besides. Maybe this makes me sound like a dick, but V is a stranger. She'll be a stranger after we part ways tonight. It's not like I'll ever see her again.

I just have a bad feeling about this that I can't shake. Maybe that's why I finish the water and most of the Manhattan by—I check my watch—five till.

Shit. It's not even time yet. I just want to get this over with already.

Leaving the CD on the table just in case V happens to arrive while I'm gone, I dart to the bathroom, praying all the while that this goes smoothly so I can head home to talk to Emma. I haven't seen her since this morning, and I miss her. Yet another sign that what I'm about to do is the right call.

Just as I'm closing the stall door behind me, my phone rings. My stomach flips. Is it V? Did she somehow get my number?

Or is it Emma?

God, I hope it's Emma.

I dig my phone out of my pocket, furrowing my brow when I see it's Chef Katie calling.

That can't be good.

"We have a situation here," she says without preamble. "We're out of butter."

"What?" I let out an aggravated sigh. "What the fresh hell is this shit?"

"I don't know, Samuel. Could be half our suppliers are shut down. Could be we're at full capacity. Or it could be people carb loading on bread and butter in their rooms. Whatever the case, it is definitely hell."

Plucking at my closed eyes with my thumb and forefinger, I slam down the toilet cover and land heavily on top of it. "All right. Let's talk this through."

Chapter Thirty

EMMA

Despite the salt that covers the sidewalk, it's still a little slippery, especially when you're teetering on four-inch heels.

By the grace of God, and with a small assist from my sister, I make it to Cucina's door. My heart is pounding. Part exertion, part extreme nervousness.

I can't tell if I want my date with Blue to be a bust or not. If it is, I can dive headfirst into a relationship with Samuel. No what-ifs, no second-guesses.

Of course, going that route puts the stability and the success I crave in serious peril.

If my date with Blue goes well, then there's a chance I won't have to face said peril, because I can possibly be with a man I don't work with, and who doesn't have the power to destroy my future and my reputation. I don't mean to sound flippant. It's just the reality of my situation.

But then I'll have to choose between Samuel and Blue. And something tells me no matter how much is at stake, I don't want to have to put an end to the incredible connection Samuel and I share. Because last night was beautiful. It was honest and raw in all the best ways, and my heart twists at the thought of abandoning him just when he's stopped abandoning himself.

Even now, dizzy with nerves, those butterflies take flight in my stomach at the memory of his words.

You live fearlessly, and you've inspired me to do the same.

What we have is once-in-a-lifetime stuff.

I wanna be inside you without a condom.

My pussy clenches at that last one. When Samuel is real, he's really fucking sexy.

But I'm not here to see Samuel. I'm here to meet Blue. And I promised myself I'd give this date a real shot.

"You okay?" Lindsey asks. "You don't have to do this if you don't want to, Em."

I nod. "No, I'm okay. Thanks again for coming. I appreciate the moral support."

"I appreciate the chance to hang with you." She loops her arm through mine and grabs the door handle. She's been hyper all day, but every time I tried to get her to open up, she closed that shit down fast. "Ready?"

Pulling back my shoulders, I take a deep breath.

"Ready."

We step inside. A warm gust of air greets us, fragrant with the scents of rosemary and a wood-burning fire. Cucina is famous for its incredible gourmet pizzas and pasta dishes, most of which are cooked in the enormous wood-burning oven custom ordered from Italy, and I wish I was even the tiniest bit hungry because the food here is *good*.

I resist the urge to pluck at my jeans and smooth my hair. I was kinda sorta able to make the beachy wave thing happen today, so I don't want to mess it up.

"All righty. I'll be at the bar." Lindsey nods in that direction. "You know the mayday signal if you need anything."

I grin at the memory of our conversation in the car. Linds

told me to give her the finger if things went south with Blue. Because that won't be obvious or anything.

"And you give me the signal if you need me to hold back your hair. You had a lot of sauv blanc today."

Lindsey shrugs. "I'm practically pickled by this point in my life. Y'all enjoy."

She sashays to the bar, greeting the bartender with a wide smile and a fifty-dollar bill.

I turn toward the dining room. I pull the green apple out of my pocket, feeling foolish. The idea seemed cute when we were chatting about it, but now the apple just feels silly.

Whatever. Too late to go back now.

I glance around the restaurant. It's mostly empty, thanks to the weather and the early-ish hour. There's a couple of chatting at a high-top table next to the open kitchen, and a few groups dining by the steel windows at the back of the restaurant.

And then there's a guy standing beside a table in a nearby corner. My stomach dips at the vaguely familiar outline of broad biceps and broad shoulders that strain against his blue sweater.

He makes a quarter turn, and the first thing my eyes catch on is the CD case in his hand.

The second thing is his face. Straight nose, square, clean-shaven jaw, full lips. Close-cropped hair that's a shade lighter than Samuel's.

Holy shit, it's Hank.

Hank is here. In a blue sweater. Holding a CD.

Holy shit, Hank is Blue. What the fuck are the chances?

A yawning roar fills my body, gathering in my ears.

Oh God, oh God, oh *God.* This is bad.

Or is it? My mind races to figure out what the hell this actually means as the saliva thickens in my mouth.

It means I've been having cybersex with Samuel's brother.

It means I've been sharing intimate truths—and even more intimate body parts—with not one, but two Beauregard brothers. It means I'm in love with Samuel because while Hank is wonderful, we definitely don't have the same chemistry that Samuel and I do. It means I may have to crush Hank, who could in turn crush my career.

It means I'm fucked.

We are all so, so fucked. Someone's going to get hurt. Badly. If not all three of us.

Grabbing the nearby hostess stand to steady myself, I try to breathe through the panic whirling through my center.

What if Hank is cool about all this? His feelings for V could very well be casual. Maybe he'll see me and laugh, and then I'll laugh, and we can agree over drinks that the universe has a very twisted sense of humor.

But I'll have to tell him about Samuel. Or will I? What will he say? What will he say to his family? The staff?

I nearly jump at the *thunk* by my feet. Looking down, I realize I dropped the apple. I look back up to see Hank staring at me.

My pulse seizes. He's got this look in his eyes—it's hurt and adoration and anger, and I know that what's about to go down will hurt. Because he's hurting.

He's also looking at me the way Samuel did last night. His eyes sweep down my body and back up again, and when they meet mine, they burn.

My mind starts scrambling again. Hank's been so kind to me. Helpful. The way he kept looking at me during my tasting with Samuel, and the way he looked at me during my tasting with him. How he always seems to be at The Barn Door when I am. *I like you, Emma.*

Maybe that like has turned into something more.

Did he know I was V? Was he lying to me this whole time? But why?

"Emma," he says, turning fully to face me.

Yup, that's definitely Van Halen's *1984* CD in his hand.

"Hank," I reply, because I have no idea what else to say.

"It's you." He scoffs. "I knew it."

I don't feel my legs as I approach him. "You knew I was V? How? And why didn't you ever say anything?"

Hank's brow furrow. "Who's V?"

Okay, now I'm really confused. I'm also on the verge of puking. "I'm V. Which means you're Blue." I nod at the CD in his hand.

I notice there's two empty glasses on the table behind Hank.

The hurt in his gaze tightens. "Guess you could say that, yeah."

"No. I mean you're MyBoyBlue4."

His furrow deepens. "MyBoyBlue4? I don't know who that is, but it's definitely not me. Samuel's number was 4 in the pros. Mine was 22."

Bile surges up my throat. I start to shake as a sense of foreboding grips my windpipe. What is going on here?

"How long?" Hank asks. A muscle in his jaw tics. Same one as Samuel's.

"Hank, I'm really sorry, but I'm not following you. What are you doing here, and why are you holding that CD?"

"Better question: why are you meeting Samuel here for what is clearly a date"—his gaze does that sweep down my body again—"when he swore up and down y'all were just friends?"

I blink. "Samuel is here?"

"Answer the question."

"But I-I'm not meeting Samuel," I stammer, heat flooding my face.

Hank scoffs again, mouth twisting in a disbelieving smirk. "Look at the three of us, lying to each other's faces."

My cheeks burn hotter. "I'm not sure what I'm apologizing for here, Hank. But if I've hurt you in any way, I'm sorry."

"I am too." He meets my eyes and lets out a breath, his shoulders falling, then runs a hand over his hair. "Fuck it. Someone has to start telling the truth. And the truth is, I'm falling in love with you, Emma."

I just stare at him, too stunned to move. To speak.

"There's nothing sexier than a woman who knows what she's doing and knows what she wants. Watching you dominate my brother and enthrall everyone with your stories about wine and food and the meaning of life—shit, Emma, competence porn is a real thing, and damn are you it. Or maybe you have it? You embody it? Whatever. All I know is I've never seen anything like it, and I think you're incredible. You're smart. You're confident. And good gracious are you beautiful." He swallows, the sound audible in the sudden quiet of the restaurant. "It was only a matter of time before I fell for you. I knew that first day we met I was in trouble."

"Hank," I blurt. People are staring, I can feel it, but I'm too—too shocked, too terrified—to move.

The anger in Hank's gaze evaporates, just for a second. Long enough to let me know I'm giving him hope.

No. No, shit, this can't be happening.

Hank takes a step forward. "I mean every word, Emma. I know it happened fast, and I tried to stop it. Honestly, I did. You don't have to tell me how much your job at the farm means to you. I would never, ever put that in jeopardy."

"But you are," I say, and his face falls. "Hank, I need you to tell me what you're doing here."

His Adam's apple dips as he swallows again. "I followed Samuel. It's fucked up and wrong, I know that, but I also know he's been lying to me. He's never lied to me before.

Ever. So I parked outside his house and waited for him to get in his car. He drove down the mountain and I did too, and now we're both here."

I glance around the restaurant for what feels like the millionth time. "Samuel's—"

"Yeah." Hank glances around, too. "But I don't know where the hell he went."

That foreboding is full-on choking me now. I glance at the CD. "Is that his? The Van Halen album?"

"Guess so. I found it here on the table, and according to the hostess, this is where she sat him."

Oh.

Oh, oh, *oh my God in heaven*.

But really, what the fuck are the chances that Blue is Samuel and Samuel is Blue?

But oh, *oh*, the dick and the honesty and the Van Halen in the car and the number and the sub stuff and the hair color and *oh* maybe Samuel was trying on honesty as Blue because he didn't have the courage yet to try it in his real life.

Maybe being Blue with Lady V was part of what gave Samuel the courage he needed to open up to me, Emma Crawford.

Which means I was the one who helped get the ball rolling.

The whole thing is lovely and tragic. Relief sweeps through me—Blue isn't Hank, thank God—followed swiftly by fear. Guilt. Confusion. Because if Samuel is Blue, why did he float the idea of moving in together when he was still intending to meet with his cybersex partner?

Is he a player after all? What am I missing?

But nothing changes the fact that Hank just confessed he's got it bad for me.

I look at Hank, eyes filming over. What the hell do I do?

"My turn to be honest. I'm here to see a guy I met on the internet."

"MyBoyBlue," Hank replies hoarsely.

"Yes. We've been chatting for a while now, and I asked him if he wanted to try meeting offline."

His eyes light up. "So you're here to meet Blue. Not Samuel."

"Yes. But I am"—I draw a shaking breath—"I'm falling for Samuel, Hank. And now that I know they're probably the same person..."

His expression crumples, and I feel his disappointment like a bullet to the chest.

So many emotions in such a short span of time. I don't know if I'll ever recover from this.

But I'm not the one getting my heart torn out.

"Right," Hank manages. "I get it."

"I'm so sorry. I would've told you, it's just—I mean, you understand why we didn't say anything, right?" I lean forward to look in Hank's eyes. "There was too much at risk for me. And for him."

"So he's in love with you too."

I stand, and I shake. "Only Samuel can answer that, Hank."

"And only you can answer this. Why him? He was such a dick to you, Emma. I wasn't."

"You weren't." I reach up and put a hand on his chest. "Thank God for that. Thank *you* for that. Hank, you're the reason I stayed. If it wasn't for you, I'm not sure I would've survived those first couple of weeks."

That jaw muscle tics again. "But you still chose him." Hank scoffs. "Nice guys really do finish last."

"No, they don't. Samuel is a nice guy. I just had to dig a little to find him." I meet Hank's gaze. "I'm sorry I wasn't upfront about my feelings for Samuel, and I'm sorry things are such a mess because of it. I just don't feel the same about you, Hank. You're a wonderful coworker and even better friend. But that's as far as my feelings go."

He dips his head in a slow nod. "Okay then."

"It's not okay. I know that. But can we at least agree to try to sort this out together? The three of us?"

Hank hesitates. Takes a breath through his nose. Hesitates some more. His eyes flick above my head. I turn around to see what he's looking at, but I only glimpse the bar. Lindsey raises her eyebrows, sticking her thumb up. If only she knew how much of a thumbs *down* this situation is.

"Okay," Hank says at last.

"Good. Now can I give you a hug?"

He scoffs again, but this one is less angry than the others. "You can always hug me, Emma. No need to ask."

I don't need to go up on my tiptoes to hug him the way I do with Samuel. But there's something weirdly familiar about the way Hank wraps his arms around my waist and holds me against him. His body is warm and solid, and I silently ask the universe to send someone his way. Someone who deserves his unique brand of awesomeness.

I start to pull back at the same moment I hear footsteps behind me. Hank's eyes flick above my head again. The look in his gaze darkens.

"Hank? Everything okay?"

He looks back at me. A beat of charged silence passes between us.

And then, without warning, Hank ducks his head and kisses me.

"*What?*" I say against his mouth, freezing. My heart bangs loudly against my breastbone, and my blood rushes cold. The sensation is awful, like what I imagine walking barefoot through the snow would feel like—a chill so deep it burns.

There is no tenderness in this kiss. Just hurt.

I jerk backward, our lips making this terrible smacking noise as I break contact. From the corner of my eye, I see my sister launching off her barstool.

That's when the voice behind me spits out, "What the fuck?"

Chapter Thirty-One

SAMUEL

That twist in my center—it's the knife. The one I thought for sure Emma would plunge into my back the second she got the chance.

Turns out it was my brother who ended up stabbing me.

Emma's eyes go wide. *What is she doing here?* She pulls Hank's arms off her waist and opens her mouth, but he beats her to the punch.

"Now you know how it feels, *brother*."

I don't need to ask Hank what he means by that. I can tell by the hard, mean gleam in his eyes that he did it on purpose.

He wanted me to see him kissing Emma. Because I lied to him. Often, though not without remorse.

But I had my reasons. Good reasons. If he'd only let me explain—

No. This fuckwad is the one who owes me an explanation.

"What are you doing here?" I growl.

Hank's nostrils flare. "I followed you."

"What the f—"

"What else was I supposed to do? You've been lying

constantly to me. You've been checked out, mentally anyway, for weeks. When I ask how you're feeling, you shove me aside like I don't matter. I was worried."

"Jealous," I snap. "You were jealous. Don't you dare confuse the two."

I stare him down, rage ballooning inside my body down to my fingertips. His face is bright red.

I ball my hands into fists.

A blonde with Emma's chin and cheekbones appears at my elbow. "What in the world is going on?"

"I'll explain everything in a minute, Linds." Emma turns to Hank, holding the back of her hand to her mouth. "Why'd you do that? Kiss me?"

"Because he wants to hurt me," I say. "Biggest dick move in the book."

The blonde gasps. Emma grimaces.

Hank just stares me down, his shoulders starting to tremble as he takes deep breath after deep breath.

I'm trembling too. I'm not used to feeling this way. Like I'm raw inside and out, bare nerve endings breaking through my skin to deliver shock after shock of agony. The depth of the pain is staggering.

It knocks the wind out of me.

This is what Emma was talking about when she said living this way, making myself vulnerable, is hard.

"Even bigger dick move?" I ask, just barely managing not to shout. "Touching a woman without her permission. Apologize, Hank. Right fucking now."

He glances at Emma. "I'm sorry," he says gruffly. "But not gonna lie, right now I hate y'all."

"Feeling is mutual," I reply.

"Stop," Emma says. "Hank, what you did was so not okay, but I won't be the reason you guys are fighting. Let's talk this through. Hank, I know you have feelings for me—"

"He said that?" I turn to my brother. "You motherfucker. You accuse me of lying, yet you're guilty of the same sin? You literally told me you didn't have feelings for Emma. What kind of bullshit is that?"

"Your kind, actually," he replies smoothly. "I learned how to bullshit from you."

Fuck.

What the hell do I say to him? He's not wrong. But this is not the time nor the place for this conversation, and at the end of the day, it was a dick move going after Emma, knowing there was something between us.

"You know what?" I manage. "You're right. I wasn't upfront about my feelings for Emma. But there's a reason for that."

"Many reasons," Emma adds, silently imploring me to... what? Stay silent? Tell him everything?

"So do it," Hank says. "Be honest. Right now. Tell me everything, both of you." The restaurant has gone completely silent. I feel everyone's eyes on me, waiting for the next line of dialogue in this ridiculous tragicomedy we've got going on.

I clench my jaw. Lock eyes with Emma for a beat. This is not the way I wanted to tell her I love her. I wanted something better for us. Something special, a memory that'd make us smile while we shuffle our walkers through the nursing home together fifty years from now.

Welp. Leave it to me to fuck that up. But I'll do what I can to salvage the moment. I move my gaze over her body, memorizing everything about her. The set of her shoulders. The color of her jeans. Her shoes—

My hand comes down, hard, on my chest. Good news: my heart is not a hole. Bad news: I think it just stopped working.

The stilettos are even more killer in person. They're sky-high, giving Emma a good boost in height. The decoration on her heels glitters in the restaurant's low lighting, making me blink.

Emma is Lady V.

I glance up at Emma and stare. "V?"

Emma's eyes glisten. She nods.

"Wow," I say like an idiot. I laugh, a hushed sound. "Wow. Now that I'm thinking about it...the '76 Riesling you talked about, and our safe word...Jesus Christ, Em, how did I not see it sooner?"

She sniffs, offering me a watery smile. "I know, right? We're blind. Or maybe blinded by our—um, witty banter."

"My God," Hank scoffs.

I ignore him and step toward Emma.

"Baby," I say, and without thinking, I reach out and cup her face in my hand. "Please don't cry. I'll fix this, I promise. And you know I don't make promises lightly. Not anymore."

"You," she breathes, tears leaking out of her eyes left and right. They're good tears. Bad tears. I feel each one like a pinprick in my heart. "It was you all along."

"The way you dominate," I say. "The bossiness—"

"Stop," Hank says.

"Please don't," the blonde says. "I want more."

I look at Emma and nod with a slight tip of my head, giving her the lead. Her chest rises on a deep inhale.

Emma explains the whole LadyV and Blue story. "And, well." She takes a deep breath. "Now here we are. He said he'd be wearing blue, and he'd have a Van Halen CD on the table."

Hank's brows snap together. "Van Halen?"

"Inside joke," I say.

Hank's expression tenses.

"You can't make this shit up," the blonde says, slowly shaking her head.

I turn to her. "Hey, Lindsey. I'm Samuel. I'm sorry I was rude and didn't introduce myself earlier, I just—"

"Had a love triangle happening in real time." She waves me away. "I get it."

I look at Emma's tears and Hank's beet-red face, and I suddenly feel very, very tired.

For a split second, I regret it all. The good things that came my way when I let her in all outweighed by *this*. A kind of misery I couldn't fathom until it hit me like a three-hundred-pound tackle.

My brother kissed a girl I love, knowing it would piss me off. That isn't like him at all. That's not what a brother does. When I'm feeling less rage-y, we'll be having that conversation.

But for now? Yeah, so much for keeping our relationship under wraps. It's only a matter of time before news of this clusterfuck reaches Blue Mountain. And then what? Emma's concerns about her reputation will be very much warranted.

I can tell she's working through the same knotty problems in her own head. She's looking at me but not seeing, gaze hazy not with lust but with fear.

"It'll be all right," I say and grab her hand.

She gives me a look that says *I'm not so sure*.

"You." I point at Hank. "Stay the fuck away from us."

Emma startles. "Samuel—"

"This is my family, Em. I'll handle it."

She pulls her hand away from mine. "I should go."

"Emma," Hank and I say in unison.

"I need some time to think." She curls her hand around the strap of her bag on her shoulder. "C'mon, Lindsey. We'll grab something to eat on the way back to my apartment."

Her apartment. Not her cottage.

I panic. "Please. Don't do this."

She meets my eyes. "Please give me time."

"Em, if I did something—"

"We all did bad things. Really bad things, Samuel. The kind of stuff that can tear apart a family. We need to be the adults in the room so that doesn't happen. Let's all take some time to cool off, okay? We could very well end up regretting the things we say now."

Emma puts a hand on my brother's chest. "I'm begging you, Hank. Go. Go back home and, I don't know, get some rest or something. We'll talk about this in the morning, okay?"

I look at Hank. Hank looks at me.

"Okay," we say.

Hank and I watch her and her sister go, the two of us frozen to the spot like big, dumb statues.

The silence that settles between us is excruciating.

"I can't believe this shit," I say, and I grab the CD and my coat and walk out of there.

Hank is hot on my heels. He follows me out to the parking lot, footfalls heavy on the wet pavement.

"You gotta believe me when I say I tried so fucking hard not to want her. But you were so cold, and I could tell she was struggling. I only meant to help her out. And, well, you know how amazing she is."

My chest clenches. The thing is, I believe him. Mostly because I *was* cold. I *was* a jackass. Hank was there for Emma when I wasn't. And she is amazing.

My hand shakes when I put it on the handle of my car door. I press my thumb into the indent on the handle, making the locks click, then yank open the door.

"Doesn't change the fact you kissed her to hurt me." I climb inside the car.

Hank rests his hand on the top of the door and leans

against it. "No, it doesn't. But it also doesn't change the fact that you lied to me. Over and over."

"Go to hell, Hank."

I shut the door, lock it, and start the engine.

My brother is still standing there when I pull out of the lot.

Chapter Thirty-Two

EMMA

I won't be the reason your relationship with your brother falls apart.

I've seen how much you love your family, and I'm not sure you can make peace with them if I'm around.

Driving up the mountain to the farm, I run through a zillion possible lines. Whatever I end up choosing, I have to make it clear to Samuel why we can't be together.

I have to make him see why I'm leaving Blue Mountain Farm for good.

I told the guys we all needed time to cool off. But it's clear I'm bad news for the Beauregard family. And if I'm the reason they're torn apart, what's left for any of us? If the family goes down, so does the resort.

Everyone's hearts will be broken. I won't do that to Samuel, and I won't do it to the people he loves.

Tears stream down my face.

"Hey." Lindsey puts a hand on my leg. "You want me to drive?"

"I got it. Thanks, though." I sniff, wiping my nose with the sleeve of my coat. I didn't bother taking it off. Now I'm burning up, my insides churning with sorrow and shame and embarrassment.

Of course my perfect older sister was there to witness the spectacle. I can only imagine what my parents will say when she tells them I quit my dream job because I was involved in a love triangle with two of the owners who—get this—are also brothers.

"I bet that kind of shit doesn't happen at the offices of Hanock, Hanock, and Brigley," I say with a scoff.

Lindsey doesn't smile, though. Giving my leg a squeeze, she looks out the window. "It's not as exciting there, no. But believe me, there's still drama."

I wait for her to finish that thought, but she doesn't. We're quiet for the rest of the drive. My embarrassment builds to the point that I'm crawling out of my skin by the time we pull up to my cottage.

I turn off the car and let my hands fall onto my lap. Closing my eyes, I take a breath. "Okay. I gotta pack up my shit and get out of here. I'm sorry you came all this way and the day ended so horribly. How about I call up to the main house for something to go for your ride home?"

Lindsey cocks her head. "One, are you sure that's the right move? Running? And two, if you are sure, then I'll get *you* food, and I'll help you pack."

The lump in my throat softens. "You don't have to do that."

"I'm your sister. Of course I do. Now talk to me about how we went from 'oh shit two dudes are in love with me' to 'I'm leaving my dream job and my dream guy.'"

Ugh, fresh wave of tears. "One, my professional reputation was just shot to hell, and now there's no way I'll be able to build a career here at the resort."

"Why not?"

"*Because.*" I stare at her. "You of all people should understand the importance of reputation. What do you think everyone will say when they hear about what just went down? How do you think they'll see me? Lemme tell you, the first thing that pops into their heads isn't going to be 'wow, what a knowledgeable and hardworking sommelier she is.'"

"Okay, that's fair. But if you give it time—"

"I don't have time!" I burst. "You saw the way Samuel and Hank just spoke to each other. They would've never said those things before I got to the farm."

"You don't know that."

"I know they hate each other. And it's my fault."

"That's not entirely true. As a matter of fact, that's, like, ninety-nine percent *not* true. They hate each other because no one was honest about how they felt. To be fair, you weren't, either, but you had a very good reason not to be. Plus, what's going on between you and Samuel is none of Hank's business."

"*That's* not entirely true. We all work together. And Hank helped me out when Samuel wasn't."

She blinks. "All right, I'll give you that point."

"Look, whoever's at fault here, it's obvious the three of us shouldn't be working together. I'm going to make the choice easy and resign."

Lindsey raises her brows. "I think that's a mistake, Em."

I lift a shoulder. "Lindsey, this is the kind of thing that destroys families. The longer I stick around, the more that hate between Hank and Samuel is going to grow. I'm just a thorn in that family's side. The family that *employs* me. You really think this story has a happy ending?"

Lindsey just stares.

I just shake my head and scoff, looking out the windshield. "I knew this would blow up in my face. I *knew* it.

Honestly, how stupid could I be? Ten years in the business and I haven't so much as laid a finger on anyone I've worked with. I should've stuck to my guns, but instead, I let myself fall for the one guy who had the power to ruin everything. And he did. I did. I was so close to having it all..."

"Em." Her voice softens. "Your life isn't ruined. You can still have it all. If you want it, which...I don't know, I'm not sure that you *should* dream of having it all."

"That's rich, coming from you. You've had it all for as long as I can remember."

Her expression contracts. "That's not true."

"Really? Isn't that what your Instagram says? 'Hello, look at my perfect life, I have the perfect everything'?"

She cuts me a look. "You're lashing out at me. You're better than that, so stop it."

I swallow. Putting my hands on the steering wheel, I lean my chest against it, suddenly deflated. "You're right. I'm sorry. I'm being a total shithead."

"You're not a shithead. You're hurt."

"I just...I don't need a perfect life. But I do need some semblance of stability. I'd like a salary, for starters. And benefits. And regular hours. I had all that and more at Blue Mountain."

"That's fair. You can still have all that, Em. Just...don't be rash."

All these fucking tears. "I'm in love with him, Linds."

She puts a hand on my back. "Which one?"

I shouldn't laugh at that, but I do. So does she.

"Too soon," I say.

"Is it?"

"How am I gonna get over him?"

My sister purses her lips. "I'm telling you, sleep on it before you make any big decisions. Here, I'll go raid the nearest wine store, and we can hang out in your super cool cottage and get shit-faced off Chardonnay and cry our eyeballs out. Then we'll get a good night's sleep so you wake up with a clear head and a heart that doesn't hurt so much. *Then* you decide if you should leave."

I shake my head. "Samuel will come over. He'll try to convince me to stay, but I can't. In my gut, I know I have to get out of here." I take a breath through my nose and straighten. "He messes with my head, clearly. Ever since we met, I've made one disaster of a decision after another. I have to go."

Lindsey slowly nods. "Okay. If that's the way you really feel, then let's get you packed up and back home."

"Can we still get shit-faced off Chardonnay?"

"Of course," she says with a smile. "My treat. By the way, despite what my Instagram says, my life is not perfect. Far from it."

But before I can ask her what she means, she shoves open her door. "If you're worried about Samuel coming over, we should hurry."

I turned off the heat in my apartment before I left, so it's freezing when we arrive an hour later, weighed down by way too much luggage for two people.

I've never thought of my apartment as drab. It's in a building that was once a textile mill back in the twenties. It has exposed brick walls, high ceilings, and enormous steel windows that overlook the city. I've always loved it.

I still do. But the evening's low light paints everything a different shade of gray. Or maybe it's just the cloud in perpetual residence above my head that's got me feeling so down and lonely.

I'm also reminded that I'm living in a rental. Will I ever be able to afford to buy my own place? I'd love to own a home, a spot I could make my own with paint, cool fixtures, maybe even a wine closet.

Will I ever not have to sweat health insurance? And what about that retirement I want (really, need) to save for?

Cybersex. Love triangles. Wearing glittery shoes to a date that ended my career.

I have never felt more like a joke than I do now.

I look at my sister through the open bedroom door. Bless her heart, she's busy unpacking my suitcase, carefully hanging up a pencil skirt in my teeny tiny closet. Watching her, I feel a surge of gratitude. Lindsey and I were close growing up. But as adults we've grown apart. Truth be told, I haven't exactly missed her over the years.

But now I'm really glad she's here. Even if her fancy clothes and car and diamonds are a stark reminder of the stability and success I definitely do not have and probably never will.

Headlights outside the window catch my eye. My stomach flips. Then clenches when I realize Samuel has no idea where I live. It's both a relief and a crushing dose of reality.

I'm really doing this.

I'm really giving up the job and the guy and the *life* I love.

Closing my eyes against a barrage of tears, I head for the kitchen. My phone vibrates in my pocket, and my stomach flips again. I know without looking that it's Samuel. He's called a dozen times and left twice as many texts.

Where are you?
Please call me.
Can we talk?
I'm so fucking sorry.
I can't stop thinking about you.
I hope you're okay.

Just thinking about them opens the floodgates all over again. I texted him earlier, telling him that I was all right but that I needed time.

I know what I'm going to do. I just need to figure out what I'm going to say. My argument has to be watertight. And because Samuel is Samuel, he's going to give me a lot of push-back, so I need to be prepared.

But I also know that Samuel is hurting right now. Badly. And I'm only hurting him more by not answering his calls.

Against my better judgment, I finally pick up the phone.

"Hey."

"Em." He lets out a breath. "Thank God, you answered. Where the fuck are you?"

The gravelly timbre of his voice makes my skin break out in goose bumps.

"You sound like hell," I say.

"I am in hell. Where are you?"

"I came home."

Silence.

"You left the farm?"

"I told you, I needed space."

"You said you needed time. It's been two hours. Can I come to you?"

"No. Not right now."

More silence. Then in barely a whisper, "How are you feeling?"

"Terrible. You?"

"Same."

"For a second, I found myself wishing I had a chat date with MyBoyBlue. He always made me feel better."

"Funny, but Lady V had the same talent. I still can't believe it was you."

"I still can't believe I didn't figure out that *you* were Blue sooner."

"Maybe we didn't want to see the signs. Maybe we needed a simple escape when our real lives got complicated. It was a good kind of complicated, though. Still is."

"I beg to differ."

"What can I do? To fix this?"

I close my eyes. "Samuel, I don't think it can be fixed."

"I beg to differ."

"Don't do that."

"Do what?"

"Throw my lines back at me."

"Why? 'Cause it reminds you how fucking perfect we are for each other?"

"It doesn't matter if we're perfect for each other if being together means hurting the people we love and burning down our lives. I didn't want to do this tonight, but...Samuel, you need to focus on your family. And I need to focus on...me."

"What? Em, no. Please don't."

I want to cry, but I steel my spine instead. "This is my two weeks' notice. I think we all know y'all are better off without me. I just witnessed firsthand how much hurt I've caused you and your family. I also saw firsthand how much family means to you. I won't mess with the special thing y'all have going on up at Blue Mountain. Also, let's be real—the chances of me building a career there went up in smoke the second I walked into the restaurant tonight. That spectacle? Samuel, everyone's going to know about it if they don't already. I've worked too hard to live under a cloud of rumor and judgment and so have you. One of us needs to go, and it makes the most sense that it's me."

Several beats of awful, bottomless silence fill a handful of heartbeats. I grab the nearest bottle of wine—an Arneis, perfect—and, tucking my phone between my ear and shoulder, try to dig my thumbnail inside the foil.

"You're resigning," he says.

"I am."

"Well, too damn bad because I don't accept your resignation."

I sigh. "This is exactly why I didn't want to talk to you until—"

"Until what, Em?"

"Until I was ready. But I guess I'll never be ready to leave you, so now's as good a time as any." I glance over my shoulder and find Lindsey a few steps behind me, arms crossed, expression serious. "Hey, I gotta go. I asked for time, and I need you to respect that. We'll work out the details of my transition at the restaurant tomorrow, okay?"

"I'm begging you, baby, don't shut down on me. Don't I have a say in this?"

I hand Lindsey the bottle and close my eyes. "I'm sorry, but my decision is final. It's better this way. I'll call Beau when I hang up with you."

"Let me tell him. Please. I need to be the one who explains…everything. When I'm done I'll let you know so you can give him a call. Sound good?"

"Okay. I'll see you tomorrow, then."

"Em?"

"Yeah?"

"I'm not letting you go without a fight."

I curl my fingers around the edge of the countertop, pressing the pads of my fingertips into the granite until they turn white. "Samuel, I already left."

The silence that follows makes me want to die.

"Whatever happens," he says at last, "I want you to know that I loved you before I found out you were V, and I love you now, and I'm pretty damn sure I always will love you, Emma Crawford. Because of you, I found myself again. I'm proud of who I am now. I like who I am. I'm focused on the right things, and that's because I met you. You're magic." He clears his throat. "The time we've spent together has been fucking magical, baby, and I hope you'll at least never regret that because you changed my life. Good night."

Jesus Christ, I can barely breathe.

"Night, Samuel."

Chapter *Thirty-Three*

SAMUEL

"I should fire your ass."

I meet Beau's gaze across his kitchen table. He's in sweatpants and a T-shirt, and he's got a snoozing Maisie curled into the crook of his arm. Clearly, he was on his way to bed when I barged into his house half an hour ago.

It's no surprise he's looking at me with daggers in his eyes.

I clear my throat, praying my words don't catch on the lump there. "I'll save you the trouble. I'm resigning."

Beau rolls his eyes. "Dude, now is not the time for jokes, okay? I'm tired as fuck, and Bel—"

"Is impatiently waiting for you in bed," she calls from the bedroom. "I may or may not be wearing pajamas."

I let out a silent sigh of relief at the much-needed humor warming Bel's voice.

"For shame, y'all, there's a baby present," I say, loud enough for her to hear across the family room.

"There won't be when Maisie goes to bed." Beau glowers at me. "Which won't happen until you get the fuck out of my house. If you wake up in hell tomorrow, you'll know who killed you. Hint: it was me. I shot you right between the eyes because you did exactly what I told you not to do and slept with Emma. Only the sommelier I've been trying to hire for two fucking years. The one woman who can not only expand our wine program, but who can take it to the next level. Take the entire resort to the next level and put us in a class of our own. Goddammit, Samuel, I could wring your neck."

My entire being burns with shame. I will the floor to open and swallow me in a single gulp.

"I knew it," Annabel yells. "Samuel, from the moment I saw you and Emma together, I knew y'all were trouble."

"I should've seen it. Maybe I did see it, but I was otherwise occupied." He looks down at Maisie and smiles, then looks up at me and scowls. "You should go."

I dig the letter out of my jacket pocket and slide it across the table. "I'm serious, Beau. This is my letter of resignation, effective immediately. I've included my recommendation for my replacement."

"I'm not dealing with your bullshit right now."

"I'm not bullshitting." I nod at the letter. "Open it."

"Jesus Christ," he mutters, grabbing the paper. He scans it, eyes going wide. "Holy shit, Samuel. Just—holy shit."

"Told you I'm serious."

"But the cellar. The staff. No one can shut up about how great your little scone and martini breakfast icebreaker thing was. Brother, you were just hitting your stride."

I flatten my hands on the table to keep them from shaking. I'm scared as fuck, but I'm going in anyway.

After I got off the phone with Emma, I didn't hesitate. I knew exactly what I had to do.

It means leveling everything I've worked for. Everything that's kept me sane since my retirement. But I will not see Emma lose her shot at happiness on my account.

It hurts like hell, giving it all up. But I'd like to think it's what Daddy would do.

I'd like to think I'm making him proud.

"I hit my stride because I had Emma working beside me. Now that she's gone—"

"Wait." Beau stares at me. "Don't tell me Emma is resigning, too? I thought you said you wanted her as your replacement!"

I swallow. "She's gonna try. To quit, I mean. But you can't let her. Emma, Hank, and I—the three of us shouldn't be working together. Someone has to go, and of course she was the first to volunteer."

"Such a Katniss move," Bel calls.

I pull my brows together. "Who's Katniss, and why do I have a feeling she has something to do with that sparkly vampire guy?"

"Clearly, you need to brush up on your YA love triangles. Anyway—I could wring all y'alls' necks right now. I'm not accepting this." He tosses the letter back at me. It flutters awkwardly through the air, landing somewhere on the floor next to his chair.

"Too bad. I'm not working for Blue Mountain Farm anymore."

Beau lets out an aggravated sigh. "Why can't the three of you work together? You're adults. Y'all just need to swallow your pride and get over your damn selves."

I dip my head. "That's exactly what I'm trying to do here. But there's a lot of hurt feelings involved—"

"Have you talked to Hank? Reached out to him?"

My chest tightens. "No."

"You need to figure that shit out."

"He's the one who kissed my girl."

Beau narrows his eyes at me. "You showed your ass when Emma got here. Now he's showing his when she leaves. Really, you're both at fault, and you both have shit to atone for."

"Maybe," I sniff. "Maybe not. Either way, I don't trust myself to talk to him without it ending bloody."

"What? Who do you think you are, Jax Teller? This isn't a motorcycle club. This is a *family*. And I won't see it come apart on my watch. Make things right with Hank, you hear? I'm telling you as a boss, but first and foremost, I'm telling you as a brother. We've all come too far and been through too much shit to give up on each other now. Besides, what do you think is gonna happen after you resign? Will you really never talk to Hank again? Are you going to skip Sunday supper from now until forever so y'all don't have to see each other? The problem is still gonna be there, Samuel, whether you leave or not. Find Hank and talk to him. Right now. Walk out that door"—he nods in the direction of his foyer—"find your brother, and make this right. Don't freeze him out until you've heard his side of the story."

By the way my gut seizes, I know that's exactly what I should do. I *should* let Hank explain himself. I *should* at least attempt to make things right. The thought of missing out on a single Sunday supper, much less all of them from now on, makes me short of breath.

But my anger is the only thing keeping me from drowning in my pain. Anger is easy.

Forgiveness is not.

I know it makes me a hypocrite, asking Emma to forgive me for being a bonehead while refusing to forgive Hank for the same sin.

Then again, he was more than a bonehead. He was malicious. He knows my history, which means he definitely knows how painful his betrayal would be.

He knew exactly where to sink his dagger to hurt me most. So yeah. If Hank wants to come to me, I'll talk. But I won't be the one extending the olive branch. That's up to him.

"Let me figure out things with Emma first, okay? Then... yeah, we'll see what happens with Hank."

Beau rises with a groan. "Don't you play that game with me, Samuel Joseph."

"You know, using my middle name to get me to listen only works when Mama does it."

"You don't figure your shit out, I'll get Mama to kick your ass. How about that?"

"You wouldn't dare."

He points at the door. "Oh, I would. Now get gone so I can put this nugget to bed."

"I'm sorry," I say, running a hand over my face. "I really am, for being such a douchebag to Emma in the beginning. I thought you didn't trust me to handle everything. The food and the wine programs."

That gives Beau pause. He frowns. "Of course I trusted you. This—right now—it's the first time I've ever questioned that."

The knife twists.

Aw, fuck.

I don't know what to do with myself when I get home.

Usually I'd check my email. Fire off some calls about John and Celeste's big wedding, which is next weekend.

But I'm unemployed now, and not exactly in my right mind, so no point in doing that.

Usually I'd decant a bottle of something good. The cellar really is my happy place. But now wine just reminds me of Emma.

God, if only she were here right now—

We'd be in the kitchen. She's sitting at the island, glass of Amarone in front of her as she watches me cook at the stove.

I'm making comfort food, maybe breakfast for dinner? Eggs Benedict, Southern style, with fried green tomatoes, grit cakes, and Mama's creamed collards. Homemade hollandaise and a side of crispy sweet potatoes.

The fire's going, and Emma's smiling, and everything is warm and cozy as it should be. We'd eat, then we'd fuck. The kind of sex that takes all night and leaves you shaking.

Instead, I'm standing in my dark kitchen alone, starving but feeling too sick to eat. I put my hand on the countertop. The marble is cold to the touch, and I start to shake for a different reason.

I can't.

I can't face the fucking enormity of what I'm feeling. The truth is killing me now, and if I don't stop it, I'm afraid it's just gonna leave my mangled body for dead.

The gym. Yeah. Maybe that'll help. Always clears my head, and I need to come up with a plan for how to clean up this mess.

I throw on some shorts. Don't bother with a shirt. I head downstairs to the basement. The trophy case is usually lit up, but tonight, I'm glad it's dark down here. I can't look at that stuff right now.

I blast music while I push my limits on one machine after another. I put on the TV. I even talk to myself in the mirror like a lunatic. But it's still too quiet. Nothing drowns out the voice in my head telling me I'm being a fuckwad. Not the sweat dripping in my eyes or the pounding of my heart or the acute burn in my muscles.

Nothing makes me miss my girl any less.

I was annoyed my brothers showed up the other day. But now I miss them. I need someone to talk to, but they all kinda hate me right now, and I hate them right back. It's a disaster, and I don't know how to fix it.

One problem at a time. I'll figure out how to get Emma back on the farm and go from there.

Emma is V. I still can't believe it.

I want her. So badly.

I love her, deeply.

I love being the beta to her alpha.

I love her courage.

I love her adventurousness. I want to be her bastard forever and always.

But we fucked up and now I'm alone in my gym, and I'm worried sick I've done things and said things I can never take back or make amends for.

I have to get her back.

An hour and a half later, I'm still shaking, but I'm hoping I've exhausted myself to the point that I can get some sleep.

My sister calls. I ignore it. Rhett calls, and I ignore him too. Even Annabel sends me a text, asking if I'm okay, but I don't respond. I tell myself it's because I need to focus on Emma. Then I'll deal with my fucking family.

But deep down I know I'm just hanging on to my rage for dear life.

I get in bed and wait for sleep to come. It doesn't. I lie there, the silence so loud it screams.

I'm right back where I started.

Alone.

Chapter Thirty-Four

EMMA

The next day is bright and warm. Springtime in the North Carolina mountains, where seventy-degree days follow freak snowstorms, and no one bats an eye.

I'm surprised when Lindsey says she'll stay another night.

"But don't you have to work?" I ask, trying valiantly to choke down some cereal. It's the only thing I have in the house for breakfast, and it's stale.

But even if it were Samuel's lemon scones, I don't think I'd be able to eat. I'm nauseous to the point that I wonder if I'll be able to make the drive up to Blue Mountain without puking.

"I took a few days off to celebrate my promotion." She tips back her mug. "Needed to charge my batteries before I dive back in, you know?"

I feel a prick of envy, and not the good kind, either. My sister is taking time off to celebrate moving up in her world, while here I am, free-falling through mine. It's only a matter of time before I hit rock bottom.

Still, I try my best to put on a brave face.

"Good for you," I say thickly. "I'll try to get off as early as I can. I'll bring home some dinner."

"I got dinner. I'll make us something good, okay?" She reaches across the sofa and gives my arm a squeeze. "You got this, Em. It only gets better from here."

I get in the car and blink back tears. I'm nervous about telling the staff I'm quitting. I'm really nervous about running into Hank.

Most of all, I'm nervous about seeing Samuel.

But crying isn't going to fix my problems. So on the drive up to the farm, I manage not to puke and come up with a plan instead. I make a mental list of people I can call: former managers and restaurant group heads. My friends at the big box wine store in West Jefferson—maybe I can land there while I figure out my next move. Fellow sommeliers at the top restaurant and wine spots downtown.

Do I want to stay in Asheville, though? I've lived in the mountains for more than a decade. I've lived in the Carolinas my whole life. I love it here.

But maybe it's time for a change. Nashville has a booming hospitality scene. There's always Charleston too. Would it be wrong if I gave Elijah Jackson a call? I could ask Beau if he'd be cool with it.

The freefall happens inside my chest too, when I think about that being the last conversation I have with Beau.

How many more times will I get to drive through the resort's front gate?

The snow's melted, except for a few spots in the shade beneath trees and the hollows of hills. Everything is suddenly vibrant green, the sky wide open and clear, a shade of blue so intense it makes your heart turn over to look at it.

The farm glitters beneath the springtime sun. I crack my windows, the smells of grass and earth filling my lungs. Horses in the field to my right toss their manes. Chef Katie's line cooks are in the enormous garden to my left, baskets on their hips as they gather whatever produce wasn't squashed by the late spring snow. I wonder what alterations Chef has had to make to tonight's menu. Did the asparagus make it? If not, what is she subbing in the agnolotti? That Tuscan kale, maybe?

Oooooh, if that's the case, then that spicy Napa Valley Cabernet Franc would be *perfect* with it.

I'm gripped by sharp-edged longing. I love my job here.

I love it here, period. So much.

But I can't stay. If it was meant to be, it would've worked out, right?

I want to turn around when the barn comes into view. I may love my job, but I do not love the idea of facing the mess I've made. Still, I park in the lot behind the restaurant and march through the door, determined to show up anyway. If I only have two weeks left, I'm going to try to enjoy them. A tall order, considering I'll have to see the man I love but can't have every damn day.

Still, I have to try.

Guests are eager to escape their rooms after being cooped up, so we're slammed right from the get-go. It's a nice distraction, but my heart is lodged somewhere in my throat as I wait to run into Samuel or Hank or any Beauregard, really.

I'm distracted to the point that I can barely function. I drop a tray carrying a bottle of Pinot Grigio and four glasses. The shatter brings the noise in the restaurant to a temporary standstill as everyone stares. I mix up a Chardonnay and a Sauv blanc I have chilling at the wait station and end up serving two tables the wrong wines. It's not the end of the world, but when the bottle of Chardonnay you're serving costs upward of two hundred dollars, your customers aren't going to be very happy.

I totally bungle not one but two tickets. I get well-deserved side-eye from Chef Katie when I pick up a hot plate without a towel and burn my hand.

I'm a mess, and it's embarrassing. Also embarrassing? The way I catch staff looking at me every so often. It's obvious they know something's up. Makes me wonder how much they know. Are they looking because I'm fucking up? Or are they looking because I fucked my co-director?

Brunch service passes, then lunch. Dinner's around the corner, but Samuel is still nowhere to be found.

At quarter till five he walks in. He's wearing a suit, as usual, but this one is alarmingly subdued for him. It's black, no pinstripes, no pocket square. His simple white button-down is open at the neck.

His eyes find mine across the restaurant, and I'm hit by a tidal wave of emotion.

He is so fucking handsome. And he looks so distraught. His eyes are red, and his scruff is scruffier than usual, like he hasn't shaved in a day or two. The naked hurt in his gaze has me putting a hand on my chest to keep my heart inside its proper cavity.

He immediately comes to me.

"Hi," he says.

I smell his skin and want to cry. "Hey."

"My office? Just for a minute."

"Sure."

I trail him upstairs. A few pairs of eyes follow us. My face burns.

Samuel closes the door behind me and moves to stand at his desk. I stay put by the door. Not wanting to stay but not wanting to go, either.

"I've resigned," he says.

I startle, my heart falling. "But you can't!"

"I did. Effective immediately. You're my replacement."

Dizzy, my hand moves to my stomach. I try to breathe

through the shock roiling my gut. "I can't replace you if I've resigned too."

"You said one of us has to go. It's not gonna be you. I have no idea what the fuck is going on with Hank, and quite frankly, I don't care. So that leaves me." His eyes soften. "We need you, Emma. The farm's gotta move forward, and you're the only one who's up to the task. That much has become clear."

I'm blinking back tears, wondering what in the world is happening. Wondering when the hell I'm going to stop crying. I was so good at managing my emotions before I met Samuel. I had control over the people in my life and how they made me feel.

But ever since he came into my life, my feelings are a runaway train. It's terrifying.

"But the staff," I say. "Our reputation—"

"If I'm gone, they'll forget. Out of sight, out of mind kind of thing. Y'all can work together to push this program to heights even Beau hasn't dreamed of. Em, this job—it was meant for you. You love it. It lights you up. It gives you what you want, so take it. I'm begging you."

I close my eyes and just breathe. Because that's all I can manage at the moment.

"But what will you do?" I say.

"Don't worry about me. I'll be fine. No, that's a lie, I won't be fine. Not until I know you're okay." He curls his hand into a fist and sets it, knuckles down, on the desk. "Right now, I'm not going to ask you to take me back. That's not what this conversation is about. But I meant it when I said I'm going to fight for you. Being in my bed alone without you—I couldn't sleep. I can't eat."

Opening my eyes, I draw a trembling breath. "Sounds familiar. But how are you going to put your family back together if I'm here?"

"Let me figure that out. It may take some time, but my family and I have been through tough shit before. We made it out alive, and we can do it again."

"Have you spoken to Hank since—"

"I haven't." His expression falls. "I'm not ready yet. You said you need time, and maybe I need that too. Time to let my relationship with my brother heal."

I shake my head. I'm watching the damage to Samuel's family happen in real time. I've already caused too much hurt. The sooner I leave, the sooner Samuel and Hank can reconcile, and the sooner they can all move on.

"I'm sorry. I can't accept your offer."

Then I turn and go before Samuel can convince me to stay.

I walk into my apartment and immediately stop in my tracks.

Lindsey is spread out on my sofa, an enormous, half-eaten pepperoni pizza in a box on the coffee table in front of her. She's got a glass of white wine in one hand and the remains of a slice in the other. Her hair is in a messy knot at the top of her head, and she's wearing leggings with one of my oversized sweatshirts. Mascara is smeared in blue-black halos around her eyes, making them look like two burn holes in a sheet.

Paul Hollywood is eviscerating some poor redhead's raspberry pavlova on TV. *The Great British Bakeoff?* Really? Last we talked, Linds and Palmer "don't have time to watch TV." Much less something light and fluffy like *GBB*.

"Lindsey?" I say slowly, my heart beginning to pound. "What's going on?"

She doesn't look at me. Just rips off a chunk of pizza and says, "Tried to cook. Couldn't. Sorry."

"I mean what's going on with you?" I gesture at her

disheveled person. "I've never seen you wear a sweatshirt. I've *never* seen you eat carbs. Did someone die?"

I mean it as a joke, but the hurt I see in Lindsey's eyes when she finally meets my gaze makes *me* want to die.

"How'd it go today?" she asks.

"It sucked. Tell me what's wrong, Lindsey, or I'm going to call Palmer and have him explain why you're having a mental breakdown on my couch."

Lindsey's face crumples. Panic unfurls inside my stomach.

"Palmer is leaving me," she says. She leans forward and drops what's left of her slice back into the box. Then she covers her face with her hand and starts to sob, shoulders shaking.

"Linds." I sink onto the sofa and wrap an arm around her shoulders. "Oh my God. I'm so sorry."

"He"—sob—"fell in love with our CrossFit coach."

I blink in shock and reach for a napkin on the coffee table, offering it to her. "Fucking CrossFit."

"I know," she scoffs, and takes the napkin and wipes her nose with it. "Came out of nowhere. I was totally blindsided."

"What in the world happened?"

Lindsey folds the napkin in half, then in quarters. Her face crumples again. "Shit, that's a lie. I'm lying, Em, I don't know why, I just...I'm sorry. Let me start over." She takes a deep breath. "Things with Palmer haven't been great for a while now. If I'm being honest, our marriage was off to a rocky start from the beginning. We were so perfect on paper, but in reality, we didn't have a lot to connect over, you know?"

I grab a napkin for myself. I'm crying now too. It's the surprise. The pain of seeing my sister hurt so much.

"I don't know, actually," I say, carefully picking my words. "Y'all were a picture of perfection from the second y'all met. You were both successful. Beautiful. You took these incredible trips and had this, like, insane wedding that was the most fun party I've ever been to. When I saw the two of you together, you seemed to always be smiling and happy. You were definitely always smiling for the camera, even when you were doing your workout of the day together. Hashtag WOD, hashtag the couple that slays together stays together."

"Hey. I work hard in the gym. There's nothing wrong with being proud of that."

I squeeze her shoulder. "You're right. I'm sorry. I don't mean to poke fun. Guess a part of me is jealous you have the time and money to do that stuff."

"No, you're right." She takes another breath. "The hashtags were obnoxious. Hell, my whole feed is obnoxious. But what was I supposed to post? 'Hey, Palmer and I are at a five-star resort in Vietnam, but we haven't talked in two days'? Or, 'hey, Palmer and I just burned eight hundred calories at the gym, but no matter how hard I try, he never looks at me the way he looks at Coach Cindy'?"

"Aw." I hand Lindsey another napkin. "Aw, Linds, that's fucking awful."

She puts her elbows on her knees and leans forward, nodding. "It's such a cliché, showing the world a highlight reel when the reality is a total dumpster fire. But the pressure to be perfect, and to be happy—it's real, Emma. I mean, don't you feel like there's no space for the messy parts of life? To show them and to actually live them? It's like, hey, shit's not great in my life right now, but I'm gonna sweep it under the rug and paste on a smile and snap a picture, and maybe if I keep doing that, the reality will finally start to look like the highlight."

"But it doesn't," I say. "The disconnect only grows."

Lindsey grabs her wine and gulps it. "Yup. You're a much smarter cookie than I ever was—"

"Hey, you're the one with the Ivy League degree."

"And you're the one with a sensitivity for bullshit. Your

own and others' too. So, yeah, you've always known that's magical thinking—believing that if you just try hard enough, you can be as perfect as your Instagram feed says you are. But I guess I had to learn that lesson the hard way." She refills her glass with a hand that shakes. "Palmer loved CrossFit. I hated it, but I did it because I wanted to have a shared hobby or whatever. And I hate my job, but I wanted us to be in the same profession so we'd always have that to talk about. Because we didn't really have much else in common other than that."

"What?" I widen my eyes. "You hate your job?"

"Em, I work eighty-hour weeks putting together prospectuses for structured product deals. Of course I hate my job."

"What the hell is a structured product?"

"Trust me, you'd fall asleep long before I finished explaining that. But it's boring, draining, never-ending work, and I fucking *hate* it. So, yeah. Now I'm alone, with a job I hate and a dream house I have to sell, and I just want to quit it all." She laughs, the sound hard and unhappy. "I just might."

"But you have it all. You're the dream, Linds. The success story."

Lindsey looks me in the eye for the first time since the conversation started. "If living a lie is the dream, then I want no part of it."

"Wow." I give myself a minute to let her words sink in. "Just...wow."

"Look. If my life falling apart has taught me one thing, it's that perfection is a Ponzi scheme. You rob yourself again and again of the truth so you can show the world something pretty but fake. The more you do it, the worse you feel. But the world tells us if we just keep trying, if we just get that trip or that ring or that dollar amount in our bank account, we'll get to the top of the pyramid where pretty is finally real, and it will finally make us happy. So we keep stacking the bullshit blocks, ignoring the voice inside us that screams *wrong* over and over again. When I finally listened to that voice"—she draws a shaky breath—"it was too late."

"My God." I swallow, hard. "That metaphor is beautiful. And awful."

"No shit. My life feels like one giant joke. Only the joke's on me."

I lace my fingers through hers. "I know exactly what you mean."

"What?" She arches a brow. "You think you're a joke?"

"Everything about me is a joke. My profession. My love life. My future."

She sets down her wineglass on the table and turns on the couch to look at me, folding her legs underneath her. She takes both my hands and looks me in the eye. "Listen to me, Em. And listen carefully. Have you ever considered it's our world that's a joke and not you? You left a lucrative future in law to follow your dreams. Not our family's dreams, *your* dreams. Look at me. I don't even know what my dreams are. I've spent my whole life trying to become what the world told me I should be. According to that world's rules, yeah, I was successful. My social media feed was perfect. But now I'm fucked. I'm going to lose most of my money in this divorce. All the partners at my firm are friendly with Palmer and have worked with him in the past, so God knows what they'll think of me now. Mom and Dad are going to be devastated. But more than that, I've wasted whole *decades* of my life doing things I hate with people who aren't my people. If that's not a joke..."

"Well, I haven't been happy all the time, either."

"No one's happy all the time. If they are, they aren't telling themselves the truth. I mean, what if success looks less like a highlight reel and more like a life you don't have to share with the world to feel good about it?" She searches my face. "I don't want perfect anymore. I want real. I want what you have with Samuel."

I'm so startled I start to cry all over again. "What? Why would you *ever* want the hot mess that we are?"

"Because," she says softly, "you took a risk last night that, if I understand it correctly, was extremely brave. The connection you have with Samuel is inconvenient and scary, but it's real. Samuel is in love with you, and if he wasn't, this wouldn't have accelerated the way it has. Take it from me—that sort of connection I picked up on in the space of, what, ten minutes between you and Samuel doesn't happen very often. It's worth another act of bravery. Another leap of faith. It's worth risking everything for. Even your job. Because at the end of the day, it's not a job that makes us happy. It's relationships. It's our people, the ones who love us for who we really are."

I let that sink in for a minute. Lindsey's right, of course. If I didn't know that deep down, the burning sincerity in her eyes would convince me. But the reminder makes me feel mushy inside nonetheless.

It softens the shell that's formed around my heart.

"But what about Samuel's people?" I manage around the lump in my throat. "He loves his family, Lindsey. Like, *loves* them, more than anything. And I messed that up. I'm the wedge that came between Samuel and Hank."

She offers me a small smile. "No offense, but if the Beauregards are as tight as you say they are, I don't think your accidental love triangle situation is going to bring them down. Mistakes were made, sure. People were hurt. But I think you're only going to end up hurting them more if you leave. Ever consider you might be more of a bridge than a wedge? What if this was always meant to happen, and Samuel and Hank were supposed to have this falling out so their relationship could become better and stronger and more true, the way it was always meant to be? Because it doesn't sound like they're very honest with each other. Maybe you were the nudge they needed."

I feel the tiniest twinge of relief, and I let out a soft laugh. "What are you, a lawyer or something?"

"Meh. Not anymore, I don't think."

"But I fucked up so bad tonight, Linds. Isn't that, I don't know, exhibit A of why working with the man I love a bad idea?"

She shakes her head. "I don't think so. One, y'all are extra-ordinarily upset right now, so of course you're going to fuck up. And two, who knows what the future will bring? If the resort is expanding like you said it is, then maybe you guys will evolve into new roles. Ones that don't require you to work side by side seven days a week. Maybe you don't have a dream scenario right now, but you could down the line. And even if it's a dream, it still won't be perfect. Which isn't a bad thing, because even perfect stories can have bad endings."

She's right. Again. I keep waiting for just the right posi-tion at just the right place with just the right pay, benefits, coworkers, hours...and while I don't think I should ever stop working toward a better situation, I do need to accept that it won't ever be perfect, and that's okay.

I guess a part of me always believed if I landed a top job, I'll finally be enough. I'll make enough money and have enough stability to not be considered a joke anymore. That I'd make my parents proud the way Lindsey always does.

When really, I wasn't a joke all along. I was just a woman working toward what her heart told her would make her happy.

I still am that woman. And I'm proud of myself for following my heart, even if most people don't understand it.

But Samuel does understand. He appreciates it too. And that, more than anything else, is real and right.

"Just think on it, okay?" she asks. "I wouldn't be a good

sister if I let you just walk away from something that's clearly so special. Have faith in yourself, and have faith in Samuel to make things right with Hank. Y'all know what you need to do. It's just a matter of whether you have the courage to do it." She gives me a tight smile, then whispers, "Spoiler alert, I think you do."

Chapter Thirty-Five

SAMUEL

I open the door to find Hank and Milly on my doorstep.

"I'm here to mediate," she explains before I can politely but firmly ask her to leave. She holds up a silver flask, monogrammed with her initials. "I also brought celebratory whiskey for when y'all make up. Which is going to happen."

I roll my eyes and step aside to let them in. "Are you here to mediate or meddle?"

"Both." She offers me a shit-eating grin. "You're welcome."

I catch Hank's gaze as he moves over the threshold. He looks as tired and anxious as I feel. I haven't slept much, and I've eaten even less.

Can't remember the last time I felt this bad. Actually, I can, and I do not want to go there.

My first impulse is to stoke the anger churning in my gut. Anger toughens my outer shell. It's armor that keeps me safe from scarier feelings, like sadness and pain.

But isn't armor ultimately bullshit? It can't protect me from myself. It certainly can't protect me from the fallout of breaking my family apart by not letting my brother in.

The idea that I can choose to set my armor aside makes me feel soft and strong and scared.

I think about what Emma said the day after Sunday supper. *Your family is great. I'd kill to have that kind of relationship with mine. You know that's rare, right?*

I know Hank and I aren't going to forgive each other right away. But I guess we gotta start somewhere. I hate Milly for taking the first step, but I'm also grateful she's forcing our hand.

"Screened-in porch," I say, pointing toward the back of the house. "I got the fire goin'."

I let Milly have the chair closest to the fire. It's definitely springtime here on Blue Mountain, but it's still a little chilly in the shade. Hank and I take opposite ends of the sofa across from her. For a second, no one says anything, and my chest tightens.

If I can't make this better, I really will have lost it all. My girl, my brother. My job.

Again, my instinct is to let anger win out. I'm no saint, I own that, but Hank definitely committed the greater sin. He should be the one to start the conversation.

But he doesn't. Instead, he stares into the fire, his hand on the ankle resting on his knee.

Milly clears her throat. "Okay then. We're gonna do this in reverse and start with the drinks. Maybe that'll get y'all talking."

She unscrews the cap and tips back the flask. In true Milly style, she doesn't so much as blink at the bite of the whiskey. I smile. My sister may be the South's preeminent wedding planner, but she's a country girl at heart. She can drink even the biggest of us under the table, no problem.

"Thanks." I swirl the whiskey around in my mouth before swallowing. Hickory chips, hint of cinnamon. "That Appalachian Red?"

"Of course it is," Hank says, taking the flask from me. "Milly and Nate Kingsley are thick as thieves these days."

Nate Kingsley owns Asheville's famous distillery down the road. Our families had a beef in the past—as in a whole feud Kevin Costner may or may not have made a TV series about —but I guess Milly's spearheading the effort to patch things up now.

"Thick enough that he's giving you thousand-dollar bottles of whiskey to sip on?"

Milly just shrugs. "Once you taste the good stuff, you can't go back."

I watch Hank take a swig, then another. Screwing the cap back onto the flask, he looks at me and says, "I did want to hurt you, Samuel. I wanted you to feel what I'd been feeling since Emma arrived on the farm. It's fucked up, but it's how I felt. I never intended to catch feelings for her. I just wanted to help her out at first."

"But you did intend to kiss her."

He winces. "I did. Not my proudest moment." The hand on his ankle balls into a fist. His voice is hoarse when he speaks again. "I regret it. Deeply. I know you're struggling to forgive me, but trust me when I say I'm struggling harder to forgive myself. I got lost in the moment. I was desperate and sad. On top of that, I've been feeling kinda...lost lately. Like I'm bored or something."

My heart contracts. How did I not see that? Was I too wrapped up in my own shit?

Thinking back, I can see the signs. But I didn't say anything. I just assumed everything was okay.

No one said anything, and now we're in a huge fucking mess because of it.

"I'm sorry you've felt lost," I reply. "And I'm sorry I wasn't looking out for you the way I should've been. That's a huge failure on my part."

From the corner of my eye, I catch Milly nodding. "I'm sorry too. Hank, why didn't you say anything?"

Hank shrugs. "I wanted to figure it out on my own. Everyone's got such full plates around here. Beau got his diagnosis, then Annabel came up to the farm with Maisie, and we all know what happened there. And Milly, you always have your weddings, and Samuel...well. Needless to say, I didn't want to bother anyone. So I muscled through the best I could. I had no way of knowing it would lead to this." His eyes are pleading. "If I did, I would've done it all differently, Samuel. I swear it."

"I believe you. I'll do better going forward."

"I appreciate that. I will too."

"Me three," Milly says with a frown. "Sounds like we all have work to do."

Hank swallows, an audible sound. "Me most of all. I know I need to move on. From Emma, I mean. But it's hard when I'm still in love with her."

I bite the inside of my cheek. "You are?"

"I am." He finally meets my eyes. "I know it's not what you wanna hear, but it's the truth. We need to be done lyin' to each other, Samuel."

Swallowing, I hold out my hand for the flask. I take another sip, welcoming the fire that trails down my throat. "I agree with that. No more lies. You told your truth, now I'm gonna tell you mine. I love you, brother, more than anything in this world. I want to see you happy. I want to see this family and this resort thrive. We've dedicated our lives to each other, and that trust—it's gotta be real, and it's gotta mean something. But right now, I don't trust you. I don't trust myself around you. And I think the only thing that's gonna make that better is time."

"Samuel," Milly warns.

Hank shoots her a look. "No, it's okay. I appreciate you

being honest. I know I can't just make this all go away, as much as I want to. That's not how forgiveness works. But I think we do need to get to a place that allows our family to function."

"I agree," Milly says. "We need to keep the business running. But more than that, we need to keep the family safe, and we need to stick together."

"I'm sorry," I say. "I don't see how we can do that with the three of us in the picture. Emma and Hank and me. How the fuck do we stick together when I feel like I'm gonna be stabbed in the back every time I turn a corner? And how do you think Emma's gonna feel, being in the same room as the two of us?"

Hank's brows shoot up. "I heard Emma was back. But Beau said she resigned?"

"She did. But I'm determined to change that. She says one of us has to go if we're going to make this work. And of course she thinks it should be her."

"No," Hank says. Voice barely above a grumble. "*I'm* the one who should go."

My gut seizes.

Milly's head snaps in his direction. "Go where?"

"I don't know. Anywhere but here."

"I disagree," Milly replies. "Running away isn't going to solve anything."

Hank pushes off the sofa and gets to his feet. "Neither is staying, Milly. Look, maybe we all just need some time to cool off and process. Samuel's right. I can't be around Emma right now, and Emma shouldn't have to be around me."

I agree with him on all points. But that doesn't stop me from feeling guilty. And regret—that's what keeps catching inside my stomach.

Yes, Hank should go, but I'm going to miss him. How fucked up is that?

Then again, families are fucked up, even the best ones, so maybe this is just par for the course.

"Are you resigning?" Milly asks, eyes wide as she stands too.

Hanks shrugs. "Sure. If that's what y'all need me to do."

"Hank," I say.

He cuts me a glare. "This is my call, Samuel. As a matter of fact, it's something I should've done a long time ago. You need to be on the farm for that big wedding we've got coming up. Besides, I'm not sure I fit in here."

"That's not true."

"Admit it. The farm, the business—that show belongs to you and Beau. Y'all won't miss me when I'm gone."

I grab at him, but he yanks his arm out of my grasp at the last minute. "Stop talking crazy."

He rolls his eyes. "I'm not gonna hurt myself. I'm just gonna get gone for a while. Go on that retirement bender I never got around to last year."

"But you'll be back, right?" Milly asks.

Hank looks me dead in the eye. "You say you need time? Take it. I'm giving you all the time you need to learn to trust me again. Me being out of the picture, it'll give us all space to breathe. Think." He slides his hands into the front pockets of his jeans. "Give you and Emma time to be together without me around."

"You sure?"

"If that's what it takes to keep our family together, yes. I'm sure."

Wow. Here's my baby brother, showing way more maturity than I think I'm capable of.

Milly puts a hand on his arm. "If you don't come back, you better believe I'll hunt you down and drag your ass back to this mountain."

Hank laughs. "Oh, I believe it, all right." He looks at me.

"I know we're not good. We're not even okay. But this is my good faith gesture here, Samuel. I love you, and I want you to be happy, and I'll do what it takes to make that happen. If I get to figure my own shit out in the process, well...guess that's a bonus."

He's right. Despite my anger, in some respects I'm proud of my brother. I just hope Mama doesn't whoop me for causing a rift between us. Or even worse, I hope she doesn't take out her frustration on Emma, because she's not guilty of anything.

But what Beau said is true. I need to fix my relationship with Hank. Our family needs to stay strong. Focused.

"Okay," I say. "Come to tomorrow's Sunday supper. Then you can go."

He nods. "Okay."

And then he turns and leaves.

Milly glances at me. She's got tears in her eyes.

I open my arms. "C'mere."

She buries her face in my chest. I wrap my arms around her and press a kiss onto the crown of her head.

"You sure this is a part of your happy ending with Emma?" Milly asks. "Watching your brother walk out the door on his way to God knows where?"

"It's not the end. Not for me and Hank, anyway. I promise I won't let our story end without a happily ever after, okay?"

She nods. "Okay."

I hold her for a while like that, each of us lost in our own thoughts. At last, she draws a quick breath through her nose and straightens. "Now, what's this about Sunday supper? You've got a plan, don't you?"

"Girl, you know me too well. Course I got a plan. Wanna help?"

She grins. "Like you even need to ask."

CHAT #5

MyBoyBlue4: Hi. I don't know if you'll even get this, but coming here seemed right. Better than sending a text, anyway. This is where we started. And I hope this is where we'll keep going for years to come.

[No reply]

MyBoyBlue4: Okay, well, on the off chance you check the chat, I'd like to invite you to Sunday supper tomorrow. I would really like to talk to you. I'd also like you to see that my family may be bruised, but we're not broken. Hank and I are actively working on our relationship, and I want you to witness that firsthand. To sweeten the deal, I'll make Emma's Cornbread (yes, it's yours now) and open a bottle or five of that 2016 Screaming Eagle. I'll do anything to make you feel better. I'm so sorry about how shit went down, Em, and if you'll let me, I'd like to make it up to you. I'd also like to convince you to stay on at Blue Mountain, but baby steps. Bring your sister if she's still in town.

[No reply]

MyBoyBlue4: I'm sitting here at my computer and

thinking about all the times this chat made me smile. You made me come, but you also made me think, Lady V. That's one hell of a combination. You're special, and you're smart, and you're creative in ways I wish I could be. I love your pervy brand of intelligence. I love the way your legs look in your sensible heels as much as I love the way they look in V's stilettos. I dream about the way you describe wine, and how fucking sexy your mastery is (in AND outside the bedroom). I love to think about all the cool things we could do together at the resort. I want you to dominate me day and night, and then I want to return the favor. I want to taste you again, baby. I can't stop thinking about you.

[No reply]

MyBoyBlue4: So, yeah. Tomorrow. If you can swing it, I'd love for you to come early. Say around 4?

LadyV76 has accepted your chat request
LadyV76 is now in the chat room

LadyV76: Hey.

MyBoyBlue4: Oh my God you're here. THANK YOU. How are you feeling?

LadyV76: Like death. You?

MyBoyBlue4: This bastard got burned. Not by your dragons or anything, but by life I guess. I can still bend the knee to you, though.

LadyV76: I do like you on your knees.

MyBoyBlue4: There she is. I've missed you, baby.

LadyV76: I've missed you too.

MyBoyBlue4: Sorry for coming to the chat with this, but I thought you might appreciate it?

LadyV76: Don't apologize. I'm glad you came to the chat. I think if I spoke to you on the phone I would just burst into tears.

MyBoyBlue4: I'm sorry. So fucking sorry about everything.

LadyV76: I know. And I'd like to come to supper tomorrow. What can I bring?

MyBoyBlue4: You've just made me the happiest man on earth, Khaleesi. Just bring yourself. My only request is that you leave the dragons at home, okay?

LadyV76: You have a deal. Lindsey is still here, so I'll bring her too?

MyBoyBlue4: Awesome. Can't wait to introduce her to the rest of my family. Please tell her all seven of us are indeed in love with you. There will be no more awkward kisses, however. That I can promise.

LadyV76: So it's not necessarily a love triangle as much as a love...heptagon?

MyBoyBlue4: Of course you'd know what that is.

LadyV76: You forget that I'm the professor.

MyBoyBlue4: And I am always an eager student. Can you come early?

LadyV76: Yes. So everything is okay with your family?

MyBoyBlue4: I wouldn't say things are okay. But Hank and I had a productive chat earlier today, and we're starting the process of healing. I wish I could tell you things are back to normal, but they're not. I don't think they will be for a while, and that's just the reality of the situation, sucky as it may be. Still, I'm trying. Hank's trying too. If you'd be willing to sit down with us to work something out, we'd really appreciate it.

LadyV76: Okay.

MyBoyBlue4: Wow, I wasn't expecting you to say that.

LadyV76: I'm still learning to let perfection go. I think it'll take me a lifetime to figure that one out. But as much as I wish things were normal, I'm going to work on being okay with complicated.

MyBoyBlue4: And as someone once told me, complicated can be delicious.

LadyV76: That someone must be very wise.

MyBoyBlue4: She is.

LadyV76: See you tomorrow, Blue.

MyBoyBlue4: See you then. Sweet dreams, V.

Chapter Thirty-Six

EMMA

Lindsey links arms with me as we walk up to Samuel's front door.

"I'm proud of you," she says.

She's smiling for the first time in days.

I smile back. "Thanks. I'm proud of you too."

She snorts. "Proud of my train wreck of a life? Thanks."

"I mean it." I nudge her with my elbow. "You got out of bed today, didn't you? That's no small feat. We need to celebrate the small things when the big things get overwhelming."

"Eh..."

"Fine. Can we at least celebrate the fact that the gallon of wine you're about to drink is the best in the world?"

"That I can get on board with."

"See? It's the small things."

Lindsey glances at my stilettos. "Like those shoes?"

"Like these shoes."

Truth be told, I didn't know how I should dress. So I went with what I felt best in: stilettos, jeans, and a bun. Little bit V, little bit me.

Judging by the way Samuel's eyes light up when he opens the door, I'd say I got the balance just right.

The late afternoon sun slices across his face, catching on the ends of his neatly parted hair. He smiles, the skin around his eyes crinkling, and the world goes still at the same moment my heart does.

He's sporting the same puffy eyes and dark circles I am. His cheeks are a little sunken, and I wonder how much weight he's lost over the past few days. I don't own a scale, but I can tell by the way my clothes fit that I'm definitely down a few pounds. Knowing he hasn't been able to eat or sleep either makes my chest hurt.

"Hey, baby."

A full-body rush of want moves through me at the deep timbre of his voice. I dig my teeth into my bottom lip. "Hi, Samuel. It's so good to see you."

"You look beautiful."

"You look handsome as hell."

"I know."

I pretend to roll my eyes. "I thought Beau always hosted Sunday supper."

"He does, but tonight he and Bel and Maisie made an exception at my request."

I nod. "Thanks for having us."

"Thanks for coming. Lindsey, it's great to see you again. My family and I promise to behave better this time. Can I get a mulligan? I'd like to start over with Em's family. Y'all are just as important to me as my own. Hopefully, you're a little less nuts, though."

"Don't count on it." Lindsey's smile grows. She holds up her arms. "Hi, I'm Lindsey, and I already love you because I can tell how much you adore my sister."

Samuel accepts her hug. "I'm Samuel, and I already love

you because I'm starting to think you may have talked Emma into giving me a second chance."

"How'd you know?" I ask with a grin.

He lifts a massive shoulder. "Lucky guess. Y'all come in, please. I have a couple of bottles of that drunk nun Albariño with your names on it."

"It's a sign," Lindsay says, following Samuel inside. "That's what my next career move should be. I can go from attorney to drunk nun, no problem."

The familiar smells of Samuel's house fill my head—soap, something savory in the oven—and my heart skips a beat.

I can hear Van Halen playing in the kitchen—"Dance the Night Away" this time.

Lindsey gawks at Samuel's house, but I just gawk at Samuel. The way his fingers move as he expertly uncorks a frosty bottle of the Albariño. The easy charm of the questions he asks Lindsey as he hands her a heavy pour. How fucking adorable he looks with a kitchen towel slung over his shoulder and that earnest gleam in his eye.

He's learning how to be charming without being full of shit. The transformation is breathtaking to witness.

"So I'm going to give myself a tour of this insane house," Lindsey says. "I won't finish until y'all tell me I'm done, okay?"

Leaning back against the counter, Samuel smiles and crosses one leg over the other. "Give Em a call if you get lost."

"It's not *that* big," I tease.

"Yes, it is," he teases right back. "Biggest you've ever seen, including all the ones you've peeped on the internet."

Lindsey wags her eyebrows at me. "Lucky girl." Then she disappears into the dining room.

The space between Samuel and me thrums the way it did that first day we met. Only this time, Samuel's looking at me with soft eyes and a smile.

"We're really gonna do this," I say, throat swelling with emotion.

He holds up his glass. "If you'll have me, yes. What changed your mind?"

"Lindsey was actually a big part of it. We talked for a while last night, and I realized I was trying to build this perfect career. But like the perfect life, it doesn't exist. The dream is still there. The dream of enjoying my work and earning enough money to live the life I want. But maybe the dream is messy, and maybe it's never going to look the way I thought it would. I'll never know everything there is to know about wine or success or money. I'll never know everything there is to know about *myself*." I move across the kitchen to stand in front of him. "One thing I do know? I've got a long road ahead of me, and there's no one I'd rather travel it with than you."

He searches my eyes. "I want to be on the road with you, every damn day. And, shamelessly, I really, really want you to be here for John and Celeste's wedding. I'm already giddy about crushing that event with you. But that still leaves your concerns about your reputation. The staff—aren't you worried what they'll think?"

"I still am. But if we can figure out a way to work together after you basically froze me out, I think we can come up with a plan to move forward in our careers while maintaining the respect of our employees."

His lips twitch. "If you think it can be done, then yeah—yeah, it'll get done."

"You have that much faith in me," I say.

"You say that as a statement and not a question, and *that*, baby"—he leans down and nudges his nose against my throat —"is one of the five thousand reasons I love you."

I unfurl my fingers into his hair. Give it a tug. He groans. I grin. "I want to be cybering with you until I'm shuffling around using that walker you were talking about."

He goes still. "You mean that?"

"I do. If I can figure it out, I want to cyber with you *while* I'm shuffling."

"Think we can do it one handed? The shuffling?"

I shrug. "I'm willing to try."

His eyes get serious. "Me too. And hey, maybe that's all we're gonna need then, and that's all we need right now. A willingness to try."

"I love that idea." I tilt my chin and kiss his mouth. "I love you."

"Would you be willing to try to think about moving in with me?"

I set down my glass on the counter and slide my hands onto his waist. "I don't need to think about that. Yes. Yes, I'd love to move in with you, Samuel Beauregard."

"Good. 'Cause I'd love to cook for you every night, Emma Crawford. No more protein bars."

I laugh. "No more protein bars."

Samuel kisses me, the taste of his mouth and the depth of his desire for me turning me inside out. Just like he did that first time, he holds nothing back. He drinks me in with slow, deep sips that say as plainly as words could that he wants me and only me, and that this is the first kiss of the rest of our lives.

My hand is halfway down his jeans when a cacophony of voices burst into the kitchen.

"Emma, are you groping my brother?"

"Oh yeah, she's definitely groping him. Mama, get over here, I gotta cover your eyes."

"Look how freaking adorable they are together. I hope this means Emma's decided to stay?"

That last one is Milly. I turn around, discreetly blocking

Samuel's very obvious erection while I grin at the Beauregard family.

Everyone's here: Beau, who's covering June's eyes, and Annabel and Maisie. Rhett, Milly, and yes, Hank too. His smile is more subdued than usual, and his eyes are a little red. But he *is* smiling. And that's something.

That's a start.

A willingness to try.

"I'm staying," I say, and I'm immediately wrapped into four tight hugs. Five if you count Maisie's tap on my cheek. My sister magically appears and hugs me too before refilling her wineglass.

Samuel also gets a hug from everyone but Hank. He hangs back, busying himself with the grocery bags June brought over.

"I'm so glad," Beau says, meeting my eyes. "And so sorry, Emma. You know I told Samuel not to lay a finger on you."

"Well." I glance up at Samuel. "I was the one who laid a finger on him first, so..."

"So yeah, she started it," Samuel says, still smiling. I can tell by the way his expression softens that he wants to kiss me, but he's holding back. For Hank, I realize. He's fine being with me while Hank is around, but it'd be pretty cruel to rub it in his face with PDA.

My heart is so swollen and so full I'm worried it'll burst. There's a lot of hurt in this room. But there's also a lot of love. And I'd like to think at the end of the day, love wins.

I hope love always wins in this house.

Our house.

As loud and unafraid as the Beauregards can be, they do know how to read a room, and they herd out onto the screened porch, leaving Hank, Samuel, and me alone in the kitchen.

Samuel holds out a hand to his brother. Hank takes it without hesitation.

"Glad you came, brother," Samuel says.

Hank nods. "Thanks for having me." He glances in my direction. "Thanks for giving my brother another shot, Emma. Thanks for giving me another shot. I want to apologize again for kissing you. It was a stupid, hurtful move, and I'm sorry." He looks back up at Samuel. "I'm leaving Blue Mountain."

My stomach does a backflip. "Hank—"

"It was my decision. And it's only temporary. I needed a break before you got here, Emma. Doing what I did"—he shakes his head and looks at his feet—"just proves my head isn't screwed on straight. I gotta fix that, and I think some time away will help me get there."

I look at Samuel. Samuel looks at me.

"If that's what you think is best, then I wholeheartedly support you," I say, turning back to Hank. "You'll let us know if you need anything?"

"I will," he replies, and the emphatic way he says it makes me believe him.

The alarm on Samuel's phone goes off, and less than a minute later, the rest of the Beauregards reappear in the kitchen. Samuel pulls a gigantic beef tenderloin out of the oven—"Look at that beautiful herb crust. *Damn* I'm good"—while I decant a couple of bottles of Cabernet Sauvignon. Hank grabs a pair of potholders and lifts a pot of mashed potatoes off the range, setting it on the dining room table. Maisie pulls Rhett's hair, and June, Milly, and Lindsey gawk over the antique silverware Milly brought before setting it on the table too. Annabel slides a spoon into a dish of squash gratin, biting her lip when Beau presses a quick kiss to the back of her neck.

"You." Samuel points at me. "Fill your wineglass and sit

your ass down at the table. You're our honored guest, so no more working, you hear?"

I smile. "You gonna make me?"

"Y'all really are adorable, but you're also kinda dirty," Milly says. "It's gross, but awesome."

Samuel meets my eyes. "Milly, you got no idea. In the bedroom, in the shower, on the internet..."

"Eww, can you not please?" Beau asks. "Maisie's taking a mental note of every damn word you're saying. How much you wanna bet her first sentence is gonna be, 'Uncle Samuel and Aunt Emma get dirty on the internet'? I'll disown all y'all, I will."

I catch Lindsey's gaze across the dining room. She's got this big, happy smile on her face, like she knows how cool it is that Beau just called me *Aunt Emma*.

I just became an aunt.

We haven't started eating yet, but I'm already full.

Full of love.

Full of gratitude.

Full of this bone-deep contentment I've never experienced before.

Milly has clearly worked her magic: the table is set with gorgeous floral arrangements, and the china, glassware, and cloth napkins all sport a matching lavender-and-peacock blue theme.

Sitting next to Samuel at the table, surrounded by our family and friends, I feel safe. I feel seen.

I feel loved for who I am. And that might just be the best kind of love of all.

Samuel reaches under the table and grabs my hand. "So do I call you Emma now, or V, or Lady..."

"Why choose?" I flash him my shoes. "I'm all three."

"You're *you*." He gives my hand a squeeze. "And you've shown me how to be me."

338

I arch a brow. "How much are *you* gonna show *me* tonight?"

His eyes flash with a familiar heat. "How much you wanna see?"

"All of it. Whatever's real."

"It's yours," he says. "I'm yours."

A few hours later, he makes good on that promise right there on the dining room table. And again in the kitchen. And twice in his bed, and three times (yes, three) in the shower.

If that's not a happy ending to Blue and V's story, I don't know what is.

THE END

EPILOGUE

Hank

I have to get the fuck out of here.

Yanking my sweater over my head, it's the first thought I have when I walk into my house after Sunday supper. I'm a little drunk and a lot worn out from playing nice.

From pretending that seeing Samuel and Emma so damn happy together doesn't make me feel like dying.

I grab a fifth of Appalachian Red whiskey from my liquor cabinet and take a pull straight from the bottle. It burns a trail of fire down my throat.

It does nothing to lessen the intense ache inside my chest.

Doesn't stop me from taking another swig before I set down the bottle and wipe my mouth with the back of my hand.

I glance around my pristine, silent kitchen. Not so much as a glass or napkin out of place. Probably because I don't really live here.

Sure, I sleep in the bed every night and get ready in the gleaming master bathroom every morning, but otherwise, I'm hustling around the resort.

Work has become my life. And it took falling in love with my brother's girlfriend to see how much I'm missing out on.

So fuck it. What do I have left to lose? I'm gonna stop putting my family first and give myself the top spot instead. I'll do what I want when I want to do it.

I want to travel.

I want to fuck around.

I want to meet people who've never heard of Blue Mountain.

Tomorrow, I'll get with my team and work out the details of my leave from guest relations. Then I'll get on the phone with my travel agent and book a private jet to—

Where?

As far away as I can get, I guess. Thailand? South Africa? Madrid?

All I know is my broken heart ain't gonna heal if I'm anywhere near this place.

I can't stop thinking about how Emma looked at Samuel over the dinner table tonight. She was lit up. Eyes glowing and full, like she was so happy she might cry. I heard them flirting, talking about all the ways they'll fuck tonight.

A slice of searing, urgent pain rips through my torso. I grab the bottle and drink, and drink some more.

"Hey." I startle at the voice behind me. I turn to see Rhett looking at me, his brow furrowed with concern. He gently takes the bottle from my hand and sets it down. Crossing his arms, he leans his back against the counter. "I'm sorry that happened, and I'm sorry you're hurting."

I nod, swallowing hard. "Me too."

He dips his head toward the whiskey. "Please tell me you aren't going to cope by drinking yourself into a shame spiral."

"I'm giving the shame spiral twenty-four hours, max. Then I'm hitting the road."

"Oh? Where ya going?"

I lift a shoulder, eyeing the bottle. "Not sure yet. Someplace where there's a bar on the beach and beautiful women."

"The best distractions in the world." Rhett nods. "Let's start in the Bahamas. Paradise Island."

"We?" I arch a brow. "Who said you're invited?"

Rhett grabs the bottle and takes a swig, smacking his lips. "I did. I have three months until training camp starts. Besides, someone needs to babysit you at that beach bar. You won't be able to pick up all those beautiful women if you're wasted."

I laugh, the tightness inside my breastbone loosening ever so slightly. "Stop. You just wanna be my wingman."

"Well, yeah." My younger brother grins. "If I happen to meet a lady or two while I'm making sure you don't give yourself rum poisoning...well, I won't hate it."

"Okay." I take the bottle from him. Take a sip. "The Bahamas. Then where?"

"We'll go around the world, obviously. Hop from the Bahamas to Ibiza. Then Mykonos, and the Seychelles... Bangkok. Australia. Hawaii. Final stop—"

"Vegas," I say.

Rhett's grin deepens into a smile. "My adopted hometown. Perfect."

He plays for the pro football team that recently moved from California to Las Vegas. Rhett's got a definite wild streak, so the new location suited him just fine.

Me? I'm an old soul. While I had my fun in Sin City, I never really got why my teammates and college friends were so obsessed with it.

Maybe this trip will change that.

I hold up the whiskey. "Let's do it. Think you can leave tomorrow?"

"Hell yeah, I can."

I take one last pull of whiskey before handing the bottle

back to Rhett. He drinks too, and for several beats we stand there in silence.

I don't know what he's thinking about, but as usual, I'm thinking about Emma. How I don't want to go on this trip, and I don't want to leave Blue Mountain, because she's here. She's been the bright spot in my days. The reason I jump out of bed in the mornings more excited and invigorated than I've felt in years.

It happened really fucking fast, me falling for her.

I don't fall easily. Not like that. Not for someone who doesn't want me back.

But it happened, and now my head won't stop spinning, and I can't stop hurting. The embarrassment is real. So is the pain. This is horrible.

I never, ever want to feel this way again.

I want to forget.

"Make me a promise," I say.

"Shoot."

"Don't let me do anything really stupid."

"Like?"

I look him in the eye. "Like fall in love again. That shit—Rhett, it hurts something fierce."

Rhett frowns. "Hank," he says softly. "You can't punish yourself like that. Yeah, you obviously need to give your heart time to heal, but don't cut yourself off that way. You're a good guy, and you deserve to be happy."

The words he doesn't say hang in the air between us. *You deserve to be happy the way Samuel and Emma are happy together.*

I swallow again. Look down at my feet and shake my head. "Just—promise me, okay? That's all I ask."

I feel his eyes on me. A heartbeat passes. Then another.

"Okay," he says at last. "But that promise expires at the end of this trip, you hear? Then all bets are off."

I wave him away. "By then we'll be in Vegas, and who falls

in love there? I'll send over the flight details when I have them."

It's a gamble, running away like this. What will happen to my job? And what about my relationship with Samuel? Will me being gone really help all of us heal?

I have no idea. But leaving is a bet I'm willing to make.

Want a Samuel + Emma bonus scene that may or may not include more kitchen sex AND a proposal? Grab your free bonus epilogue by signing up for my newsletter at www.jessicapeterson.com!

What happens in Vegas definitely doesn't stay in Vegas in SOUTHERN SINNER, Hank's story. Keep reading for a juicy excerpt.

SOUTHERN SINNER EXCERPT

Hank

Kygo ends his set with a banger of a Whitney Houston remix. The place goes nuts. Confetti cannons go off, arms are raised, and drinks fly everywhere.

Stevie's got one hand on my nape, fingers playing with my hair—fuck, I love when she does that—and the other on my waist.

My hands are on her ass, where they've been since she put them there a while ago.

The girl has ass for days and days.

The song ends, and Stevie leans back to look at me. Our eyes meet, and hers smile, and I know I'm this fucking close to popping the woody I've been fighting all night.

"A hand of blackjack?" she says. "And then . . . bed?"

A piece of confetti lands on the tip of her nose, and I grab it, thumb grazing her cheek. "Yes, ma'am."

Taking her hand, I head for the exit. Rhett cuts me a look, eyebrow raised. *You good?*

I nod. *I'm good.*

Stevie waves to her girls, and then a bouncer escorts us to the VIP exit just off the stage.

We spill onto the casino floor, the two of us blinking at the sudden onslaught of light and the chime of slot machines. I check my watch.

It's almost four, but the casino is packed. People crowd the tables, jockeying for a seat, and guys wait four deep for drinks at the nearby bar. The energy in the place is palpable.

I'm wide-awake. My ears are ringing, and so is my body.

Looking at Stevie for the five hundredth time tonight —*Jesus fuck*—I wonder if I've ever been more turned on in my life.

"One hand," I say. "Just one."

Stevie turns her head to glance at me, digging her teeth into her bottom lip. "But not just once in bed, surely?"

I let out a bark of laughter. "Naw, honey, I hope you didn't have plans to sleep tonight 'cause I sure as hell ain't gonna let you."

We manage to nab a seat at a five-hundred-dollar-minimum table. I start to pull out the chair for Stevie, but she presses her breasts against my chest and shakes her head. "You play."

"You're the expert."

"And you're the student. You only get better if you practice."

I smile. I cannot fucking wait to put my mouth on those tits.

I wanna put my mouth all over her. That is something I'd definitely like to practice.

"If you say so." I take the seat and grab a wad of cash from my wallet. Stevie stands behind me, hands curled over the back of my chair.

This dealer is a lot less fun than Helen was, so I'm glad we won't be staying long. I still play my hand with him the way Stevie taught me, setting a few chips closer to the center of the table so he can gamble with me.

"Fast learner," she says behind me, swiping a finger across my shoulder blade.

"Easy enough when you learn from the best."

My first card is an eight. Waiting for my second, I hold my breath.

Another eight.

I glance over my shoulder at Stevie. She's smiling, and I'm struck dumb the way I always am by this Julia Roberts thing that's wide and real and nothing short of beautiful.

Yeah, probably should be careful with this one. There's a reason I gave Rhett explicit instructions at the start of our trip not to let me fall for anyone. I've played the love-sick asshole before, and it's a sucky role.

Especially when you're lovesick for your brother's girl.

A girl who's now his fiancée. A month or so ago, Rhett gave me the news that Samuel and Emma had gotten engaged.

I wait for the way my chest clenches anytime I think about them and how badly I fucked up.

I wait some more.

Stevie's finger moves up my nape. My skin ignites.

Wow. Wow, the awful tightness actually isn't happening. Guilt is still there, don't get me wrong. It sits on my breast-bone like a goddamn gorilla night and day. But longing, for Emma at least, doesn't rise to meet it.

Halle-fucking-*lujah*. The relief's been slow to come, but tonight—being with Stevie—it's hardly even a thought.

She's setting me on fire.

Reaching behind me, I give Stevie's thigh a quick grab. She responds by pressing her tits into my back.

Fuck careful. Where's the fun in that? I've been careful my whole damn life. While it's paid off in some respects, it didn't stop disaster from happening in others.

"You know what to do?" Stevie asks.

"Split 'em," I say to the dealer.

I split my cards and put more chips on the table. And whaddya know, the dealer busts, and I end up winning north of three grand.

"Hot damn!" I stand and give Stevie another high five. Our fingers twine like we've done it a hundred times. "You know your shit, honey."

"And now you know yours. Shall we celebrate in my suite?"

"I'm sure a high roller like you has a nice room. But mine is nicer."

"I did hear you might be famous."

"Might be?" I smirk. "How about this? Let *my* suite do the talking, and then you can decide if I'm famous or not."

"So cocky."

I lift a shoulder. "Well, yeah. How could I not be now that I know how to crush it at blackjack?"

Stevie's hand in mine, I flash my player card at the door to the Tower Suites. The sounds of the casino fade as we step into the private lobby, a gleaming, perfumed oasis for Encore's most exclusive guests.

Another couple is waiting in the elevator bank. But because lady luck is on my side tonight, two elevators arrive at the same time. The other couple takes one. Stevie and I take the other, turning around so we're facing the doors. I hit the button for 35. The doors glide shut with a hushed *whoosh*, and I join Stevie at the back of the elevator.

We're alone for the first time. For half a heartbeat, the silence between us swells.

I turn to face her and press her against the elevator wall with my body. I grab her wrists in one hand and pin her arms above her head. Her chest rises on a sharp inhale, and I imagine her nipples dragging up my chest.

My dick is in agony.

Her dark eyes are fire.

I lean in and press my lips to hers. Her hips roll forward to meet mine, and I open my mouth to groan, the kiss deepening when I lick my tongue over the seam of her lips. She opens her mouth too, letting me taste her.

She's breathing hard, and I am too.

I work my mouth over her jaw, and her head falls back, eyes catching on the far corner of the elevator.

"There's a camera," she pants.

I kiss the freckle on her neck. Her skin tastes clean. "Don't care."

The guy I was back home would care. As (former?) head of guest relations at Blue Mountain Farm, he'd care very much if people were making out in the resort's elevators.

Good thing I'm not that guy in Vegas. Hell, I don't know if I'll ever be that guy again.

Good thing Stevie makes it easy to live in the moment. This feeling—the one that keeps my mind from wandering—is the whole point of my retirement bender.

It's what I've been chasing from day one, when Rhett and I boarded a plane for the Bahamas back in April.

I kiss a trail down her neck, her chest, kissing the swell of her breasts through the fabric of her dress. She shudders when I lick her there, and I glance up to see her sucking in a breath, eyes fluttering shut for a moment before she opens them, determinedly meeting my gaze.

Huh. Almost like she's . . . I don't know, fighting the surrender.

Like she's playing it safe. Why?

Fuck that. I wanna drive this girl wild.

I kiss her one last time, a bruising caress that has her moaning into my mouth, before the elevator doors open on my floor.

"Come," I growl and grab her hand.

I try not to walk too fast. Stevie's wearing killer heels that can't be comfortable, especially after a night of dancing. But I'm impatient to disappear into the privacy of my suite. I gotta get her naked, now.

My hand shakes when I slide the key card into its slot. It takes me two tries, but the door finally swings open. I gesture for Stevie to enter first, and she stops three steps into the room.

"Oh, Hank," she breathes. "This is unbelievable."

The living and dining area of the suite is a two-story behemoth, ridiculously grand in true over-the-top Vegas style. It's decorated in shades of cream, brown, and white with pops of bright red. An enormous chandelier hangs overhead, and cushy furniture dots the space: velvet couches, marble tables, and a leather-clad bar.

But that shit isn't what catches Stevie's attention. Instead, she stares at the wall of floor-to-ceiling windows that gives us an incredible view of the Strip below. She walks over, touching her fingertips to the glass.

I sidle up behind her, slipping my arms around her waist while I press a kiss to her neck. Her body is warm and soft, and I love the feel of it against mine.

Our reflections are visible in the glass. Our gazes lock there, our bodies a shadow over the lights of the neighboring Wynn.

"Okay, you're famous," she says and reaches behind her to slide her fingers into the hair at my nape.

I begin to gather her dress in my fist, hiking it up her legs. "That gonna be a problem?"

"No." She looks to the side. "Actually, it works better."

"Because you wanna fuck an athlete?" I nudge her nose with mine.

Her brows snap together. "No."

"Hey, I'm not here to judge you."

"And I'm not here to chase . . . whatever you are. I'm just

making a very rude assumption that, because you're famous and hot, you like to play the field. Pun intended."

I've got her dress hiked up over her hips. I run my hand over the tops of her bare thighs, reaching for the place between her legs.

"That *is* a rude assumption."

"Is it true?"

"Maybe."

"Are you"—her breath falters when I cup her pussy through the second layer of her outfit, the bodysuit thing —"going to do rude things to me for making it? The assumption?"

"Yes." Even through the silky fabric, I can feel how hot and damp she is. My dick goes full mast. "I got three bedrooms in this place, plus a billiards room, and I'm gonna fuck you in all of 'em. But first, you gotta tell me how to get this thing off you."

She laughs, turning around to face me. Her eyes flash, playful and hot, and she grabs the hem of her dress and slowly pulls it over her head, mussing her ponytail in the process.

Eyes on mine, she holds up the dress between her pinched forefinger and thumb. She releases the pinch, fingers straightening as the dress drops to the floor beside her. She plants a hand on my chest and gives me a firm shove, sending me backward so I can take her in.

For several beats, I just stare. I wonder vaguely if I've experienced cardiac arrest and am now floating somewhere between heaven and hell.

The bodysuit has suddenly become the sexiest lingerie ever. Combined with the stilettos and her slightly swollen lips, it is a sight to be savored.

And when she starts walking toward me, swaying her hips and smirking?

I am definitely a dead man.

I'm also a giver. I grab her hand and lead her to the billiards room. My butler (yes, the suite comes with twenty-four-hour butler service) must've swung by while I was gone because the lights are on and the balls are racked up on the table, ready for a game.

Again, Stevie's gaze moves to the view outside the windows. Lights twinkle in every color and rhythm, and the outline of the mountainous desert beyond is just visible.

I shove the rack and pair of pool cues aside with my arm. They somersault over the lip of the table and land on the floor with a clatter. Stevie jumps, then smiles.

She plays right into my hand, resting her ass against the edge of the table with a come-hither look in her eyes. I settle my hands on the table on either side of her hips and lean in, drawing my nose up her throat.

"Hey, honey," I breathe, relieved to finally, *finally*, have her all to myself.

She takes my face in her hand. "Hey," she says and covers her mouth with mine.

The kiss is savage, deep, our lips and tongues moving in tandem. I lick my tongue into her mouth again, drawing her chin up as I sip her, then drink her in deep, long pulls that have her fisting my shirt in her hands.

I cup her breast, massaging it. Gently, cursing with the effort to be patient, I work the cup of her bodysuit down, propping her tit above it. I thumb her nipple, and she bites down on my lip.

We both look down at the same time, foreheads touching. We watch as I work the other breast free, both tits propped up for us to savor.

They're generous, soft, with large, dusky pink nipples.

I groan and duck my head, leaning in to take her right nipple in my mouth. I suck, lathing my tongue over the pebbled point, and she hisses.

Her head falls back. She digs a hand into my hair, panting, and rolls her hips.

She's begging.

"This too." I reach around to her back, searching for a clasp, a zipper. "How—"

She reaches behind her and finds my hand, leading it to the zipper at the top of the garment. "Like this," she says, and together, we guide the zipper down.

Getting on my knees, I help pull it over her hips and down her legs.

My gaze is level with her pussy. Her pubic hair is dark and lush.

It glistens with her arousal.

I look up at her. She's beautiful, naked save for her heels, and I resist the urge to reach into my pants and give myself a stroke. I'll come in five seconds flat if I so much as graze my dick, much less jack off.

I put my hands on her thighs and say, "Can I?"

"Can you what?" she pants, cheeks burning pink.

"Here." I touch my middle finger to the place just beneath her belly button and drag it down, sliding it between her legs. Parting her lips. She's swollen and soft and *perfect*. "Can I kiss you here?"

She hesitates, just for a second. Her eyes gleam with something I haven't seen before. Vulnerability?

Her fingers find my hair again. "You're famous, you're hot, and you're considerate?"

"Total package. I know. Now get on the table and spread your legs."

Stevie hikes her ass onto the table and gives me a gorgeous view of her pussy. She's so wet my fingers make a slick, crude sound as I circle them over her clit.

"Hank," she breathes, brows snapping together as she watches me.

I curl my hands around the backs of her knees and spread her wider. Stop to admire the dimples along the inside of her thighs. I lean in.

The first taste is rich. Warm. I go slowly, deeply, and Stevie moans, hips rolling again. I lick her slit front to back, then dip my tongue inside her, savoring her heat.

Christ, it's gonna feel good to be inside her.

I suck on her clit. Press my lips to it. Slip a finger inside her. Reach up and gather her nipple between my thumb and forefinger.

Her moans get louder. She pulls my hair. Pulls it harder, making my heart thump.

"What is it?" My eyes go wide. "Did I hurt you?"

She shakes her head, breathless. "No. I—bed. I'm close, but I don't—I want to make it last—"

"I got you." I stand, and she takes both hands I offer, rising to her feet. She sways a little; I hold her, steady her, and she kisses my jaw. "Let's go to bed."

Read the rest of SOUTHERN SINNER today!

Thank you so much for reading SOUTHERN HOTSHOT! I hope you enjoyed Samuel + Emma's smoking hot story.

Check out the next book in the NC Highlands Series, SOUTHERN SINNER. It just might be my sexiest, most fun book yet. Keep reading for a steamy excerpt!

I love nothing more than hanging out with readers. I spend the most time in my r**eader group on Facebook, The City Girls, where we talk about anything and everything**—PPD, butt stuff, what we're having for dinner. It's a fun place.

You can also follow my not-so-glamorous life as a romance author and new mom on Instagram @JessicaPAuthor.

ALSO BY JESSICA PETERSON

THE STUDY ABROAD SERIES

Studying Abroad Just Got a Whole Lot Sexier.

A Series of Sexy Interconnected Standalone Romances

ACKNOWLEDGMENTS

Huge thanks to everyone who made this book happen. I'm so proud of the work we've done together.

Thanks to my PA and right-hand woman, Jodi. You're a bright spot in my days, and I'm so grateful to have you on my team.

To my publicist, Nina, and all the gals at Valentine PR. Thanks to you, this cover (and this book!) are my hottest yet. Thank you!

To my beta readers, Jodi, Quinn, Heather, and Julia. Y'all consistently amaze me with your attention to detail and your generosity.

Thanks to my reader group admins, Emily, Tara, Ingrid, Julie, and Kenysha. You guys absolutely rock, and I appreciate you guys holding down the fort while I disappear to write.

To my ARC team, for your unwavering support, and your incredible enthusiasm for my books. I truly appreciate it!

To my editing team, Marion, Jenny, and Karen. You gals truly make my books shine.

Thanks to my incredible cover designer, Najla, and her team for always knocking it out of the park.

Thanks to Nick Erik, for your help with ads.

Finally, thanks to my readers and my family. You are the reason I get to sit down at my dream job every day, and I can't thank you enough for being on this journey with me.

ABOUT THE AUTHOR

Jessica Peterson writes smokin' hot romance set in her favorite cities around the world. She grew up on a steady diet of Mr. Darcy, Edward Cullen, and Jamie Frasier, and it wasn't long before she started writing swoon-worthy heroes of her own. She loves strong coffee, stronger heroines, and heroes with hot accents.

She lives in Charlotte, NC with her husband, Ben, her sweet baby, Grace, and her smelly Goldendoodle, Martha Bean. You can check out her books at www.jessicapeterson.com.

Printed in Dunstable, United Kingdom